THE
TOPAZ

OTHER BOOKS AND AUDIO BOOKS
BY JENNIE HANSEN:

Abandoned

All I Hold Dear

Beyond Summer Dreams

Breaking Point

Chance Encounter

Code Red

Coming Home

High Stakes

Macady

Some Sweet Day

Wild Card

OTHER BOOKS AND AUDIO BOOKS
IN THE BRACELET SERIES:

The Bracelet

The Emerald

THE TOPAZ

a novel by

Jennie Hansen

Covenant Communications, Inc.

Cover image The Topaz © Dave Malan
For more information on this artist please visit www.davemalan.com

Cover design copyrighted 2007 by Covenant Communications, Inc.

Published by Covenant Communications, Inc.
American Fork, Utah

This is a work of fiction. The characters, names, incidents, places, and dialogue are products of the author's imagination, and are not to be construed as real.

Printed in Canada
First Printing: October 2007

13 12 11 10 09 08 07   10 9 8 7 6 5 4 3 2 1

ISBN 978-1-59811-456-0

This book is dedicated to the Covenant editors who taught me, befriended me, and encouraged me to be better than I thought I could be. Thank you Darla Isackson, Giles H. Florence Jr., JoAnn Jolley, Valerie Holladay, Shauna Humphreys, Christian Sorensen, Kirk L. Shaw, and Kathryn B. Jenkins. And thanks too to my family, who have journeyed with me through good times and bad. A special thanks to Janice and Lezlie for their proofreading.

PROLOGUE

The mounted knight pinned the old man against an ancient, twisted fig tree with his lance. One thrust would end the infidel's life, yet something stayed the knight's hand. Whether it was the sobbing woman in rags at the old man's feet or the knight's general disgust for a quest that had fallen far short of his expectations, he could not say. As he hesitated, the old woman, nearly obscured beneath yards of black fabric, rose to her feet and with tottering steps approached him, one trembling hand extended.

A glint of gold in her clenched fist was all that kept the knight from dispatching the old man and then drawing his sword on her. She spread her fingers, and he stared in awe at two shimmering golden stones on her palm. She said something in some heathen tongue, but her words were meaningless to him. She gestured frantically, repeating the sounds she'd made before. At last the knight understood. She was attempting to exchange the stones for the old man's life.

The knight knew he could easily kill them both and take the stones, but almost two years of slaughter and deceit hadn't completely wiped away the shining honor with which he had set forth from Britain to drive the unbelievers from the Holy Land. There was little left of their original divine purpose among the battle-worn knights, but this one Crusader had grown weary of bloodshed. Thus, he made his choice. His gauntleted hand closed around the offering, and his lance tilted away from his prey. The Crusade was at an end, and though he carried no honor or glory back to his king, and though barbaric infidels still defiled the Holy City of Jerusalem, some instinct whispered that he held in his hand a fortune worth a king's ransom, a trophy beyond his wildest dreams.

He watched the elderly pair stumble away, then turned his eyes back to the glittering jewels. A strange peace filled his breast, assuring him that his holy purpose was not the failure he had supposed. The sun-bright stones that turned to fiery red as they caught the sun's rays would surely be his amulet, providing him with strength and clear vision.

* * *

Along with the title, the new Viscount Burton inherited from his father an estate, a sizable fortune, and a casket of jewels. Prominent among the jewels was a set of large topaz cuff links, the gems carried back from the Crusades by a long-forgotten ancestor who had been knighted, thus bestowing a title on his descendants. Lord Burton's father and grandfather had made the twin topaz jewels the hallmark of their rank and position in the realm. He vowed to wear them proudly, but they were more frequently seen at gaming tables and sporting events than in the halls of parliament. About the time his own second son was killed aboard an American vessel in London's harbor and vile rumors linked the young man to various nefarious activities, he noticed one of the stones seemed to lose its luster. When his older son's wife and his younger son's widow both gave birth to healthy males within the year, he became convinced the duller stone had regained its brilliance.

1 ~ℓ

A cloud of dust at the far end of the street caught Serenity's attention, and she watched two somberly dressed young men alight from the public stage and make their way across the street to the general store. Accustomed to the plain, dark clothing of her Quaker neighbors, Serenity felt little interest in the two men until they left the general store and walked toward her papa's shop.

She couldn't say for certain how she knew the two men weren't Quakers. Perhaps it was their hats. Though black, they were taller and had narrower brims than those worn by the Friends. The men weren't soldiers making their way back home either—they were too well dressed for that. It had only been a few weeks since Papa had brought home a newspaper announcing that General Lee had surrendered to the Union's General Grant at a place called Appomattox, and already the village had seen a steady flow of ragged, half-starved soldiers drifting down its main street on their way back to wherever they called home.

She considered slipping through the door that separated the family's living quarters from the store to satisfy her curiosity about the strangers, but she couldn't leave her task. Her arms ached, but she continued to raise and lower them in the age-old rhythm required to turn cream to butter. Two loaves of bread were cooling on a wire rack in front of the window. The butter was a surprise for Papa. She'd traded a bucket of apples from last autumn's crop for the cream.

The murmur of male voices coming from the store continued as she finished churning. *So Papa's still conversing with the two strangers,* Serenity mused. *Perhaps they'll make a purchase that will raise his spirits.* Business had been poor during the war. Few people had been able to afford the fine things displayed on Papa's shelves. Fortunately for her and Papa, he had put away a comfortable sum before the war and, by being frugal, they had managed.

She considered placing her ear next to the door, but then she shook her head. She was much too grown up to indulge in such childish behavior. Instead, she set the table in the dining room the way her mother had taught her when she was a little girl. As it always did, the simple ritual brought back a flood of memories. A little more than five years had passed since that awful night before the war when Mamma was murdered, but time hadn't eased the ache in Serenity's heart—nor the one in Papa's. He'd grown thin, his hair had turned gray, his shoulders slouched, and he seldom laughed. Often she caught him standing in the doorway, staring off toward the west with great longing in his eyes. Serenity had also changed during those years, from a carefree child to a somber woman.

"Serenity?" The door opened between the house and the store, and Charles Caswell stepped inside the long room adjoining the kitchen that served as parlor at one end and dining room at the other. "Set two more places at the table. We have guests tonight." There was a light in his eyes she hadn't seen for a long time.

Cutlery dropped from Serenity's hands and clattered against the plate she'd already set at Papa's place. She'd been right. There was something unusual about the strangers.

"Yes, Papa," she managed, then watched him disappear back inside the store. She couldn't remember more than a handful of times when Papa had invited guests to dine with them. A neighboring Quaker farmer had sat stiffly at the table with Papa on rare occasions, and twice Timothy and Caleb, the two former slaves, had traveled from upper New York to pay their respects at Mamma's grave. Papa had insisted they share their table, though the black men were clearly uncomfortable doing so.

Serenity hadn't been pleased by these latter visits. She'd caught glimpses of Caleb and Timothy several times before Mamma's death, but she'd never been in the same room with them until the night they came in carrying her mother's body. She suspected they knew more about the man who shot her mother than they let on. Papa said her suspicions were nonsense, but she'd still worried when Timothy had come alone just before joining the 8th Cavalry in Philadelphia and Papa had treated him as though he were family, spending hours walking and conversing with him.

Serenity gathered up the plates she'd already set on the table and replaced them with the four matching plates Mamma had called her "company dishes." This was only the second time Serenity had used them. She frowned, recalling the time six months ago when Bernard Tolson and his son, Percival, had arrived at their door just as she and Papa were preparing to eat their evening meal. Papa had politely invited the Tolsons to join them, and she'd rushed to reset the table. Their visitors had gorged themselves, leaving greasy fingerprints on Mamma's tablecloth and an astonishing amount of food and debris under the table. To Serenity's dismay, Percy had somehow managed to steadily move his chair closer to hers until he brushed against her each time he lifted his fork to his thick lips. She'd been so busy trying to avoid him without making a scene, she hadn't listened to Mr. Tolson's conversation with Papa, but after the Tolsons' departure she'd noticed that Papa was distracted and annoyed all evening.

Tonight wouldn't be like that. Papa had invited the strangers to eat with them and was pleased by their acceptance, so they surely had much better manners than the Tolsons. Serenity felt a small shiver of excitement at the prospect of sitting at the table with two young gentlemen. Had she prepared enough food? Would the gentlemen be disappointed to discover that their supper consisted of one fat hen, dumplings, and root vegetables? Serenity was glad Papa had accepted the hen in trade for the plain gold wedding band that had sat in his display case since his last trip to New York before the war. Papa had laughed when he told her the ragged soldier who purchased it had probably caught some farmer's runaway chicken and counted it an answer to prayer as he returned to his sweetheart with a wedding ring.

The sound of an opening door alerted her that Papa was returning with their guests. She watched them file into the room and noted that though the strangers were better dressed than the returning soldiers, their trousers and shoes showed signs of much use. The men appeared to be no more than twenty-five years of age. One was tall with a thick thatch of yellow hair. The other was shorter, though still above average in height, with straight brown hair parted in the center and combed to each side. Perpetual mischief seemed to sparkle in his eyes, and Serenity felt inclined to respond to his warm smile.

"Serenity, dear." Papa bustled forward to make introductions. "These young men have recently come from Denmark. They traveled some distance out of their way to inquire about your mother. This one—" he indicated the taller, more fair young man—"Mr. James Holmes, was acquainted with your mother. This other gentleman is his friend and companion, Edward Benson."

"How do you do, Miss Caswell?" Mr. Holmes offered. "It was kind of you to offer us dinner tonight."

"Pleased to meet you, miss," Mr. Benson said with a slight bow.

"How do you do?" Serenity attempted to play the gracious hostess in spite of feeling flustered by their warm greetings.

"We received instruction a short time ago that your father might be able to tell us something of Hannah Waterton," Mr. Holmes said. "I was deeply saddened to learn of her demise." There was a look of genuine sorrow in his eyes.

Serenity's smile disappeared and she drew back, welcoming the solid wood of the table that separated her from the two men. By the time she was five years old, she'd known that she shouldn't speak of her mother to strangers and that her mother's sudden and frequent disappearances had something to do with the soft taps on the back door that came late at night. She'd known, too, that because of her mother, she wasn't quite welcome in the Quaker community nor at the village school the sons and daughters of other merchants and businessmen attended. But the war was over and President Lincoln had freed the slaves, so why were these men looking for Mamma now? Could it be because she had been a Mormon? What did it matter anyway? Mamma was dead.

"My mother died shortly before the war began," she said in a stilted voice. She glanced toward her father, silently begging him for help. He merely smiled encouragement.

"I can't believe I've actually found Sister Hannah's daughter," said Mr. Holmes with excitement. Serenity nodded in hesitant acknowledgment, causing her long sable curls to bounce. She blinked to clear away unexpected moisture from her eyes. She wasn't accustomed to speaking of her mother or of hearing Mamma's name spoken aloud. Unbidden tears threatened to fall.

"I'm sorry," Mr. Holmes said quickly, noticing Serenity's reaction. "She was a good woman and my family owes her much. My mother, especially, will be sad to hear of her death. But she will also be thrilled to learn of her daughter."

"How did you know my mother?" Serenity knew little of her mother's life before marrying Papa, other than that she was a Mormon and that her family had gone west to the Rocky Mountains without her. If Papa knew more of her past, he never spoke of it to Serenity.

"Our mothers were friends in Nauvoo, Illinois, twenty years ago. Your grandparents were comfortably situated, but my mother was a poor widow with two small children. Miss Hannah secretly left gifts of vegetables from her family's garden on our doorstep that summer and fall. We owe our lives to her generosity."

Not knowing how to respond to the young man's frank admiration of her mother, Serenity gestured toward the table and the chairs gathered around it. "Come, won't you sit down?" she invited. Her father seconded the invitation. Serenity hoped Mr. Holmes would tell her more about Mamma. She still missed her mother and thought that if she knew more about her, she might be better able to accept her tragic death.

When the men were seated, she hurried to the kitchen to serve the meal she had prepared. She carried the steaming platters and bowls to the table and took care to place the freshly churned butter before her father before accepting the chair Mr. Benson held for her. She was about to begin passing the platter of chicken when Papa spoke up.

"Do you wish to say grace before we proceed?" He directed the question to Mr. Holmes.

"I would be honored." The young man bowed his head and spoke a simple prayer, causing Serenity a brief moment of remorse. Mamma had always prayed before meals, but she and Papa had let the practice drop during those first grief-filled days following her death and had never resumed it.

Once plates were filled and the first bites sampled, Serenity voiced the first of the questions crowding through her mind. "Did I understand Papa to say you've come from across the ocean, all the way from Denmark?"

Again it was the blond man who spoke first. "We're both from Salt Lake City in the Utah Territory, where we've lived since we were young children," he explained. "We've been away preaching the gospel in Denmark and are now on our way home."

"You're Mormon preachers?" Serenity asked.

"Not exactly," Mr. Benson answered her. "Most Mormon men accept a call to preach the gospel for a few years, then they return to their families and professions. We've completed our missions and are now preparing to resume the plans for our futures made before we journeyed to Denmark. Fortunately for me, Elder Holmes had a promise to keep, which brought us here." His smile seemed to hint that the good fortune he alluded to was more than a plate heaped with chicken and dumplings.

"Miss Caswell, before I left for Denmark, I promised your uncle, Reliance Waterton, that upon my return I would try to find his sister, as I would be passing through Pennsylvania," Mr. Holmes explained. Turning to her father, he added. "He told me he had written numerous times to acquaintances in the village where he and his sister had lived as children, but his letters were always returned unopened. He believed it was because when his family left the Quaker faith to become Mormons, the village elders ordered their congregation to shun them. It was Reliance's hope that I might find a way to locate his sister, since I had devoted several years to the study of law before accepting a call from the Lord to preach the gospel."

Serenity's hand shook, almost spilling the contents of her fork. She'd never considered that her mother's family could have been shunned by the Quakers. She was aware that most people in their community, both Quakers and Protestants, disapproved of Mormons, and she had assumed that bias accounted for her and her mother's limited acceptance among them. But to cut off all communication with the Waterton family? Hannah's return to Pennsylvania must have presented quite a dilemma to the Friends who worked in the cause for which Mamma gave her life.

"I have an uncle?" That aspect of James Holmes's message gradually sank into Serenity's mind, giving rise to eager excitement. For the last five years she'd longed for more family than just herself and Papa, and now she had many questions about her mother's family. Papa had told her long ago that he was an orphan and that he'd never met his wife's family, who had moved west without her. He'd been reluctant to discuss the matter further, leaving Serenity's curiosity unsatisfied.

Mr. Holmes appeared amused by her question. "Not only do you have an uncle, but through him you also have at least fourteen Waterton cousins. The oldest of them is a man a little older than myself, then an even dozen females, followed by a small boy who was an infant when I left for Denmark. There may be more cousins by now. Your mother had but one brother, and he is a stalwart in his community in Utah and in the Church. He has a farm some miles south of Salt Lake City where he raises onions and potatoes."

"Goodness!" Her hand fluttered to the neckline of her plain, worsted gown. "Please tell me my cousins' names and all you know of them."

"I remember Miss Hannah brought Andrew, her brother's oldest child, to my birthday party when I turned four . . ."

James seemed happy to oblige her with tales of her cousins, whom he seemed to know well. She laughed and was delighted to learn of their exploits.

"And do Mamma's parents live near Uncle Reliance?" she asked at length. "I remember Mamma spoke of my grandparents with longing a few times."

"I'm sorry to be the one to inform you that they died before reaching Zion. Your grandfather was ill before they left Nauvoo. They both contracted a fever on the journey to Winter Quarters and succumbed to their illnesses during that first difficult winter. Reliance feared Hannah had met the same fate, as he never heard from her after her departure from Nauvoo."

At this, Papa entered the conversation. "You speak as if she left the Mormon settlement before her family did. It was my understanding that her family left without her, leaving her to fare for herself."

"No, Hannah left first." James appeared uneasy and looked around as though assuring himself no one could overhear his words. "She left Nauvoo four or five months before her family started west. She was strongly opposed to slavery, and when she discovered a black child being whipped on the property where my family lived, she and my mother took steps to protect the boy. When the slave owner threatened to separate the child's family, Miss Hannah made arrangements for the family to run away and she left with them. She told my mother she was taking them to Canada and that she meant to settle among the Quakers in Pennsylvania to work for the abolitionist cause once the family was safe."

Serenity's father cleared his throat. "My wife was deeply committed to abolishing slavery." Serenity glanced at her father. She suspected the conversation was difficult for the private man she knew her papa to be. A more mature woman would graciously change the subject, but she couldn't bring herself to do so. She'd yearned to know more of her mother for such a long time, and now it was no longer a crime to support the emancipation of slaves. After another quick glance at her father, she voiced the question that troubled her.

"I always wondered where she got the money to bring that family so far and help them begin a business of their own." Her fingers played over the carved sides of the table, and she avoided looking at the two young men or Papa. She didn't want them to know her suspicions about two members of the family Mamma had helped run away from Nauvoo—the two colored men who'd brought Mamma's body home after she'd been shot. She suspected that they had stolen a valuable ring from her.

Mr. Holmes's reply to her question put to rest one of Serenity's suspicions but not the other. "Hannah had some money of her own," he said. "A dear lady, whom I called grandmother, gave the slave family her small savings, and my mother had a large topaz gem she tried to give to them. They refused it, fearing that if they were caught with it in their possession, they would be hung as thieves. When they wouldn't accept the stone, Mamma gave it to Hannah to help them get started in their new life."

Serenity's eyes opened wide. James Holmes knew about the topaz! Then another thought hit her. She hesitated. Then, as if she couldn't help herself, she continued in jerky phrases. "Papa said he bought the topaz . . . from someone who was helping . . . escaped slaves reach Canada. He never said it was Mamma who brought it to him."

2

"That topaz brought your mamma and me together." Charles reached across the table to place his hand on his daughter's. "The first time I saw your mother was the day she entered my store just after sunset, when I was preparing to lock up for the night. She appeared exhausted and glanced frequently over her shoulder as though she expected someone threatening to suddenly appear. She held out her hand, and on her palm rested the biggest topaz I had ever seen. It had a medium golden hue with a faint blush of pink. I knew by its color and clarity that it was worth far more than I could give her for it. Still, I offered her all of the cash I could lay my hands on, and she accepted it."

"Didn't you wonder where she'd gotten such a gem?" Mr. Benson asked.

"I know what you're implying, but no. The moment I saw Hannah Waterton I knew she was a woman incapable of stealing and that however she'd come by the gem, it was through no dishonest action."

Mr. Benson turned to his friend. "You said your mother gave it to Miss Hannah, but how did a poor widow acquire a valuable gem?"

Serenity leaned closer to hear Mr. Holmes's answer.

"It was on the ship on which our family took passage to America when I was a small boy. A woman, a complete stranger to us, made certain my mother would find the jewel where she'd hidden it. We never saw her again, though my mother searched for her at length."

Mr. Benson asked Charles another question. "Did you suspect Miss Hannah would use the money you gave her to help slaves escape their master?"

"I suspected as much. I had been purchasing trinkets from escaping slaves for years to help them on their way. Often a Quaker intermediary made the actual exchange. Other than a trusted Quaker friend and my wife, no one, not even my daughter—" he squeezed Serenity's fingers—"knew of my involvement with the Underground Railroad, though there were many who were suspicious of my wife."

"Papa, why didn't you tell me?" She watched her father draw his lips together and close his eyes briefly.

"At first it was because of the need for secrecy, then it just became a habit to never speak of your mother guiding those slave families to safety, nor of my efforts to finance new lives for them. I knew you had pieced together many things concerning your mother's involvement in the Railroad, but it never seemed the right time to tell you of my own involvement. After she . . . died, I couldn't speak of her. At least not until today."

"But what is different today?"

"These gentlemen . . ." He paused. "When you were born I promised your mother that I would look into her belief that families could still be together as families in heaven, but then I never did much to keep that promise. Almost a year ago I took her Book of Mormon from the drawer in the little table beside our bed and began to read it. As I read I thought of her, and you, and the many families torn apart by war, and I found myself hoping that God really did have a plan to bring families back together. A couple of months ago, I started praying that someone would come who could teach me more about this concept, and today Mr. Holmes and Mr. Benson arrived at our door."

"We'd be happy to teach you, Mr. Caswell," Mr. Holmes offered. "Whenever you wish."

Charles smiled. "How about right after we finish my daughter's delicious pudding?"

* * *

Serenity cleared the table and retired to the kitchen to wash the dishes while the men gathered in the front room. When they spoke of a sealing power given to their prophet that united families for eternity through a ceremony performed in a temple, she remembered that when she was very young, Mamma had told her about a beautiful temple, which she said was God's house. For years Serenity had dreamed of the temple, imagining it to be a castle filled with magical wonders like Mamma's topaz ring. Whenever Mamma had spoken of the temple, she'd looked sad. Young Serenity had decided it must be because her mother was really a princess who was forced to leave the castle by wicked intruders. When Serenity got older she began paying attention to snatches of conversation between her parents, and she began to understand that the wicked people hated Mamma because she was a Mormon and an abolitionist.

She wasn't sure why some people hated Mormons, but she understood that the Mormon leader had married a Pennsylvania girl and that many Pennsylvanians didn't think much of him or the church he had started.

In time she'd learned more about slavery and about the Mormons. Slavery had ended because President Lincoln had signed an emancipation law, making the secret doings of people like Mamma no longer necessary. The Pennsylvania newspapers generally applauded the president's action. Most of the things the papers had to say about the Mormons weren't so favorable.

From the next room, she heard Papa say, "My wife believed families were meant to be together in heaven. I've thought long about this, and it seems to me that she was too alive to just die from a single shot by a slaver. Lately, I've had a powerful feeling that she's not really far away and that she's waiting for us to go to the temple she used to talk about, so that someday we can be with her in heaven. That feeling keeps getting stronger. Now that the war is over, I'm thinking of going west to see if the Mormons have built another temple."

"Another temple?" Serenity whispered in puzzlement. She had never considered the possibility that her mother's people might build another temple. In her mind there was only the one, and it had been taken over and burned by the Mormons' enemies.

When she finished washing the dishes, she meant to sit on a wooden chair in the kitchen and continue listening to Papa and the Mormons, but Papa called to her and made room for her beside him on the horsehair sofa. Their guests sat across from them on comfortable chairs.

She was surprised to see Mamma's Book of Mormon on Papa's lap. She hadn't thought about that book for a long time. Almost five years ago, not long after Mamma died, she had found it accidentally while looking for her mother's topaz ring. Mamma had asked Serenity to promise that when she died, Serenity would wear the ring as a reminder of her mother's love until God found a greater need for it. Remembering her promise and being anxious to keep it, she'd gone looking for the ring and had found the book instead. It was inside a hidden drawer in a little table that Mamma's sewing basket sat under.

Seeing the basket had brought a lump to her throat and memories of the many evenings her mother had sat before the fire stitching dresses for her and dolls for the children she helped escape to freedom. After stitching for a time, she'd always set the basket aside and pick up the book. Often she read aloud to Serenity.

For a long time after that day, when Serenity was feeling particularly sad or lonely, she'd sit on the side of Papa's bed and run her fingers across the worn spots on the book Mamma had loved. Many times she'd prayed, asking God to help her find Mamma's ring so she could keep her promise.

Papa spoke of the book now in response to a question from Mr. Benson. "Yes, I've read it through several times. It has given me a great deal to think about. I've considered that Joe Smith might have been right when he declared that God speaks to men as clearly today as in Bible times."

Serenity was still thinking about her mother's ring. Even as a small child, she'd understood there was something mysterious about the huge, yellow stone. Mamma had told her that the Egyptians believed topaz to be an amulet that protected the faithful against harm. She'd wondered more than once if Mamma had died because she hadn't been wearing the ring the night she was killed. Serenity vowed that if she ever found the ring, she'd never take it off.

"There's a room off the stable you're welcome to use." Serenity blinked and forced her attention back to the conversation going on around her. She was disappointed to find the discussion at an end. She'd been so wrapped in her thoughts, she'd heard little the two former missionaries had said. But if Papa was inviting them to spend the night in the stable, perhaps she'd get another opportunity. Like her father, she wanted to hear more about Mamma's beliefs. And, though it didn't seem possible, she wanted to know if there was a chance she'd see her mother again.

Papa saw their visitors to the door. When he turned back into the room, Serenity watched him make his way back to the book he'd left on the sofa. Summoning her courage, she asked, "Papa, did Mamma leave her ring behind the night she was killed?"

Papa looked startled for a moment, then sat down heavily. He was silent for a long time before speaking. "The ring is gone, probably stolen," he told her. "I searched everywhere for it and at last concluded that her murderer stole it. I didn't want to tell you until you were older. Though I made an effort to keep the circumstances of Hannah's death a secret, word spread among the Quakers that she had been shot by a slave hunter. Our neighbors were much kinder to you after they believed your mother died supporting a cause they were passionate about. They were willing to forget she was a Mormon and treat you as the daughter of a martyr. If they thought she had been killed by a mere thief, I think they wouldn't have been so willing to reach out to you."

"But surely Mamma was killed by a slave hunter. Those two black men said—"

"They didn't actually see who shot her. Her ring wasn't on her finger when Caleb and Timothy brought her here that night. At first I thought she might have left it home so that she would have less chance of being identified if she were captured, but I never found it among her things. I long ago concluded that whoever shot her must have taken her ring, and that robbery may have had more to do with the shooting than her work with escaped slaves."

"Do you think, Papa, that when Caleb and Timothy found Mamma and saw that she was dead, they took the ring? They might have thought their claim to the stone was greater than ours."

"I did consider that possibility. Before Timothy left to join the army, I followed him to your mother's grave and put that question to him."

Serenity held her breath. "And did he confess?"

"No. He said that when he and his uncle reached her side, she was lying face down with one hand outstretched as though she were pointing. She usually wore riding gloves on all her forays, but he didn't give any thought that night to her gloves and the ring being missing. He did notice, however, that the ground appeared to have been the scene of a scuffle and that her saddlebag was gone."

Long after Serenity crawled into her warm featherbed, she lay awake thinking about the things her father had told her, and about their visitors. Eventually she drifted to sleep. Some time afterwards she sat bolt upright and listened intently. She'd been dreaming about her mother, but then she'd heard the back gate squeak, followed a few seconds later by a soft tap on the back door.

She must have cried out, because moments later Papa pushed her door open and peered inside.

"Are you all right?" he asked.

"Yes." Papa came to sit on the edge of her bed. "I thought I heard the back gate squeak, then a tap on the door—like all those nights when I was a child and watched from my window as Mamma rode away into the black shadows. Oh, Papa, why did you let her go? You must have known how dangerous it was."

Papa sighed and bowed his head. For long minutes he cradled his head in his hands. His voice was almost a whisper when he spoke. "Speaking of your mother tonight has upset you. I should have told you more about her years ago. I always meant to tell you of that day your Mamma came to my store with a huge jewel in her hand. She took the cash I gave her for the gem and disappeared. Shortly after, I set out for New York. There I learned the jewel was a unique and extremely valuable gem, the kind of jewel that once seen would never be forgotten, much like your mamma herself. I found I couldn't part with the stone, so I had it set in a ring.

"Upon my return to our village, I learned of a woman living alone at the edge of the Quaker settlement. I was delighted when I discovered that she was the same woman who had brought me the topaz. When I asked her to be my wife, she was reluctant to accept my offer. She said that after much prayer, she'd received the direction that her life was to be devoted to uniting slave families and helping them obtain their freedom. I gave her my word I would never interfere and sealed our bargain by placing the topaz ring on her finger."

"Thank you for telling me, Papa."

Serenity drifted back to sleep only to dream a tangled dream in which her mother looked at her reproachfully for not wearing her topaz ring. When she tried to explain that she couldn't find it, the two dark-coated missionaries appeared and said she hadn't searched hard enough—that she'd have to keep searching or her family would never be reunited in the new Mormon castle.

* * *

Over the next week, Mr. Holmes and Mr. Benson were frequent visitors in the Caswell home. Serenity often spotted them strolling with her father through the orchard or leaning across the counter in Papa's store engaged in earnest conversation. The gentlemen were effusive in their compliments toward her cooking, especially Mr. Benson, and sometimes she found herself blushing furiously when he paid her particular attention. Though she enjoyed their company, she wasn't so sure about their constant discussions with Papa concerning their beliefs.

One morning as she sat across from Papa at the breakfast table, he announced plans to travel to New York on his first buying trip since before the war. She remembered his once-frequent trips to New York to trade items he'd acquired and to buy merchandise for his store.

"I shall only be gone a short time, but there is business I must see to there."

"May I go with you, Papa?" Even as a small child, Papa's trips had inspired a world of wonder in Serenity's dreams. Surely New

York City must be the most wondrous place in the world, and she longed to go there.

Charles shook his head. "Not this time. I'll need you to keep the store open while I'm gone. And there could be some danger for a young lady with so many vagabond soldiers on the roads. Besides, this isn't just a business trip. It will even be dangerous for me—and I wouldn't dream of exposing you to such danger."

Serenity looked at him worriedly, so he continued.

"With the war starting so soon after your mother's death, I was unable to make inquiries about her ring in New York. I shall take that opportunity now since I am quite convinced that anyone having seen that exquisite imperial topaz could never forget it."

"Papa, I could stay at your hotel while you make inquiries."

"No, dear child, but upon my return we shall undertake a journey together. I am quite convinced we should make our way to Salt Lake City to meet your uncle's family and to learn more about this sealing power James and Edward speak of so convincingly." She noticed that her father now referred to the two men by their given names.

Hoping to quell her disappointment in hard work, Serenity donned her plainest gown and retired to her garden. After spading the ground for a short time, she heard whistling. Looking up, she saw Mr. Benson walking toward her with a spade in his hands.

"It looks like you could use some help," he called out and soon was beside her, turning the soil with swift, deft strokes.

"I can do it," she protested, but she didn't really mind when he continued turning the soil. After observing him for a few moments, she resumed her self-appointed task.

A short time later, he paused beside her and wiped his brow with a large handkerchief from his pocket. She stopped too. When his eyes met hers, she felt a strange flutter behind her ribs and quickly looked away.

"James and I shall be leaving for a few weeks," he announced. "We've been invited to visit with a family a few miles upstream who wish to hear more of the gospel. We shall return before James begins his journey west and I take up my studies again."

A strange sense of gloom descended over Serenity. Isolated from both the Quaker children and the village children, she'd grown up with few friends or playmates and was finding the attention of the two young men gratifying. But now they were leaving. And in a few days Papa would be leaving too. Serenity hadn't spent a night apart from Papa in the past five years. She would be lonely without him. And now she wouldn't even have the company of the two young men who had arrived a week ago to lighten her and Papa's solitary existence. *Yes, that's all it is,* she assured herself. She'd grown accustomed to their company, and that was the only reason their imminent departure filled her with melancholy.

3

Serenity leaned both elbows on the counter and sighed. She'd be glad when Papa returned. This was his first trip East since Mamma's death, and the two weeks he'd been gone had seemed to drag. She wished he'd allowed her to accompany him. His argument that she needed to keep the store open in his absence had proved to be absurd. Even with the war at an end, no one had money to spend on pretty ornaments for their homes or for themselves. In two weeks' time, she'd sold one simple picture frame, four scented candles, a bar of fine-milled soap, a single leather-bound book, and half a dozen hand-painted napkin rings.

The bell over the door tinkled and she looked up to see Mr. Holmes and Mr. Benson enter the store. A glad smile lit her face, and if she wasn't mistaken, Mr. Benson winked at her.

She found herself blushing and looked away to hide her confusion from the handsome young man who seemed about to burst into laughter. She couldn't guess what he found so amusing unless he was laughing at her.

"Has your father returned?" Mr. Holmes asked.

"Not yet, though I expect to see him ride in any minute. Would you care to join us for supper?"

Mr. Benson was quick to respond. "Yes, we would be pleased to accept your kind invitation."

Mr. Holmes directed an appreciative smile toward her. "You are as gracious as your mother."

"I didn't know your mother," Mr. Benson chimed in, "but if she was half as pretty as her daughter, I consider it my loss."

Serenity's eyes widened as it dawned on her that Mr. Benson was flirting with her! She didn't know whether she was pleased or annoyed. She wasn't accustomed to receiving attention from young men—except for Percy Tolson, who was nothing short of a bother.

Serenity didn't miss the annoyed frown Mr. Holmes sent his friend before saying to her, "I truly am sorry for your loss. My family will want to know all I can tell them about your mother's life and yours here in Pennsylvania."

Serenity took a few steps away from the counter before pausing to look back at her visitors. "Papa and I seldom talk about Mamma to anyone other than each other." She hesitated then continued. "But I feel you truly cared for her, and it doesn't seem right to be less than truthful." She took a deep breath and faced Mr. Holmes squarely. "When Papa married Mamma he returned the topaz to her in the form of a ring. She always wore it. A short time before the war began, she escorted a young black couple with a small child to their next contact point on the Underground Railroad. As she began her return journey, she was shot, presumably by a slave hunter, though her assailant may have been nothing more than a thief. She was already dead when her body was returned to Papa and me, and her ring was gone."

"Your father told us she had been murdered," Mr. Holmes said, pacing the short distance between them, "but did not give us the details. I cannot fathom the reasoning behind taking the life of such a kind woman. Was the murderer apprehended?"

Serenity shook her head slowly.

"Surely there was an investigation," he exclaimed.

"No. Papa let everyone think Mamma was expecting a child and that she died from birthing complications. Many in the Quaker community knew how she really died, but they helped Papa keep it a secret."

Mr. Benson joined the discussion, his confusion evident. "But why? The murderer should be punished."

"The shooter could claim he was only protecting his property. Aiding runaway slaves was illegal, and if it were known that Mamma was involved with the Underground Railroad, Papa and I would not have been safe. Both our lives and Papa's property would have been in danger. Papa feared for Mamma's contacts as well, for their lives would also have been jeopardized if it became known she was helping slaves escape from their masters."

"It seems your mother led an adventurous life," Mr. Benson said, shaking his head. Fearing she might see mocking laughter in the eyes of the jovial young man, Serenity glanced at him suspiciously. The sympathy she found in his steady gaze went far to ease her uncertainty about him. It also increased the self-consciousness he seemed to stir in her.

Slightly flustered, Serenity broke eye contact with him and turned her attention back to her responsibilities. "Papa will be coming soon, and it is almost time to close the shop," she said. Though she'd been looking toward the window at frequent intervals, she'd seen no sign of her father. She wanted Mr. Holmes and Mr. Benson to stay for supper, but she had little experience entertaining, and it would be much easier and likely more proper if Papa were at home. When she'd extended the hasty invitation, she'd felt certain her father would be home long before the supper hour. She hesitantly glanced toward the door leading to the house.

"We don't wish to intrude," Mr. Holmes began as though he sensed her hesitation.

"No, it's not an intrusion," she assured him. She really didn't want them to leave.

Mr. Benson smiled roguishly. "I never pass up an opportunity to eat with a pretty young woman."

Feeling flustered again, Serenity hurried back behind the counter to close the cashbox, then turned toward the door to lock it and pull the shade. She glanced up the empty street one more time as she did so.

The two men followed her through a side door into the home she and Papa shared. During their first visit she had sensed they were surprised to find a home of such high taste and quality attached to a store. Again she noticed their appreciative perusal of the art objects, paintings, and fine fabrics that filled the home.

Mamma had appreciated fine things, but it was Papa who had collected the valuables. Until the start of the war, he'd not only bought many treasures from desperate fugitives, but he'd purchased family treasures from people heading west who needed cash more than they needed heirlooms. He'd taken many of the items to New York to sell or trade, but he'd kept a few of them.

Serenity busied herself preparing supper. When she reached for the empty coal bucket, Mr. Benson took it from her hand and asked directions to the coal shed.

"It's there beside the stable." She pointed through the open doorway to the small building beyond the back gate.

"I'll be back in two shakes of a lamb's tail," he said before hurrying down the path, his cheerful, tuneless whistle following him. She stared after him feeling quite bemused.

"Miss Caswell."

She turned back to face Mr. Holmes and noted from his serious demeanor that something was bothering him.

"I know when your mother left Nauvoo she brought a slave family this far," he began, "but do you know anything of what became of little Timothy, the youngest member of that family? When I was a child little Timothy spent his days in our home while his family worked for the Rundells, who were the property owners. We grew attached to him, and I have wondered about his well-being all these years. I meant to ask your father, but it never seemed to be the right time."

"My parents never talked about the people my mother helped." Serenity began peeling potatoes. As though it were a natural thing to do, Mr. Holmes picked up another paring knife and reached for one of the potatoes. She'd never seen a man peel vegetables before and wondered if she should protest, though his assistance would certainly speed dinner preparations. As he began to remove the peel and she could see it was a task he'd performed before, she grew more comfortable speaking to him.

"I do know something of the family. Timothy and his uncle, Caleb, were deeply involved in the Underground Railroad. My mother had just turned a runaway family over to them and bid them farewell when she was shot. They were the ones who brought her body home." She finished peeling one potato and reached for another as she continued. "Caleb is a preacher now. Timothy was anxious to enlist when the war began, but Caleb insisted that his nephew was too young and that the Union didn't want black volunteers anyway. Three years later, when two black regiments were formed and Timothy was seventeen, he stopped here to pay his respects to Mamma's grave on his way to enlist."

"He's a buffalo soldier then?"

"No. When he learned there were colored regiments being recruited in New York and Philadelphia, he went to Philadelphia to join a cavalry unit. Papa read in one of his papers that his unit took part in the Battle of Richmond."

"Is he safe? Has he returned home?"

"I don't know how he fared. We pored over the papers each time one was published, looking for his name among the dead and wounded, but did not see it. But many of the colored soldiers were not even listed by name. Papa has remarked several times that he wished he'd made Timothy promise he would stop by to let us know of his welfare on his return from the war."

"Do you know anything of his family and where I might contact them?"

"I don't know where they settled. Mamma kept no records, and I never heard the name of their town mentioned, but I think it's in upstate New York. Papa may know something of their whereabouts. When he comes, you can ask him."

"I'll do that."

Serenity added lard to the flour for the biscuits she was preparing and thoroughly mixed the two together with her hands. She wondered if she should tell Mr. Holmes about her suspicions concerning Timothy and Caleb. Her conversation with her father hadn't fully resolved her concerns. But she could be mistaken, so she decided to say nothing.

"Is something troubling you, Miss Caswell?"

She jumped. She'd been so deep in thought, she'd almost forgotten her visitor. "I was thinking about Timothy and Caleb. When they brought my mother home, she wasn't wearing her ring. I thought . . . I wondered . . . We looked everywhere for it but never found it . . . and . . ."

"You think they might have taken it?"

She looked away, feeling embarrassed. Subconsciously she began scraping dough from her hands, then scrubbed at the remaining dough with a damp cloth.

"I suppose it is possible, but the Caleb I remember wouldn't have touched that gem even if he thought he had a right to it, since Mother first offered it to his family."

"But what could have happened to it?"

"One bucket of coal coming up!" Edward shouted as he appeared at the door. He walked across the room and set the heavy bucket on the floor near the large cookstove. "I'll add a chunk to your fire, then step outside to wash up." He reached for the handle to lift one of the round stovetop lids and quickly thrust another lump into the hot coals. Then he held up his hands, displaying the coal dust and smears. "I'll be right back." Smiling, he backed toward the door, turning only to reach for the latch. He was brought up short when the door opened almost in his face and Charles stumbled into the room.

"Hannah's saddlebag—" The hoarse whisper broke off abruptly. The man staggered, sank to his knees, and then fell backward. A pool of red spread from beneath his body and ran across the floor. His shirt and hands were smeared with blood, and his face was ashen.

"Papa!" Serenity screamed, running toward the fallen figure.

She knelt beside her father, her hands going to his closed eyes. "Papa, what happened?" She pulled off her apron and pressed it against the dark red spot on his shirt in an effort to halt the flow of blood.

"Miss Caswell, let me check him." Mr. Benson gently moved her aside so that he could get a better view of the injured man. He left her apron covering the wound while he looked for other injuries. Mr. Holmes handed his friend a towel he'd dampened with a dipper of water. Absently, Mr. Benson used it to wipe the coal dust from his hands before touching Charles.

"Help me turn him over," he ordered. Before Serenity could move, Mr. Holmes knelt beside Mr. Benson and the two men turned Charles. Serenity gasped when she saw the wound in his back. Edward pressed the clean end of the towel to the wound and called for more towels. "It appears he's been shot in the back. Let's lift him to the table, where I can examine the wound more thoroughly," Mr. Benson instructed. Mr. Holmes obeyed quickly.

Serenity rushed about, snatching dishes from the table and fetching a pillow as the two men placed her father on the table. Mr. Benson's words beat a frantic rhythm in her mind, seeming to freeze her capacity to think. *Shot in the back. Shot in the back.* She'd lost her mother to a bullet in her back. Surely she wasn't going to lose her father that way too.

"Can you stop the bleeding?" Mr. Holmes asked.

"I don't know. It doesn't look good. Hurry with those towels and bring some soap and warm water."

Mr. Holmes rushed to do his bidding. When he returned with the basin, Mr. Benson plunged his hands in the water and lathered the soap between his hands. Mr. Holmes handed him a fresh towel he'd grabbed from a stack Serenity kept near the wash basin.

Mr. Benson scrubbed at the wound in Charles's back and then pressed a towel against it before enlisting James's assistance in turning his patient over again.

Serenity watched, wringing her hands helplessly as Mr. Benson pressed his ear against Papa's chest. "He has lost a great deal of blood, and his lungs don't sound good."

"Papa." Serenity hurried to stand at his head and began stroking his temples. "Open your eyes. Oh, Papa, please don't leave me too." She turned to Mr. Holmes. "Should I fetch the Quaker midwife? Our village's only doctor hasn't returned from the war."

Mr. Holmes shook his head. "Your father is in good hands. Mr. Benson studied with an excellent doctor in Salt Lake City and assisted him with many of his cases, then spent two years at the medical school in Philadelphia."

"The bullet passed through him," Mr. Benson announced. "It may have pierced a lung, as he is having difficulty breathing. It sounds as if the left one is filling with liquid." He turned to his friend. "Would you go for my bag in the front room?"

Mr. Holmes sprinted from the room, letting the door bang shut behind him.

"Serenity." Her name came out gargled as Charles struggled to speak.

Serenity leaned closer to her father. "Don't try to talk," she said. "There's someone here who can help you."

"Just be still, Mr. Caswell," Mr. Benson soothed.

"Must tell . . ." Charles's voice trailed off in a strangled cough. After a few moments, the coughing ceased and he lay still. His chest rose and fell, but his breathing was ragged and harsh.

"Papa, oh Papa, please don't go!" Serenity lay her cheek against her father's, her tears wetting his face. He seemed to rally for a moment and again struggled to speak. His words were slurred, but she thought he told her he loved her before his voice disappeared behind the bubbling sound in his throat and he lost consciousness. She stroked his face and did her best to stay out of the way of Mr. Benson's efforts to stop the bleeding.

About the same time Mr. Holmes burst through the door with a black bag in his hand, Charles opened his eyes again. Mr. Benson extracted a packet of white powder from his bag. He sprinkled it liberally on the wound he'd finished cleaning.

Charles appeared confused for a moment, then he met Serenity's gaze. He tried to speak, but at first no words came out. With great determination, he finally managed to say, "Hannah . . . doll . . . take to Timothy . . ." His eyes closed, then opened wide. His whisper sounded more urgent. "Go Salt Lake . . ."

Serenity struggled to make sense of his garbled words. It seemed he was concerned about their planned journey to Salt Lake. Tears slipped down her cheeks as another possibility came to mind.

Perhaps he didn't expect to survive and wished for her to go to her mother's family.

He lapsed into unconsciousness, and then the harsh sound of his breathing became erratic. Serenity panicked. Papa couldn't die. There was so much they still needed to say to each other.

"I love you, Papa." She grasped his hand as tears ran unchecked down her cheeks. A glow lit her father's face, and he seemed about to smile. He applied faint pressure to her hand, then the gurgling noises in his throat stopped. His hand fell limply to the table.

"No, no," she sobbed. She felt an arm around her shoulders and let herself be led to the rocking chair. Numbness took over. For the next few hours, though she saw people come and go from the room, she felt detached, as though she were watching from a distant window.

4

The next two days passed in a blur. Women from both the Quaker community and the town brought food. Patience Hobson, a Quaker woman of Serenity's acquaintance, stayed with Serenity for two nights. The pastor from the town church came to call, as did the sheriff. They spoke with the two Mormons, who presented themselves as friends of the family. Serenity was scarcely aware of their presence.

"We must discuss funeral arrangements," said the pastor. He had seated himself across from her and now spoke to her in hushed tones as though she were ill. When she ignored him, he turned to Edward, who was never far from her side.

"We shall assist her with the arrangements," Edward said. "And we'll contact you if that is her wish."

When it became clear that Serenity wouldn't or couldn't discuss a funeral, Edward and James quietly planned a simple service, then set about coaxing her to eat.

Serenity would never recall when she began thinking of them as Edward and James instead of Mr. Benson and Mr. Holmes. In fact, she remembered little of those days at all. Details of the burial preparations seemed to pass her by. When James suggested Charles be buried beside his wife, Serenity merely nodded her head in agreement.

The service for Charles Caswell was to be held on the orchard hill. A grave had been dug next to Hannah's.

Patience Hobson dressed Serenity in a black gown for the service, and both James and Edward called for her. As the three of them walked through the orchard, a cold wind sprang up, sending apple blossoms fluttering toward the mound of dirt waiting beyond the trees. Edward stood beside Serenity, his arm supporting her, and James led the stalwart Quaker men who had stepped forward to carry Charles's coffin to its final resting place. James also conducted the service, and he and Edward each delivered a brief sermon to the surprisingly large crowd that had gathered to bid Charles farewell. A stirring of awareness half-awakened Serenity, and she struggled to absorb the messages James and Edward delivered. Though her mind tended to drift to a faraway place, some instinct told her she would someday wish to remember this day.

James spoke of something he called the "plan of salvation," a plan instituted by the Father to provide His children with a way to be awarded places in the kingdoms of glory. He also told the gathering of Hannah's kindness and compassion toward his family and his conviction that Charles was a noble spirit because no one of lesser stature could have won the love of Hannah Waterton.

Edward spoke more briefly. Referring to the recent civil war, he spoke of the need for healing—the healing of the nation, the healing of an abused people, and the healing of broken hearts. He referred to his unsuccessful attempt to heal Charles Caswell's broken body, then expressed his conviction that Charles was alive and whole in a far better place and that all could be healed of their hurts if they turned to God, the Great Healer. "I've no doubt his beloved wife was there to greet him when he breathed his last mortal breath," he concluded.

On some level, Serenity was aware of the Quakers standing stoically throughout the service and of an occasional amen coming from the townspeople as Edward and James spoke. Around the edges of the crowd could be seen a number of tearful black faces. A great gulf of emptiness threatened to swallow her, and she became painfully aware that no family or dear friends surrounded her. Though her father was respected in the community, he'd never cultivated close friends and had probably always been a bit of an enigma to the townspeople. She was his only family.

Most of the people left quickly when the last amen faded away. Two of the black women remained, standing near the orchard fence. When James noticed the women, he hurried toward them, and they greeted him like an old friend. Serenity felt a moment's gratitude that he was taking over the task of speaking to them, then she dismissed them from her mind.

Serenity knelt beside the coffin long after the crowd had gone. She almost envied Papa—surely he was with Mamma now, while she was left to make her way alone. At length someone reached for her arm.

"Come." Edward helped her to her feet. "I'll walk you back to your house. You can come back later after James and I have filled in the grave."

With Edward's arm around her waist, she walked slowly, stopping several times to look back. When they reached the house, he led her to the rocking chair beside the fireplace, where he made her comfortable with a quilt around her shoulders. He picked up a cup from the table beside her chair and ladled warm soup into it from a kettle hanging inside the fireplace. He pressed it into her cold hands before hurrying back outside.

Patience Hobson was gone, and Serenity was alone for the first time since her father's death. She held the cup but didn't sip from it. Unaware of the passing of time, she became lost in memories of her childhood, where she and Mamma and Papa had shared a loving home, a safe haven from the rest of the world.

When Edward and James returned to the house, they weren't alone. The two black women Serenity had seen earlier accompanied them. The older one hurried forward and knelt beside her. Resting her hands on the arm of Serenity's chair, she spoke words that seemed to come from deep within her heart.

"Yo' mamma an' Mistah James's mamma save my granbaby's life a long time ago. They was good people an' I owe 'em. Yo' pa was good man too. He give money and blankets to most all the slaves come this way, an' he signal when it be safe to move on an' which way to go. No question, the Lord God welcome him an' yo' mamma straight into heaven. Now I worry about the chile they leave behind. I plans to stay with you an' look after you 'til our Timothy come home. Don' you worry none. Julia will look after you like you my own dear chile."

"Child?" She was vaguely annoyed by the disturbance to her inner world of memories. It was like struggling against a river current to force herself to focus on the old woman's words.

"Yes, ma'am. Our Timothy tole me you the only chile our dear Miz Hannah have. Now your pa gone to his reward, you be all alone. What you gonna do if Julia don' look after you?"

The other woman stepped forward. "I'm Rosie. Timothy is my son. I'll be here to help you too, just like your mamma help me and my Timmy."

The older woman stood and retreated a few steps to stand beside Rosie. She looked at Serenity as though she were looking for something in particular. After watching her for several minutes, she said, "I knowed your Mamma. She was somethin'. She never give up or act scared no matter what. She make up her mind to do somethin', she do it. When she missin' her family an' times be hard, she work and she pray. You be like yo' mamma, a strong woman. You ain't got no time be sittin' around feelin' sorry for yourself. Yo' pa afraid he cause trouble if he track down man shoot yo' mamma. He ask questions, but never go to the law. Times change. Now it up to you to find coward shoot yo' pa in back. When you get the answer, then you tell the sheriff the whole story. Maybe the same man shoot yo' mamma."

Serenity sat up straight as though a bolt of lightning had gone through her. Was it possible both her parents had been killed by the same person? But why? Before the question was fully formed in her mind, she knew the answer. *The topaz ring! What if Papa had uncovered evidence that could identify the person who killed Mamma and stole the ring? He'd planned to ask about the ring in New York. Was it possible he'd learned the identity of the shooter after all this time? And if that person knew that Papa had uncovered something that might incriminate him . . .* Her mind raced on, taking on a clarity that had been absent since her father's death.

"You're right," she said to Julia. "I've been so busy thinking about my loss, I never asked why he was killed or who would do such a terrible thing." Shame flooded Serenity's mind. She looked around, and her attention centered on the missionaries.

"Does the sheriff have any suspects or plans to find the person who shot Papa?" she asked. "He had no enemies, so the person who shot him must have been intent on robbery."

Edward spoke up, eager to share what he and James had learned. "After he was shot, your father traveled a considerable distance by foot—almost a mile—even though he was bleeding steadily. At first light the morning after your father died, James and I followed the trail of blood back to where the shooting took place. We thought it best to keep in touch with the sheriff over what we found, so we asked him and his deputy to accompany us to a wooded place we had discovered where the road passes beneath a bluff about a mile outside of town. We figured the shots came from up on the bluff, and when we climbed up there, the sheriff found empty cartridges on the ground."

"Shots? But you said there was only the one wound."

"Your father was only struck once, but we found a dead horse that appeared to have been shot as well."

"Papa's Cindy Lou?" Serenity blinked back fresh tears. "I never thought to ask about Papa's mare. I should have inquired about her before now. Neither Mamma nor Papa would have been so weak-minded as I have been."

"You suffered a shock," Edward defended her.

The kind old black woman also spoke up. "Don' you worry none, Miz Serenity. Sometimes folks' minds go away for a little while when things get too bad for them to handle. That's all. Don' you worry. You be fine now."

Serenity studied her. Papa had described Julia Hayes, Timothy's grandmother, as the strong and brave matriarch of the Hayes family.

James's voice interrupted her musings. "We brought your father's saddle and a traveling case that was attached to it," he said. "Unfortunately, the bag seems to have been thoroughly ransacked."

"When Papa first stumbled through the door, he mentioned Mamma's saddlebag. I know he searched for it after her death but never found it."

"Do you suppose he found it in New York and that's what he was trying to tell you?" Edward asked.

"He planned to ask a few questions while in New York, but as far as I know, no one there knew of Mamma or her connection to the Underground Railroad." Serenity took a sip of the now cold soup she still clutched in her hand. She grimaced and set the cup on a low table beside her chair.

Julia frowned at the fireplace where the forgotten fire had gone out. "I 'spect you ain't et a thing for days," she surmised. She scooped up the cup Serenity had set down and bustled toward the kitchen with it, calling over her shoulder, "I'll have something hot in no time. Thinking be easier with a full belly."

"Don't fuss. Bread and cheese will be fine," Serenity replied.

"Land sakes! I never seen such a mess!" Julia stood in the doorway leading to the kitchen, her hands resting on her ample hips.

Edward hurried toward her, followed by James and, more slowly, Serenity. Serenity looked around the kitchen, aghast. Flour was spilled across the floor, the contents of the cupboards were toppled, and the door to the pantry stood open, showing the shelves there in complete disarray.

"Surely Patience Hobson didn't do this!" James exclaimed.

Edward looked grim. "Indeed she didn't. She was tidy to a fault."

"Then we'd best check the rest of the house." James turned toward the closed door that led to what had been Charles's bedroom. Edward picked up the fireplace poker on his way to join his friend. Serenity followed them at a distance.

James thrust the door open, then cautiously stepped inside. Serenity peeked into the room and let out a gasp. This room was worse than the kitchen. Feathers from the feather tick that had been slashed covered everything. Clothing was flung about the room, and holes had been knocked in the maple armoire. Cushions and pillows were emptied of their stuffing, and Hannah's sewing basket had been upended. Charles's books and papers were scattered everywhere.

"Who could have done this?" Serenity cried. Chills washed over her as she remembered sitting alone before the fireplace earlier as the fire burned itself out. She'd been oblivious to all around her. Anyone could have sneaked in or out of the house without her notice.

"I suspect whoever murdered your father didn't get what he was looking for, so he came here to search while we were holding the funeral," Edward suggested, and Serenity let out a sigh of relief. Surely he was right. The intruder had come while they'd been in the orchard for the funeral.

Julia peered over Serenity's shoulder, shaking her head in disgust. "What he lookin' for?"

Serenity decided to share her theory with the black woman. "Do you remember a large yellow jewel my mother brought with her from Nauvoo?"

"Indeed, I do." Julia nodded her head emphatically. "Mistah Caswell give Miz Hannah big handful of money for that thing. Most money I ever see. 'Nuff money to buy us a store an' a house, with plenty left over for Caleb to build a church."

"Papa had that topaz set in a ring and gave it to Mamma for a betrothal ring."

"Yes, I seen it when they visit us on the way back from they wedding trip to New York City."

"When Caleb and Timothy brought Mamma home after she was shot, the ring was gone. Papa believed the slave hunter who killed Mamma saw the ring and took it." She didn't add Papa's alternate theory that Hannah had been killed by someone who had already known she had the ring and had killed her to steal it.

Julia scowled as she tried to fathom the puzzle. "But if the ring already be gone, why somebody be lookin' for it now?"

"There are a couple of possibilities," James noted. "What if the person who killed Hannah put the ring up for sale and Mr. Caswell learned of it while he was in New York? Or perhaps Hannah hid the ring and the thief was unable to find it, so he assumed Mr. Caswell had it or had hidden it, so he made another attempt to get the ring as soon as the war ended?"

Both of James's theories were plausible—at least to some extent. But if someone were still searching for the ring, might

Serenity be the next victim? Little fingers of fear played at the edge of her mind. James's second theory would explain why someone had ransacked the house—which, she realized, still needed to be fully checked. She moved reluctantly toward the stairs leading to her attic bedroom and the storage room across the hall from it.

Edward moved to join her. "You shouldn't go up there alone."

"I have to know . . ."

"I'll go with you."

"I will too." James hurried toward them while Julia remained behind, shaking her head at the mess left by the intruder.

Dreading the prospect of seeing her own room torn apart, Serenity opened the storage room door first. A trunk was lying on its side, and old dresses—her mother's and her own—lay heaped on the floor. A trail of debris spread from the trunk to an open window, suggesting someone had left the room in a hurry through the window. James dashed toward it, stuck his head out, and examined the tree that grew close to it before closing the window and locking it.

"It appears the intruder had only begun to ransack this room before he fled rather suddenly," Edward said. "I assume he heard us come in and move about downstairs, so he beat a hasty retreat through the window."

Serenity backed out of the storage room and stepped across the hall, then flung open her bedroom door before her courage could fail her. When she looked inside, she nearly wept with relief. Nothing in the room appeared to be out of place. "It seems he hadn't reached my room yet."

A knock sounded from below. Before Serenity could start down the stairs, she heard her name spoken.

"Miss Serenity." Julia's voice floated up the stairs. "The sheriff be at the door. He be askin' for you."

"I'll be right there." She left the door to her bedroom standing open and quickly descended the stairs.

"Sheriff Compton, please come in." She held out her hand to the big man with a droopy mustache and thick sideburns who stood in her doorway. He stepped inside and looked around, appearing ill at ease among the vases and figurines that adorned the parlor. At another time she might have smiled to see his discomfort. Instead, she simply ushered him in. "Have a seat there beside the fire," she said, pointing to a sturdy chair that faced the rocking chair she preferred.

He looked past her and nodded a greeting to the two young men just entering the room.

"I sent a couple of men up the road to remove that dead horse," he began. "They found something interesting in the bushes a short distance from the animal." He held out a worn leather saddlebag. "It appears Charles may have tossed this into a thicket before his horse went down."

5

"Is this your pa's bag?" the sheriff asked Serenity.

She reached out to touch the worn leather, finding it stiff from lack of use. Her fingers closed around it, and the sheriff released it to her. She knew it wasn't Papa's bag, but there was something familiar about it. With shaking hands she lifted the flap to peek inside.

"Mamma!" The word escaped her throat, sounding much like the child she'd been when her mother had been murdered. There was no doubt the bag was the one Serenity and her father had searched for, the one she'd suspected Timothy and Caleb of keeping. Slowly she sank into the rocking chair, holding the bag tightly against her chest. "It's my mother's saddlebag," she murmured.

"How that bag come to be by her pa's dead horse?" Julia asked, puzzlement clear on her dark face.

"I'd like to know that too," Edward said, looking to the sheriff for an explanation.

"Maybe he couldn't find his own bag, so he took hers," the sheriff theorized, ignoring Julia and looking directly at Edward.

"No." Serenity shook her head. "This bag has been missing since Mamma's death."

"New York is a big place," James added. "I wonder how Mr. Caswell found it there? Or did he find it somewhere on his journey between there and here?" He turned to Serenity. "Open it up and see if your mother's ring is inside."

"Ring?" The sheriff frowned and edged closer to Serenity for a better look at the contents of the bag. "I remember that big shiner Hannah Caswell wore on her hand. How long has it been missing?"

The other men and Julia moved nearer as well, their eyes on the bag as Serenity's hand crept inside it. Feeling something soft, she pulled it out and stared at a doll with button eyes and long, yellow, yarn hair. She knew this doll. Tears dimmed her vision, and she had to wipe them away with the back of her hand before she could examine the doll more closely.

"Your mother carried a doll in her saddlebag?" Edward asked in surprise.

"It's not just any doll," Serenity tried to explain, not knowing whether to laugh or cry at the memories the doll brought rushing back to her. "My mother made it for me when I was just a baby. She often made dolls and stuffed toys for children. Before she died, I put my doll in her saddlebag with the other toys that she had made or collected to give to children who were too poor to own any toys. I was almost twelve then and feeling quite grown up— much too old to play with dolls. I thought it time to pass it on to a younger child who might have need of it."

James moved closer and knelt at her side. "Was that the only thing in the bag?" He picked up the doll and examined it closely.

"No, there's another doll. Mamma made this one from scraps left from her new black dress." She sat the round-faced black doll beside her childhood memento. Next she pulled out a tiny scotch-plaid puppy and a wooden soldier. The next item she withdrew was a miniature covered wagon. The bag also held an empty water-skin, a candle stub, and a few coins.

"I had a wagon like that when I was a boy," James said, sounding wistful. "An old man I called Grandpa, though he wasn't really my grandfather, made it for me."

Rosie brushed at her eyes. "Mistah Soren was a kind man. He made a wagon for Timothy too. And he also made this soldjah for my baby." She picked up the wooden soldier, caressing it in her hands. Serenity could see the longing in the woman's eyes for the return of her soldier son.

"Those are mighty strange items for your ma to be carryin' around with her." The sheriff's voice turned stiff and suspicious. Serenity remembered the sheriff had been one of those charged with hunting for runaway slaves before the war. He'd sided with President Lincoln concerning holding the Union together, but he'd had little sympathy for those fleeing slavery and had mercilessly pursued runaways.

Serenity tried to assuage his suspicion. "Mamma liked to sew. As I mentioned, she often made toys to give to poor children. Stitching them gave her something to occupy her time while Papa went on his buying trips."

The sheriff's pleasant demeanor disappeared and he glared at Serenity. "There were some who suspected your mamma was involved with the folks that were sneaking runaway slaves into Canada. They say she was shot because she was breaking the law."

"I believe my mother died in childbirth," Serenity responded. Seeing the scared expressions on the two black women's faces, she added, "But if she had died helping families who only wanted to stay together and be safe from abuse and torture, I'd be very proud of her."

The sheriff thrust out his jaw, taking a firm stance. "Aiding in the loss of property is criminal behavior—same as stealing."

"People aren't property," Serenity snapped back. "Besides, it's all in the past now. President Lincoln signed papers that abolished slavery in America."

"He made a mistake. Once more territories are made states and the South is voting again, it'll be corrected."

"I don't think so," Edward interjected, stepping into the fray. "None of the territories have any use for slavery, and the war opened people's eyes to the evil of the practice. This country will never tolerate slavery again but has set itself upon a course to heal the wrongs the war laid bare."

The sheriff grunted. "I only came by to ask about the saddlebag. Good day." He then turned toward the door, his abrupt dismissal of their arguments making his opinion clear. The discussion was at an end. Serenity suspected he'd spend little time in the future investigating her father's death.

After walking the sheriff to the door, Serenity sat down at the bottom of the stairs and looked around. From her position, she could see some of the wreckage that had been made of Papa's bedroom. How would she find out who had searched her home, or who had killed Papa? What could one young woman do? Even if she didn't agree with the sheriff's opinion about slavery, she should have told him about the intruder and the damage done to her home. She wasn't certain she could explain to the others why she'd remained silent, nor did she know whether they'd even noticed her omission.

Edward soon made it clear he had noticed her silence on the subject. "I don't think the sheriff will be much protection for you should the intruder who ransacked your home return," he said. "You didn't mention the intrusion to him, and I can only assume your reasoning is the same as mine. But even if he did know about it and wasn't prejudiced toward your mother, he still might not be able to prevent the intruder from returning."

Serenity paled as she realized her home might not be safe. Who knew what might happen if the intruder returned when she was home alone?

"Miz Serenity not goin' to be alone in this house," Julia announced. "Me and Rosie plan on stayin' right here 'til the man who shoot her pa be caught."

"But what about your store?" Serenity asked.

"I've got another daughter. Trixie and her man be right happy to tend the store. They don' need our help," Julia assured her. "So don' you worry none."

"Thank you." Serenity bowed her head, touched by the two women's generous gesture.

"And we'll be close by," James told her. "We took the liberty of bedding down in your stable again the last two nights and will continue to do so if you've no objection."

Again Serenity felt embarrassed. She'd given no thought to where the two men were sleeping at night; she'd been too absorbed in her grief to think of her guests' needs.

"As an extra precaution," James added, "I think I'll collect your papa's hammer and some nails to make certain the villain can't return the way he left." He stood and made his way to the kitchen on his way to the stable. Serenity heard the back door open, then James gave a shout.

Edward leaped to his feet and dashed toward the kitchen. The three women followed more slowly, and when they reached the back door, they were surprised to see the men leaning over a trail of footprints outlined in flour from the barrel that had spilled inside the pantry. On the back stoop were several clear prints indicating that the person making the tracks had made his way to the back door, stepped outside, then reentered the house.

A careful perusal of the tracks showed that the person making them had worn shoes unlike the rough footgear the farmers and tradespeople about town wore. The prints were also smaller than those James's shoes would make, but larger than Edward's.

"A fellow with fancy shoes like that should be easy to spot," James suggested.

"Maybe not," Edward countered with a frown. "With the large numbers of soldiers making their way home from the war, there's bound to be a wide variety of shoes leaving prints of every description."

* * *

Evening had come and lamps had to be lit before Serenity and her friends could finish cleaning the rooms damaged by the intruder. Charles's bedroom was turned into a bedroom for Julia and Rosie. They were reluctant to accept this arrangement at first, but Serenity assured them that returning the room to the condition in which her father had left it would only be a painful reminder of her loss.

Edward and James brought down the trunk that had been tipped over upstairs, and Serenity filled it with papers and mementos of her parents to keep in her bedroom. She tucked the saddlebag inside the trunk as well. She then had them carry her mother's writing table and sewing basket upstairs along with the trunk.

"Whew!" Edward exclaimed when the cleaning and reorganizing was finished. "I'm glad that's done."

Serenity knotted and broke the thread where she'd just finished mending the feather tick. "I think that will do," she said. She and Rosie had gathered all the feathers they could find to stuff back inside it, but it still wasn't as fluffy as it had been.

"Something smells good," James announced upon returning to the house. At Serenity's insistence, he had carried quilts to the stable for Edward and himself. Julia had set about preparing an evening meal as soon as the kitchen had been returned to order.

Noticing only three places set at the table, Serenity asked Julia to add two more settings, but no amount of coaxing would persuade Julia and Rosie to join the others at the big oak table. So while Serenity, James, and Edward ate in the dining room, the black women sat at the small kitchen table where Serenity and Charles had eaten most of their meals since Hannah's death.

The three at the dining table ate in silence for several minutes. Their hard work acted as a stimulant to their appetites. For Serenity, it was the first meal of any substance she'd eaten in three days.

"How long are you staying?" Serenity asked her guests after the first pangs of hunger were sated. She braced herself for the answer. With all that had happened, she'd almost forgotten that they had only planned to make a brief stop to inquire about her mother and Timothy.

James described his plans with some reluctance. "I'll be leaving tomorrow. In two weeks' time, I'm scheduled to meet a steamship of Scandinavian converts to the Church at Erie to help them make arrangements to travel west. Then I'll accompany them to Salt Lake. I wish I could stay longer and see you settled, and perhaps meet up with Timothy before continuing west, but if the new settlers are not on the trail by the end of June, they risk running into snow before they reach the valley."

Serenity nodded her understanding, then turned to Edward. She felt even more anxious to learn of his plans.

"I won't be going on with James," Edward told her. "I have plans to continue studying medicine and will begin surgery classes in Philadelphia at the end of the summer. There isn't enough time for me to reach Salt Lake and return before classes begin in September. My stepfather has already paid for my classes, but I will be looking for temporary work for the next few weeks to help finance my living expenses."

"I shall miss you when you go," Serenity said. "I don't know how I would have managed without your help."

"I'm glad we were here." James smiled at her, then glanced toward the kitchen. "I'm pleased, too, that Julia and Rosie will be staying to help you adjust and provide you with some protection. They're good women."

"I've been thinking," Edward said thoughtfully. "I might look for work in this area. If you've no objection, I could turn the tack room in your stable into a comfortable place to stay for the summer. By living there, I could be available to assist you in discovering who ambushed your father and to aid in discouraging the return of the person who searched your home. I'd be willing to chop wood, haul water, and carry out any tasks you might need done to pay for my room."

Serenity felt an easing of her concern. "You are most welcome to stay," she said with a smile, "and I shall include meals in our bargain. There are a few pieces of furniture in the storage room you may move to the tack room to make your stay more comfortable."

"Thank you."

"One other thing." Serenity looked down at her plate nervously. "I've been trying to remember everything Papa said in those last moments of consciousness before he died. I know it was his wish that I go to Salt Lake City to seek out my mother's family. He had no family other than me, and I think he did not wish for me to be alone."

"I could make arrangements for you to travel with the train of immigrants I will be accompanying," James offered.

"Thank you, but it would be impossible for me to leave so quickly. Papa's business will need to be inventoried and sold. I will also need to check into his financial affairs and discover whether I have access to his funds. If I don't, I may have become a penniless pauper."

"If your father had no relatives and owned his store and this house, why should you become a pauper?" Edward asked, puzzled.

Serenity sighed. "Ah, so many men just don't understand how laws concerning money and property affect women. It is generally assumed that women aren't capable of handling their own financial affairs. Papa spoke to me several times after Mamma's death about what I should do if he were to die. He said he would leave a will with Mr. Tolson, who is the only attorney in town, outlining his wishes that I inherit all of his assets and make the necessary decisions myself concerning financial matters. Knowing Mr. Tolson as I do, I'm sure he'll find every reason possible to keep me from controlling my inheritance myself."

"But how can he keep you from inheriting what your father clearly meant for you to have?" Edward was indignant and appeared ready to do battle for her.

"Oh, he won't prevent me from inheriting, he'll just insist that I'm too young to be without the guidance of a guardian or husband. He'll likely have himself appointed as my guardian in spite of the fact that Papa chose Mr. Nixon, a Quaker farmer, as a potential guardian for me many years ago. Unfortunately, Mr. Nixon died a short time ago." Serenity's hands clenched in her lap. "Mr. Tolson and the local judge are considered to be warm friends. The judge generally rules in his favor, so I'm certain I shall fall under his guardianship. Mr. Tolson will dole out household expenses with great stinginess and charge the estate enormous fees for his services."

"If the court is made aware that you have an uncle, couldn't Reliance Waterton be appointed your guardian?" James asked.

Serenity looked up at him with a hesitant hopefulness. "Do you suppose he would be willing to take responsibility for a niece he's never seen?"

"I'm certain he would welcome you to his household with open arms," James assured her.

Serenity almost smiled, but then she sighed. "There's just so much to think about." Her head drooped. "I miss Papa so dreadfully. Since he was in excellent health, we thought we had plenty of time to concern ourselves with what I should do in the future. Before going to New York, Papa spoke to me of journeying west to meet Mamma's people and to further study their religion. I think I would still like to do that. If the only way I can go is by imposing myself on an uncle who doesn't know me, then that is the request I shall have to make."

"I assure you, Reliance is a fine fellow, and the women in his household are happy and quite independent," James said.

"I think you'll find matters of female independence much different in the West from what you are accustomed to here," Edward informed her. "My father died when I was just a boy. My mother took over the management of his farm and stock until she remarried three years later. Even after her marriage, she still runs the farm and has converted half of the land to peach orchards. Her husband has a fine home in a settlement north of Salt Lake, but she prefers the farm and spends most of her time there, though they visit each other.

"It's not just Mormon women," James added. "Women in Wyoming, Utah, and the Idaho Territory are strong advocates of women's rights, and many men there are supportive of their agenda."

"Of course there are those who adamantly oppose these ideas," Edward noted with a grin. "But women like my mother are quite determined to help them see the error of their ways."

Serenity smiled, enjoying the chuckles of the two men. She liked the picture they painted of Mormon women and wished such attitudes prevailed in Pennsylvania. However, she was a practical woman and felt certain the judge would insist on appointing Mr. Tolson as her guardian. She could only hope that when she came of age, there would still be enough of Papa's funds left to finance a trip west. Her head began to nod, and she became aware of a curtain of fatigue settling over her. The day had been filled with too many emotionally and physically draining challenges.

She rose slowly and began gathering the dishes from the table. To her surprise, both men jumped to their feet and began assisting her. When they carried the dishes to the kitchen, Julia took the plates from their hands and scolded them for cleaning up.

"Rosie, take Miz Serenity to her room an' make sure she tucked in tight for the night," the older woman instructed her daughter.

"I'm all right," Serenity insisted.

Rosie took her arm to lead her toward the stairs." It don't do any good to argue with Mamma," she explained.

Serenity followed meekly, but just as she placed a foot on the first step, a knock sounded on the back door.

6

It wasn't a loud knock, but one that stopped Serenity short. It brought back memories of the nights she'd lain in bed as a child and heard the soft staccato tap, followed by the swish of Mamma's skirts and the opening and closing of the back door. It was also the sound she'd heard the night Timothy and Caleb had brought Mamma's body home. Turning, she dashed toward the door.

"Wait! It might be . . ." Edward's voice trailed off as she flung open the door to reveal an emaciated, disheveled, and ragged soldier standing on the back stoop. He appeared solemn and hesitant as he stared back at Serenity with his cap in his hand.

"Miss Serenity?"

"Come in, Timothy." She gestured him inside. Two steps from the door, Serenity was forced to step aside as the soldier was engulfed in the arms of his mother and grandmother, who both embraced him, laughing and crying at the same time.

"Timmy! Oh Timmy, I've been so worried about you." Rosie wiped at her eyes with her apron while clinging to her son's arm.

"Don't you ever go off like that agin!" Julia scolded.

With his mother and grandmother each on an arm, Timothy turned to face the other occupants of the small kitchen with a tired but happy smile on his face. When his gaze fell on Serenity, his smile disappeared and was replaced by deferential solemnity.

"I came to pay my respects, Miss Serenity. Your pa was a good man and he always treated me fair."

"Thank you, but how did you know . . . ?"

"I was on my way home from the war and I stopped in Scranton at one of the old stations run by the Friends. The folks there told me that I'd just missed Mamma Rose and Mamma Julia and that they were on their way to care for Miss Serenity because her pa had been murdered. I rode straight here to see if I could help."

"Timothy, that was very kind of you." Serenity felt a lump in her throat. She hadn't always harbored the kindest feelings toward Timothy, but she found his gesture sincere. "I'd like you to meet two friends of mine who have been more than kind in helping me deal with Papa's death. One of them is an old friend of yours."

"Of mine?" Timothy looked askance at the two young men who stood just behind Serenity.

"This is Edward Benson," she said, taking the shorter of the two men by his arm. "And this—" she took James's hand and drew him closer to Timothy—"is James Holmes."

James thrust out a hand toward Timothy. "When you knew me I was called Jens Jorgensen," he explained.

"Jens? You are Jens?" Timothy was clearly taken aback. "I barely remember playing with two white-haired children a long time ago, but all while I was growing up Mamma told me stories about you and your sister to keep my memories of you alive. She said she didn't want me to ever forget the family who saved my life and helped keep our family together."

Timothy extended his hand to meet James's, but James bypassed the out-stretched hand to embrace the tired young soldier. Timothy hesitated only a moment before returning the bear hug. Serenity saw Julia and Rosie wipe tears from their eyes.

"You may not remember me too well," James said as he stepped back without releasing his grip on Timothy. "But I remember you. The day I discovered you were gone, I made a promise to myself that someday I would find you and make certain no one ever whipped you again."

Seeing the puzzled look on Serenity's face, Edward whispered, "James told me on the way here about the little slave boy who was ordered to be whipped because he cried for his mamma. To make matters worse, his mother's teenage brother was ordered by their mistress to do the whipping. James's mother and yours saved the little boy, and from then until his family ran away, he spent all of his days in the Jorgensen household playing with James and his sister, Lisa."

Serenity looked back and forth between Timothy and James, surprised to learn the extent of the past they shared.

Timothy still appeared a bit puzzled. "Why are you called James now instead of Jens?"

"My grandfather, back in Denmark, was looking for us. He was a cruel, spiteful man who treated us about like Mrs. Rundell treated you and your family. We were runaways too. We changed our names to evade the detective he sent to find us and drag us back to his farm in Denmark."

"I'm glad you got away."

"I am too, but I'm also glad that I've been able to spend the last three years in Denmark, learning more about my heritage and discovering that the people there are not all like my grandfather. Edward Benson and I made some good friends there and found it to be a beautiful place."

"You didn't fight in the war then," Timothy concluded.

"No, most members of our church pretty much stayed out of the fighting, though our sympathies were mostly with the North. I've heard a few men were involved with protecting the telegraph lines and some of the mining interests of the Union in the West, but mostly we've been building new settlements and establishing a strong base in the Rocky Mountains."

"Timothy," Serenity broke in, "you look as tired as I am. You're probably hungry, too. We just finished eating, but I think your mother could find enough left to prepare you a plate of supper. Then you can bed down in the stable with James and Edward. There's feed for your horse there too."

"Yes, miss, and thank you. I do be knowin' my way around that stable." They shared a soft smile filled with memories.

* * *

Serenity didn't fall asleep as quickly as she'd expected. She lay for some time thinking about her father and the changes his death was thrusting upon her. She didn't want to leave her home to live with a guardian. And even if the judge allowed her to go to her uncle, she dreaded traveling alone to his home in the West. The two-story house attached to the side of Papa's store was the only home she'd ever known. The aloofness of her neighbors and the no-nonsense frankness of the Friends was all she knew of the world beyond her childhood home and the orchard where Mamma and Papa were buried.

She wondered if she would be welcomed by her uncle and his large brood of children. Would his wife be her friend, or would she be anxious for Serenity to marry and leave their household?

Serenity climbed out of bed and lit her lantern. She couldn't sleep, so she decided to write a letter to Uncle Reliance instead. James was leaving soon and would surely carry the missive for her. It was only courtesy that she should tell her uncle a little about herself and explain about her parents' deaths.

She sat at her writing table and worried her pen between her fingers, lost in thought for some time. At length she managed a brief note, promising a longer letter to follow. She folded the paper and melted a drop of wax to seal it before blowing out the lantern and returning to her bed.

As she drifted toward sleep, she wondered if she would be able to take any of her possessions with her, or if Mr. Tolson would find a way to appropriate her entire inheritance. If he became her guardian, would she be forced to live in his ramshackle house, or would he and his loathsome son move into her tidy home?

A scratching at her window caused her heart to pound, but then she chuckled at herself. An old lilac bush had grown to the height of a tree near her window, and when a breeze rustled the blossom-laden bows, they scraped softly against the glass. On many occasions, she'd thrown the window open to inhale the scented air. She wondered if she would find lilacs in Utah Territory—if she were able to escape to that far-off place.

* * *

The next morning Serenity awoke with a start to unexpected sounds. A rich alto carried the melody of an unfamiliar hymn up the stairs, accompanied by the clatter of pots and pans. Men's voices could be heard in the garden. An air of life and vitality, which had been missing since her mother's death, seemed to fill every corner of her home.

She dressed quickly and made her way downstairs to find Julia at the stove preparing flat cakes she called hoecakes. Eggs and bacon sizzled in a large skillet. Rosie sang as she swept, dusted, and took frequent proud glances through the window at her son, who stood with the two Mormon missionaries near the gate, deeply engrossed in conversation.

Serenity felt awkward, almost like a child again, to find other women cooking in her kitchen and dusting the furniture she'd had sole care of for more than five years. Seeming to sense her feelings, Julia allowed her to set the table, and for this meal Serenity was adamant that Julia and Rosie sit at the table with the others.

Breakfast was a pleasant meal that almost made her forget the tragedy that had struck. After the meal, James invited her to walk with him, and they made their way to the two graves at the far side of the orchard. Serenity carried an armful of fragrant lilacs. Bees buzzed among the tree blossoms, and the scent of spring filled the air. The trampled grass and freshly turned earth spoke of the newness of her father's grave. Serenity knelt beside the mound of earth and prayed.

Mamma had taught her to pray, and she'd often found comfort in kneeling beside her bed before her mother's death. But at the loss of her mother, she'd ceased praying. As time had tempered her pain, she'd gradually resumed the practice. More recently she'd felt an overwhelming urge to pour out her heart to God.

When she finished, she searched in her pocket for a handkerchief to wipe her eyes. James offered his hand after she dabbed at her tears. She then rose to her feet to stand beside him. He was silent, his hat in his hand, for several moments. Then he said, "I shall be leaving in an hour's time. Should I tell your uncle that you shall be arriving in Salt Lake with one of the later wagon trains?"

"Yes, I think it would be best to give him some warning. I wrote a short note for you to carry to him, if you would, please." She drew the note from her apron.

He took the paper she offered him and tucked it in his pocket. "I hope you will forgive me," he said, "but I already took the liberty of sending a wire to Reliance, informing him of your orphaned state." He handed her a small square of yellow paper. "A response arrived this morning expressing his sorrow for the loss of his sister and requesting that you join his family at your earliest convenience."

"He truly wishes me to make my home with him?"

"Indeed he does. Church trains leave from several cities along the Missouri during the summer." He handed her another slip of paper. "The trains will take travelers as far as western Iowa, where wagon companies are formed. Present this to any of the wagon masters and you will be permitted to travel with the immigrants headed west. Any family with room for one more person will readily accept a single traveler who can pay for her own supplies. Don't wait too long. Snow comes early to the Rocky Mountains, and the wagon trains must leave Iowa early enough to pass through the mountains before the winter storms begin. If the season grows late, you will have to wait until spring."

"I am grateful to you and Edward," Serenity said, attempting to express her feelings. "Without your assistance, I don't know how I should have managed."

"You're stronger than you think. You would have managed. Indeed, I feel I should thank you for your hospitality and for giving me an opportunity to assist Hannah Waterton's daughter in some small way. I only regret that she isn't here to hear my mother's message of gratitude for the service she rendered our family all those years ago."

"Mamma didn't often speak of her life in Nauvoo. I think it pained her to be reminded of all she left behind. That's not to say she wasn't happy with my father and me—she loved us dearly and

I think she considered freeing the slaves a calling from God—but sometimes she got a faraway look in her eyes and appeared to be unbearably lonely." Serenity managed a small smile as tears pooled in her eyes.

"Her faith in God ran deep," James interjected. "I suspect she missed associating with other members of her faith and having the opportunity to hear the Brethren speak. She and her mother were close, and it must have pained her greatly when she was cut off from her family. It took great courage to set aside her own needs and devote her life to securing the freedom of a downtrodden people."

Serenity looked up at James. "I'm glad you came. I think I needed to be reminded of my mother and her faith at this time. I've never stopped missing her, and with Papa gone now too, I feel like a toy boat that has been pulled along by a string until the string breaks and the little boat is tossed about and swamped in heavy waters. I wish I could have had both of my parents longer."

"You *can* have your parents longer." James reached above his head and broke off a small twig of apple blossoms. "Your papa spoke with Edward and me at length concerning eternal families. Being with you and your mother forever was of great importance to him. I regret that I shall not be here to teach you more, but I feel certain Edward would be pleased to answer your questions until he must leave too." He glanced down at the graves stretched out side by side. "I would like to have known your father better. I am convinced he was a person of integrity and honor like Hannah. You would do well to pattern your life after theirs."

Serenity nodded, then furrowed her brow. "When I was a little girl, I was fascinated by the big golden stone in Mamma's ring. She said there was an old legend about a stone that was colored by the power of the sun. Those who carried a piece of this powerful stone with them would be protected from harm and be clear-sighted. I wish that I had Mamma's ring and that the legend was true. I think I shall have great need of protection and clarity."

"I wish you had the stone too, not because of its reputed power, but because it was dear to you. Will you believe me if I tell you there is a power you can trust that is greater than a legend? That power is faith in our Lord Jesus Christ. The topaz you speak of once belonged to my mother, and she believed with all her heart that God put it in her hands because He knew her need. She knew He wanted her to pass it on when someone else's need for it was greater than hers. She believed then, and still believes today, that faith and prayer are the greatest jewels of all."

James's words filled Serenity with warmth, and she felt encouraged. Her heart longed to believe in something even more precious than her mother's topaz.

When they returned to the house, they found a carriage parked on the street in front of her papa's shop.

"Oh, no!" Serenity whispered in dismay.

"What is it?" James asked as he drew her into the shelter of the lilac tree. "Do you have some reason to fear the owner of that carriage?"

Before she could answer, Edward appeared beside them.

"I've been watching for you," he whispered. "There are a couple of fellows here to see you. They claim that one of them is your father's attorney and that the other is betrothed to you."

Serenity felt the color drain from her face. It was worse than she had feared. Mr. Tolson, as her guardian, would force her to marry his odious son in order to take over Papa's property.

"I am not betrothed to anyone," she declared with vehement bitterness. "The attorney is Bernard Tolson. He is the only attorney in town, so Papa used his services to draw up his will. Papa gave me the original document of his will, which I can retrieve from its secure hiding place at any time. It's quite clear that he wished for me to inherit his property should he die while I was still unwed. If his death occurred after I married, my husband, of course, would have the management of my property."

"You shall be fine then," James attempted to assure her. "Reliance will protect your assets until you are of age."

"It won't be that simple." She tried to keep her voice from trembling. "I have no doubt the magistrate at the county seat will appoint Mr. Tolson to be my guardian. Mr. Tolson will then insist I wed his son to ensure Papa's property remains in his hands."

"You must tell him arrangements have already been made for you to come under the supervision of your uncle, Reliance Waterton," James advised her. "As long as you have a family member who wishes to take responsibility for you, Mr. Tolson has no authority to dispose of your property, nor to take charge of your person."

A coach clattered by and James lifted his head, then looked at Serenity in some agitation before turning to his friend. "The public coach has arrived, and it has but a brief layover. Edward, I shall trust you to look after Serenity's interests and see her on her way to join Reliance before you depart for school. I wish I could remain to handle her legal affairs, but I must fetch my bag and be on my way."

Turning back to Serenity, he took her hands in his and briefly brushed her cheek with his lips. "I must go, but I shall forever be grateful for our meeting. Trust in God to keep you safe, and allow Edward to be of assistance. He is set on becoming a physician, but I believe he has absorbed enough of my prattle concerning the law to serve you well."

After saying farewell, Serenity stood watching James's long strides carry him toward the stable to collect his bag. He emerged in short order and loped toward the stage, which had halted in front of the general store. A stranger, wearing a jacket that looked much too heavy for the unseasonably warm morning, stood beside the coach and gestured toward the luggage piled atop it. James threw his bag up, tipped his hat to the driver, and clambered aboard the conveyance. Serenity wondered if she would ever see him again and was amazed at how dear he had become to her in such a short period of time.

After James disappeared from sight, she turned to Edward. Taking a deep breath and squaring her shoulders, she said, "I suppose I must face Mr. Tolson."

7

Edward tucked her hand in the crook of his arm. "You won't be alone," he said with a charming smile. "I just returned from Denmark, an enchanted land filled with dragons and mysterious monsters, so I'm well prepared to come to the aid of a damsel in distress."

Serenity giggled and felt some of the tension seep away, which, she surmised, had been precisely Edward's intention. When they reached the door, he made a gallant gesture and ushered her ahead of him.

She stepped into the room and instantly came to a halt. On the settee sat Mr. Tolson in his black broadcloth suit and shiny city shoes. His hat rested on one knee, and his chin wobbled as he drank from one of Mamma's china tea cups. Beside him sat Percy, similarly attired but in a suit at least two sizes too small for his portly figure. His hair, parted in the center, was plastered to his round head, and beads of perspiration ran in the direction of his tall, starched collar. He stared nervously at the fragile cup he held to his blubbery lips.

Bernard Tolson stood. As he did, he nudged his son with his foot, reminding him of his manners. The lout stumbled to his feet, sending his cup clattering against its saucer and causing Serenity to fear for the precious piece of fine Dresden. To her relief, Julia stepped forward to pluck the fragile china from his hand and march it to the kitchen.

"We have come to offer our condolences," the elder Tolson intoned. Percy nodded his head in agreement.

"Thank you, Mr. Tolson, Percy," Serenity responded with forced politeness.

"We also came to assure you that you needn't worry about your future," Mr. Tolson continued. "I have arranged for Mrs. Townsend, a widow of impeccable reputation, to act as your chaperone until you wed. She shall handle your household accounts and present the bills to me for payment."

Serenity had to force herself to remain calm. "Your offer is generous," she replied, "but I shall not need Mrs. Townsend's assistance in handling my household. I have had the charge of running this house since I was twelve. My father instructed me well in the art of handling accounts and managing our home." Serenity kept her voice sweet and low. She didn't wish to provoke a fight.

Mr. Tolson looked annoyed, but forged ahead. "It is not seemly that a lass of such tender years should be so burdened. The matter has been arranged."

"No, it has not," Serenity said. "I have no room for another houseguest. Mrs. Hayes and her daughter, dear friends of my mother, are occupying Papa's bedroom. My bedroom is too small to accommodate a second cot, and the other room in the attic is quite given to storage. Even the stable is filled to capacity."

"Then I shall give your guests until Monday to depart." The pompous man drew himself up as though his was the final word.

Serenity's voice turned haughty. "Mr. Tolson, why ever would you think you have a say in the matter? My guests shall stay as long as they wish."

At that point Edward stepped forward to address Serenity. "Am I correct in assuming this gentleman has arrived for the purpose of reading your father's will?" he asked in a businesslike tone.

"Oh, forgive me, Mr. Benson," Serenity said formally. "I should have introduced Mr. Tolson and his son to you at once." She gave a slight nod toward the older man, but went on speaking to Edward. "Mr. Tolson practices law here in town and Percy is his son. Mr. Tolson drew up Papa's will several years ago. Since I have the original document and Mr. Tolson a mere copy, I did not think there was a need for a formal reading." Turning back to the Tolsons, she continued, smiling sweetly. "I'm pleased to introduce Edward Benson, a friend of the family. He has been commissioned to act for my uncle in any matters with which I need assistance."

"It might be well if you went ahead and read the will in order to conclude that formality," Edward suggested.

"This is highly irregular, sir," Mr. Tolson sputtered. "Mr. Caswell gave me to understand that he had no relatives."

"That is technically true, but his daughter has a considerable number of relatives," Edward informed him. "At the time Mr. Caswell drew up his will, he had no knowledge of his brother-in-law's whereabouts. And until the war ended, Mr. Waterton was unable to contact his sister's family."

"And where is Mr. Waterton? I find it quite suspect that he should send a youth in his stead to take charge of his niece's affairs."

"I may appear to be but a youth, but at four and twenty, I am of legal age." Edward's eyes twinkled. "And as for Miss Caswell's uncle, though born and reared in Pennsylvania, Mr. Waterton made his way west twenty years ago. At that time, he and his sister lost contact with each other until Mr. James Holmes and myself were asked to seek her out as we passed through this area. Discovering conditions here, we arranged at once for a telegram to be sent informing Mr. Waterton of the deaths of his sister and her husband and the orphaned state of his niece. He was greatly grieved to learn of his sister's passing. He instructed us at once to arrange for Miss Serenity's transportation to Salt Lake City, where he will meet her and welcome her into his household."

"This won't do at all. The West is a dangerous place filled with savages, wild beasts, and Mormons. Miss Serenity is far too young and innocent to make her way across the country alone, and she will need assistance in disposing of her father's store and its contents. I shall speak to the magistrate, who I'm sure will wish me to continue with preparations for the auction scheduled for Saturday next. It had been my intention to allow the lass a period of mourning before posting banns for her marriage, but I can see now that with her future happiness at stake, we must proceed with wedding preparations at once."

"Wedding! Auction! You are much too presumptuous, Mr. Tolson," Serenity sputtered. "I will not be wed against my will, and there will be no auction until I have had time to inventory Papa's treasures. He taught me much about the value of the items he has for sale, and he kept meticulous records of how much he paid for each. I shall need time to establish a catalog."

"I'll not tolerate female interference," Mr. Tolson spat. "Such matters are best left in my hands."

"It is none of your concern, sir!" Serenity felt her temper rising and knew that in minutes she would be unable to stem its eruption. It was just as she feared. The Tolsons, father and son, had every intention of taking over both her and her inheritance.

"Percy has known you since you were an infant and is eager to accept you as his bride. There's no reason to put off the marriage that your father and I have had planned since you were in your cradle. You will be spared a tedious and dangerous journey to live among strangers, and you shall have the benefit of my experience in the handling of your financial affairs." Mr. Tolson spoke as though the matter were settled.

"I do not believe my father wished me to marry your son," Serenity responded through clenched teeth. She would run away and make her way west secretly if necessary rather than marry the odious young man who sat on her sofa, drooling at the prospect of acquiring her and her property. She could almost feel sorry for the great, useless lump; he didn't seem to comprehend that even should he manage to marry her, it would be his father, not him, who would control the considerable amount of money she should realize from the sale of her father's property.

Edward spoke up again. "Mr. Tolson, I think it would be wise for you to leave now and cancel any plans you have made concerning Miss Caswell and her property. The drawing of a will does not automatically entitle one to serve as executor. Perhaps we should leave this matter to a magistrate."

Mr. Tolson sniffed. "Come, Percy. I shall not countenance this upstart's interference any longer. We shall meet with Judge Detweiler and return with a constable."

"Then can I marry Serenity?" Percy scooted to the edge of the settee before launching himself to his feet. Serenity shuddered as the two men saw themselves to the door and let themselves out.

Julia suddenly appeared to close the door behind the Tolsons. Timothy and Rosie hovered by the kitchen door, and Serenity guessed they'd heard the entire exchange. As soon as the door was shut, Edward turned to Serenity. "Who is Judge Detweiler? And where is he? We need to get to him first."

"He lives in the next township but serves as justice of the peace for the entire county. He sides with Mr. Tolson more often than not. Even if we might persuade him to take my part, how should we get there? We cannot walk as quickly as the Tolsons can drive their buggy."

Timothy stepped forward. "My horse don't look like much, but she's a prime runner, and after sleeping in a stable for an uninterrupted night with plenty of hay and oats, she's rarin' to go. She could carry both of you to the judge, no problem."

Serenity looked at him with admiration. "Thank you, Timothy." She gave him a quick embrace before turning back to Edward. "It will only take me a moment to don my riding clothes." She excused herself and made a dash for the stairs.

"Bring along your papa's will, the telegram your uncle sent, and any other papers that might help your cause," Edward called toward her back as she fled upstairs. Seconds later the back door slammed, signaling that Timothy was fetching his horse.

* * *

Riding double behind Edward was not Serenity's idea of a pleasant excursion. At first she'd been occupied pointing out directions, then reading aloud Papa's will to acquaint Edward with its contents. But Timothy's horse was on the bony side, and after perching on its sharp spine for nearly two hours with her arms clasped around Edward's waist, she was anxious for a rest. At last he drew the animal to a halt and pointed ahead.

"There's a town on the other side of the stream we've been following. Is that our destination?"

"Yes. I came here a couple of times with Papa. Right in the center of town there's a large stone building with a clock tower. That's where we need to go."

Edward pressed his knees against the horse's sides and they hurried on, crossing a covered bridge to arrive at the top of the town's main street. Finding the courthouse was a simple matter, and in a short time Edward was tethering the horse to a rail while Serenity drank deeply from the nearby public pump. She was flushed from the heat of the long ride under the midday sun. When Edward finished with the horse, she handed him a dipper of the refreshing cold water. A few drops spilled down his chin, which he wiped away with the back of his free hand. The small gesture mesmerized her unduly.

Moments later, they climbed wide stone steps to a large double door. Edward pressed on the massive latch and pulled until one of the doors swung open. He held it wide for Serenity to step inside, then hurried after her.

Once inside the building, they scurried from room to room, looking for the magistrate. At length, a fussy gentleman with ink-stained cuffs pointed them toward a door that stood open at the end of a long hall. "You'll find Judge Detweiler in that room."

Serenity cringed at the noise their footsteps made on the polished floor, but at last they reached the doorway indicated. They peered inside to see a large man, with his hair tied back in an old-fashioned powdered queue, seated behind a tall desk that rested on a dais. Edward rapped on the door frame. When there was no response from the gentleman, he rapped again and cleared his throat.

With an air of annoyance, the man looked up and motioned them forward. With some trepidation, Serenity preceded Edward down the center aisle to stand before the judge.

When neither Serenity nor Edward spoke immediately, the judge looked at them over wire-rimmed glasses in a peevish manner. "Well?"

"Sir—Your Honor," Edward began. "This is Serenity Caswell, and I am Edward Benson. We've come to acquaint you with the facts surrounding the matter of her inheritance from her recently deceased father, Charles Caswell."

The judge straightened, removed his glasses, and polished them on the full sleeve of his black robe. "I am somewhat acquainted with the matter of Charles Caswell's demise. Shot in the back, I heard, but a mile from his own door. Regrettable!" The judge shook his head. "Has the ambushing bounder been apprehended?"

"No, Your Honor." Serenity felt tears threaten to break free. "He has not, though the sheriff has assured me he will continue to search for the culprit." She thought it best not to mention her suspicion that the lawman wasn't searching very diligently. "We've brought you my father's will for probate and a telegram from my uncle, Reliance Waterton, stating that he wishes me to go west to live with him. As you will see when you read the document, Papa intended for me to sell his business and inventory and to have the use of the funds garnered to support myself until I reached my uncle's home."

The judge took the papers she held out to him, adjusted the glasses on his nose, and scowled at the paper for a long time while Serenity and Edward fidgeted nervously.

"Where is Bernard Tolson?" The judge looked around as though he expected the lawyer to suddenly materialize before him. "He usually attends to these matters."

"That is the problem, Your Honor," Edward volunteered. "Tolson is of the opinion that he should arrange the sale of Miss Caswell's property in a simple auction. He knows nothing of the art pieces and valuables Mr. Caswell bought and sold. It is my opinion that Miss Caswell, who has studied such matters since a small child at her father's knee, should have the opportunity to approach dealers in Philadelphia and New York City to obtain the best prices for the items."

Judge Detweiler glowered at Edward. "It wouldn't be seemly for a woman of Miss Caswell's tender years to engage in such an action."

"Neither would it be seemly for her to accept the paltry amount Mr. Tolson's plan would net when a knowledgeable buyer would pay many thousands for such valuable items," Edward argued.

The judge's demeanor lightened noticeably, and he straightened at the word *thousands*. "Allow me to consider this conundrum for a time." The judge stared off into space for several minutes before speaking again. "It does appear that an attempt should be made to garner the best price for Mr. Caswell's estate. Perhaps Miss Caswell's guardian will find it acceptable to send a representative to a larger center of commerce to make an appropriate sale of the more valuable items."

"That's another matter we wish to discuss with you. Since Miss Caswell is approaching eighteen and is particularly sensible, why should she be encumbered with a guardian? A youth of the same years would be expected to fend for himself."

"Being young yourself, you know little of the female mind," Judge Detweiler replied, taking on a stern demeanor as he lectured Edward. "Women's minds are more fragile than those of men and are incapable of understanding business matters. Therefore, benevolent laws have been devised through the years to provide a means of protecting the rights and property of women, especially of those who are young and particularly vulnerable, by appointing trustworthy males to look after their interests. In most instances, this responsibility is assumed by a male relative."

Serenity decided to rejoin the conversation that had been going on about her as through she weren't present. "As you can see from the telegram I handed you," she said, struggling to present a calm face, "my closest male relative, my mother's older brother, lives in Utah Territory." She stopped. Instinct warned that giving in to frustration and anger over the insults Judge Detweiler had just delivered would cost her far more than the satisfaction she would receive from informing him that he was a bigoted fool. "It is his wish that I join him as soon as possible. In the meantime, he has appointed Mr. Benson to assist me with whatever arrangements I need to make. However, when Mr. Tolson was informed of my uncle's decision, he dismissed Uncle Reliance's guardianship and appointed himself my guardian, then announced that he has already set a date to auction off my father's business assets. He also informed me that I must marry his son."

A commotion erupted at the rear of the room. Serenity turned her head and a sinking sensation settled in the pit of her stomach.

"What is the meaning of this?" Bernard Tolson almost yelled as he waddled down the aisle toward them. His breath came in short gasps, and he mopped at his brow with a broad square of linen. Percy followed, gasping and wheezing and red-faced, with large circles of perspiration darkening his shirt beneath his arms.

"At great inconvenience and hardship to myself, I have traveled all this distance to expedite matters concerning this young lady's father's will, and here I find her and this imposter attempting to subvert her father's instructions. I won't have it. I won't!" Mr. Tolson waved his arms and shouted as though volume might prove his assertion.

"Quiet! This is *my* court!" Judge Detweiler's roar and his vigorous hammering of a wooden mallet against his desk silenced Mr. Tolson, but only for a moment.

"Your Honor." Tolson executed a gallant bow. "Five years ago, following the death of Mrs. Caswell, Charles Caswell approached me to draw up his last will and testament because he was concerned for his only child's welfare should he also die early. Unfortunately, his fears were realized and he was laid to rest two days ago."

"A funeral you didn't bother to attend," Serenity muttered just loud enough for the judge to hear.

"And this is the document you drew up for him?" The judge lifted the papers Serenity had handed him.

"The same, though you may wish to examine it to ascertain whether there have been any alterations."

The judge's thick brows drew together in annoyance. "I know my business." Perhaps the magistrate wasn't as close to Mr. Tolson as the latter had so often suggested. "There have been no changes.

Can you say the same for the paper you hold? I assume that is a copy of the document in question." He held out his hand.

"Yes, of course." Tolson appeared flustered for a moment but then handed the judge his copy of the will and pressed on. "If you'll look at the fourth paragraph, you'll see Mr. Caswell acknowledged that a guardian must assume responsibility for his daughter and his business. I have attempted to take this matter in hand but have met with insult and interference." Tolson attempted to look wounded.

"Nowhere does the will state that *you* should be either Miss Caswell's guardian or the one to arrange the sale of her father's business," Edward interjected.

"If I may quote the document my father dictated," Serenity said, then launched into quoting from the will without waiting for the judge's permission. "'As the whereabouts of the family of my late wife, Hannah Waterton Caswell, are unknown at this time, Sufferance Nixon shall be appointed to the guardianship of my daughter, Serenity Caswell, until such time as she reaches adulthood or marries.' It seems quite clear his first choice for my guardian was someone from my mother's family."

"Order! Wait until I ask for rebuttal." The judge hammered the desk with great vigor once again. Serenity knew at once she'd made a mistake in attempting to counter Mr. Tolson's argument without first receiving permission from the touchy magistrate.

"Where is this Sufferance Nixon?" he demanded of Mr. Tolson.

"He managed to get himself shot at Richmond less than a year ago." Bernard wiped his face with his handkerchief and Percy sidled closer to Serenity.

"Shot? With a name like Sufferance, I thought he was surely a Quaker."

"He was, but he signed up to help Doc Johnson. Confederates stole his horses early in the war, so he couldn't farm. Figured he might as well help the wounded, and he and the doc were close as brothers."

"Why didn't Caswell appoint another guardian?"

"He figured the girl would be marrying her childhood sweetheart right away, making the assignment of a guardian unnecessary."

"That's a lie." Serenity thrust out her chin. "Papa and I had plans to go west looking for Mamma's family. He made no plans for me to marry Percival Tolson."

"Miss Caswell, I won't have you interrupting these proceedings," Judge Detweiler admonished.

"She only speaks the truth," Edward said. "She is sufficiently well-educated to manage the disposal of her father's estate. However, she recognizes the law's prejudice against women and is willing to subject herself to her uncle's guardianship. She is merely asking you to recognize her uncle's superior right to her guardianship over Mr. Tolson's claim, and his choice of me to guide her until she is under her uncle's roof. She wishes to halt the sale of her father's assets until a qualified evaluator can ascertain their worth."

"Such foolishness," Bernard Tolson scoffed. "I already have an offer for the business, stock, and household goods from a former business acquaintance of Mr. Caswell who arrived a short time ago from New York. Since plans are underway for Serenity's marriage to Percy in three weeks' time, it is only reasonable to act in my future daughter-in-law's interest until such time as her husband can take control of her affairs."

Serenity found it impossible to hold her tongue. "No! Your plans to force me to marry Percy are nothing but a scheme to get your hands on my father's money! Besides, Papa's business associates in New York never come here. Papa has always gone to them."

Judge Detweiler sighed heavily as though he were exercising great forbearance in dealing with a headstrong female. "Now Miss Caswell, I've known Bernard Tolson a long time," he said. "I'm sure he has your best interests in mind, since he was personally acquainted with your father. And it does seem rather foolish to travel all the way to the territories when an eligible suitor is so close at hand."

"I will not marry that repulsive toad!" Serenity stated in flat defiance, folding her arms. "I believe the laws of this state forbid the forcing of a woman to accept a marriage arrangement that is distasteful to her. Percy Tolson is extremely distasteful to me as a marriage prospect."

"You're lucky to get me," Percy wheezed as he attempted to take her hand.

"Don't touch me!" she hissed, moving to Edward's other side, where Percy was blocked from further amorous attempts.

"Young lady, I've shown great patience with you considering your recent bereavement, but I have reached the end of my tolerance. You will leave this courtroom today either as a ward of Bernard Tolson or as a married woman. As Bernard's wife is long since deceased and there are no female relatives resident in his household to act as chaperone, I firmly recommend the latter."

8

Serenity stared at the judge in shock. His stern expression told her that he wouldn't back down. How could she accept either alternative? Actually, there was no alternative, she thought with deep bitterness. Either way, she would become a slave in the Tolson household, just as poor Emily Tolson, Percy's mother, had been before she fell in the river and drowned. Papa's money would disappear into Bernard Tolson's pockets, and she would eventually be forced to share Percy's bed.

Her eyes shifted left and right, and she caught sight of the triumphant smirk on the elder Tolson's face and the leer on the younger's. She couldn't do it. There had to be another way.

Edward gripped her arm as he addressed the judge. "Miss Caswell just buried her father. It is unconscionable to require her to marry without a decent period of mourning."

"She's headstrong and needs to be taken in hand at once." Judge Detweiler turned to Serenity. "I'll have your answer, young lady."

Defiant to the last, Serenity met the judge's disapproving glare. "I'll marry . . . Mr. Benson."

She felt Edward's hand tighten on her arm, but she didn't dare glance at him. She held her breath, expecting him to repudiate her proposal.

A strange smirk lifted one corner of the judge's bushy mustache. He turned to Edward. "Does that meet with your approval?"

"Yes." He spoke quietly, but there was a firmness to his voice that lent strength to her resolve, and she slowly released the breath she had been holding.

But for the judge's whiskers, Serenity might have thought the stern magistrate actually smiled as he said, "Well, then the Tolsons can act as witnesses." It definitely seemed the judge really wasn't as enamored with Bernard Tolson as the man had implied.

"Your Honor!" Bernard gasped. "Surely you can see how unsuitable this match is. We know nothing of Mr. Benson's background. He may abandon Miss Caswell and abscond with her father's fortune."

"Pa, you said *I* could have Miss Serenity," Percy whined. "You can't let her marry this fella."

Wham! Once more the judge pounded his gavel, reminding everyone that he was in charge of his court. "My decision is final," he bellowed. "If you gentlemen prefer not to remain as witnesses, please send in my secretary and the bailiff as you leave."

At that moment two gentlemen dressed in dark suits entered the room. Serenity recognized the one with ink-stained cuffs as the man who had directed them to the courtroom. She suspected that since no one had yet summoned them, they had been nearby, listening to the exchange that had just occurred.

"I'll have the marriage annulled and sue for breach of promise!" Bernard threatened.

"You'll do no such thing," the judge growled. "Now go home. I have a marriage to perform."

Bernard reached across the judge's desk to retrieve his papers, but Edward stayed his hand. "I think those papers belong to my bride." Serenity winced at the slight emphasis Edward put on "bride." She'd have a great deal of apologizing to do when they left the courthouse.

Judge Detweiler's hand came down atop the papers. "I'll determine who gets these."

Bernard Tolson turned to stomp up the aisle. "Come along, Percy," he ordered.

"I'm not leaving Serenity here," Percy sniffled, sidling next to her.

Edward turned back to Serenity just as Percy grabbed her about the waist and attempted to drag her toward the exit. Caught by surprise, she screamed, then began to struggle. Edward was on Percy almost immediately, struggling to loosen his grip. Serenity heard something rip in the scuffle. She attempted to land an unladylike kick to Percy's shins.

A fist landed squarely in her left eye, and she felt the room sway and begin to dim. The next thing she knew she was sitting on the floor, looking up at a half-dozen male faces exhibiting various degrees of anger or concern. She recognized Bernard's loud threats and Percy's sniffling whine, and then she saw Edward kneeling beside her.

"You're going to have a beaut of a shiner," he said. Putting his arm around her, he helped her to her feet. The room gradually righted itself in time for her to dimly view the Tolsons being escorted through the door by the bailiff and secretary.

The judge returned to his desk, where he picked up a large book. "Let's get on with it. It's time to go home, and Mrs. Detweiler gets out of sorts if I'm late for supper. Stand there." He pointed to a spot directly in front of him. Edward took Serenity's hand and together they approached the designated spot with some reluctance. Serenity noticed that Edward limped slightly. A door slammed, followed by the sound of scurrying feet. In seconds, the now rumpled bailiff and secretary took their places on either side of the soon-to-be bride and groom.

The judge began to speak, and Serenity felt the room begin to sway again. She was barely conscious of the words he said. Her mind filled with the dreams she'd once harbored of a lovely church wedding. She had imagined herself in a gown of satin and lace, her uncooperative hair for once cascading in perfect curls about her shoulders. Instead, she stood before a judge rather than a preacher. Her hair was mussed, she wore a torn, black mourning gown, and her left eye was very nearly swollen shut. Worst of all, she was marrying a man she'd only known a month and who hadn't even proposed to her. He didn't look any more ready for a wedding than she did. His jacket was ripped under one arm, his shirt was crumpled and sported splatters of blood, his hair was wildly disheveled, and he walked with a decided limp. She was too tired and confused to contemplate the larger issues involved in this impromptu marriage.

She must have managed the correct responses, because the judge was soon pronouncing them man and wife. In a blur, she signed her name beneath Edward's signature as instructed, then saw Edward collect the stack of papers they had brought with them, along with the ones Bernard Tolson had been forced to leave behind. He took her arm, and she stumbled along beside him on the return trip up the courtroom aisle.

As they left the courthouse, she was vaguely aware of Edward scrutinizing the street as though he expected trouble, but there was no sign of the Tolsons. When they reached the hitching rail, Edward took a moment to soak his handkerchief in the cold pump water. He mounted Timothy's horse, then extended a hand to Serenity, who had climbed onto the edge of the watering trough to make mounting easier.

"Here," he said, handing her the handkerchief. "Press this to your eye. It might ease the swelling and the pain."

"Thank you." She did as he instructed and discovered the cool water did relieve some of the throbbing in her eye.

They rode slowly toward the bridge. Edward kept quiet, and a cloud of gloom settled over Serenity's shoulders. She couldn't blame him for being angry with her. He'd been kind to her ever since the day he'd arrived at Papa's store, and she had repaid the kindness by embroiling him in her personal problems and saddling him with an unwanted wife.

The horse plodded back up the trail they'd come down with so much haste earlier in the day. The shadows grew longer, suggesting nighttime would soon be upon them.

Finally Edward spoke. "Are you hungry? Julia packed sandwiches for us."

"Yes," she answered in a small voice. She'd had too much on her mind to think about food, but now that Edward mentioned sandwiches, she discovered she was indeed hungry. She realized how long ago the pleasant breakfast had been that began their day.

Edward pulled back on the reins, bringing the horse to a stop in a small wooded glen. He dismounted and helped Serenity do the same before removing a small packet from the saddlebag. After waiting for Serenity to be seated on a grassy spot, he opened the cloth-wrapped package and offered her a sandwich before helping himself to one. They ate silently for several minutes before he broached the subject uppermost on both their minds.

"Have you thought about what we're going to do when we reach your home?"

"Edward, I'm so sorry. I never really thought of anything except saving myself from the Tolsons. I looked at Percy and knew I couldn't be his wife, so I said the first thing that came to mind."

"What's done is done. And looking at it from your perspective, I can see that you couldn't marry Percy. But we need to think about what we're going to do now. I don't think the Tolsons are going to let your defiance go. They'll be looking to exact revenge, and I certainly don't wish to be part of events that include making you a widow."

"A widow? Surely you don't think they would try to murder you?"

"I don't know. Someone murdered both of your parents. Whoever did that wants something a great deal, and the Tolsons are the only suspects I've seen thus far who have made an attempt to secure either you or your property. The only way to gain control of you and your inheritance now is to eliminate me."

"I never thought I might be placing you in danger. I only thought that if Papa was shot because he found out the identity of Mamma's murderer when he went to New York to ask about her ring, the murderer might try to silence me too. He might fear that Papa told me his name. Now I've made matters worse by putting you in danger too."

"I've been thinking about that ring." Edward stuffed the last of his sandwich into his mouth, chewed quickly, and swallowed. "Tolson could have shot your mother, then sold her ring to a jeweler in New York. He was safe enough during the war because your father never traveled to the city. But when the war ended, he may have decided to kill your father to keep him from discovering from one of his contacts that the ring had been sold. On the other hand, what if the person who shot your mother really was a slaver and took the ring as an afterthought, thinking it merely a pretty bauble? Your family kept the circumstances surrounding her death quiet, so Tolson may not be aware the ring is even missing. If he has fallen on hard times, as most people have because of the war, he may have shot your father to gain custody of you and your possessions to pay his debts and ensure a comfortable life for himself. The two crimes may not even be related."

"I don't think Bernard Tolson would actually shoot someone himself, but he might hire someone to do it for him," Serenity mused. She didn't like the Tolsons, but it was difficult to think that someone she'd known all her life might actually be a murderer.

"I'm not so sure. He was definitely out for blood when he attacked me back at the courthouse."

"I noticed you limping. Did he hurt you badly?" She raised her dark brown eyes to meet his lighter ones.

"Actually, I think you can take the credit for my bruised shin. I'm pretty certain it was a woman's boot that clipped me." His old grin surfaced briefly, but then he grew serious again. "Your would-be father-in-law drew a knife, with which he attempted to slit my throat. Thanks to the judge's bailiff, he only succeeded in drawing enough blood to ruin a perfectly good shirt."

"I was aiming for Percy's shin." She ducked her head in embarrassment. "And to think you were wounded with a knife because you sought to protect me! I wouldn't blame you if you rode off and left me in these woods. I've done nothing but cause you more trouble and pain than you can possibly forgive."

"For the past four years, I've been preaching repentance and forgiveness, so don't underestimate my capacity in that respect. But that is something we can discuss later. For the present, it might be best to approach the village as quietly as possible and spend the next few days crating up for shipment to Philadelphia those sale items you consider most valuable. Items you wish to keep, we can ship to James and ask that he transport them to Utah. Then, if you agree with my plan, you should pack one small, easy-to-carry bag to take with you on our journey to Philadelphia. There, you can dispose of the valuables as you see fit."

"I'll be going to Philadelphia with you?"

"I begin medical school at the end of summer, and I wouldn't dream of leaving my wife behind." His grin looked a little uncertain this time.

"Then you don't mean to abandon me?"

"No, I'll not abandon you. But just so you know, if you wish an annulment of our marriage once we're safely away, I'll do nothing in the meantime to cause forfeiture of that possibility. The decision will be in your hands." He stood and reached for her hand. "I think it best that we proceed with haste now. I don't wish to be caught in these woods after dark."

In the absence of a mounting block or a convenient-sized rock, Edward tossed Serenity into the saddle and mounted behind her. Reaching around her, he gathered the reins in his hands and urged the horse onward.

Serenity found Edward's arms around her a bit disconcerting. They seemed to cause a strange flutter in her stomach at the same time they lent a comforting sense of safety.

It was dark when they reached the stable, and Serenity lingered with Edward as he unsaddled the horse and brushed the animal until her coat shone. Serenity held the lantern for him so he could better see his task, and she glanced around the stable while she waited. She'd been in the stable many times before at night, but this night something about the small barn made her uneasy. The lantern sputtered and nearly went out. Shaking it gently, she discovered it was almost empty of oil and made a mental note to send more oil for it with Edward and Timothy when they retired for the night.

As she gazed around the familiar barn, she attempted to dismiss her uneasy feeling as merely the culmination of the day's trying events. The door to the tack room stood open, and she could see two bed rolls on the floor, a valise that she assumed belonged to Edward, and a flour sack that likely held Timothy's few possessions. On one pillow rested two dark, leather-bound books. They closely resembled the pair of books that rested in the secret drawer of the writing table that had been moved from her parents' bedroom to her own just yesterday.

"I'm finished," Edward announced. He left the horse's stall and hung the brush on a nail while Serenity turned down the wick of the lantern until the flame was extinguished. She then hung the lantern on a nail in its usual place.

"I'll send more fuel for the lantern the next time you or Timothy come this way," she promised. He looked at her with a wry smile and took her arm without speaking. Together they walked toward the house. Serenity could smell the lilacs even though she couldn't see them in the dark. She would miss that lilac tree when the time came to leave her home.

She thought of Edward's concern that the Tolsons might seek some kind of revenge and moved closer to him. They approached the house, cautiously peering in windows to ascertain that no unpleasant surprise was awaiting them, then stepped inside to a chorus of greetings from the Hayes family.

"Land sakes, child! What happened to you?" Julia exclaimed. She took one look at Serenity's bruised and swollen eye along with her disheveled clothing and shook her head, muttering something Serenity couldn't quite make out.

"Did Mr. Tolson do that to you?" Timothy demanded. He stood, a look of grim determination on his face, and reached for the rifle he'd leaned in a corner upon his arrival.

Edward gently pushed the rifle aside. "I daresay Tolson looks worse than she does." There was a note of grim satisfaction in Edward's voice.

"I've much to tell you," Serenity said and sighed with pleasure when Rosie placed a cold compress on her eye.

Julia insisted they all sit at the table before explanations began. She had a warm supper waiting. While they ate, Serenity told them about the day's events. When she finished there was a stunned silence.

"Married?" Timothy finally broke the silence. "Now you is really in big trouble." He was looking at Edward.

"Don't I know it!" Edward slowly swung his head back and forth. This time his grin was the familiar one Serenity quite admired. It took her considerable effort to avoid kicking his shin beneath the table.

When they were finished clearing away the dishes, the men prepared to return to the stable for the night. Julia stopped them.

"If that lawyer man be set on causin' trouble, he'll be watchin' to see if you and Miz Serenity act like married folks. If he see you sleepin' in that barn, he cause trouble. You best be stayin' in this house."

Serenity's eyes met Edward's, and she could see he agreed with Julia. She had no idea what prompted her to add, "I think you both should stay in the house tonight. If there's trouble, we'll be needing your help, and I don't think it's a good idea for Timothy to be alone in the stable. I noticed earlier that there are a couple of cots behind an old wardrobe in the storage room upstairs. We could clear enough space for you to make use of them."

Timothy and Edward gathered their bedrolls and their few possessions from the barn. Serenity fell asleep while they were still sliding trunks and furniture about in the room across the hall to create enough space to set up the cots.

A few hours later she awoke to screams and slamming doors. A flickering light illuminated her room. She dashed to the window and parted the curtains to see flames leaping in the air beyond the lilac tree. The stable was engulfed in flames.

Snatching up her robe, she ran barefoot down the stairs and emerged in the back garden in time to see someone leading a blindfolded horse through the smoke. Edward appeared beside the rescuer she assumed was Timothy, taking the bridle in his own grip and pointing the man toward the house.

Timothy staggered and stumbled to his knees, coughing and retching. Struggling to breathe and wiping at her eyes, Serenity reached him only seconds before Julia and Rosie did. Together the three women dragged him out of the smoke. His mother and grandmother then took over his care while Serenity turned back to view the burning stable. It quickly became clear there was nothing she could do to save the stable.

Keeping her back to the smoke, she walked as quickly as she could in the direction she'd seen Edward and the horse disappear earlier. She found Edward in a corner of the orchard where a thick tangle of currant bushes grew. He was tethering Timothy's horse to a tree beside the trickle of water that meandered through the grove.

"The horse will be safe here. It's far enough from the flames to calm her." He clasped Serenity's hand and they began running back toward the inferno. When they emerged from the orchard, they found a line forming and buckets of water being passed from hand to hand. A dozen or more townspeople manned the bucket brigade, clearly fearing the fire might spread to the house or to their own homes and businesses.

The fire was almost out and the line had grown to several dozen men when the first wagon load of Friends arrived. They lost no time forming a second line and relieving the exhausted townspeople. With the farmers' help, the fire was checked before it could spread, though it was too late for the stable.

Once the fire seemed to be extinguished, Serenity, with Edward at her side, circled the smoldering heap of rubble. Edward paused several times to be certain no embers remained. When they reached the weary members of the bucket brigade, they stopped to thank Serenity's neighbors for their prompt response.

Sheriff Compton approached Edward, ignoring Serenity. "You're fortunate you got out of there, young man. You and that darky could have been burned alive. In the future, you best be more careful about leaving a lantern burning. If old Mrs. Ross hadn't looked out her window and raised an alarm, the whole town might have burned."

"Neither Timothy nor I lit a lantern in the stable tonight," Edward replied through clenched teeth. "The lantern was out of oil, and we neglected to refill it when we went to the stable to feed and water Mr. Hayes's horse."

The sheriff's brows knit together as he attempted to discover another explanation for the fire.

"Sheriff," Serenity said stiffly, "my husband slept in the house tonight. Mr. Benson and I were married today. And not wishing for Mr. Hayes, who has been absent from his mother and grandmother for some time, to spend the night alone in the stable, we invited him to also spend the night in the house. I suspect this fire was no accident. I trust you will be looking into it."

Edward lightly touched her elbow. "Serenity, my dear, why don't you check on Timothy while I speak with the sheriff," he said, urging her toward the house. For a moment she resisted, then, recognizing the futility of expecting the sheriff to listen to her, she hurried down the path leading to the door of her home.

Timothy was sitting at the kitchen table with a tablecloth covering his head, and she could see the outline of the teakettle under the cloth as well. Mamma had used the same sort of steam-tent therapy for Serenity's childhood colds. She didn't know if it would ease Timothy's discomfort from breathing smoke-laden air, but she didn't know anything else to suggest. He heard her steps and lifted his head.

"Is Susquehanna all right?" he asked.

"Susquehanna?" She wasn't sure what the wide, shallow river that ran a short distance from the village had to do with the day's events.

"My horse," Timothy clarified. "I pulled that horse out of a mud and ice hole in the river right after she was born. The farmer she belonged to said the filly's mother was dead and if the baby survived she wouldn't be worth much, as her legs were cut up. He said I could have her if I wanted her, and I did. I named her Susquehanna for the river I pulled her out of. The last few years she pulled me out of more than one far worse hole and saved my life. I'm right fond of that horse."

Serenity smiled. "She's fine. Edward tethered her near the little stream that runs at the far end of the orchard."

"I best be seein' about her." Timothy rose to his feet, and though his mother fussed, he continued to the door with only an occasional cough. The door opened almost in his face.

Edward grasped the black man's arm. "Timothy, I think you'd better hide. That fool sheriff is coming to charge you with arson."

9

"Go out the window in my room," Serenity advised. "The lilac tree will hide you."

"I'll gather some vittles you can take with you," Julia said and rushed toward the kitchen.

"It don't seem right to run when I ain't done nothin' wrong," Timothy complained.

"It isn't right," Edward agreed, "but Bernard Tolson showed up just as the bucket brigade people were preparing to leave. He got the people all worked up, and the sheriff said he'd arrest you. I fear there might be a lynching before we can prove you had nothing to do with the fire."

Angry voices approaching the house galvanized them into action. Timothy darted up the stairs with his mother and grand-mother following. "Don't worry about me," Serenity heard him say. "I'm still in the army, and my unit is heading west to Fort Laramie to keep order where some of the tribes are still causing problems."

Hammering sounded on the front door. Serenity and Edward looked at each other. "We better stall as long as we can," Edward whispered as he released the lock on the door.

Together, they stepped onto the porch. The sheriff, taken by surprise, stepped back, allowing Serenity to close the door behind her before confronting the crowd. Edward raised his arms, and after some shouts and grumbling, the crowd became quieter.

"My wife and I are grateful for your help tonight," he called out. Several people in the crowd exchanged startled looks, and some looked at Serenity as though asking for confirmation that the pair were indeed wed. She stepped to Edward's side, and he placed a hand at the back of her waist and continued talking in a relaxed manner. "Contrary to what may have been reported, no one was sleeping in the stable tonight other than a horse, which I was able to lead to safety."

"Get out of the way," someone shouted. "The house should be searched."

"Ain't none of your business to go searchin' any houses," the sheriff shouted back, and to Serenity's surprise, he came to stand beside her and Edward.

"We heard accusations directed toward a young man who stopped to offer his condolences to me when he heard my father had been murdered," Serenity called to the crowd. "He's a Union soldier on his way to meet up with his unit, and we wish to assure you he had nothing to do with setting the fire." At the edge of the crowd she spotted a number of Quaker farmers whom she suspected of working with her mother and the Hayes family in the Underground Railroad. "Some of you know Timothy Hayes," she added. "He has stopped here a number of times in the past to visit with my parents."

She knew her guess had been correct as the bearded farmers looked at each other and then scowled at the gathered townspeople.

"That boy is no troublemaker," one of the farmers shouted.

"His unit was at Richmond," another added. "General Grant said those boys conducted themselves admirably and aided in bringing about the end of the war."

A few muttered remarks came from some of the townspeople, especially those who had opposed freeing the slaves.

"The sheriff found a smashed lantern, and we smelled kerosene," Bernard Tolson shouted.

"You didn't arrive until after the fire was out and there was no more heavy work to do," Edward scoffed. "You wouldn't know whether there were kerosene fumes or not."

Several men chuckled, and Bernard Tolson glared at Edward with hate-filled eyes. "I'd still like to talk to that—"

"He isn't here," Serenity interrupted. "He already left to catch up with his unit."

"What about this fellow?" A finger pointed toward Edward. Serenity couldn't see who called out the question, but Bernard Tolson quickly added, "He's been hanging around ever since Charles was shot and seems to be awfully interested in Miss Caswell's inheritance."

"Edward Benson is my husband and you know it," Serenity countered sharply.

"Seems to me that if I were interested in the Caswell property, I wouldn't be burning it down," Edward said with a chuckle, and several men in the crowd guffawed loudly. Laughter broke up the tension, and men began to wander away with comments about getting some sleep before it was time to get up again.

Seeing the crowd was deserting him, Tolson stomped away. Just as he reached the trees, someone stepped out of the shadows to join him, but he was too far away for Serenity to identify.

"Mr. Benson," the sheriff said to Edward, "it might be wise to watch the rubble until morning to make certain a hot spot doesn't reignite a blaze."

"I'll do that," Edward agreed.

"I don't know what got into old Tolson tonight." The sheriff scratched his head. "He's always been a windbag, but for a while there I thought I might have a lynching on my hands. I sympathize with folks who paid good money for slaves then lost everything because of the war and Mr. Lincoln's proclamation saying they ain't got no right to their property. But that's the law now, and my job is to see that folks obeys the law. It wouldn't have been easy, but I wouldn't have let them hang that boy."

"Mr. Tolson was mighty upset earlier today because I married Mr. Benson instead of Percy," Serenity told him. "He had big plans for handling the money from the sale of Papa's store. I think it would be a good idea for you to investigate where Mr. Tolson was the night Papa was shot and discover why he didn't show up to fight the fire tonight until it had been put out. It appears he might prefer me being a widow to a bride."

"Females!" The sheriff shook his head and chuckled. He turned to Edward, "I don't know where they get their foolish ideas, but I hope you're man enough to teach your wife to leave the thinking to men and to hold her tongue when she ain't got nothin' to say." He turned to walk away.

Serenity knew it would be futile to say anything more. Sheriff Compton had always dismissed women as a silly lot, which probably explained why he'd never married.

"The man's a fool," Edward muttered after the sheriff had left. "I'd punch him in the nose, but I doubt he'd be able to figure out why I did it."

Serenity appreciated his sentiment, but rather than discuss the sheriff's shortcomings, she thought it best to return to the house. "I'd better check on Julia and Rosie," she said.

"I'll watch for embers until the sun comes up," Edward told her. "Then I plan to go over every inch of the burned-out area to see if I can find any clues as to who set the fire."

* * *

The sun was just turning the mist above the river to pale pink when Serenity sat down beside Edward at the edge of the orchard. He'd chosen a spot where the ground rose slightly and he had a good view of the burned-out stable. From his position he'd be able to see if any coals turned red or any flames sprang to life.

"Is everything all right?" he asked.

"Yes, but I couldn't go back to sleep. I kept thinking about Timothy and how he fought in the war to give his people a new beginning, but he had to sneak away in the middle of the night or be blamed and maybe lynched for a fire he didn't start. Rosie said when Timothy was a little boy, they lived in a tent and one night a mob set it on fire while he and his family were in it. They barely escaped with their lives. Even with the end of the war, she says, nothing has changed much since that night. Ignorant, hate-filled people still think they can make themselves look big and important by attacking those who are weaker, and the colored people are still a handy target."

"It will take a long time for attitudes and prejudices to change."

She thought about Edward's observation and suspected he was thinking of his own people, who had been driven from their homes by a hate-filled mob. She knew he was right, but it still didn't seem fair. After a few minutes, she changed the subject.

"Why is everyone so sure the fire was set? Could it have been an accident?"

"At first, everyone was more concerned with extinguishing the fire than with its cause. I don't recall anyone mentioning arson until Bernard Tolson arrived. Now almost everyone seems to believe the fire was set."

"I have to admit, I believe it was deliberately set too. Perhaps I might have accepted that the fire was an accident if Mr. Tolson hadn't shown up here and acted the way he did. Though he was clearly wrong in who he accused, reason tells me there was no lightning, I put out the lantern myself and it was out of fuel, and there was neither hay nor kerosene stored in the barn."

Edward turned to look at her. "Do you think Bernard Tolson started the fire?"

Serenity could see Edward's face now and knew he suspected the lawyer. She took her time answering his question. "I don't know what to think," she said finally. "He was angry yesterday, and he might have thought he could expose our marriage as a sham and still force me to marry Percy."

"Or, as you told the sheriff, make you a young widow. No, I don't really believe that. If he'd been snooping around and knew Timothy and I had been sleeping in the barn, he may have thought he could scare me away. I can see him setting the barn on fire out of revenge or to scare me, but I don't think he could have killed me or your father. Bernard is a heavy man and somewhat clumsy, too. I can't see him climbing to the bluff from which your father was shot. The two incidents may not be connected."

"Somehow I think they *are* connected. I just don't know what that connection is. The worst part is, I don't know who to trust anymore."

"Trust no one until this is resolved," Edward advised.

"That's what Julia said. She's a wise old woman and knows much more than I do about people. She wants me to leave here as soon as possible."

"I agree with her. I've spent the last couple of hours thinking about your situation, and I've concluded you're not safe here. My instincts tell me it all goes back to your mother. Until we know why she was murdered, I doubt we will discover who or what was behind your father's death. Somehow, last night's fire ties in too. But getting answers isn't worth your life."

"This might be just one of those silly female starts the sheriff accused me of, but I think it's all connected to Mamma's topaz ring. If we could find it, I think we would find answers to the other puzzles."

"You may be right. In spite of Tolson's bad behavior, I don't think he's guilty of much more than being obnoxious. He may have started the stable fire to scare me away, but I don't think he intended to kill anyone. It would have been easy for him to determine that no one was sleeping in the barn."

"I don't feel so generous toward him." Serenity thrust out her jaw and scowled, recalling what she knew of the man. "He's greedy, and he's mean. Don't forget he drew a knife on you at the courthouse, and his late wife was frequently bruised. I've never been certain her death was an accident, nor that she drowned herself, as most folks believe. The Susquehanna isn't deep, and the place where she died is only knee-deep in August. It seems unlikely that she could have held her own head under water that shallow long enough to drown, as she supposedly did."

"That makes him a stronger suspect than I first thought," Edward conceded. "But it's also possible that the fire may have been a warning, having nothing to do with our lawyer friend. I can't help thinking Tolson is an opportunist and that someone smarter than him planned your father's murder."

Serenity sighed. Her eyes lingered over the charred beams and wreckage, now visible in the early-morning light. "If whoever started the fire had wished to kill you or Timothy, it seems logical that he would have torched the house when he discovered you weren't in the stable. I doubt murder was the intent behind the fire, in spite of what I said to the sheriff. It may have been a ruse to distract us so he could search the house again, but his plan failed because Julia and Rosie stayed inside taking care of Timothy. If someone believes the topaz is in my house or that something there might expose the murderer, he could be anxious to scare us away and will try again."

"We'll need to be cautious," Edward agreed. He stood to walk closer to the burned stable. Taking a long stick, he poked at several lumps but found no answers. There were too many footprints to be certain any matched the ones found in the trail of flour just two days earlier.

Julia's voice reached them from the kitchen stoop where she stood waving to them. "Breakfast be on the table," she called.

Enticing aromas lured them to the dining room, where Julia had set the table for four. Serenity and Edward seated themselves, then Rosie entered the room from the kitchen and sat across the table from them. Serenity could see that her eyes were swollen, and there was a slight tremble to her hands when she passed the pitcher of syrup. After the terrifying tent fire long ago, seeing her son once more suffering from the effects of a fire and then being forced to flee seemed to have thoroughly upset the poor woman.

Serenity turned to Julia. "This looks and smells wonderful, Julia, but you don't need to wait on me. You're my guest. I've been cooking and cleaning since I was a child, and I'm perfectly capable of continuing to do so."

"I know that," Julia said. "But yo' mamma was awful good to me, an' I always wanted to help her some way."

Serenity rose from her chair to give Julia a hug. "I appreciate all you and Rosie have done for me, but last night's fire convinced me there is no need for you to stay here and put yourselves at risk. Timothy shouldn't have had to leave the way he did, and I don't want anyone causing trouble for you. Edward and I will be fine here by ourselves until I can make arrangements for Papa's valuables and sell this property."

"She's right," Edward agreed. "You've been more than kind to both of us, but we don't think you should take chances. I'll ask around to see if any of the farmers are heading north soon and if they have room for a couple of passengers."

"First, you needs to sleep," Julia admonished. "Neither you nor Miz Serenity scarce had a chance to close yo' eyes all night. Rosie and me will keep our eyes open while you rest, then we can talk 'bout other things."

Serenity knew that, as usual, Julia was right. Her head was nodding with fatigue and Edward had gotten less sleep than she had.

* * *

In the coming days, a continual train of visitors came to Serenity's door, some to offer sympathy and some to make offers to purchase goods. Edward accompanied her to the telegraph office to inform her uncle of the change in her marital status. And two gentlemen—Joshua Brown from Boston and Loyal Ochendorf, the son of the farmer owning the field adjacent to the orchard—made offers to purchase her home, Papa's store, and the small acreage that included the orchard.

"I'm aware of the buryin' place for thy folks on the other side of the orchard," Loyal Ochendorf stammered as he wrung his hat in his hands. "I give thee my word, I'll fence off that bit of land and leave it undisturbed if thou accept my offer."

Joshua Brown was another matter entirely. He approached Edward in front of the small building that housed the telegraph and Mr. Tolson's law office and offered to purchase the property and its contents for what he claimed was a generous sum. He then announced that he would arrive to inspect his future property early the following morning.

Later, Edward reported to Serenity the answer he'd given. "I told him he'd have to discuss the matter with my wife. That didn't sit well with the gentleman from Boston," he said with a mischievous grin.

* * *

It had been two weeks since Charles Caswell's burial when Serenity sat in the tall orchard grass, weaving a daisy chain beside her parents' graves. The past week had been peaceful, without the kind of excitement her unexpected wedding and the frightening fire of the previous week had brought. She'd seen nothing of Bernard Tolson or his son, nor of Joshua Brown. So far Mr. Brown hadn't approached her, though she'd seen him about town.

She and Edward, assisted by Julia and Rosie, had spent long hours sorting and cataloging Papa's possessions, and a crate of her favorite items had been taken by one of the Quaker farmers to Erie for James to transport to her uncle's home.

Her fingers moved rapidly and seemingly without direction. Her mind was far away, remembering the days when Mamma had taught her her letters and Papa had insisted she learn sums as well. Papa had continued teaching her right up until the day before he left on his last trip to New York. She was grateful for the education they had given her, especially now that she was alone and greatly in need of being able to understand her business affairs. In spite of all of Papa's expensive trinkets and valuable property, she was completely without funds. Mr. Barnes at the bank refused to discuss Papa's account with her, and even though Edward had shown him the marriage certificate Judge Detweiler had given them, he insisted he couldn't release any funds to either of them without Mr. Tolson's approval. Remembering the banker's haughty attitude, Serenity seethed with anger for several minutes, then her thoughts returned to her parents.

She'd missed Mamma for a long time, but now the sharpest pain was for Papa. For almost a week now, she'd been handling his treasures and attempting to assess their value. Figuring a value for the items from the shelves in his store had proved simple, as he'd thoroughly discussed those items with her and she knew what he expected to realize from the sale of each. It was the items in the storage room at the back of the store and in the upstairs room where Edward slept that gave her trouble and made her long for Papa's wise counsel.

Charles Caswell had collected paintings and sculptures, jewelry, laces and tapestries, elaborate carvings of both wood and ivory, and a multitude of unique household items ranging from china to silver. He had also stocked candles, barrels, perfume, and practical leather items of his own design. Some of the items were of great value, and some were only valued according to their usefulness.

The ones that puzzled Serenity most were found in a trunk in the upstairs room. This strange collection consisted of paste jewels, clumsy copies of art pieces, and metal objects that had turned green. They were worthless, and she wondered why Papa had kept them and how he had acquired them. She knew very well that with his keen ability to appraise such items, he couldn't have been cheated so many times. When she'd mentioned the matter at the dinner table, Julia had looked at her strangely and supplied the only possible answer.

"Yo' pa," she said, "was as much involved as yo' mamma wif helpin' black folks. Whenever runaway slaves sneak up his back step hopin' to trade somethin' for enough cash for the next leg of they journey, yo' pa buy whatever treasure they have. Sometimes they only have junk. He know that, but he trade anyway."

The explanation brought a lump to Serenity's throat, and she wondered how she'd failed to see that Papa's involvement with the Underground Railroad was as great as Mamma's. There had never been a time when she'd been unaware of her parents' devotion to each other, and she should have realized they also shared their commitment to the cause.

She looked up at Julia and felt tears stinging her eyes. She would miss Julia and Rosie terribly. She'd come to depend on their friendship and blunt practicality. Through their eyes, she'd come to know her parents more fully too. But true to his word, Edward had found a farmer who would be traveling to upper New York late that evening and had secured a place in his wagon for the two women.

Serenity draped the daisy chain over the stone Edward and James had placed at the head of Papa's grave. A shadow fell across her. She looked up, expecting to see Edward. Instead, a carefully dressed stranger stood watching her.

"Good day." He removed his hat, pressed it against a wide expanse of lawn shirt, and bowed courteously. "You must be Serenity Caswell," he said. "I am Rupert Montague, your father's friend and the executor of his estate."

10

Rupert Montague appeared to be around fifty. He was fastidiously dressed, with silver streaks in his hair and a thin mustache. His hands looked soft, and his shoes had recently been polished. He looked entirely out of place in the orchard.

Serenity rose to her feet, ignoring the hand the gentleman extended to help her rise. "I am Serenity Caswell Benson." She gave the last name slight emphasis, wishing to communicate that she wasn't without protection should the need for such arise. Though neither she nor Edward had spoken of it, she was aware that Edward lingered among the trees nearby while she visited her parents' burial place.

When she said nothing more, her visitor cleared his throat and looked more closely at her. He frowned, and she knew he had noticed the dark smudge that still underlined her eye. He appeared momentarily ill at ease but did not comment on his observation.

"Miss—Ma'am," he corrected. "You are the daughter of Charles Caswell?"

"I am." She volunteered nothing further. She assumed the man standing before her was the gentleman she had seen at some distance who had approached Edward almost a week ago. He also was likely the man Bernard Tolson had told the judge would come to make an offer on her father's business. His arrival just days after her father's death and his association with Mr. Tolson did nothing to encourage Serenity to trust the stranger.

"Your maid said I would find you here," he said. Though it caused her some discomfort to allow him to assume Julia was her maid, Serenity didn't correct him.

"I received word last week," he went on, "that your father died on his way home from New York, where we conducted considerable business together. There was a notice in the New York papers, submitted by a Mr. Barnes, apparently a local banker and personal acquaintance of your father. I wish to offer both my condolences and any assistance you may need in dealing with your father's business interests. I am completely at your service to acquaint you with his considerable stock and assets as well as the conditions of his will."

"Stock and assets? Mr. Montague, I am not certain I know to what you refer, but my husband and I have already begun compiling a catalog of Papa's collection. It is our intention to dispose of all those items we do not wish to take with us when we eventually establish ourselves farther west."

"Your father spoke of your intended visit to Salt Lake City and was at pains to arrange his affairs for the possibility of a protracted stay."

"He told you we planned to go west?" This surprised Serenity. She hadn't known Papa had spoken to anyone other than herself of his interest in finding out more about her mother's people.

"Your father and I have been friends and business colleagues for many years. It was his habit to stay at my family's estate while visiting New York, since we attended school together in Oxford many years ago and he was, for a time, my father's ward. I only met your mother once, when he brought her to New York on their wedding trip."

Serenity felt her defenses crumble. Papa had told her he was orphaned at a young age, but beyond that, he never spoke of his family. She began to hope this man really had been acquainted with her father and could tell her more of his family.

"I'm sorry I haven't been more welcoming since your arrival in town," she apologized. "Had I known . . ."

"Did you not receive my telegrams?"

"I've received but one telegram since Papa's death," she told him. "My uncle in Utah Territory telegraphed his condolences and an invitation to make my home with him."

"That's odd." Mr. Montague quirked one eyebrow in a fashion that made him appear skeptical. "I wired you my deepest sympathies as soon as I learned of Charles's death, and a few days later I wired you again to acquaint you with my arrival date. I brought several papers that await your signature, and there are decisions that need to be made. I can advise you, or perhaps your husband . . . ?" He let his voice trail off in a question.

"Perhaps we should adjourn to the house and wait for Edward to join us." Her mind was in turmoil. *Why didn't Papa ever speak of this man? And what papers could I be required to sign?* She prided herself on her excellent education and her independence, but she didn't have an inkling of the matters Mr. Montague mentioned.

Edward joined them before they reached the garden gate, and Serenity introduced the two men. They shook hands, then Mr. Montague noticed the rubble from the burned stable. He raised one eyebrow and seemed about to ask a question, then chose to remain silent.

Once they were seated in the parlor and Julia had fetched a tray of beverages, Edward turned to Mr. Montague to ask, "What business do you represent and how were you acquainted with my father-in-law?"

Mr. Montague took a long swallow from his glass, then set it down. "More than thirty years ago, Charles and I found ourselves sharing a room at Oxford. I was far from home and lonely, while he had been recently orphaned and was my father's ward. Though we hadn't expected to like each other, we became fast friends. My father had founded one of the first banking establishments in New York City, and Charles's father had been one of his clients. When the elder Caswell died, he left his fortune to his son, but due to Charles's tender years, my father administered his inheritance and sent him to Oxford to await his majority.

"Charles was always more interested in art and philosophy than in finances. He showed no interest in investing or spending his father's money, though I suspected early on that he channeled most of his allowance into the eradication of slavery. After graduating, he was content to leave the handling of his money to me, except where the buying and selling of his treasured art pieces was concerned. There were, on occasion, rumors concerning the true ownership of some of the pieces he produced for sale, but no charges were ever made that anyone could prove. Then one day he brought a lovely young woman to New York with him and introduced her as his bride. Hannah had a keen grasp of finance and insisted that Charles draw up a will concerning the disposition of his inherited fortune upon his demise."

"Inherited fortune?" Serenity had never heard anything about the fortune her father supposedly possessed. She had assumed that their family's living was produced by Papa's store. Agitated, she rose to her feet and paced to the window. "Why was I never told about Papa's inheritance?"

Mr. Montague looked around as though fearing someone might overhear, then in a softer voice explained. "Charles never knew his father's fortune was amassed through the slave trade until after the senior Caswell's death. He was appalled and swore he would never touch a cent of his father's money. Upon leaving school, he moved here to this frontier town, opened his store, and managed to eke out a meager living until he chanced upon the Underground Railroad and learned that many of the runaways carried trinkets and small artifacts they had appropriated or been given to finance their trips. A few of the braver ones approached him, hoping to trade the items for food."

"Papa bought those items, then traded them in New York," Serenity finished for him and returned to her chair.

"He paid handsomely for them, far more than their worth in many instances." A slight smile twitched one corner of the gentleman's mouth. "At first, he came to me for funds from his trust to buy items he referred to as family treasures, but his business was soon flourishing and he was amassing a comfortable living of his own from eager buyers who recognized the worth of the more valuable items he acquired. Through my advice and that of his wife, he invested wisely, accruing a small fortune, which is also on deposit at my bank."

"Does Bernard Tolson know about the money in your bank?" Serenity asked.

This time, Rupert Montague did smile—a wide, wolfish grin that suggested he wasn't the complete gentleman dandy she had supposed. "I've never met Mr. Tolson, but from Charles's description, I suspect he's not the saintly country lawyer he would have others believe him to be. Your father didn't trust him, so he kept only a small amount of money in your local bank and wrote a will that placed you beyond Tolson's reach until such time as you chose to marry." He gave Edward a questioning look.

"We married quickly to prevent Mr. Tolson from being appointed Serenity's guardian," Edward said.

"I am surprised to learn of your marriage, since your father did not make mention of any gentleman who had captured your attention." Mr. Montague quirked that one eyebrow upward again as though asking a question, then went on when neither Serenity nor Edward offered further explanation of their courtship.

"Charles told me of the will he'd allowed Tolson to write and of the gentleman selected to serve as your guardian. He never intended that his Quaker friend assume permanent responsibility for you. He didn't trust Tolson, but he thought the will he'd drawn up would ensure that his estate couldn't be disposed of before my arrival, should I find travel difficult because of the war. The original plan was for Mr. Nixon to send a messenger to me so that I could present a more recently dated will. Charles intended for me to become your guardian."

"You?" Serenity and Edward spoke at the same time.

"As I told you, we were friends since our youth. On his recent trip east, he was a guest in my home. On that occasion, he updated his will once more." He passed a sheaf of papers to Serenity.

As her eyes skimmed the paper, her hands began to shake. Surely Papa hadn't been so wealthy! They hadn't lived as paupers, but there was nothing in their way of living that suggested he had access to such a great fortune. Seeing her agitation, Edward moved closer, placing an arm around her shoulders for support. Mr. Montague went on speaking to her.

"Your father left his personal fortune to you, as you had every right to expect, but for his inherited fortune he made other arrangements."

"I brought papers with me that require your signature so you can draw limited drafts as you choose until your twenty-fifth birthday, when you will receive unfettered control of the remainder of your money. He placed your funds in a trust with a set amount to be forwarded to you each quarter beginning at once." He handed her a draft for an amount that seemed excessively large to her. He eyed Edward for a moment, then continued on.

"As long as your money remains in New York, you will have the control of it, but should you choose to transfer any or all of it to almost any other state, your husband or guardian will have control of it. It was my intention to invite you to make your home with my wife and myself in New York, but your marriage alters this prospect."

Serenity lifted her eyes to Edward's. She felt certain he was thinking that their marriage could easily be annulled. An annulment would free him to go on with his plans without concern for protecting her interests. She should offer him his freedom at once, but what if Mr. Montague wasn't telling her the truth? After all, Papa had never mentioned him or an account at his bank. Besides, she didn't wish to live in New York. She wanted to go west to find her uncle. And if Papa had stayed at Mr. Montague's estate in New York during his recent visit there, that might be where he found Mamma's saddlebag or perhaps learned something of her ring.

"I'm curious," Edward said. "What is to become of the money Serenity's father inherited from his father?" Serenity watched her visitor's face. For just a moment, he appeared uncertain. She found that she too was suddenly curious about the disposition of those funds—if they existed. Mr. Montague recovered his poise so quickly she wondered if she'd imagined that slight hesitation.

"When Charles arrived at my home, he was excited about the war ending and the slaves being set free. But he was also concerned about what would become of those people who possessed no education or property. In many instances, there weren't even any family bonds to encourage the former slaves to work together. He wanted the money his father derived from placing those people in bondage to be used to build schools and purchase tracts of land for those who wished to farm. He said the only way he could atone for his father's greed was to use the money to better the lives of those who suffered because of it."

Serenity could easily believe her father would have elected to use the money in the manner Mr. Montague stated, but why hadn't he chosen her to carry out his wishes? And could Mr. Montague be trusted to use the money as her father wished? She sensed he was leaving something out. She cautioned herself to remember the saddlebag Papa had been bringing back from New York.

"I don't know what to say," she said hesitantly.

"We need time to discuss this," Edward added.

Mr. Montague appeared disappointed, but he didn't protest. He set the glass Julia had given him on a side table and rose to his feet. "I shall be happy to call on you tomorrow," he said with a slight bow.

Edward walked their guest to the door and accompanied him as far as the front gate. They stood together talking for a few minutes, then Edward turned back toward the house. A single shot rang out, and Rupert Montague dropped to the ground, followed by Edward. Serenity could see that Edward was alive as he scooted forward, clasped Mr. Montague's legs, and pulled him into a shallow dip behind the boardwalk that fronted the Caswell house and store. In minutes, both men disappeared beneath a clump of shrubbery. Serenity was about to run to their aid, but Julia gripped her arm.

"Stay here," the older woman warned. "Mistah Edward be fine, an' he take care of that other gentleman."

Serenity peered desperately into the shrubbery but saw no movement nor any indication from which direction the shot had come, though the thickly wooded area across the road was the most likely hiding place for the shooter. She paced the parlor, occasionally stealing a glance at the street from behind the edge of the parlor curtains. Rosie rushed upstairs to see if there was a better view from the upper hallway window, then reported there was nothing to be seen but the dusty street. Julia armed herself with a poker and took up a position near the front door.

Hearing a sound behind her, Serenity whirled about to see the kitchen door slowly opening.

"Julia!" she shouted as she reached for a brass candlestick. With candlestick and poker, the two women rushed the door. Serenity's heart was pounding as she raised her weapon.

"Serenity, wait!" The split-second warning kept her from smashing the heavy object against Edward's head.

"Gracious, you frightened us!" Julia exclaimed as Edward and Mr. Montague stumbled into the room.

"Careful with that candlestick," Mr. Montague cautioned. "It's really quite valuable."

"Are you all right?" Serenity asked the older man, who no longer looked so fastidious. His coat was dusty, twigs adorned his hair, and a long scratch ran along his right cheek.

"I was startled more than injured." He brushed at his coat.

"Nevertheless, I intend to take a look at that cut on your cheek," Edward insisted and hurried upstairs for his medical bag.

"Edward isn't a doctor yet," Serenity explained. "But he has apprenticed with a licensed doctor for several years."

Edward returned in moments and proceeded to clean and apply a bandage to Mr. Montague's cheek. "Did you see who shot at you?" he asked as he worked.

"No, but I estimate the shot came from that wooded lot across the street. I turned to bid you farewell, else you might have had a corpse to bury."

"I'm not certain the shot was intended for you," Edward stated in a surprisingly calm manner. "Someone who apparently believed me to be sleeping in the barn set fire to it a week ago." He didn't mention the brawl that had occurred at his and Serenity's wedding.

"Who's behind this?" Mr. Montague demanded.

"We wish we knew," Serenity told him. "I suspect Bernard Tolson, who was upset when I married Edward and spoiled his plans to become my guardian."

"It might be more accurate to say his plan was to become your money's guardian," Edward interjected wryly. "And that was before we learned there's more at stake than this property and the contents of your father's house and store." He finished bandaging Mr. Montague's cheek and returned his supplies to his bag.

"There's a stranger in town who made arrangements with Mr. Tolson to purchase Papa's store, but I've seen nothing of him," Serenity added. "At first, I mistook you for him."

"And there's one more disappointed party." Edward grinned and winked at Serenity, bringing a flush to her cheeks. "Tolson's son Percy seems to think he had a prior claim to Serenity herself. He assumed she would agree to marry him and was quite distraught to learn she'd rather marry me." Edward launched into an edited version of their trip to the courthouse, which left both men chuckling, though Serenity failed to see anything humorous about that disastrous day. She quietly left the room.

"Miss Serenity, where you going?" Julia asked in her strong voice. Serenity winced. She'd hoped she could slip out the kitchen door while the men were busy discussing her would-be suitor.

"You can't go outside where someone is roaming about with a rifle," Edward remonstrated as he hurried to her side.

"Where did you plan to go?" Mr. Montague asked in a calmer voice.

"To the telegraph office." Serenity frowned at those intent on keeping her inside the house. "You said you sent me a telegram advising me that you were coming. I'd like to know why I didn't receive it—and who was charged with delivering it to me."

"I'll go. You stay here where you'll be safe," Edward argued.

"I sent the telegram," Mr. Montague interjected. "I have a right to demand an answer as to why it wasn't delivered." He settled his hat firmly on his head and started toward the door.

Serenity opened the door. "You're not leaving me behind."

Edward sighed. "Lock the doors behind us," he whispered to Julia before he and Mr. Montague exited the back door with Serenity between them.

11

Edward led the way, staying in the shadows of trees and buildings until they reached the telegraph office. One after another they slipped into the small room. The telegrapher looked up as they approached his desk. Serenity came right to the point.

"Mr. Miller, who picked up the telegram that was sent to me from New York after Papa was laid to rest?"

Mr. Miller leaned back in his chair, scratched his nearly bald head, and thought for several minutes before asking, "Which one?"

"You mean more than one telegram has arrived for me in the past couple of weeks?"

"I can't rightly say how many, but there's been a good number of condolences and such. Young Frederick has been kept busy running them messages to you."

"But I haven't received them, not one."

"You must be mistaken. Frederick comes in before and after school to pick up telegrams to deliver. I leave them in that box right there for him." He pointed to a wooden box on the counter that separated his chair and the telegraph key from the remainder of the office. Serenity glanced toward the box Mr. Miller indicated. It sat where anyone might glance inside and see the messages.

"When my father wired me to report his safe arrival in New York, you delivered that message in person to my home. And I received a telegram from my uncle a few weeks ago. Why are you entrusting my telegrams to someone else now?" She'd have to find the boy, Frederick, and demand her telegrams.

"The telegram from your father was delivered before I hired Frederick, and the first one from Salt Lake came quite late in the evening after Frederick had already gone home to bed. I don't have an assistant, and since the war ended, I've been awfully busy sending and receiving messages, especially during the daytime. A few weeks ago, several folks could see I couldn't be available to work the key if I was away delivering telegrams, and they suggested I hire a boy to do the running. Frederick is a good boy, and I haven't had any complaints about him until now."

Edward stepped forward. "Where can we find Frederick? Those messages are important."

The office door opened and a freckle-faced lad of about twelve whistled his way inside. "Afternoon, Mr. Miller," he called and went straight to the box waiting on the counter.

"Frederick," Mr. Miller said sternly. "Miss Caswell, er, Benson has informed me she hasn't received any of the telegrams you were supposed to deliver to her."

The boy appeared startled. He looked at Serenity, then back at his employer, clearly confused.

"What did you do with them?" Mr. Montague gave the boy a severe look.

"I gave them to Mr. Tolson. He said he was representing Miss Caswell since her pa passed on and that all telegrams addressed to her should be given to him. I've given them all to him. Except one. I delivered a message to Sheriff Compton last week, and he saw I had one for Miss Caswell. He said he was on his way to the Caswell house and would save me the bother. Did I do something wrong?" The boy's face turned red, and he looked to be fighting the urge to cry.

"From now on you are to deliver telegrams to the person addressed and to no one else. Do you understand?" Mr. Miller continued to speak to the boy in a stern voice. Frederick nodded his head and swallowed hard.

Serenity smiled at the boy, and he seemed to perk up a little after seeing her pleasant face amid all the sour ones.

"I'm sure Mr. Tolson just forgot about the telegrams." Mr. Miller appealed to Serenity. "He's sure to take them to you on his next visit."

"Sir, Mr. Tolson does not represent Serenity Caswell Benson in any way, and he is not welcome in our home." Edward matched Mr. Miller's severe tone. "He lied to Frederick when he said he did. I believe you have a responsibility to reclaim my wife's messages from him and turn them over to her immediately."

Mr. Miller sputtered, expressing his surprise on learning that Mr. Tolson didn't have the authority to act for Serenity. He then donned his coat with a promise to retrieve the missing telegrams.

"Thank you." Edward took Serenity's arm. "I believe we shall call on the sheriff."

As they crossed the street to the sheriff's office, the telegrapher scurried in one direction and Frederick in the other.

Sheriff Compton had only just arrived at his office when Serenity, Edward, and Mr. Montague walked through the door. He turned from placing his hat on a rack. "I just came from your house," he said, addressing Edward, much to Serenity's annoyance. "That black woman said someone shot at you."

"We're not certain whether he was aiming at me or at Mr. Montague," Edward admitted. "I wasn't injured, but as you can see, Mr. Montague sustained a minor injury to his cheek."

"Did you see who shot you?" the sheriff asked as he turned to Mr. Montague. When the gentleman shook his head, the sheriff added, "Doubtless it was a hunter who got a little careless."

"I don't think carelessness had anything to do with it," Edward disagreed. "I doubt Mr. Caswell's death and the fire were due to carelessness either. I think someone wanted something from Serenity's father and now thinks I stand in the way of his obtaining it."

"Bernard Tolson appropriated telegrams meant for me," Serenity added.

The sheriff sighed and looked disgusted. It was obvious to Serenity that he wouldn't take seriously anything she said, so she might as well leave the discussion to Edward.

"I believe you also have a telegram that belongs to the young lady," Mr. Montague said, speaking up for the first time. "It seems certain persons in this town are not only lax in delivering telegrams, but also in protecting its citizens."

"Now, see here!" Sheriff Compton's face turned red and he puffed out his chest. "I forgot all about that telegram when I saw Miss Caswell's barn was on fire last week. I remembered today and took it to her house, but she wasn't there, so I left it with her housekeeper. You got no call findin' fault with me or my town. What business is it of yours anyway?"

"Mr. Montague is the man Serenity's father picked to be her guardian, had she not married me." Edward seemed to relish letting the sheriff know Bernard Tolson had lied. "Montague is a longtime friend of the Caswells and a big-city banker. Mr. Barnes at the bank placed a notice of Mr. Caswell's death in the New York City papers, and seeing it, Mr. Montague traveled here at once."

Mr. Montague stepped forward. "I also sent Miss Caswell a wire letting her know that I had a copy of her father's updated will and that I would be arriving to assist her in settling her father's affairs this week. She didn't receive that telegram, and the boy working at the telegraph office said he gave all of her telegrams except one to Mr. Tolson to deliver to her." He finished Edward's explanation with a censuring frown directed at the lawman.

"It seems I'll need to have a talk with Bernard." Sheriff Compton squared his shoulders and picked up his hat once more. "I'll collect the telegrams from him and let him know he's not to meddle in Mrs. Benson's affairs anymore, since she has both a husband and a family friend to see to her well-being." He left his office wrapped in aggrieved dignity.

* * *

"Have you a place to stay tonight?" Serenity asked as she stood facing Mr. Montague on the plank walk in front of the sheriff's office. After all that had happened concerning Mr. Montague, she felt she owed him greater hospitality.

"No, but surely a town this size must have a hotel or inn."

"There's a boarding house two blocks over," Edward advised him. "But it might be well for you to spend the night with us."

"Please do," Serenity echoed the invitation. "Our guests, the Hayes, are leaving this evening, which leaves a bedroom open."

"I'll accept without argument. It seems there have been a few too many unfortunate coincidences around you of late, and should there be another one, I think Charles would wish me to lend a hand."

Serenity found herself walking between Edward and Mr. Montague on the way back to her house. There was something in their bearing that made her feel protected and safe, though she knew full well that if someone decided to shoot at them there was little either man could do about it.

Julia peeked through a window before permitting them entry. As soon as they stepped into the kitchen, they spotted the bundles that were Julia's and Rosie's luggage. Julia wiped her eyes with the corner of her large apron. "I been worried," she stated bluntly.

"We took good care of Miss Serenity, and we appreciate the responsible way you took care of this house while we were away," Edward told her. "The sheriff told us he had been here and that you hadn't allowed him entrance without first being certain it was indeed he."

Serenity rushed to give Julia a hug, followed by one for Rosie. "I'm going to miss you both," she said.

"It's time we be gettin' home," Julia replied. "That Trixie an' her man most likely broke by now, an' they needin' me to set the store straight agin."

"And what are your plans?" Edward asked Rosie.

Julia answered for her. "Moses Jackson ask her plenty times to marry with him, but she keep sayin' no." She laughed her hearty laugh. "Now the war be over, she say she start a school for black children for sure."

"Is that right, Rosie?" Mr. Montague asked.

Rosie nodded. "Not many black children, grown-ups neither, can read or write. Most can't do simple sums. Miss Hannah taught me some, then she sent me books so I could learn more. I kept all those books, and it just seems right to use them to help those who want to learn." Rosie looked at the floor and twisted her hands as she talked. It was the longest speech Serenity had ever heard her make.

"I have a crate of books and several slates you can have to help in your classroom," she offered the future schoolteacher.

"Oh, thank you." Rosie smiled and glanced up with her eyes full of gratitude.

"Where do you live?" Mr. Montague questioned.

"We never quite made it to Canada," Julia answered. "We found a pretty place in upper New York. Us an' some other black folks built our own town and was careful to keep an eye out for trouble, but we never had no school. Caleb took to preachin', and sometimes he help a few folks learn their letters."

"It seems to me that building a school in your town might be a good project for a certain philanthropic fund," Mr. Montague said with a pointed look at Serenity. "I'll speak to a few people, then let you know what is decided. A man of my acquaintance, a free man of color, has plans to begin a university for freed slaves. If I can get you a scholarship, Rosie, would you be interested in attending college in your off-season to get a teacher's certificate?"

"Me?" Tears welled in Rosie's eyes. "You think they let a plain black girl like me in that school, Mr. Montague?"

"I think it's time all of you begin calling me Rupert, just as Charles did. And yes, Rosie, you and many more like you will now be able to attend college. I'm not saying the end of the war is the end of problems for your race, because it isn't. There's a lot of healing that needs to take place before we're truly one nation again and black people can take their place alongside whites as brothers and sisters. But there are some people, like Miss Serenity's father, who have the foresight to start preparing for that day."

The sound of a team and wagon pausing at the gate halted their conversation. Edward pulled the curtain aside to get a good look.

"It's the farmer come for Miss Julia and Miss Rosie," he announced.

Serenity rushed upstairs for the box of books from her school-room days. She was pleased to see Edward and Rupert reach past Julia for the two women's bundles. When she returned with the books, Edward was there to take them from her arms and hoist them onto the wagon. Julia was already seated by the time he turned to assist her to the back of the wagon, and Rupert helped lift Rosie to sit beside her mother.

"Now, you be careful, Miss Serenity. Somebody be fixin' to cause you trouble for sure," Julia warned. "You best stay close to Mistah Edward. Oh, I almost forgot. The sheriff bring you this." She fumbled in her apron pocket and at last produced a crumpled piece of yellow paper, which she passed to Serenity.

The wagon lurched forward and Serenity stepped back. She waved and Julia and Rosie waved back until the wagon was out of sight.

Taking her eyes from the empty road, Serenity noticed that dusk was falling. Dark shadows made the trees across the road appear shadowy and indistinct. She felt a slight chill as she remembered that earlier that day someone had fired a shot at the two men who now stood on either side of her. They must have been recalling the same incident, because they each took one of her arms and hurried her toward the house.

Once inside, she felt slightly bereft. The cheerfulness that had existed in the house as long as Julia and Rosie had been there was noticeably missing now. She'd never felt ill at ease being alone while Papa had conducted his business in neighboring towns, but today she was grateful for Edward and Rupert's presence. She realized she would no longer care to be alone in her house on the edge of town.

Serenity busied herself dishing up the stew Julia had prepared earlier, and she visited Papa's room to be certain all was in readiness for Rupert. The room looked bare and lifeless now that Papa's treasures and books no longer covered every surface.

"Come, you need to eat." Edward took her hand and led her to the table. When she was seated, he said grace, and they began to eat. Hearing the crackle of paper in her pocket, she reached for the telegram Julia had handed her. She looked at the paper, turning it this way and that without reading it for several minutes.

"It won't bite," Edward teased.

"I wasn't certain it was proper to read it at the table."

"You've waited long enough. Go ahead and read it," Rupert encouraged.

It took a moment for her to focus on the brief message, and when she finished it, she wiped away a bit of moisture that crept from her eyes. Smiling slightly, she said, "It's from a Mr. Tiffany in New York. He expresses his condolences for the loss of my father, then asks if I wish to return for a full refund the items Papa purchased from him a few weeks ago."

"Who is Mr. Tiffany?" Edward asked.

"He's a gentleman Papa spoke of quite highly," Serenity responded. "He has a store in New York."

"He deals in fine jewelry and delicate glass works," Rupert added. "He designed your mother's incredible topaz ring."

"He must be extremely gifted, because Papa wouldn't have allowed any artisan but the best to handle that gem, and it truly was a remarkable piece of workmanship. But I don't know what items Mr. Tiffany is referring to. Papa had nothing with him when he was attacked—or if he did, the items were stolen." Serenity wrinkled her brow. "I don't know what he might have purchased from Mr. Tiffany."

"The items might not be lost," Rupert said. "When your father left to transact some business two days before his scheduled departure, he left a number of bundles at my estate. Previously, it had been his habit to buy a pack animal or arrange for teamsters to deliver objects too large for his saddlebags, but no one ever came for them. That was why I expected he would return to my home before leaving New York. I didn't bring his packages with me because I thought you would be accompanying me back to New York."

"I remember—" A knock sounded at the door, bringing Serenity's words to a halt. She began to rise, but Edward placed a hand on her forearm, suggesting she remain seated while he saw to the door.

She watched him cross the room and felt the shiver she'd felt earlier. "Be careful," she whispered.

He paused as he passed the parlor window to brush aside the curtain and look out, then he quickly dropped it back in place. "It's the telegrapher," he announced before opening the door.

Edward ushered Mr. Miller into the parlor, and Serenity rose to offer the visitor a chair. Mr. Miller scraped his hat from his head and nodded in a half bow.

"No, I must get right back. There's no time to dawdle." He thrust a handful of yellow papers toward her. "Mr. Tolson was greatly offended when I asked for the return of the telegrams he hadn't delivered. He promised to deliver them to you tonight, but not wishing any more trouble, I insisted he turn them over to me at once."

"Thank you." Serenity reached for the papers.

"I expect they're all here, though it seems a smaller number than I remembered," he added as he relinquished the telegrams. "I'll be off then." He slapped his cap back on his nearly bald head and reached for the doorknob. The sound of his footsteps disappeared almost at once.

Serenity sank down on the parlor sofa, the telegrams clutched in her hands. She spread them across her lap and just stared at them for a time. She knew most would be kind expressions of sympathy for the loss of her father, but it was conceivable that one might hold a clue to the identity of the man who shot Papa. With trembling fingers, she drew one slip of paper from the lot, then lifted it to catch the light from the ornamental lamp on a small table at her side. She began to read.

12

Serenity read each telegram silently, then passed it to Edward. Rupert read over his shoulder and occasionally commented on a sender whom he knew.

"This one is from Uncle Reliance." Serenity held up one of the papers, and there was a catch in her voice. "He says he's anxious for me to come to Utah and asks if I'm in need of funds to make the journey."

"Uncle? Your father mentioned that you had relatives who joined the Mormon church and traveled to the Rocky Mountains twenty years ago. He said he'd never met them, but he planned to look them up when the two of you visited that area. I'm glad you've made contact with them." Rupert's approval sounded genuine.

"A friend of Edward's passed through here a few weeks ago and put us in touch." She didn't clarify further. Though her trust in Rupert had grown, she still felt he was holding something back, and she decided not to confide in him completely until she knew him better.

"Two of these telegrams are from people who wish to buy some of your father's stock," Edward pointed out.

"They're both small, reputable dealers whom your father has dealt with for many years," Rupert added. "Both can be trusted to pay you fairly. I'm surprised there are no offers from larger dealers who could make offers on the entire lot."

"I recognize both of their names from Papa's records." Serenity sighed. "There are seven telegrams, counting the one from Mr. Tiffany, and only one is from a gentleman whose name I don't recognize. And there's no telegram from you, Rupert."

"I noticed that." Rupert frowned. "Neither of my messages are in this stack. I suspect Mr. Tolson kept those messages for some reason, possibly to cast doubt on my credibility."

"He may have destroyed them, along with any from representatives or brokers from the larger companies, to keep me from learning I had an alternative to marrying his son." Serenity didn't doubt that discovering someone else was authorized to handle her business affairs had set in motion Bernard Tolson's plan to rush her into marrying Percy.

"If the telegram hinted that a large fortune was at stake, I've no doubt Mr. Tolson took matters into his own hands to secure your dependence on him," Edward concurred.

Heavy pounding rattled the front door, causing all three to jump. They'd been so engrossed they hadn't heard footsteps on the porch.

"Take cover behind the sofa," Edward whispered to Serenity. She darted behind the heavy piece of furniture while both Edward and Rupert approached the door. Edward snatched up the same brass candlestick she'd used previously for an impromptu weapon. She didn't miss the pained reaction his gesture brought to Rupert's face.

Edward took the precaution once again of peeking outside from behind the curtain. He indicated to Rupert that he didn't recognize the caller. While Rupert hid behind the door, Edward cautiously opened it a crack. Serenity was startled to see a small pistol appear in Rupert's hand. Truth be told, the gun was so small she wasn't certain it could truly be classified as a weapon.

"I say, is this the Caswell residence?" a hearty voice boomed from the front stoop.

"And if it is?" Edward asked.

"I've come to meet with the heiress, appraise that which she wishes to make available for purchase, and make an offer for the whole of it." The voice was loud and a mite arrogant.

"You might as well come in." Edward opened the door wider, revealing a large, barrel-chested man with a little-boy face who was attired as finely as Rupert Montague, though his suit appeared more than a little snug. And there was an aroma about him that caused Edward to wrinkle his nose.

"It is past the dinner hour. What possesses you to approach Mr. Caswell's daughter at this late hour?" Rupert spoke with some irritation. Serenity noted his gun had disappeared. His expression too became one of disgust as he came closer to the visitor.

"It was not my intention to appear on your doorstep so tardily," the man defended himself. "I stopped to ask directions when I arrived on the morning stage. The gentleman I spoke with directed me in a woefully inadequate manner. He said the Caswell estate was some distance in the country. Following his directions to the letter, I found myself in some farmer's hog wallow. As I endeavored to remove the taint from my shoes in a nearby stream, I was beset by a pair of hounds. Not until a shrill whistle sounded toward the end of the day was I able to make my way back to town."

The man told a woeful tale, but something didn't ring true to Serenity. Other than the stench that hovered about the man, he didn't appear to be the sort who might have been so easily made the fool.

He bowed upon seeing Serenity leave the shadows and come to stand beside Edward. "Fenton Simmons, at your service, miss."

She introduced herself. "How do you do? I am Serenity Caswell Benson."

"It is indeed a pleasure to meet you." He gave another jerky bow. "I am sorry for your great loss. However, I am aware of some of the fine pieces your father purchased over the years and am most anxious to add some of them to my own collection."

"If you'll call again tomorrow—"

Once again she was interrupted by a heavy hand on her door. "Mr. Benson, are you and your wife all right?" There was no mistaking Sheriff Compton's bellow.

Edward met her eyes and appeared puzzled. His glance seemed to say, "Why would he wonder if we're all right or not?"

Rupert, who was standing closest to the door, opened it so abruptly the sheriff stumbled inside. After righting himself, he glared around the room, taking in its occupants.

"Bernard Tolson has been murdered," he announced without preamble. "Shot in the head. That blubbering idiot son of his said the telegrapher was the last person to see him alive. Miller isn't in his office, and I thought I might find him here."

"Tolson's been killed?" Rupert asked in disbelief.

Serenity's eyes were wide. "Mr. Miller left some time ago," she said, "after delivering my telegrams as promised."

"He said he needed to get back to his office," Rupert added.

"Well, he ain't there. I already looked," the sheriff grumbled. "You folks got an alibi for the time since you left my office this afternoon?"

Edward quickly summarized. "The three of us have been together the whole time. We came back here, saw Julia and Rosie Hayes off on their journey home, and ate dinner. Mr. Miller arrived as we were finishing our meal, and since then we have been reading the telegrams Mr. Miller obtained from Bernard Tolson."

"And who's this fellow?" Sheriff Compton pointed to Fenton Simmons. The gentleman hastily introduced himself and produced a calling card.

"He arrived just moments before you did," Serenity said.

The sheriff glared at the newcomer. "Were you acquainted with Bernard Tolson?"

"I've met few people since my arrival in your fair city," Simmons responded, but after a few minutes of questioning, they all, including Simmons, became convinced that Tolson was the person who had given him the false directions.

"Seems a trivial excuse for killing a man," the sheriff said, "but just in case, I suppose you better spend the night in my jail where I can keep an eye on you." He wrinkled his nose in distaste upon coming to the conclusion that it was his responsibility to arrest the stranger.

"But sir!" Simmons protested. "I have business to transact with Miss Caswell, and I am expected in New York posthaste."

The mention of New York seemed to cement the sheriff's resolve to arrest Simmons. "Come along." He prodded the reluctant art dealer through the door with the tip of his gun. After the door closed behind them, Serenity nearly collapsed onto the horsehair sofa. She buried her face in her hands and tried to think.

Edward sat beside her, moving her skirt out of the way so he could sit close enough to gather her in his arms. "Don't cry," he soothed. She hesitated a moment, then relaxed against him. It felt good to have Edward's arms around her. It made her feel safe and secure like when Papa had held her when she was a little girl—but different. That difference had her raising her head to insist she was only thinking, not crying. Edward released her but didn't move away.

"You don't suppose he really did it, do you?" she asked. There was no need to explain whom she meant.

"No, but a simple test will verify whether or not Mr. Simmons set foot in Mr. Tolson's house." Rupert delicately sniffed the air.

Edward chuckled, and even Serenity found herself attempting to smother a smile. The unmistakable and unpleasant scent of hogs lingered on the air.

"It might do to air this room before we find our beds," Edward suggested. Suiting action to words, he lifted a window sash and breathed deeply of the fresh night air.

"I can't help thinking Mr. Tolson's death is somehow connected to Papa's death," Serenity said when they were seated among the telegrams again.

"I agree," Edward concurred, "but I'm not sure *how* they are connected. Do you suppose Tolson was working with someone, they quarreled, and his partner shot him?"

"Until the shooter is caught, I doubt we'll know the connection," Rupert speculated.

Suddenly Edward froze. "Hush!" he whispered. "Did you hear that?" He then stood and hurried toward the open window. Serenity strained to hear whatever sound had alarmed Edward.

The sound came again, and Edward flung open the door. Rupert was beside him in seconds. "Where did the sound come from?" he asked.

"There. In those bushes." Edward leaped from the porch and burrowed his way into the thick shrubs that grew beside it. After a moment, he announced, "There's a man here. He seems to be unconscious."

"Here, let me help you." Rupert wormed his way into the narrow space between the shrubbery and the porch.

Serenity followed the sounds of great exertion, then saw a body slide onto the porch. Edward and Rupert scrambled after it. Edward lifted the unconscious man by his shoulders, and Rupert grappled with his legs. The unfortunate man groaned several times, and in moments his rescuers had him inside the house.

Serenity barred the door, then turned toward the men, who were leaning over the unconscious form they'd placed on the sofa. She hurried to turn up the lamp and gasped when she recognized Mr. Miller, the telegrapher, sprawled across the sofa. Dried blood indicated that the lump on his temple had bled profusely.

Edward disappeared into the kitchen to collect his bag from where Julia had stowed it in a cupboard, and Serenity filled a basin with warm water from the teakettle. She gathered up several rags and hurried back to the injured man.

Edward cleaned the wound, then fashioned a bandage out of one of the rags Serenity had produced. She stayed at his side, seeming to anticipate each of his needs. Mr. Miller groaned several times and mumbled something inaudible.

"I think he's about to come around," Edward said. "Perhaps a cool cloth will help to speed up his awakening."

Serenity rushed to dip a cloth in cold water and wring it out. A few moments after she applied it to his forehead, their patient opened his eyes. He blinked several times, then looked around, appearing amazed by his surroundings.

Rupert leaned forward. "Do you remember what happened?" he asked.

Mr. Miller looked confused for a moment, then gingerly raised his hand to touch the bandage that circled his head.

"I don't." He blinked owlishly, then tried to sit up.

Edward put out an arm to stop him. "Easy," he said. "You've quite a lump on your head."

"I remember now" Mr. Miller exclaimed. "I was in a hurry to get back to the telegraph office. I started down the steps, then I heard something rustling in the bushes. I turned my head to look and someone hit me."

"Did you see who hit you?" Edward asked.

"Are you sure you were hit and that you didn't simply trip?" Rupert asked at nearly the same time.

"I was hit. Of that I'm certain, but I didn't see the face of the person who struck me. There was something—I can't remember. But there was something important I *should* remember."

Serenity tucked a lacy pillow beneath his head. "Maybe it will come back to you after you rest for a bit."

"Someone was waiting in the shadows when I stepped outside," Mr. Miller asserted after only a few minutes. "I'm certain of that."

Rupert addressed him again. "Now, here's a question. Was he waiting for you specifically or was he waiting to cause trouble for someone inside this house and your exit merely took him by surprise?"

Mr. Miller groaned. "What difference does it make? He hit me powerful hard."

"The sheriff came here looking for you," Serenity told him. The already confused man blinked rapidly and appeared unable to follow what appeared to be a shift in topic.

"What did he want?"

"Bernard Tolson was murdered, and you're the last person known to have seen him alive," Serenity informed him.

Mr. Miller was still while his mind processed this new information. Then, bewildered, he asked, "Sheriff Compton thinks I shot Bernard?"

"He only said he wanted to ask you some questions," she reassured him.

This time Mr. Miller did succeed in sitting up, though he swayed precariously before leaning back against the cushions. "I didn't see anyone but Bernard when I reached the Tolson house.

Not even that mooncalf son of his was around. You think Sheriff Compton suspects me?" He repeated his concern.

"He only said he wants to talk to you," Serenity reminded him.

"It'll have to wait until morning," Edward said, shifting his patient back to a reclining position. "You're in no shape to go anywhere, and neither Rupert nor I is willing to leave Serenity alone while we conduct you there. Even if one of us could get you home, I'm not inclined to walk back alone, and I wouldn't want Rupert to attempt it."

"So, what are we going to do now?" Serenity asked.

"Find a blanket to cover Mr. Miller, and the rest of us will retire to our beds." Edward walked to the open window and closed it with a decisive slam and secured the latch. He then checked the other windows and the doors in both the parlor and the kitchen.

When all seemed secure, Serenity and Edward walked up the stairs side by side. Reaching the top, Serenity turned to face Edward.

"With all that has happened, I'm a little nervous about going to sleep. What if someone breaks in and murders us all while we're sleeping?"

"I doubt I'll sleep much either, but we do need to rest. Would you like me to tell you how I deal with sleepless nights?"

She nodded her head, and he took her hand, leading her to the door of her room. "I don't know how much your mother taught you about her faith, but we believe strongly in prayer. When I feel the need for guidance or protection, I get on my knees. I'm certainly planning to spend some time on my knees before going to bed tonight. Would you like me to pray with you?"

"Yes. Mamma always said praying made her feel better, and she taught me to say my prayers each night, but after she died I didn't pray for a long time. I was just too angry with God. After a year or so, I began to pray again. Though my efforts may be clumsy, praying does bring me great comfort."

Together they knelt beside Serenity's bed. Edward clasped her hand, and he began to speak as though God stood right before him. At first she felt a little uncomfortable, but as the words sank into her heart and echoed in her mind, peace began to settle over her. When Edward said amen, she said the word as well, remembering Mamma had always added a soft amen to her childhood prayers.

When the prayer was finished, Edward stood and helped her to her feet. He didn't release her hand at once. "I'm just across the hall if you need me," he said in a soft whisper.

"Thank you," she murmured. "But I feel I shall be fine." She did feel better—at least until he released her hand and she watched him walk away and disappear into the room across the hall. She was left wondering whether it was their shared prayer or Edward's presence that had calmed her fears.

* * *

"Serenity, wake up." Someone was shaking her shoulder. "Serenity, I need your help."

Groggily she opened her eyes, then struggled to a sitting position. Edward was in her room, and from the urgent sound of his voice, something was terribly wrong.

"What is it?" she whispered back.

"I heard the sound of breaking glass coming from the store. Evidently Rupert heard it too. I hurried downstairs in time to see him disappear through the door that leads to the shop. I was about to follow when I heard something behind me in the room Rupert had vacated moments earlier. It may have been an intruder. I need you to stay with Mr. Miller while I investigate."

Soundlessly, she slipped from her bed, snatched up her robe, and followed Edward downstairs. They were both barefoot and took care to avoid making any sound. Tiptoeing to the sofa, Serenity sat on the floor beside the sleeping patient and watched Edward's shadow move toward the closed bedroom door. A faint line of light shone beneath the door, as though the intruder was using a shuttered lamp.

Edward thrust the door open. The light blinked out and Serenity heard the sound of running feet, followed by a crash. Leaping to her feet, she hurried to the bedroom door, but in the darkness she could only barely discern two figures grappling with each other. After a moment, one separated itself from the other and disappeared through the broken window while the other remained on the floor.

Not knowing whether Edward or the intruder was still in the room, she flattened herself against the wall until she heard Edward's voice. "Light a lantern, Serenity."

Before she could follow Edward's instructions, she heard the door leading from the store behind her open. Fearful of an attack from behind, she whirled about only to see Rupert emerge from the store, a lighted lantern in his hand.

"I wondered if anyone else was awakened by the sound of breaking glass," he said. "There was no one in the store, and I don't think whoever broke the window had time to steal anything before I arrived. I found a large stone lying on the floor."

"Breaking the window was just a distraction, I fear, to lure us into the store and away from our thief's real intent." Edward took the lantern from Rupert, turned up the wick, and held the light high to illuminate the bedroom. The room was awash once again in floating feathers.

13

Serenity stared at the feathers in dismay. "Not again! I just stitched up that feather tick," she cried.

"Someone broke the store window just so he could secretly cut open a feather tick?" Rupert's voice was filled with incredulity.

Edward shook his head. "Not to cut open just any feather tick."

Serenity knew what Edward was implying. Her father had slept in that room and on that feather mattress. Whoever cut it open was looking for the topaz ring.

"What's going on?" Mr. Miller asked. His voice revealed groggy confusion. Groaning, he pulled himself to a sitting position.

"Go back to sleep," Edward admonished him. "Someone attempted to break in, but he's gone now."

"Need to get back . . ." Mr. Miller's head sank toward his pillow once more. "I remember now. He was wearing freshly polished shoes . . ."

"Who was wearing shoes?" Edward asked, confused. There was no answer to his question, as Mr. Miller had gone back to sleep.

"Should I try to wake him?" Rupert asked.

"Let's secure the broken windows, then talk," Edward suggested. He and Rupert collected boards, nails, and a hammer, then set about boarding up the broken windows. They moved first to Rupert's window, where they hammered boards in place. Then they headed toward the door leading to the store office. Serenity made her way to the kitchen. She could inspect the damage to the store tomorrow. At present, it seemed best to watch for the intruder lest he return to the house while Edward and Rupert were occupied in the store and poor Mr. Miller was nearly unconscious on the sofa.

* * *

The sheriff arrived on their doorstep shortly before noon the following day. Edward saw his approach and suggested they meet him on the front porch. "I would prefer that he not see Mr. Miller until that gentleman is better able to defend himself," he explained. He sauntered outside with Serenity and Rupert following, timing his arrival to match that of the sheriff.

Sheriff Compton was accompanied by Fenton Simmons, whose attire hadn't weathered a night in jail overly well. Seams across his shoulders showed gaps, and his wrinkled trousers appeared to have shrunken several inches. His hair stood on end, and he was in need of a shave.

Seeing Rupert's arched eyebrow, the sheriff mumbled something about ordering a hasty bath in the horse trough before allowing the odoriferous man to spend a night in his jail. Mr. Simmons parted his lips in a cherubic smile.

"Ain't got no evidence to hold him, so I have to let him go," the sheriff explained, then turned to Simmons. "But I'll be keeping an eye out, and if you take one wrong step, you'll be back in my jail," he warned the man.

"I don't aim to cause any trouble. I just came to make a few purchases," Mr. Simmons said. He made Serenity a short bow and asked, "Might I take a look at some of your father's lovely pieces?"

"No, you may not."

Serenity hadn't noticed the arrival of another man until Edward introduced him as Joshua Brown. Without acknowledging Serenity in any way, he informed Mr. Simmons that he had a prior claim to all of the Caswell holdings.

"Indeed you do not," Serenity bristled. "I have not yet granted any individual a claim to any of Papa's possessions."

"Perhaps it would be best if you and I conduct our business inside," Mr. Brown suggested to Edward, "where we won't be interrupted by interlopers or those who don't know their place."

Edward chuckled. "You have it all wrong, sir. My wife is her father's heir, and the disposition of his property is entirely in her hands." His smile was a little too innocent.

"Ridiculous!" Joshua Brown looked affronted. "No reasonable man would leave the settlement of an estate to a woman."

"Are you saying Charles Caswell wasn't a reasonable man?" Rupert demanded as he stood, adopting a more formidable manner. Both Sheriff Compton and Fenton Simmons also shifted their positions, as though hinting they wouldn't permit this stranger to browbeat Edward.

Mr. Brown took a step back as though he'd just realized that three of the men confronting him were significantly taller than he and that both the sheriff and Mr. Simmons outweighed him by a considerable amount. Only Edward was of a similar height.

Edward wasn't the least bit intimidated. He wore a broad grin and seemed to be enjoying himself. He lounged against the porch railing and winked at Serenity. The intimate gesture buoyed her courage, and she clapped her hands together to gain the other men's attention.

When they finally looked her way, she announced, "Gentlemen, it is my intention to place those items I wish to sell on display in Papa's store tomorrow. If I do not receive offers commensurate with their value, I shall take them to Philadelphia to sell." She didn't mention that most of the items she'd chosen to keep were already on their way to her uncle's home in Utah Territory. "The land, house, and store will most likely be purchased by a neighboring farmer's son who wishes to establish a home separate from his parents. Those who wish to make offers on the available goods are invited to meet me at the door to the store at eight o'clock sharp tomorrow morning."

"Anyone who doesn't behave in a gentlemanly fashion will be escorted off the premises," Sheriff Compton added with a pointed glare at Joshua Brown.

Mr. Brown turned to the lawman, his anger evident. "Sheriff, you cannot permit this travesty. I've already paid a considerable

sum for this property, the remainder to be paid upon taking possession of it. The only business left is for Mr. Benson and myself to
determine which trinkets his wife should be allowed to keep as
personal mementos of her father. Naturally, she shall be allowed to
keep her wardrobe, but jewelry by law is part of the estate."

"And to whom did you pay this 'considerable sum'?" Rupert
Montague asked.

Mr. Brown turned his back on Rupert. "My business is no
concern of yours."

"You are mistaken. If you think you have any claim on Mrs.
Benson's estate, then it *is* my concern. I am the executor of Charles
Caswell's will, duly appointed by Mr. Caswell himself to manage
his estate until such time as his daughter is prepared to assume
control of her inheritance," Rupert asserted.

"Miss Caswell has a husband who can speak for her," Mr. Brown
sneered.

"A husband who has made no arrangement with you," Edward
pointed out.

"Your approval wasn't necessary." Mr. Brown produced a paper
and held it up for the sheriff's inspection. "My arrangement was
entered into before Miss Caswell's marriage. It is signed by Bernard
Tolson and duly witnessed by Percy Tolson and Floyd Jones,
blacksmith."

Serenity placed both hands on her hips and glared at the
presumptuous Joshua Brown. "Mr. Tolson was never my guardian
nor executor of my father's estate. Your papers are worthless."

She turned to the sheriff, then thought better of appealing to
him. He was likely to side against her just because she asked.

Edward had no such qualms. "It is well known that Mr. Tolson
made a number of erroneous assumptions concerning my wife in
the days following her father's death," he calmly told Mr. Brown.
"If you care to journey to Harrisburg, a distance of some two hours
from here, Judge Detweiler will acquaint you with his ruling in
this regard." Edward smiled. "If you wish to participate in
tomorrow's sale, be here promptly at eight."

"But my money . . . I signed in good faith with Mr. Tolson."

Serenity turned to him again. "You'll have to take that up with Mr. Tolson." She gave Mr. Brown her most innocent smile, relishing the prospect of the loathsome man traveling to the nether regions to meet with Bernard Tolson.

"Tolson's dead," Sheriff Compton growled. He directed a less-than-pleased scowl at her before addressing the aggrieved Mr. Brown. "The old fool overstepped himself. You'll have to take your claim up with his son. The boy ain't up to much, but he might be able to refund your investment. I can't help you out as far as the Caswell property is concerned. Mr. Benson has legal title in Pennsylvania to the whole of it, and I can't stop him from allowing his wife a say in its disposition."

Fenton Simmons cleared his throat. "I will be pleased to meet with you tomorrow morning," he announced and executed his familiar little half bow in Serenity's direction.

"I'll be there too," the sheriff promised, "to keep an eye on proceedings." He cast a baleful glare first at Brown, then at Simmons.

"Am I too late?" A tall, rail-thin man wearing a ruffled shirt and knee britches dashed up the path that led to Serenity's home. Spectacles bounced precariously on his nose. "I met with an unfortunate incident yesterday that delayed my arrival." He stopped and looked around. Spotting Fenton Simmons, his face turned a deep shade of red and he shook an angry finger at the man. "You! You . . ." he spluttered, seemingly unable to finish a sentence. "My suit is ruined. Just look at it."

Mr. Simmons, looking sheepish, began to back away.

"Arrest that man!" The newcomer demanded of Sheriff Compton.

"What's he done—other than making a blamed nuisance of himself, that is?" the sheriff demanded to know. "Stop right there!" he shouted at the retreating man. When Simmons broke into a run, he shook his head and said, "Just the same, I'm sure he'll be back tomorrow for the auction." He turned back to the angry accuser. "Go on."

The man looked incredulous. "But . . . but . . ." he stuttered. "Fine. I was on my way to meet with Miss Caswell yesterday when I took a wrong turn. My buggy became stuck in a filthy mire. I waited for some time, hoping another traveler would come to my assistance, but I saw no one until that man happened along." He pointed in the direction Simmons had gone. "His attire was not nearly so fine at that time. I begged his assistance, and he proceeded to roll up his pants and wade through the mire to my side. He carried me to the edge of the mire, then returned to talk to my horses and put a shoulder to the back of my conveyance. In short order he freed the stuck wheels and I climbed back in the buggy, prepared to travel on."

"Quite commendable, it appears to me," Edward said.

"But then he asked what business I was about and I made the mistake of telling him that I was on my way to attend an auction of the late Charles Caswell's property and to make an offer for a fabulous topaz gem the man owned that I had seen but once."

Suddenly Serenity was deeply interested in the man's story. She suspected the loquacious man had told Mr. Simmons far more than the bare minimum he offered now about her mother's topaz. "So what did he do?" she asked.

"He drove my buggy straightway back into the bog, released my horses, then waded back to shore, taking my portmanteau with him. In full view of myself, he helped himself to my best suit and left his foul garments lying where they fell. He then walked away, whistling, leaving me stranded with none but a herd of swine for company."

"Did he take your money or valuables?" the sheriff asked.

"No. Though I carried considerable funds with which to buy the topaz, he left the money untouched."

The sheriff scratched his head. "It appears he performed a good deed, then regretted his action. I don't know of any law that says a man can't change his mind about helping someone. Did you offer him compensation for his ruined clothes and the trouble he went to in getting you out of that hog wallow?"

"Indeed I did. Two bright copper pennies seemed more than adequate."

Edward grinned. "Seems Mr. Simmons didn't agree."

"I don't think you have cause to demand Mr. Simmons's arrest," the sheriff said.

"But he stole my suit!"

"I never had anyone charged with stealing a suit of clothes before, but it seems to me that you were the cause of damage to his clothing so you owed him a change of apparel. I'll look into the matter. You'll be staying at Mrs. Burton's boardinghouse, I assume, until the sale tomorrow morning, should I have any further questions, Mr. . . . ?"

"Stephen J. Rappleton, of Graham, Hennessy, and Rappleton Jewelers in New York City," the prissy scarecrow responded. "If you will direct me to the boardinghouse, I shall retire until tomorrow morning's sale."

The sheriff gave him precise instructions, then stood shaking his head as he watched him disappear up the street.

"I suppose we will see more of him tomorrow," Rupert sighed. "I've heard him mentioned but had been fortunate enough to avoid meeting him until today."

"I'm not sure about his story," the sheriff mused. "Seems to me he could have walked out of that bog as easy as that Simmons fellow did." He looked around. "Hey, where'd Brown go?"

Edward gave every indication that he was laughing at some joke. "He seemed just as much in a hurry to leave our presence as Mr. Simmons was."

The sheriff snorted angrily. "They're all three hiding something, if you ask me. That Brown fellow has been hanging around town for two weeks and has been seen with Bernard Tolson a number of times. He didn't seem surprised to hear about Tolson's death, neither. I got the feeling he already knew. Simmons is a flim-flam man. He's up to something. I just don't know what yet. I ain't sure whether he put Rappleton back in the pig wallow because he was sore over the priss's behavior or so's he could beat him back to town. And Rappleton . . ." He shook his head. "I'll be keeping an eye on them. Any of them might have killed Tolson, though I haven't ruled out Miller. I checked and he still ain't in his office."

Serenity and Edward looked at each other, and Serenity gave Edward a slight nod.

"We know where to find Mr. Miller," Edward said. "He's sleeping on Serenity's sofa." He proceeded to tell the sheriff of the previous night's events, and then Compton insisted on going inside the house to see Mr. Miller for himself.

It wasn't long before Sheriff Compton and Mr. Miller left the house together, the sheriff supporting the still-weak telegrapher, who was adamant about returning to his duties.

* * *

"Edward and I can handle this," Rupert told Serenity the next morning when he caught her staring at her bowl of oatmeal rather than actually eating it. "I know something of the fine pieces Charles collected. We could bring the items back here and consult with you if we feel uncertain about whether an offer is sufficient."

Serenity looked up. "No, Papa would wish me to do this myself." She roused herself to clear the table, then retired to her room to brush her hair. As she passed the room where Edward slept, she noticed the door stood open. She paused to look at the room that was almost bare now save for a narrow cot, Papa's trunk of worthless items he'd purchased from runaway slaves, and Edward's traveling case.

Feeling guilty for peering into the room, she hurried to her own room to brush her hair and smooth her shirtwaist before descending the stairs and approaching the door that led to the store. Edward and Rupert met her just inside the store. She noticed Rupert took care to leave the connecting door open, no doubt to prevent another unauthorized entry to the house while they were occupied in the store. Papa's store seemed darker than usual, which she supposed could be blamed on the boarded up window. She lit a few lamps and placed them about the room.

Fenton Simmons was the first of her potential buyers to arrive. He was followed shortly by the fastidious Mr. Rappleton, who was so anxious to view the items for sale that he merely glared at Simmons before becoming absorbed in the various displays. Sheriff Compton stepped into the store moments before Joshua Brown arrived. He took up a stance in the center aisle with his big pistol prominently displayed on his hip. Brown was followed by Loyal Ochendorf, the young farmer, and John Barnes, the banker. Serenity invited them all to wander freely about the store examining Papa's wares. Conversation was stilted and businesslike as the buyers laid claim to various items. Neither Simmons nor Brown bought as much as she had expected, and all three buyers argued vociferously over the prices she set and pointedly ignored each other.

"Don't back down any," Rupert whispered in her ear. "Dealers in New York will be happy to meet your prices."

"Simmons, Rappleton, and Brown are all wearing shoes, not boots," Edward noted in a barely audible aside. "But any one of them could have left the flour footprints we found outside your kitchen."

By noon the art dealers had gathered their selected items into three areas, with Rappleton claiming the largest portion. Rupert showed interest in a couple of pieces, including a brass candlestick almost identical to the one Serenity had used as a weapon. The banker expressed his pleasure in obtaining a painting he said he had been eyeing for some time.

"There's not much jewelry," Rappleton complained as he examined the small display case that held a pair of pearl studs, a couple of gold pieces, and a smattering of faux gems in attractive settings. There were no rings at all. The few Serenity's father had had in the case at the beginning of the war had all been sold for wedding rings during the long siege.

"Papa had planned to replenish his stock of jewelry while in New York," she explained.

"When I was an apprentice at Tiffany's," Rappleton said, "Mr. Caswell brought in a magnificent imperial topaz to be set with diamonds in a ring. I have never seen another jewel so fine. Is it not for sale?"

Suddenly Serenity thought of something. "It's been almost twenty years since my father had that ring made. What leads you to believe he didn't sell it long ago?" she asked.

Rappleton opened his mouth to answer but then seemed to think better of it. He frowned and glanced toward Mr. Brown and Mr. Simmons, who were lingering nearby, paying particular attention to the conversation.

Serenity sighed. "You're correct, though. My father didn't sell the ring. He gave it to my mother. But it is not for sale."

At this Mr. Rappleton regained his voice. "There has been much speculation among the art and jewelry dealers in New York that the ring would soon be placed on the market," he said. "I personally have an interested foreign buyer willing to pay a sum beyond your greatest imagining for that ring. Indeed, it is enough to provide you with a comfortable living for the rest of your life, Mrs. Benson. Are you quite certain you will not reconsider?"

Mr. Brown stepped forward. "I too have heard of that ring," he said. "I shall better any offer made by this man."

"I'll not be outbid," Mr. Simmons warned.

"Gentlemen," Rupert interrupted. "The lady has told you her mother's ring is not for sale. Now might we return to the business at hand?"

None of the three buyers persisted in an attempt to buy the land or buildings, so Serenity informed the young Quaker farmer that she would accept his offer. She told him that she would vacate the property within a week, after the other buyers removed the items they had purchased and the remaining items were shipped to New York. Rupert assured her he could draw up a bill of sale. Though not an attorney, he had experience with such paperwork through his bank.

"Might I just see the topaz before I go?" Mr. Rappleton whispered as he bid her farewell. She shook her head and turned to the next gentleman. Joshua Brown ignored her and spoke to Edward.

"You shall regret allowing your wife to keep that ring," she heard him mutter.

Mr. Simmons kissed her hand. "I shall return, my dear."

When everyone else was gone, Serenity, Edward, and Rupert returned to the house. While they were eating lunch, Rupert said, "Serenity, I could see you were troubled by mention of the topaz ring. Please don't harbor any guilt because you have chosen to keep it rather than sell it to the highest bidder. Had I such a lovely gem, I wouldn't part with it either, if I didn't need to, and I can assure you that you don't need it to support yourself. Your father left you well situated."

"I don't *have* the ring," Serenity said. "It disappeared five years ago when my mother died."

Rupert's astonishment seemed real. "Was it stolen?" he questioned.

"My father and I believed it to have been stolen, but with all the recent interest in the ring and with the mystery surrounding Papa's death, I've become convinced my mother's murderer didn't find the ring. Edward and I suspect Papa discovered something while he was in New York concerning the topaz, Mamma's murderer, or both, and that's why he was killed."

"What do you think he discovered?" Rupert asked.

Edward explained. "We think it has something to do with the saddlebag Serenity's mother was carrying when she was murdered. When her body was found, the bag was missing, but it suddenly reappeared near Charles Caswell's fallen horse after he was killed."

Rupert pushed his chair away from the table. "I believe I will call on Mr. Miller," he said. "If he has returned to his telegraph key, I have a few wires to send." He reached for his hat, then paused. "I've seen your mother's ring," he told Serenity. "I suspect that magnificent jewel has been the motive behind murdering and looting many times during the centuries since it was first discovered. As long as would-be thieves believe you have the gem in your possession, you won't be safe." He looked from her to Edward, who nodded. "Prudence decrees that you both stay out of sight until this matter is resolved."

14

It was late when Rupert returned, looking tired and worried. He closed the door and turned the key in the lock before seating himself across from Serenity and Edward. They waited for him to speak.

"The situation is worse than even I anticipated," he began. "I fear you are in great danger here, Serenity, and that danger extends to Edward because of your marriage. After sending several wires to New York and waiting for responses from colleagues and friends there, I learned that Mr. Tiffany dismissed Stephen J. Rappleton from his post almost twenty years ago, not long after Charles and Hannah were married. He was suspected of switching a valuable diamond for a flawed stone in a brooch brought in for repair, then keeping the more valuable gem. No one knew his whereabouts or had reason to wonder about him until he opened a shop during the early days of the war. He is suspected of fencing jewelry stolen or extorted from the South's once-wealthy families."

"He may well be the person we're looking for." Edward sounded excited.

Serenity moved closer to Edward, feeling quite unsettled. "Rappleton is a bit odd," she admitted, "but I never supposed him to be a murderer."

"That's not all. Joshua Brown is not an art dealer in Boston as he claims to be. Until the war began, he hunted runaway slaves and returned them to their masters for a considerable fee. I feel certain something beyond coincidence has brought him here at this time."

"Being involved with Bernard Tolson made him suspect from the beginning," Serenity said. "And what about Mr. Simmons?"

"Nothing. None of my contacts knows anything of him." Rupert swiped his handkerchief across his damp forehead. "That is the most worrisome news of all."

"Serenity," Edward said, turning to her, "I think you should leave here at once. One of those men likely killed your parents, and I have a feeling they'll keep coming after you until they get what they want."

"Edward is right." Rupert leaned forward until his hand touched hers. "Your life could be in danger if you stay here. We must make arrangements at once for the two of you to quietly disappear."

"But how can I leave? I need to complete the sale of Papa's treasures."

"Your father wouldn't consider any of his possessions worth your life," Edward assured her. "And knowing what we now know of your buyers, how can you trust them to pay you what they have promised?"

"Surprisingly, Brown and Rappleton both have sufficient funds on deposit with Mr. Barnes to pay for the items they chose today. I propose that both of you leave on the first stage tomorrow morning and leave me to complete the transactions. Serenity, I can place their vouchers in your father's account here or deposit them directly in an account in your name at my bank in New York."

Serenity didn't know what to do. She intended to leave, but something inside her resisted being chased from her home. And there was Rupert Montague himself. As she'd spent time with him, a growing warmth and trust had developed, but she still suspected he was withholding something from her.

"Sir," she began, addressing the older man, "I mean no insult, but I cannot leave my affairs in the hands of a man I know nothing of, other than the little you have told me of yourself."

Rupert sighed. "You are wise beyond your years, and you are your mother's daughter. Your mother insisted on certain safeguards on your father's fortune from the start. I hesitated to inform you of those matters before I knew you and Edward better, but I feel confident now that you can be trusted to carry out your parents' wishes. The distribution of your grandfather's fortune is not to be placed in my hands alone, but is to be arranged by a committee composed of five persons, each having an equal voice, with myself as the chairman. You and I are only two of the people involved. We are each to select one other person to be on the committee. The only requirement for the selection of this person is that he or she be of the Negro race. The fifth person, who was chosen by your father, is a gentleman who has been involved for twenty-five years in both educational and political matters." He went on to explain that it was her father's wish that the committee decide jointly the best way to use her grandfather's money to fund projects that would help the freed slaves become better educated and support themselves.

Rupert's explanations eased some of her concerns. It had never made sense to her that her father would completely turn over the management of such a large sum of money to one individual.

"But how can we study proposals and make decisions if we live in different areas?" Serenity asked. She was thinking of choosing Julia Hayes to serve on the committee, but Julia lived in upstate New York, while Serenity would be in Philadelphia until she could make her way west.

"That is something we shall have to resolve later. For the present, I think we must consider your safety," Rupert replied. "Once you are established in a new location, we can make plans for completing the committee and conducting its business."

Edward yawned and stretched. "It's late and we're all tired. Let's sleep on it, then in the morning we can go over the papers you brought and Serenity and I can make plans to leave," he suggested.

Serenity gratefully agreed. She needed time to consider all that was at stake in leaving her home behind.

* * *

Gunfire jolted Serenity awake. A rapid succession of shots accompanied by shouts came from just outside her home. She sat up and looked around in confusion. She was reaching for her robe when a tap came on her door. Without warning, the door opened, and she recognized Edward in the dim light coming through her window.

"We've got trouble," he whispered. "Half a dozen rowdies on horseback are shooting at the house."

"What do they want?"

"They think someone in this house murdered Bernard Tolson. They're threatening to break down the door and come in after the murderer."

"How can we defend ourselves? Papa never owned a gun."

"Rupert has a small pistol. He fired it once to warn them to keep their distance, but it won't be a match for their bigger guns. I think you should get dressed."

"All right."

"But don't come downstairs. You're safer up here." Edward left the room, and Serenity dressed in the first gown she found. She debated whether or not to obey Edward by staying in her room. What if those attacking her home decided to burn it like the stable? She moved about the room, avoiding the window, as she collected those things she wished to preserve should she be forced to abandon a burning house.

Her hand brushed her mother's saddlebag. Gathering it up, she placed inside it a change of clothing, the papers her father had considered important, and her mother's Book of Mormon. She considered removing the toys to make room for a loaf of bread but was not sure she could safely creep down to the kitchen to retrieve the bread.

As she debated, more shots rang out. A familiar voice shouted her name. The voice sounded like that of Percy Tolson. She crept into the hall, dragging the saddlebag behind her.

Flattening herself against the wall, she approached the hall window that faced the street. When she reached the window, she moved the thick drape far enough to allow a peek at the street. Percy's unwieldy shape lurched into view atop a horse. It appeared he had little control over the animal and could easily find himself pitched onto the street. She thought she recognized several other men who had reputations for drinking and carousing.

Hearing a commotion coming from downstairs, her heart leaped with fright until she heard a hoarse whisper calling her name. Hurrying to the stairs, she saw Sheriff Compton kneeling beside Rupert Montague at the front window. Both men were firing through broken panes of glass. Standing beside Edward at the foot of the stairs was Loyal Ochendorf. Edward came to meet her as soon as he saw her.

"Friend Ochendorf came through the orchard when he heard the gunfire. When he saw what was going on, he went for the sheriff and found him already on his way here. He has a team and wagon waiting beyond the trees. He and the sheriff think they can calm that bunch and save the house if we leave. Can you pack a bag without lighting a lantern?"

"I already have." She lifted the saddlebag and draped its strap over her shoulder.

"I don't hold with fighting," the young farmer said, "but if the sheriff will loan me a gun, I can fire a few shots into the air to help thee escape. Give the horses their head and they'll take thee to my pa's house. He can outfit thee with supplies for thy journey."

"Thank you," Edward whispered and dashed past Serenity and up the stairs.

Thinking she might need a weapon, Serenity snatched up the brass candlestick.

"Serenity Caswell is mine!" Percy roared outside. She could see him, dimly outlined just beyond the gate. "Benson, ya stole my intended, then ya shot my pa. I'm gonna see ya hang, then I'm gonna marry yer widder." Serenity shuddered.

"Percy!" the sheriff shouted back. "Edward Benson didn't kill your pa. He wasn't anywhere near your house that afternoon. Now you and your friends need to go home and sober up."

Percy fired a shot toward the house in response.

It was obvious he'd been drinking. He was none too stable when sober, but drunk he was a dangerous fool. Serenity despised the lout, drunk or sober. He had followed her around obsessively since she was a child, but now she saw something far more dangerous in him than the annoying harrassment she'd known all her life. A strong impression of danger filled her, telling her Edward and Rupert were right. She must leave.

Edward took her hand. "This way. We'll slip out the back." He was carrying a bag now, too.

"Collect what supplies you need from Ochendorf, then keep going until you get to one of the larger towns," Rupert cautioned. He sprang to his feet and thrust a purse into her hands. "Take this. It should be enough to cover your expenses until you get settled in Philadelphia. I'll find you in a couple of months at that hospital where Edward plans to finish his training."

Serenity nodded and dropped the purse into a deep pocket of her cloak, then gripped the candlestick tighter.

Rupert turned to Edward with a final whispered admonition. "Take care of her."

Edward inched the kitchen door open, looked around, then stepped out, pulling Serenity behind him into the shadows of the trees. Taking care to make no sound, they moved from one deep shadow to the next until they reached the back fence. Edward lifted their bags over the fence, then scooped her up in his arms and followed suit.

More gunfire came from the street in front of the house. Shouldering her bag, Serenity glanced behind them. Her heart filled with regret to leave her home in such a manner. A shadow separated from the blackness beneath the lilac tree that wound its way upward to her bedroom window. Had they been discovered? Clapping a hand to her mouth to prevent a scream from erupting, she jerked Edward's arm with the other and pointed. He turned in time to share her startled reaction at seeing a man sprint around the corner of the house. The man was not moving toward them, but away. As he disappeared around the front of the house, the sound of gunfire intensified.

Clasping Serenity's hand, Edward made a dash for the orchard. Once within the shelter of the trees, they slowed to a fast walk but stayed alert for any sign of being followed. They paused for just a moment when they reached the graves of Serenity's parents. She tried to stay calm as she bid her loved ones a last farewell, but a small sob escaped and she turned away, fearing a collapse of the resolve that was keeping her upright.

"This way," Edward whispered. He took the candlestick from her hand and dropped it into his valise. "I can just make out the outline of the wagon and horses."

When they reached the wagon, he helped her scramble onto the high seat, then picked up the reins and signaled for the animals to go. They took off at a rapid walk that soon changed to a jolting trot. Serenity clasped the side of the wagon seat and held on with all her might. She didn't dare speak for fear the jarring movement of the wagon would cause her to bite her tongue.

It didn't take long to reach the farmhouse. Light streamed from the door that opened as the wagon rattled toward the barn. The senior Mr. Ochendorf met them at the barn and halted the team.

"My son?" he asked.

"He'll be along shortly," Edward said.

"There's a drunken, unruly crowd intent on harming my husband," Serenity told the farmer she'd known all of her life. "Your son and the sheriff sent us ahead. Loyal said we could buy some supplies from you to continue our journey."

"Yes. I'll have my wife prepare a sugar sack of vittles. Come to the house while she gets it ready."

The house was clean and orderly, reinforcing Serenity's conviction that selling her house to the farmer's son was the right thing to do. It was comforting to know her home would be well cared for, and she didn't doubt Loyal would tend her parents' graves as faithfully as if his own loved ones lay there.

"You remember my wife, Patience," the farmer said of the older of two women who waited inside a snug kitchen. "And this is Charity, Loyal's wife." He motioned toward a plump young woman who was clearly expecting a child in the near future. She acknowledged them with a hint of fear in her eyes.

Serenity went to her and took her hand. "The sheriff will protect Loyal, and he'll be along soon," she said. "I'm very pleased to meet you, and I am pleased you and your husband will be living in my house. It holds many dear memories. It will ease my mind greatly to know that good people are living there and that a new generation of children will sleep upstairs under the eaves and play in the orchard."

The woman blushed, and her hands strayed to her apron. "I shall be pleased to have such a fine house to care for," she said.

It was an hour later when Loyal opened the door, almost without sound, and stepped into the room. He looked tired and dusty but pleased with himself.

"The sheriff locked three of those fellows in jail for the night," he reported to Edward. "Percy and a couple of others ran off, but the sheriff said he'd find them in the morning and charge them with drunk and disorderly conduct. Thy friend and the sheriff plan to stay the night at thy house, and with thy permission, I'll move into it tomorrow." He passed an envelope to Edward. "I was instructed to give thee these papers."

Edward looked the papers over and saw that they were a bill of sale for the house and any furniture that remained in it. He showed them to Serenity, who nodded her head. He then asked for a pen and signed them before handing them back to Loyal. Loyal then fetched a thick roll of bank notes, which he counted out to Edward.

"There's just one other thing . . ." Serenity spoke hesitantly. "My mother owned a beautiful topaz ring. It has been missing for many years. If you should come upon it, I would request that you send it to my uncle." She carefully noted Reliance Waterton's address on the back of the bill of sale.

"I shall be pleased to do so," Loyal promised, and Charity nodded her head in agreement, a promise Serenity knew they would keep. "Now we need to proceed to set thee on thy journey before daylight. I shall gather a few items thou wilt need and meet thee at the barn."

A short time later, Serenity and Edward huddled beneath a canvas tarp while Loyal drove the wagon. Serenity discovered that the sheriff and Rupert had discussed the matter of their leaving town with Edward and Loyal. Together they had determined that it was best for Serenity and Edward to leave unseen on a raft rather than wait for a stage. Their enemies might be watching the stage, but since the river was used so little for traffic because of its shallowness, there was less likelihood of anyone keeping watch on it.

The road to the river was rough, but Serenity still thought it somewhat of an improvement over their earlier ride across the Ochendorf fields. They had been traveling for close to an hour when they heard the sound of running horses approaching from behind them.

"Halt! Or I'll fire!" a voice shouted. The wagon slowly shuddered to a stop.

"I have no valuables," Loyal offered in a calm voice.

"Isn't it a little late for a farm wagon to be on the road?" the sneering voice asked.

"'Tis not late, but early. Farmers have need to begin the day before dawn."

Taking care not to move a muscle, Serenity listened to the exchange between Loyal and the rider. She was so terrified, she thought she might become ill. She felt Edward's fingers squeeze hers in an attempt to offer support, and she returned the gentle pressure.

"I think I'll just see for myself." A hand ripped away the tarp, and she found herself staring into Joshua Brown's face in the bright moonlight.

"Well, what do we have here?" He reached for her, but before he could lay a hand on her, Edward launched himself upward, knocking Brown from his horse. They hit the ground hard and rolled, locked together in the dust. As Serenity grasped the side of the wagon and prepared to go to Edward's aid, a hand clasped her upper arm and she was dragged onto the back of a nervous horse that pranced and shifted around the two figures struggling on the ground.

An arm circled her neck, drawing her back against a man's chest. Screaming and kicking, she attempted to break free. She heard a click and felt something hard dig into her temple.

"Back off or I'll shoot your wife," the man holding her shouted at Edward.

Edward looked up. "I think we have a stalemate," he said, dragging Joshua Brown to his feet in front of him. In Edward's hand was a dangerous-looking pistol. No doubt he had appropriated it from Mr. Brown during their scuffle.

15

"Hold still!" Suddenly Serenity recognized the voice of the man holding her. Rappleton's bony arm was far stronger than she might have expected. She hadn't considered that he and Brown might be working together.

From the corner of her eye, she saw Loyal sitting quietly with both arms raised.

Edward thumbed back the hammer on the gun in his hand. "Turn my wife loose and ride out of here," he demanded.

"If you shoot Josh, I'll eliminate your wife and the dumb farmer before you can fire again." Rappleton slid from the horse's back, taking Serenity with him. "The lady has something I want," he sneered, tightening his hold on her throat. She gasped for breath and feared she was about to lose consciousness.

"What do you want?" Edward shouted back. "If it's money, we'll give you the little I have." He didn't mention that Serenity had a great deal of money in her mother's saddlebag, which was where she'd stashed the money from the sale of her home and the store, along with the purse Rupert had given her.

"Oh, you'll give us that and more. I want that big topaz ring your little bride's ma used to flash around. It should have been mine a long time ago," Joshua snarled in defiance of the gun Edward held.

"That ring is gone. It was stolen when her mother was murdered."

Joshua Brown gave a sharp bark of laughter. "That's a lie. Sweet little Serenity has it, and I mean to get it."

"Did you send Percy to shoot up my house?" Loyal interrupted, asking his question without directing it to either man specifically. He spoke as though he had all the time in the world and was merely curious. He now sat with his team's reins laced through his fingers. Serenity suspected both Edward and Loyal were stalling, hoping time would bring them an advantage.

Rappleton turned and noticed that Loyal's arms were no longer raised. "Get your hands up like I told you!" he shouted. The slight movement caused the barrel of Rappleton's gun to grind painfully into Serenity's remple. She held her breath, waiting for the explosion that would end her life.

Brown answered Loyal's question. "That Tolson kid's a bigger fool than his greedy pa," he said with a smirk. "A few drinks and a suggestion or two is all it took. He's going to be right disappointed when he learns the love of his life ran off with her husband." He indulged in a snorting laugh, apparently amused by his own wit.

Serenity felt the hard metal against her temple slide to her ear then slip to her chin. It wavered back and forth with Rappleton's laughter, sometimes aiming away from Serenity altogether.

Suddenly a shot exploded next to Serenity's ear, stunning her. She waited for pain, expecting blood and death. Instead she saw Edward spin away from Joshua and the gun he held fly toward a thick stand of trees. Edward landed on his knees and quickly rolled toward a clump of bushes. She screamed, thinking Edward had been hit, but then she saw Mr. Brown slowly buckle toward the ground.

"Josh!" Rappleton cried. "The gun just went off by itself."

Rappleton fired a second shot, sending leaves and twigs flying from the place where Serenity had last seen Edward. This shot she knew was deliberate. A riderless horse, most likely Joshua Brown's, tore past her, and the one Rappleton had ridden on danced nervously, as though eager to join the running animal. With the gun no longer at her temple and Rappleton preparing to shoot again toward Edward's hiding place, she lowered her head and bit down hard on his gun arm.

Rappleton yelled, and his shot went wild. He shook her off, knocking her to the ground. Before he could take aim again, she clasped her arms around his knees and pressed her weight against the backs of his legs. He sprawled in the dirt while Serenity rolled her body over the gun he'd held in his hand. Before she could retrieve it, a volley of shots rang out and she lifted her head to see the silhouettes of three men riding toward them against the glare of the rising sun.

Thinking help had arrived, she started to rise. But then recognition brought keen disappointment. Percy and his friends had stumbled onto the holdup scene. She sank back down, averting her face in hopes he wouldn't recognize her. She'd as soon take her chances with the robbers as with Percy.

"You double-crosser!" Percy screamed when he spotted her lying on the dusty road almost beneath the wagon and Joshua Brown struggling to his feet a few feet away. She cringed from his anger. "You're just like Pa. You lied to me." He fired at Brown, and Serenity realized Percy wasn't speaking to her but to Joshua, who collapsed back to the ground.

"No, he didn't lie. He was just getting the girl for you and asked me to help him." Rappleton stretched out his arms as though pleading. "She was running away, but we caught her." Clearly he was hoping to ingratiate himself with Percy.

"Serenity wouldn't run from me. She likes me. It was Pa's fault she married that Mormon. He wants her money just like Pa did, so I gotta kill him. Where is he?" He waved the gun about in a frightening manner.

Serenity felt her strength returning and her vision clearing, but dismay filled her heart. Percy had never been like other boys, but now she feared he was truly insane. As she reached that conclusion, she became aware of Stephen Rappleton cowering behind the wagon. He was genuinely afraid of Percy. Was it because he sensed the boy's insanity as she did? Or did he know something that was just beginning to dawn on her? Percy, she now realized, was the one who had killed Bernard Tolson, his own father!

A creeping sense of horror told her that Percy had killed his father because of his obsession with her, and that he would kill any man he thought might interfere with his determination to claim her. She glanced nervously toward the bush where she'd seen Edward disappear and prayed he would stay out of sight. Her eye caught a movement—Joshua Brown was still very much alive, and he was creeping toward Percy to get the drop on him. Without his pistol, however, she didn't know what he could do. Percy's friends were occupied with restraining Loyal and Rappleton, who weren't putting up any opposition to the ropes being used to tie their hands.

Her hand moved slowly beneath her body until her fingers touched the butt of Joshua's pistol. Slowly she slid it into her pocket.

"You can get up now, Serenity," Percy called to her. "I'll take care of you."

She hesitated. If she rolled beneath the wagon, perhaps she could escape on the other side and make a run for the woods. On the other hand, Percy was just crazy enough he might start shooting. She felt no fondness for the men who wished to steal her mother's ring, but she didn't wish to be responsible for their deaths either. And she wouldn't be able to live with herself if Loyal died because of her. Anyway, she was none too sure Percy wouldn't shoot *her* if she tried to escape. Slowly, she stood. Unconsciously, she dusted the dirt and twigs from her skirt.

"Come here," he beckoned to her.

She took a few cautious steps, more to the side than forward, maneuvering to keep one of Loyal's restless horses between herself and Percy. Arms closed around her. She'd forgotten about Joshua and had passed too near him. Now Joshua was using her as a shield to protect himself from Percy.

She felt her captor's hand slide toward her pocket. While she'd been absorbed in trying to find a way to escape Percy, Joshua had noticed that his firearm wasn't on the ground and had correctly interpreted the sagging line of her skirt. They'd both be killed if he and Percy engaged in a gun battle.

Percy's angry shriek frightened his friends' loose horses into running. Even Loyal's team charged forward, knocking the two bound men to the ground as the wagon clattered down the road, leaving a cloud of dust in its wake.

Percy urged his horse forward. "I'll kill you!" he screamed at Joshua. "You aren't fit to touch my woman's skirt."

Joshua's hand flashed downward, delving into Serenity's pocket, and a shot ripped into Percy's shoulder. Enraged, the wounded youth dug his heels into his horse's side and charged toward them. Serenity felt her skirt rip as Joshua tore free the gun he'd fired from her pocket moments earlier. He shoved her aside, causing her to stumble back a step. Joshua fired once more as Percy's horse's hooves knocked him to the ground. A streak of red appeared on the horse's flank. The pain, added to Percy's screams, drove the horse into a frenzy.

Scrambling to evade the crazed horse's plunging hooves, Serenity began to run without thought to direction, only to escape. Hearing running footsteps behind her, she clutched her tattered skirt and ran faster.

When a hand grasped the back of her dress, she fell backward and sat dazed for a moment in the dust. Then she gasped for breath and shoved her hair out of her eyes. She could hear a horse charging madly toward her. Before she could regain her feet, Joshua Brown dragged her upright. Clasping her hands together behind her back, he held them in one of his.

"I'm not going to hurt you," he whispered in her ear. "My gun is gone, and I have a bullet in my side. Neither of us can reach the woods before that fool is on us. Just play along and don't scream."

Serenity stood still. She didn't trust Brown, but going along with whatever plan he had thought up would be preferable to being carried off by Percy.

Percy gave a vicious yank on the reins, and his horse slid to a stop in a cloud of dust that settled across Serenity's feet and made her sneeze. He raised his pistol.

"She almost got away again," Brown said in a surprisingly calm voice. "You can have her, but I'll need your help catching my horse."

"What!" Serenity sputtered. Joshua Brown had no intention of helping her. He was willing to turn her over to Percy to save his own hide. She'd been a fool to believe him.

Percy tossed Joshua a length of rope. "Tie her hands with this."

Serenity twisted and fought, but she was no match for the much larger man. He wrapped the rope around her wrists, tying her hands in front, then handed the trailing end of the rope to Percy.

"You dolt!" she snarled at Percy. "Joshua Brown isn't your friend or mine. He only turned me over to you so he can steal my mother's ring."

Percy blinked, looking confused. "I always liked your ma's big, shiny ring."

"If you let him escape, he'll get away with stealing it." Serenity was so angry, she didn't care if Percy shot Brown.

"Hey! He's gone!"

Serenity looked around. Percy was right: Brown was gone. He'd disappeared while she'd distracted Percy. She'd played right into the thief's strategy.

Abruptly she was jerked forward and almost lost her balance. She couldn't believe what was happening. Percy was urging his horse toward the trees in pursuit of Joshua, heedless of the tether that forced her to follow. As the horse picked up speed, she had to run. She couldn't possibly keep up with a horse, but if she tripped, she'd be dragged to her death. Brush tore at her clothing and yanked her hair.

"Percy! Stop!" she screamed. But he kept going. She stumbled to her knees, then fell prostate. Pain ripped through her shoulders, and rocks and brush tore at her face. She tasted blood and grass.

In a blur she saw a figure step in front of the horse, leaping for its bridle and bringing the terrified animal to a stop. The abrupt halt sent Percy tumbling to the ground. He fumbled for his pistol, only to discover it had flown from his hand. Serenity saw it at the same time he did. Her attempt to reach it fell far short. Through a red mist of pain, she saw a boot kick the gun beyond Percy's reach.

Percy reacted quickly, grasping Serenity in a strangle hold.

"Let her go, Percy." There was no mistaking the steel in Edward's voice. Serenity's eyes swam with tears of relief when she recognized it. At least he was alive.

"No, she's mine!" Percy snarled. "I always had a hankering for her, and Pa said I could have her." He tightened his hold, threatening to cut off her ability to breathe. Soon he'd have nothing but a dead, battered body to claim.

Edward moved closer. His heavy boot caught Percy in the ribs with a high kick, leaving him writhing on the ground. A hand went out to Serenity, and she grasped it. With Edward's help, she managed to rise to her feet. He never glanced at her but kept his eyes on Percy, who was still screaming and threatening to kill him.

"Can you get that rope off?" Edward asked without looking at her.

"I don't think so. The knots were pulled tight when he dragged me after him."

"I can." Loyal Ochendorf trotted toward them, the rope that had bound him dangling from one hand. "But I think it would be wise to attend to Percy first." He knelt and with a few quick twists immobilized Percy's hands behind his back and lashed his ankles together. For good measure, he stuffed a handkerchief in his mouth.

Serenity took a good look at Edward for the first time since their capture and was shocked by what she saw. His face was covered with blood and welts, and his left arm hung at an awkward angle. Before she could say anything, Loyal drew a knife from his pocket and sliced through the rope that bound her hands.

The pain of returning circulation made her gasp. Her shoulders throbbed with excruciating pain. She rubbed at her bruised and swollen wrists for only a moment, then stumbled toward Edward. His good arm came around her, gently massaging her shoulders and upper arms.

"Thank you. You saved my life." She blinked back tears. "You've been hurt. Let me—"

"There isn't time. Joshua Brown is out here somewhere, and I've no idea what shape Rappleton is in, and then there are Percy's friends." Edward took her hand, attempting to draw her toward cover.

"The skinny one is still hog-tied," Loyal reported as he followed them into the woods, dragging Percy by the rope that secured his hands and feet. His horse had already disappeared. "I don't think either of thee is going to get far, in the shape thou art in. I suggest we stay out of sight until Pa gets here, then return to the farm with him to patch thee up."

"What makes you think your pa knows we need help?" Edward staggered, and Serenity helped him to a fallen log, where she collapsed beside him.

"The horses know where their feed bags be. They'll return to the barn, and when Pa doesn't see me, he'll come looking."

Serenity attempted to look at Edward's arm, but he wouldn't allow it. "It's not broken, merely dislocated," he said.

"If thou art sure," Loyal began, "I could help thee set it in place."

"When we get back to the farm. Right now I can't risk losing consciousness."

Loyal nodded his head. "I thought that might be thy reasoning." He pointed to Percy. "What dost thou plan to do with him?"

"Turn him over to the sheriff, I suppose."

Edward sounded tired, and Serenity knew he must be in great pain. Concern for his wounds overshadowed her own injuries. "What about Percy's friends?" she asked. "Can you see if they're coming after us?" She tried to peer through the bushes and trees.

"I don't think thou hast anything to fear from them," Loyal said with a faint smile. "They sobered up and decided to head back to town and their beds."

Edward also tried to offer her reassurance. "We probably have little to fear from Joshua Brown at the moment either," he said. "He's more intent on catching up to the wagon and our luggage, where he assumes your mother's topaz is hidden, than in pursuing us, though I don't doubt he'll return once he discovers the ring isn't in our luggage. And I believe he's the sort who will want to eliminate witnesses."

Serenity bit her lip to keep from crying. Their ordeal wasn't over yet.

"Instead of hiding," Edward said to Loyal, "I think we should walk up the road to meet your pa."

Loyal rose to his feet. "I was thinking I should do that. Neither of thee should be walking. I'll go—"

"No," Edward objected. "If you were to stumble onto Brown, you wouldn't defend yourself, and he'd likely kill you."

Loyal sighed and stretched out a hand toward Edward, who looked at it suspiciously.

"Thou canst not walk until that arm is as it should be," he said. "Allow me to set it in place. And do not worry. If thou faintest, I'll not leave thy wife alone with an unconscious man."

Serenity could not bear to watch as Loyal grasped Edward's arm, but when she heard Edward giving the young man instructions on just how he should maneuver his arm and shoulder and Loyal's insistence that he knew what he was doing, she hid the beginnings of a smile. A muffled yell came from Edward, and she turned to see him clinging dizzily to a nearby tree trunk. She hurried to his side.

"I'm not going to faint," he muttered. "Rip up my shirt and bind the shoulder so it won't move."

Instead of his shirt, she chose one of her tattered petticoats for the task. When she finished, he straightened, winced, and said, "Let's go." They left Percy trussed to a tree.

Their steps were slow. Edward didn't refuse Serenity's assistance when she placed an arm around his waist and encouraged him to lean on her. She winced when he brushed against her bruised ribs, but she insisted she was fine.

They paused when they reached the place where they'd left Rappleton.

Loyal scratched his head. "He's gone. I should have made certain he was securely tied."

"Seeing you work yourself free must have motivated him to do the same."

They continued walking up the road, making slow progress until they heard the jangle of harnesses and the heavy thud of

hooves from an approaching team of horses. They rounded a bend
to see the Ochendorf wagon approaching with a different team of
Belgians pulling it. Seeing the farm wagon coming toward them
brought tears of relief to Serenity's eyes. She was so tired, and she
ached in so many places.

"There's Pa," Loyal announced, but his voice sounded flat.
Seated beside his father was Sheriff Compton. And behind the
wagon seat stood Joshua Brown with a revolver aimed at Mr.
Ochendorf's head.

16

The wagon came to a halt a few feet in front of them. Sheriff Compton's face was red, and he was nearly bursting from frustration and anger. Ochendorf kept his head down. He appeared more sad than angry.

"Well, well, so kind of you to come to meet me," Brown mocked. "In the interest of saving time, I'll allow the lady to search her own luggage for that ring."

"I told you, I don't have it," Serenity cried. "When my mother's body was brought home the night she died, the ring was already gone."

"She hid it and you have it!"

"Likely she buried it before she died," Sheriff Compton suggested. "Or her killer took it."

"No!" Brown threw Serenity's bag to the ground. It landed at her feet. "Find that ring or this old farmer will be as dead as your father. I want that ring now." His voice was hard and menacing.

"The ring isn't going to do you any good," a voice called from a thick clump of trees to Serenity's right. "And if you shoot your hostage, you'll be dead before you can take a step."

Like Joshua Brown, Serenity turned toward the voice. She almost missed Sheriff Compton's swift attack that sent Brown's gun flying. The sheriff had been watching for his chance, and the voice provided just enough distraction. The gun landed on the road in front of the wagon. Edward dove toward it, narrowly missing being trampled by the heavy hoof of one of Ochendorf's Belgians. The draft horse's heavy foot came down on the gun instead, effectively ending its usefulness.

Fists flew between Compton and Brown. Both of the Ochendorf men calmly stayed where they were, but Edward struggled toward Serenity. "Run!" he shouted.

She started painfully toward the woods. Her muscles had stiffened while they were stopped, making motion difficult. Each movement was an aching reminder of the battering her body had taken while being dragged. She moved as quickly as she could, but soon was stopped by a voice shouting, "Hold it right there!"

Coming toward her was Fenton Simmons with a shotgun. She stopped, slowly raising her hands, but he walked right past her. Simmons's gun was leveled on the combatants in the wagon. Approaching them from the rear, he nimbly leaped over the wagon end. He pointed the gun, then hesitated, watching the contest between Brown and the sheriff.

Compton landed a solid blow to Brown's stomach, causing him to bend nearly double. He then brought both fists together in a powerful uppercut to the man's jaw. Brown went down and didn't stagger back to his feet. The sheriff glanced up with a satisfied smile on his face, which froze when he saw Simmons.

Simmons handed the shotgun to the startled sheriff. "Here, hold this," he said. "I'll take charge of the prisoner."

"Now wait a minute," Compton blustered as Simmons closed handcuffs around the unconscious man's wrists.

Neither Serenity nor Edward thought to run or fade into the woods. Their attention was riveted on the drama taking place in the wagon.

Simmons straightened when the task was completed. He reached for something inside his coat, and Compton turned the shotgun toward him. When Simmons withdrew his hand, it held a small leather case, which he flipped open.

"Fenton Simmons, Pinkerton Agent," Sheriff Compton read aloud, nearly dropping the shotgun. "Why didn't you tell me?" he roared.

"Our friend here is wanted for murder and theft in Boston," the agent announced. "Added to those charges will be the crime he attempted here today. I had to be sure you weren't sheltering him before I revealed my identity."

The sheriff appeared greatly offended. "I suppose you're the mysterious gunman who helped us hold off young Tolson and his friends last night."

"I've been keeping an eye on the Benson household. It seemed the most likely place that Brown would make his next move."

Edward stepped forward. "Percy Tolson is tied up in a grove of trees on the south side of a big clearing about a mile down the road," he told the sheriff. "Stephen Rappleton escaped, but with his aversion to the woods, he shouldn't be too hard to apprehend."

"They're all yours," Agent Simmons informed the sheriff.

* * *

Almost a full week passed before Edward and Serenity were sufficiently healed to continue their journey. Both Simmons and Compton asked questions throughout the week. The Ochendorfs were gracious hosts, and Rupert Montague called on them several times before departing for New York with the remaining treasures Serenity's father had loved and collected. The proceeds were to be deposited in an account for her at the New York bank.

Serenity was now a wealthy young woman, at least in New York. Rupert left her with a considerable amount of cash in addition to the money from the sale of her home, but by Pennsylvania law it legally belonged to Edward. Thus far he'd shown little interest in it. His major concern was to reach Philadelphia to continue his medical studies. He objected to Serenity sharing any of the money with him, but she pointed out that it was due to his chivalry in dealing with her problems that he'd been unable to secure a job that would have provided him with some needed cash. Grudgingly, he accepted the necessity of using her money to finance their trip to Philadelphia and to provide a place for them to stay after they reached the city. She hoped they could find a place near the hospital where he would be enrolled as a student.

Though early in August, it was too late in the year for Serenity to consider traveling west to meet her uncle, and she felt reluctant to spend the winter in New York with Rupert and his wife, though Rupert suggested she do so. After some discussion with Rupert and the sheriff, she and Edward decided to continue with their original plan of journeying together to Philadelphia, where Serenity would secure a house near the hospital and Edward would visit her whenever he had free time.

Upon the advice of both the sheriff and Simmons, they decided to begin their journey on the river as originally planned, thus avoiding a public departure on the coach and the risk of a holdup. Rappleton had not been captured, and Simmons informed them that Brown was known to work with several different partners at various times. It was therefore advisable to keep their movements hidden from any of those partners who might be in the vicinity.

Early one morning, before the stifling heat of the day began, they once more set out for the river. This time they were prepared with adequate supplies for their journey. They were each looking forward to the prospect of a tranquil float down the shallow river. They planned to journey as far as possible before transferring to the lurching, uncomfortable overland combination of train and coach.

Instead of the raft on which they'd first planned to make their escape, arrangements had been made for a small, lightweight boat. Serenity was pleased to see that the boat had not only two sets of oars, but also a long pole that would come in handy should they get stuck on a sandbar.

Once again Loyal conveyed them to the river, where they bid him farewell. The river was calm and smooth, and the clear blue sky overhead and verdant green on either bank seemed to be an omen of a peaceful adventure. They'd drifted only a short distance when Edward confessed, "I've never rowed a boat before. The only boats I've ever been on were the ships that carried James and me to Denmark and back. I was only a small boy when my family reached the Salt Lake Valley, and boats aren't something I grew up around."

"Didn't you ever travel by boat on the Salt Lake?"

"The Salt Lake isn't like other lakes. It's extremely salty, and the soil for some miles from its shore is unsuitable for farming and quite desolate. It's also some distance from the city, so it isn't especially inviting and few people travel there. Though I tried swimming in it once, there isn't much boating done on it."

"Rowing is not difficult. I shall teach you."

"I was hoping you would volunteer." He grinned and suddenly the day seemed perfect.

Amid a great deal of laughter and splashing, Serenity explained and demonstrated rowing until they were both satisfied he could handle the oars. While he worked on improving his technique, she leaned back against the luggage and lazily watched the shoreline as they drifted south. When they grew hungry, they went ashore for a brief respite.

Toward evening, Serenity began watching for a stream that emptied into the river. When she spotted one, she picked up one set of oars.

"Let's head for that stream," she suggested, pointing to where a narrow creek emptied into the river. Edward shrugged and followed her example, picking up the other set of oars. When they were a short distance up the shallow stream, she helped Edward pull the boat onto a gravelly sand bar and then tie it to a tree.

Working together, they made a shelter from the canvas Loyal had provided for them, and then they spread out their bedrolls. Edward started a small fire, and while Serenity prepared their supper, he disappeared for a time. When he returned, he was carrying three small fish on a forked willow. Supper was ready and he didn't offer to add the fish to the meal she had prepared. Instead he took his fish back to the stream, where he stuck the willow in a shallow pool and placed rocks around the fish to keep them cold until morning.

They ate slowly, enjoying the calm and solitude, something they'd known little of during the few months they'd known each other. After dinner, Edward searched in his bag until he found his scriptures, then seated himself near the fire and began to read.

"Papa was reading the Book of Mormon quite a bit before he died," Serenity commented, remembering how her father had pored over the book just before leaving for New York.

"He told us he'd been studying it for almost a year," Edward said. "Have you read it?"

"A few pages. It was my mother's book. I remember her reading it and that sometimes she cried while she was reading. After she died, Papa kept it in his room, but sometimes I took it from the drawer and found comfort in just holding it."

"Did you bring it with you?" he asked.

"Yes. It's in the large bundle Loyal wrapped in canvas and secured in the middle of the boat. He said it would be best not to unwrap that bundle until we reach our destination. I think I might read it after we get to Philadelphia."

"We could share mine while we travel. Come sit beside me and we shall begin at the beginning."

"But you're already halfway through the book. It would be unfair to cause you to start over." In spite of the protest she voiced, Serenity moved closer to the spot Edward had indicated.

"I've read it many times," he said. "It doesn't matter where I begin." He began reading, and she listened until the fire burned to coals and it was too dark for Edward to see the words on the page before him. When he closed the book, he said nothing about the chapters he'd read. She refrained from commenting as well. She wasn't certain how she felt about what she'd heard, but she found the story of Nephi and his brothers far more interesting than she'd anticipated.

"I'll bank the fire and check that our boat is secure while you get ready for bed," Edward told her as he rose to his feet. She watched him stroll toward the stream and hurried to change into nightclothes, grateful for his consideration. By the time he returned, she was snuggled beneath her blankets with her back to his bedroll.

She'd considered asking him to arrange separate shelters, but as the night grew darker and unexplained noises reached her ears, she was glad Edward was close at hand. She'd never slept on the ground or outdoors before. She had never even been on an overnight trip. The only time she could recall sleeping anywhere other than under the roof of her own home, excepting the past week spent at the Ochendorfs', was a time when Papa had been away and Mamma had been ill. Sufferance Nixon had taken Serenity to his farm, where she'd spent the night giggling beneath the covers with the four Nixon daughters.

Falling asleep was difficult, but she eventually did. When she awoke the sun was shining, though the air was still cool. The enticing aroma of fish frying in bacon fat filled the air. She scrambled into her clothes and hurried to join Edward beside the campfire.

"Good morning, sleepyhead." Edward's grin was back. "Grab a plate." He waved vaguely toward two tin plates and a couple of tin cups. She remembered she hadn't given a thought to washing them the night before, but they were now scrubbed clean. She was surprised to discover Edward had prepared a delicious breakfast. Other than simple meals like those her father had occasionally prepared, especially when she was younger, she hadn't thought cooking was something men did.

Following breakfast, they broke camp, and Serenity was impressed to see that Edward was as adept at organizing and stowing their gear as Loyal had been. Only in the matter of steering and rowing their boat was she more accomplished than he, but she could see that he was quickly picking up that skill too.

They stayed near the edge of the current and let it carry them most of the day. Sometimes Serenity dozed as they glided smoothly along, but most of the time she watched Edward with hooded eyes or thought about all that had happened since her father's death. Occasionally her thoughts drifted to the previous evening, and she hoped Edward would read more of the book to her that night. It was an interesting story. Knowing nothing of the land where Nephi and his family had traveled in the wilderness, she found herself thinking of the family traveling through a wilderness much like the one she and Edward were passing through. Sometimes she thought about her parents and the events that had brought her to be sharing a small boat with Edward. Thinking of her mother reminded her of the topaz ring.

"Do you suppose I shall ever see my mother's ring again?" she wondered aloud.

"It's not likely," Edward replied as he steered the boat away from a rock that protruded out of the water.

Trailing her fingers in the water, Serenity continued sharing her thoughts about the topaz. "I've often felt disappointed that I've been unable to keep my promise to Mamma to wear the ring. And I certainly could have used the topaz's supposed powers of greater strength and clearer vision this past month. I wonder what happened to it."

"Several things Rappleton and Brown said made me suspect at first that they were involved in your parents' deaths, but if either of them was the shooter, why would they still be searching for the ring? The only explanation I can think of is that one of them shot your mother, but she lived long enough to hide it, maybe on her person. Then before they could search her and the surrounding area, Timothy and his uncle arrived. If the ring was hidden in her clothing but wasn't secure, it might have fallen to the ground unnoticed while they were carrying her to your house. If that is the case, it may never be found."

"I guess I'll never know." She sighed, deeply disappointed at the thought.

* * *

That night, as Serenity reached for the heavy kettle she'd placed in the coals, Edward reached for it at the same time and his hand closed around hers. Jerking her hand free, she raised her fingertips to her mouth.

"Are you burned?" Edward scooted closer and drew her fingers from her mouth, examining them closely.

"N-no," she stammered, feeling foolish. She hadn't been burned, but the sudden touch of Edward's hand on hers had felt for just a brief moment as though she had been scalded. It was just because he had touched her unexpectedly, she assured herself.

She dished up the stew and dumplings she'd made and sat across from him on a corner of the cloth he'd spread on the ground. After finishing her meal, she carried the dishes to the edge of the water to scrub them with sand. When Edward offered to read from his book again, she joined him on a log before the fire. Vague memories stirred in her mind as Edward read. She recalled her mother reading about the quarrelsome brothers. She also remembered her mother's admonition to pray about life's challenges as Nephi had done, and she vowed to pray more often.

In the succeeding days, they drifted south, passing occasional farms and villages. The Susquehanna wasn't a busy waterway bearing people and trade goods as were other rivers. It was too shallow for paddle wheelers, steamboats, or barges. Still, they avoided going ashore and making contact with the few people they saw. Once a large raft overtook and passed them, and sometimes they passed other small boats or canoes. Beyond a friendly wave at these few chance encounters, they kept their distance, keeping a wary watch out for Rappleton or anyone suspicious who might have followed them.

They were alone, but Serenity never felt lonely. She missed her father but found something soothing in Edward's presence. There was always some topic to discuss with him, and though he sometimes disagreed with her perception of a matter, he never discounted her view. He often explained portions of the previous night's reading to her, though he always waited for her to pose a question before mentioning the Book of Mormon. She spent many peaceful hours quietly pondering the passages that had particularly caught her attention.

Their days passed in peaceful companionship, but the evenings brought a tiny edge of tension to their relationship. Serenity took care to avoid brushing against Edward, and he always remained outside their shelter until he was certain she was dressed and settled snugly under her blankets. Morning always brought a resumption of their ease with each other, and she easily dismissed the previous night's slight discomfort.

If her calculations were right, they were almost to the end of their river journey when a pleasant summer breeze turned to strong gusts of wind and the water grew choppy. Edward suggested they turn toward shore, and they both began to paddle vigorously. To the west, Serenity could see dense, black clouds. Thunder rumbled, lending urgency to their efforts to reach shore.

Before they could get off of the river, rain came in a deluge, drenching them and limiting visibility. There was an added cacophony of sound with its driving fury. Premature darkness further reduced visibility, except for flashes of brilliant lightning. The roar of water cascading over rocks didn't reach Serenity's ears until it was too late to change the boat's course.

Where a large creek emptied into the river, the channel they followed made a sudden drop of a foot or so. Caught in an unexpected rapid, the small boat tilted and Edward was swept over the side into the water. Serenity leaned against the tilt, and the boat slowly righted itself.

Hearing Edward calling from somewhere ahead of her, Serenity swept her wet hair from her eyes and strained to see him. She wasn't certain whether he knew how to swim. Her own ability to swim was limited, as it wasn't considered proper for young ladies to sport in the water, but when she was only five her mother had begun taking her to a quiet spot in the river to instruct her in the basics for safety purposes. Unfortunately, she hadn't been swimming since she'd turned twelve.

Spotting a flailing hand, Serenity rowed toward it. As she drew nearer, she could see Edward floundering and making little headway in an eddy near what appeared to be a deep hole. Fighting the wind and the lashing rain, she maneuvered the boat as close to him as she could. He clasped the side of the boat, causing it to rock precariously.

"Don't try to climb aboard," she shouted. "Just hold onto the side."

He didn't hear or didn't understand. He placed his other hand on the side of the boat and attempted to clamber aboard. Serenity was unable to counter his move and the boat tipped, sending her plunging over the side. Water closed over her head and she felt herself sinking far deeper than she thought possible in the supposedly shallow river.

17

Remembering her mother's instructions concerning kicking upward and reaching for the surface, Serenity came up sputtering and spitting. With one hand she scraped her streaming hair back from her eyes, and with the other she treaded water to remain afloat.

"Edward!" she screamed. She thought she heard a faint response and swam in the direction from which the sound had come. Her heavy clothing created a drag. She paused to tear off her petticoats but was unable to kick free of her shoes, which were laced tightly above her ankles. She forged on, fearful that taking time to struggle with her shoes might make her too late to find Edward.

She paused to call his name again. This time she was certain he answered. Her toe brushed against rocks, telling her she was past the hole where she'd plunged into the water. A few more strokes and she was able to stand.

"Over here," Edward called. "Stay close to the shore. There's a strong current farther out." She nearly wept with relief on hearing his voice.

She angled toward the shore, fighting the tugs of current that seemed to urge her in the other direction. In a flash of lightning she caught a glimpse of their boat, which was now tangled in the branches of a giant tree that had fallen into the water.

"Are you all right?" she called. She needed to keep him talking so she could follow the sound of his voice.

"Yes, but I'm caught and can't free myself."

The lightning made her nervous. Papa had warned her numerous times to stay away from open spaces, hills, and water in a thunderstorm. Still she struggled on, trying to find Edward.

When she reached the downed tree, it took her several minutes to find her way through the tangle of broken limbs to the boat. She couldn't immediately tell whether or not it was damaged. In any case, the boat wasn't her immediate concern. Edward was.

"Where are you?" she called, not seeing him, though she'd felt certain his voice had come from near the boat.

"On the other side of the boat." This time he sounded closer, but there was a breathless catch in his voice. "I was able to hang onto the boat until it ran into this tree, but then I lost my hold. I'm tangled in the rope and trapped between the boat and several large tree branches."

Clinging to the side of the boat, she worked her way around it, climbing over the branches that obstructed her path. Sometimes she found herself standing in mere inches of water and then dropping into uncertain depths, but she persevered in working her way toward Edward. Finally, she stood in water that reached to her shoulders with a tree branch as big around as a man's body separating her from him. All she could see of him was his head and one arm. Water lapped at his chin, and when the wind gusted toward him, small wavelets washed over his face.

"I can't free myself," he gasped. "I tried to pull myself higher, but it's hopeless."

"If I climb into the boat, perhaps I can pull you up," she suggested.

He groaned several times as she pulled herself over the side of the boat, and she feared that her added weight was pushing the boat against his chest and causing him more pain or injury. When at last she reached his side, she clasped his free hand and attempted to tug him upward. Even when she slid a hand to his trapped shoulder and pulled on it, she couldn't move him.

"The rope is so tangled around tree branches and around me, I think the only way to free me is to cut the rope," he said. A ripple of water washed over his mouth and nose, setting him choking and gasping for air.

Serenity looked around with a growing sense of panic, then dug into their cooking utensils, which thankfully were still in the boat. At last she found the knife she'd used to chop vegetables for the stew the previous night. Grasping it, she scrambled over to the rope that was attached to a metal ring at the front of the boat, but then she hesitated.

"What if the rope is what's keeping your head above water?" she asked.

"I'm more afraid that if you cut the rope, the boat will drift free and we'll lose our supplies," Edward said.

Serenity admitted it was a strong possibility, since the wind was still buffeting the small vessel, causing it to rock and bump against the large branch to which it was bound. She tried to look down into the water and tangled branches for a better solution, but it was no use. The falling tree had stirred up too much mud and silt that hadn't yet settled, and the storm-darkened sky and driving rain were making a visual examination of the problem impossible.

She climbed over the side of the boat onto the heavy tree limb, clutching the knife in one hand. She needed to cut the rope that tangled Edward, not the portion that held the boat tethered to the tree. She soon discovered that there wasn't enough room between the branch and Edward for even her hand. Reaching for a smaller branch that protruded from the larger one, she slid off the branch into the tangle of water and tree branches. Her feet didn't touch the bottom.

"Careful," Edward cautioned. "I'll never forgive myself if you become entangled too."

With her feet, she searched for a spot to stand. One shoe brushed against Edward, then found a small branch of the tree that was closer to him than her present position. She couldn't stand on it, but if she held onto it with one hand, it would place her closer to her objective. Releasing her grip on the branch she'd been holding, she slid toward the other branch, catching it with her left hand as she felt her skirt snag on underwater debris.

Her head was now barely above water, and Edward was between her and the boat. There was no way she could slash at the rope with one hand without injuring Edward. Taking a deep breath, she released her hold on the tree branch and sank below the surface, at the same time reaching out for Edward. Her hand caught his shirt, and she pulled herself closer.

Her fingers found the rope and searched for a space where she could insert the knife. Two quick slices at the rope and she knew she was running out of air. She clawed her way upward, breaking the water at long last to gulp greedily at the cold air.

"Serenity, are you all right?" There was concern in Edward's voice and something else that didn't sound right. The storm had dropped the temperature sharply, and he sounded as though his teeth were chattering. She found herself shivering in the cool air too. She had to hurry.

Sliding back into the water, she found Edward more quickly this time and returned to the spot where she'd begun cutting the rope. She had to surface two more times before she finally managed to separate the thick strands of hemp. The last time she surfaced, Edward didn't respond to her gasped greeting.

Her arms and legs ached, her lungs hurt, and she'd jerked at her skirt so many times to free it from snags that it was nothing more than ragged ribbons of cloth. Still, she submerged herself once more and tore at the rope to unwind the tangles. It took the last of her strength to drag herself onto the thick branch that pinned Edward and work her way to where his face lolled toward the water. She dropped the knife into the boat, which was bobbing behind her more vigorously than it had before. Somehow she pulled herself into it.

"Edward, you have to pull yourself up. I can't do it." She touched his face. To her relief, he slowly lifted his face and blinked his eyes.

"Cold," he mumbled, and his head drooped again.

"No, Edward." She jerked at his hair. "I cut the rope. You can pull yourself out now."

"Pull myself out . . ." he repeated slowly.

Again she jerked at his hair and pulled at his arm. Tears mingled with the rain on her face. She remembered how much he depended on prayer, and she muttered a few hasty words of supplication. She didn't know if it was the prayer or her persistence that finally reached him, but she suspected it was the prayer. He looked up, blinked several times, then seemed to recognize her.

He struggled a moment, then discovered that the boat had shifted enough for him to get his recently freed arm above it and the tree limb. The discovery seemed to energize him. Grasping for anything he could close his hands around, he clasped the side of the boat and braced his feet against the tree branch to begin lifting himself up. When he slipped a few inches, Serenity clutched at his clothes and tried to assist him. Her chilled hands had trouble maintaining a hold, as did his, but after several attempts he managed to lean his upper body across the side of the boat.

After resting a moment, he crawled and she tugged him forward. Finally, he fell into the small vessel, gasping and shivering.

"We can't stay here," she warned. "We've got to reach shore and build a fire. I don't know if I can secure the boat." She had difficulty enunciating the words as her teeth chattered uncontrollably. Nevertheless, she worked her way to the front of the boat and after several attempts managed to tie what was left of the rope to the heavy tree limb.

Edward roused himself to delve into the pack that contained their food and cooking utensils. Using their ground cloth to form a bundle, he transferred some of the most needed items to it, then fastened it to his back. He looked at the tree, and she could sense that in spite of the continuing rain, he was reluctant to leave the relative safety of the boat.

"If we climb toward the tree's roots . . . ." His voice trailed off, and she suspected he was hoping for a way to reach shore without returning to the water.

"It will be faster and much easier to wade," she pointed out. "The water is less than a foot deep on this side of the boat." She reached for his hand to lead the way. She cringed when she stepped over the side of the boat and found that the water felt deeper and colder than it had earlier. She felt Edward hesitate, then he was in the water beside her.

Feeling their way, they worked free of the tree and stumbled forward, supporting each other, until they reached a cove of sand-like silt that squished beneath their feet. When Serenity would have collapsed to the ground, Edward urged her on, past a narrow wedge of grass to the crater left by the fallen tree's roots. Finding the spot dry, almost like a cave and protected from the storm by the huge clump of roots and soil, they huddled together. After a few minutes, Edward unloaded their supplies from the tarp and spread it around them for further protection.

Leaning against his chest, Serenity could hear the steady thump of his heart beneath her ear. She found herself growing sleepy and was startled when Edward said, "The thunder and lightning have stopped and the rain has almost ceased. I'm going to venture into the woods to see if I can find dry wood."

"All right," she mumbled sleepily.

"Stay awake," he warned. "Better yet, come with me."

"I'm so tired." But in spite of her fatigue, she followed him. It was more than not wishing to be alone; she knew she was suffering from exposure as much as he was and they both needed to get warm. Then too, he possibly had injuries that they had been too tired and miserable to examine.

They hadn't traveled far into the dense forest when they found a few dry twigs under some trees and some sticks that appeared dry enough to burn. They broke out chunks of wood from the under-side of an old windfall, then returned to their shelter. Thankfully their matches had stayed dry inside a can wrapped with several thicknesses of canvas, but it took a number of tries before a small blaze rewarded Edward's efforts.

Between the heat from the small fire and the passing of the storm, they began to feel better. They were both still tired, but Serenity sensed there was something different about it. The lethargy that had threatened to cause them to give up earlier was gone, and now they were simply tired from their exertion.

After a time, Edward returned to the forest to search out more wood, and Serenity began a simple supper of biscuits and warm tea. The biscuits had almost finished baking when she saw Edward dragging a log toward the fire. He said he'd found it inside the mouth of a small cave and that he hadn't dared venture farther into the cave to see what else it might shelter.

They slept that night wrapped together in the canvas ground cloth, as near the fire as they considered safe. Serenity was conscious of Edward leaving their cocoon to stir up the fire a couple of times before morning.

When she finally awoke, the sun was up and a cloud of vapor hung over the river. Even the ground seemed to be steaming. Edward sat a short distance away, idly stirring a stick in the fire. An attack of self-consciousness had Serenity burrowing deeper beneath her stiff canvas covering. She remembered very well how closely she'd snuggled against him during the night. A cold draft on her legs reminded her, too, of how little remained of her dress and that her petticoats were long gone.

"We're going to have to check on the boat." He seemed to know she was awake.

She sat up, pushing her tangle of hair away from her eyes. She tugged the sheet of canvas a little higher too.

"We need dry clothes and something warm to eat," he said, and she became aware that his clothing was as tattered as hers. His shoes rested on a rock near the fire, but she doubted he'd be able to get them on his feet again as the leather had been damaged by water, and now by heat. They were sure to have shrunk. Her own wet shoes pinched and felt uncomfortable, but she didn't dare remove them.

She was putting off the inevitable. Lowering the stiff canvas, she rose to her feet. A blush burned her cheeks as she viewed the extent of the damage to her dress and caught glimpses of her bare legs through the tattered remnants that hung from her waist. Edward didn't comment, but she knew he was aware of her immodest attire since he kept his eyes averted as she came to stand beside him.

"We might as well wade out to the boat," she said. "Once we free it from the tree, we may have to float it downstream until we find a place where we can draw it ashore and check for damage."

"I assumed we could drag it ashore here."

"Between the current and that deep hole, I don't think we can maneuver it out of the tree and drag it this direction." She began gathering up the few things they'd brought ashore. The fire was nearly out, but she brushed wet sand over it anyway.

Edward shouldered their pack again and followed her into the water with his shoes dangling over his shoulder. They reached the boat without incident and were pleased to find that it appeared to be in fairly good condition. Serenity released the rope, and together they began working the boat free of the entangling branches.

"Climb in and use the pole to keep the current from carrying it back into the tree," Serenity called to Edward. When he was safely aboard, she joined him. That's when she discovered that the oars had been lost in the storm. Using the pole to ward off the fallen tree, they managed to work their way past the obstacle and catch the current.

On a wide bend, the current slowed. Using the pole again, they worked their way to shore. As soon as the boat bumped the gravelly bottom, Edward leaped out, clutching the shortened rope. They dragged the boat as far up the riverbank as they could get it, then spent most of the day drying their supplies and clothing. Serenity was grateful none of their supplies, nor the tightly wrapped bundle of belongings from her old home, had been lost. Edward announced that he considered it a miracle that the small boat hadn't capsized when he'd tried to board it and dumped Serenity into the river instead.

Toward evening, they heard the deep bellow of a cow, followed by the bark of a dog. Curious, they followed the sound to a farmstead located only a short distance away. A couple of children could be seen playing about the yard.

"We could call at the farm and seek a night's shelter," Edward suggested, though his voice lacked enthusiasm.

"I think I would rest better beneath our canvas," Serenity replied. Besides, she didn't relish the idea of meeting anyone with bags beneath her eyes and wild hair, and wearing her homeliest gown, which had happened to be the one to dry first. In the morning she would don a better gown and arrange her hair before beginning the last day of their journey by water.

They worked together to prepare a simple meal, then Edward read to her. The familiar ritual brought her peace and comfort, and she relaxed as he read of Jacob, who had been born in the wilderness and was now the Nephite leader.

Edward read, "'But before ye seek for riches, seek ye for the kingdom of God. And after ye have obtained a hope in Christ ye shall obtain riches, if ye seek them; and ye will seek them for the intent to do good—to clothe the naked, and to feed the hungry, and to liberate the captive, and administer relief to the sick and the afflicted.'"

Surely, that was what had happened to her father. Warmth crept over Serenity, and for a moment she imagined her father was speaking. He was telling her not to worry about money, that she would have what she needed, and that it was truly his desire that his fortune be used to better the lives and opportunities of those who had been enslaved by men like her grandfather. Calm settled in her heart, and she knew Rupert Montague and Edward Benson were to be trusted both in protecting her personal financial interests and in aiding her to find the best purposes for the money her grandfather had accumulated. Tears of joy ran down her cheeks.

Edward became aware of the tears and stopped reading. Placing the book facedown on a fallen tree trunk, he took her in his arms. He didn't speak but simply held her while she cried.

After a few minutes, she straightened, drew her handkerchief from her pocket, and dried her eyes and blew her nose.

"Do you wish to talk about it?" he asked softly.

"I'm not sad. If anything I feel comforted, as though Papa were letting me know all will be well and that I'm doing the right thing."

"Remember that feeling," Edward told her. "It's called the Holy Spirit, and it's God's way of letting you know something is true."

* * *

In spite of fatigue from physical exertion and her lack of sleep the previous night, Serenity had difficulty falling asleep that night. She lay in her blankets and listened to Edward breathe. She was warm and dry, but she missed the closeness with which Edward had held her in their precarious shelter the night before. Pictures flitted through her mind of him tugging the boat ashore, clad only in his tattered pants and a shirt that clung to his shoulders by a few stubborn seams. She felt a warmth wash over her, but it wasn't the same kind of warmth she'd felt earlier when he'd read to her.

She forced herself to think of the words he'd read, and the calm comfort of feeling her father nearby came again. With that thought, she drifted to sleep.

* * *

Less than an hour on the river the following morning brought them to a small town. While Edward arranged for seats on the coach that would take them to the nearest train station, Serenity purchased bread and apples they could eat as they journeyed.

Leaving the bakery, she spotted a cobbler's shop. She'd been right about Edward's shoes; he'd been unable to get them on his feet after they dried, so now he'd been without shoes for two days. Her own shoes hadn't fared much better. She stepped into the shop and purchased sturdy walking boots for each of them, guessing at Edward's size. She then hurried to where Edward was stowing their bundles on the coach. As Edward helped her climb aboard, she was filled with nervous excitement. Their time alone was at an end, but a whole new world was opening to her. She glanced back once and wished she hadn't. A shadow shifted in a grove of trees, reminding her that though Joshua Brown was in jail, Stephen Rappleton was still out there somewhere.

18~

"They're so big, and there are so many of them!" Serenity stared in awe through the carriage window at the buildings lining the streets of Philadelphia. Her sheltered life in a rural village had done little to prepare her for so much abrupt change. It had been dusk when they'd arrived the previous evening, and Edward had taken her directly to a hotel, so she'd seen little of the city. But even the hotel had proved a new experience for her, as had traveling aboard a car pulled by a steam engine. The past week had been filled with new adventures.

After checking into the hotel, they'd eaten in the dining room, then gone to their separate rooms. Even though she was exhausted, Serenity stayed awake for a while listening to the strangeness of the city around her. At last fatigue won out, and she fell into a deep sleep.

Edward tapped on her door early the next morning and escorted her to breakfast. Then, while she packed up her few belongings and dressed in her best gown and hat, he'd rented a buggy and called at the depot for the crates they had shipped earlier. Now they were on their way to secure a place for Serenity to stay until spring, when she could begin her journey west. Edward had already been assured of a room in a dormitory wing of the hospital, which he would share with another student.

After many hours of looking at rooms in various boarding-houses, Serenity grew discouraged until Edward pointed to a small house that had once been the gatekeeper's cottage for a large estate on a quiet street. A dozen fine homes surrounded by sweeping lawns and gardens sat back from the tree-lined street, and nestled among them were a few cottages tucked among the trees, almost out of sight. Some of the cottages likely housed servants, Edward told her, but during his earlier stay in Philadelphia, he had learned that a few cottages in wealthier neighborhoods were leased to ordinary people wishing to live in quiet, respectable areas. Something about the tiny house caught at Serenity's heart. It appeared uninhabited, so Edward drove the rented buggy past it and up a long, curving lane to a large gray house fronted by stone pillars.

A maid answered the door and ushered them into a formal drawing room, where they found a tiny, gray-haired woman who was soon joined by a stooped gentleman with bushy white sideburns. The couple introduced themselves as George and Edith Frampton.

Edward stated their business.

"We've never rented the cottage," the man said in response to Edward's request.

"It has been empty many years," the woman added. "Even though it has been kept in repair and I've sent staff to clean it each spring and fall, we never thought of renting it."

"We shall be happy to do any needed work to make it habitable," Edward promised. "I will be completing my medical studies and shall be living at the hospital once the term begins, but I wish to provide my wife with acceptable accommodations and see her settled before I take up residence in the student doctors' quarters."

Serenity knew he was anxious to be free to begin his studies. She too wished to be settled. She had imposed on Edward quite long enough, and it was time to take stock of her life and make plans for her future.

At length, an agreement was reached and the elderly couple seemed pleased to have acquired a young married couple as tenants.

"There is little furniture in the cottage other than a bed, a sofa, a table, and a few chairs," Mrs. Frampton told them. "I shall send over a feather mattress and have the maids search the attic for other pieces you may have need of."

Serenity thanked the woman, saying, "We shall be greatly obliged. I brought those household items which I could from my previous home, so I shall not be in need of linens." She thought of the crates sitting in the back of the buggy, waiting to be unpacked. They would give this strange new place a connection to her childhood home.

"I'll not be at the cottage often," Edward explained. "While finishing my medical training, I will be expected to remain at the hospital most of the time and shall have little free time."

"You needn't worry about your wife," Mr. Frampton assured him. "This is a quiet street, safe from the comings and goings of the rest of the city."

Mr. Frampton sent the maid to fetch the key to the cottage and then handed it to Edward. "Feel free to move in as soon as you like," he told them.

* * *

The cottage was an enchanting place, and Serenity fell in love with it at once. It had two rooms and was surrounded by a small garden that disappeared into the extensive grove of trees separating the cottage from the main house. Trees also offered a buffer between the cottage and the street. A stone fireplace filled one end of the larger room of the cottage, a room which would double as kitchen and sitting room. The smaller room would be her bedroom. The furniture was old, but she felt certain it would welcome the treasures she'd brought from her old home and they would suit each other nicely.

Edward slept on a lumpy sofa in front of the fireplace that night. Early the next morning he bid her farewell before making his way to the hospital to register and move into the room assigned to him. Serenity occupied herself for the remainder of the day with unpacking the crates and turning the cottage into a home. She wasn't certain how long she would be there, but she meant to be as comfortable as possible throughout the winter, surrounded by items familiar and dear to her.

Edward returned that evening to report that his classes would begin on Monday next and that he had been assigned a bed in a dormitory for advanced medical students. His quarters were to be shared with another senior student, Richard Deerfield. They'd met, and Edward expressed his belief that they would suit each other admirably.

Edward looked around at the changes Serenity had made in the little cottage. He recognized a painting, several small ornaments, pillows, scarves, a tablecloth, and even the candlestick she had used as a weapon. On a little table sat her mother's Book of Mormon. Several other books filled a small nook built into one wall.

"You've made a comfortable home of the cottage," he complimented her. "I shall envy you such a warm and inviting space while I have nothing more than a narrow cot and a trunk for my books and clothing."

"Are conditions so austere at the hospital?" she asked.

"They're plain, but I'm excited about some of the lectures I'll be attending," he said. "And there will be opportunities to practice the newest surgical methods. Philadelphia is one of the most medically advanced cities in the world. There's even a medical school for women here."

"Papa sometimes got the New York papers. I read not long ago of a Boston doctor who thinks many illnesses can be cured through the application of soap and water."

"One of my professors will speak to that subject. It's rumored that a few of the doctors who treated war wounds these past five years found that keeping the wound clean and using freshly scrubbed knives and bandages produced promising results. The old doctor I worked with in Utah was committed to cleanliness as both a healing tool and a virtue."

"Well, whether it helps in healing or not, I find being clean feels better than being dirty."

Edward chuckled, then asked, "I shall be busy with my studies, but what will you do to fill your time until we can go west in the spring?"

"My mother liked to sew, but she died before she could teach me much of the skill. I brought her sewing basket and shall endeavor to teach myself to complete several projects she began. I think too, that I shall finish reading the Book of Mormon."

"If you're interested, we could go to church tomorrow. There's an immigrant ship that arrived at the Philadelphia port this morning. The converts will be holding a service before boarding a westbound train. They'll winter over in Omaha, then continue on in the spring."

"I think I would like that."

"Good. I shall hire a carriage and be here in time for breakfast." He grinned, and she felt the little catch in her chest that this particular mischievous grin always seemed to trigger inside her. "But for now, we have all day. Would you care to accompany me on a walking tour of the city?" He stood and offered his arm. Laughing, she accepted.

Serenity had never seen any place like Philadelphia, with its buildings that had been standing for a century. She recognized names and places from her father's history lessons and was duly impressed. She and Edward laughed like children. They bought fruit and fresh bread and ate their lunch alfresco in a shady grove of trees overlooking the Delaware River.

Late in the afternoon, they stopped at a market to make a few purchases to carry back to the cottage. They were both tired from their day's excursion, and Serenity persuaded Edward to spend the night on the sofa in front of the fireplace again.

Following a hasty breakfast the following morning, they set out for the port, traveling most of the distance by railway car instead of carriage. They found nearly a hundred Saints from Europe who were hoping to make their way as far as the Missouri before winter set in. Others, particularly those from Wales, had already set out for the various coal towns in Pennsylvania in hopes of finding work to see them through the winter and enable them to travel on to Salt Lake in the spring.

With the captain's permission, the group held their meeting aboard the ship on which they had arrived. The speakers took turns standing on a barrel to speak to the crowd gathered on the deck. Serenity was surprised to learn that over four hundred members of the Church had lived in Philadelphia before the

Mormons were forced from their homes in Nauvoo. Most had moved west, but there was still a small splinter group in the state who didn't accept Brigham Young as their leader. Some of the speakers encouraged the travelers to stay strong in their faith and to continue their journey as soon as possible, while others dwelt on matters pertaining to Church doctrine. She was surprised by how much she understood from her discussions with Edward. She liked the feel of being among Mormons and was glad Edward had brought her.

Following the concluding prayer, she and Edward wandered among the travelers, listening to snippets of conversation and, in Edward's case, answering questions about Salt Lake City. She was pleased to see a large number of young people her own age in the crowd. When she reached Salt Lake, she was assured she would find contemporaries with which to socialize. The prospect delighted her, as she'd never had much opportunity to enjoy friends.

The day was growing late and the sun was setting when they returned to the cottage. Edward saw her to the door, then departed for the hospital, where he would be living and working for the next twenty weeks. He promised to stop in to check on her as often as his courses allowed.

Seeing Edward turn his back to her and walk down the lane alone gave Serenity an odd feeling. At the end of the lane he turned to wave, and then he was gone. She'd never felt so alone before—not when Papa had left on one of his buying trips and not even when her parents had died.

With dragging feet, she made her way inside the cottage. Deciding she was too tired to heat water for a cup of tea, she settled for a dipper of water and a roll left over from the previous day. When she finished eating the roll, she locked the door and crawled into bed.

She awoke the following morning determined to finish setting the cottage to rights. She polished the hearth, hung curtains, and unpacked the last of the household items she'd shipped ahead. When she finished, she sat down with the Book of Mormon in her lap and read for a time.

In the following weeks, it became her habit to ponder the things she read and to reread passages that stirred her thoughts. She took a particular liking to Captain Moroni, thinking her ideals often matched his. A warm, calming feeling much like she'd experienced during her and Edward's river journey filled her as she read Alma 48:11: "And Moroni was a strong and a mighty man; he was a man of a perfect understanding; yea, a man that did not delight in bloodshed; a man whose soul did joy in the liberty and the freedom of his country, and his brethren from bondage and slavery."

At length, she tired of household tasks, reading, and struggling to make stitches somewhat similar to the ones her mother had made. In need of supplies, she made up her mind to venture from the cottage. Her first few expeditions took her around the estate, where she viewed the gardens and occasionally chanced on a maid or gardener with whom she could exchange a few words.

By the end of her third week of living alone in the cottage, she set out to find an art dealer who might wish to purchase some of Papa's more valuable small pieces, which she'd had shipped to Philadelphia. She wandered in and out of shops, enjoying herself, and eventually found two buyers who were anxious to meet her asking price for the items. All in all, she was quite satisfied with her excursion.

On her way back to the cottage she remembered a market from her stroll about town with Edward. It was surprisingly easy to find, and she filled a bag with fresh produce and a fish the butcher wrapped in paper for her. When she reached the cottage, she found a letter in her door with a note from Edward scribbled on the envelope.

"I haven't much time," he'd penned. "Barring an emergency, I shall have Wednesday off and shall be by to see you." She felt a stab of disappointment that she had been out when he came to deliver the letter, but at the same time she felt cheered knowing it wouldn't be long before she would see him again.

She took her time putting her purchases away and preparing her supper. When all was in readiness, she sat at the table. She took a few bites, then used her table knife to open the seal on the envelope Edward had delivered. Drawing out a folded piece of fine stationery, she glanced first at the signature and saw it was Rupert's.

She read the letter through, then read it again. Rupert had written to ask about her well-being and to inform her that he had transferred a large sum of money to an account at the Bank of Philadelphia. The bank had insisted that the account be in her husband's name, not hers, but Rupert said he trusted Edward would use the money to provide for her needs. He also requested that she soon journey to New York to spend a fortnight with him and his wife. He hoped they might finalize their committee and begin determining which projects they wished to fund from her father's inherited fortune.

It would be good to travel to New York, she thought. She'd long dreamed of visiting that city. It was only four hours away by train and would give her something to occupy her time while she waited for the arrival of spring. Besides, she was anxious to carry out her father's wishes and to see Julia Hayes again, who had eagerly agreed to serve on the committee.

She thought of little else over the next few days as she waited for Edward's visit. She made a list of those causes she considered most important for preparing former slaves to obtain educations and careers. Twice she walked several blocks to purchase a newspaper, hoping to become better informed on legislation and social movements that might affect how her grandfather's money should be spent.

Wednesday finally arrived, and Serenity arose early to scrub the cottage floor and polish the furniture. Donning her best dress, she spent almost thirty minutes in front of her mirror, brushing her hair one way, then another. She prepared a lovely luncheon and waited. At length, she ate by herself and tidied the cottage once more. Still Edward didn't come. She'd almost given up hope, deciding some emergency had arisen, when she heard his cheerful whistle coming up the lane.

He rapped on the door, and it was all she could do to refrain from throwing herself in his arms when he walked in. He clasped her hands and grinned. She noticed lines near his mouth and a drooping weariness around his eyes.

"Come eat," she urged. "I baked a pie from apples I purchased at the market yesterday."

"I can't stay long," he warned as he seated himself at the little wooden table. "The hospital is short-staffed, and I have to be available for emergencies all night."

She placed a large slice of pie in front of him, and he dug in with his fork as though he was starved. Catching her startled expression, he apologized. "I don't always have time for meals. The past few days have been particularly difficult because we received a new batch of returning soldiers from a field hospital that was ordered closed. Several are near death from infections, and I don't know if the new hygiene rules we've adopted in the surgery ward will be enough to save them."

"Have all of the doctors agreed to the new rules?"

"No. Some are vocal in their objections, and many of the nurses disobey Dr. Van Wagonen's orders to scrub the wards and wash their hands between patients. They say there aren't enough nurses for even their usual tasks and the procedures take too much of their time away from patients."

Serenity sat in the chair opposite Edward. When he finished his pie, she fetched a second piece for him and added a slice of cheese to the top of it while he continued to talk about the hospital and the lectures he had attended. He spoke at length of his favorite lecturer, a Professor Wickham. Finally he asked, "Have you found enough to keep you occupied?"

"Yes, I've ventured out several times to the market and discovered the post office a few days ago. I went there to mail a letter to Rupert."

"Ah yes, I assume you received his letter. He sent me one too, telling me of the money he deposited in the Bank of Philadelphia for you. It is one of the reasons I wished to see you today." He reached into his pocket and withdrew a handful of banknotes, which he set on the table. "In his note to me, Rupert explained the peculiarities of the banking system. I visited the bank on my way here and drew out funds for you."

"Oh dear." Serenity chewed on her bottom lip for a moment. "I'm not comfortable having so much cash at my disposal. I already have the money Loyal gave me for the house and the proceeds from the sale of Papa's treasures. Rupert also gave me money for our journey, and I still have more than half of that. All together it's a considerable sum."

"You should consider depositing some of it in the account Rupert arranged for you. I know it's in my name, but you have my word that I'll not touch a cent of it myself but will draw it out only as you wish."

"Keep some of it." She picked up two bills and offered them to him. "Because you spent the summer helping me, you never had an opportunity to earn sufficient funds for your needs. And this is far more than I need at the present time."

He protested, but in the end accepted her generosity. "I drew out such a large amount," he said, "because I thought you might wish to purchase a winter wardrobe. I've been told the winters are quite harsh here, and I have no idea of the cost of women's frocks and coats."

"I have plenty left for my needs. Besides, I may go to New York for a time. Rupert said I am needed there to set up the committee to distribute Grandfather Caswell's ill-gotten fortune. He suggested that while I'm there, I should also plan a shopping expedition with his wife."

"You will be careful?"

"I'm sure I shall be perfectly safe. With Joshua Brown in jail and no sign of Mr. Rappleton, I don't expect any trouble."

"That reminds me. I've thought some about your mother's ring," Edward said. "Do you still have her saddlebag?"

"I couldn't bear to part with it."

"Since the ring wasn't on your mother's hand and the bag was missing, I can only assume the thief thought she hid the ring there. Therefore he took the bag with him."

"Only it seems the ring wasn't in the bag."

"Do you think the thief examined the dolls closely? I've been wondering if she might have concealed the ring by slipping it inside a loose seam."

"It seems logical that the thief might have checked such a possibility, but it won't hurt if we examine the dolls as well." She hurried to the bedroom to retrieve the bag from the wardrobe where she had stowed it earlier. Upon returning to the other room, she released the clasp and drew out the toys, placing them on the table. Together she and Edward examined each seam. Serenity wasn't surprised to discover that each of her mother's tiny, precise stitches still held.

While Serenity returned the dolls, the wooden soldier, and the little stuffed dog to the bag, Edward picked up the wagon and turned it one way, then another, examining it closely. "The detail is astonishing. The man who carved it must have been a master woodworker," he observed. Then he looked questioningly at Serenity. "I understand why you decided to keep the dolls your mother made, but why did you keep Timothy's wagon?"

"I meant to ask him if he wished to have it back, but then he left so abruptly I didn't have the chance. I could have given it to Rosie, but again there was too much on my mind when she left. James told me a little about the old man who carved it for Timothy. I think someday Timothy will settle down and wish to have it as a memento of the man who acted as a grandfather to him and James. Or he may wish to pass it on to his own son. Anyway, if I remember my geography correctly, we shall pass Fort Laramie on our way to Salt Lake next spring. If he's still there, I shall give it to him."

Edward handed the toy back to Serenity, then stood. "I must be on my way. I don't know when I shall be able to come again." He handed her a slip of paper. "If you have need of me, send word to this address."

"I shall do so," she promised, slipping the paper into the pocket of her apron.

"When do you plan to leave for New York?"

"I shall wait until I hear from Rupert and will send you word before I depart."

19

Serenity stepped down from the train onto the station platform and looked around at the crowds of people and luggage that seemed to be rushing in every direction. New York City was a bustling city, but it was no larger than Philadelphia. It just seemed bigger and busier because of the rapid pace, the tall buildings, and the many dialects she could hear bandied about. Rupert had wired her that he would meet her, but she didn't see him. Though the noise and confusion were startling, she did her best to look poised. She didn't wish to appear as a raw country girl.

Several people were waving signs bearing various names. One such sign caught her eye. She looked again to assure herself that the sign did indeed bear her name. Then, feeling hesitant, she walked toward the young man holding the card.

Before she could speak, he smiled appreciatively at her. "You must be Serenity Benson," he said, lowering the sign. "Father is unable to get away from his office, so he sent me in his stead."

Taking a closer look, she could see that the young man showed a definite resemblance to Rupert. He was tall with dark, wavy hair that fell across his forehead in a perfect curl. His eyes were an intense, warm brown, and one eyebrow arched in a question as he watched her appraisal of him, reminding her of his father's habit of raising one brow in just such an expressive manner.

"My name is Jerome Montague. Mr. Montague sounds so stuffy, I should be delighted if you would call me Jerome." His smile widened, and there was a twinkle in his eyes. He was a decidedly attractive young man. "Come, let us collect your luggage and we shall be on our way. Mother is most anxious to make your acquaintance."

Serenity held up her carpet bag. "I have only one small bag."

"Only one?" He stared at her quizzically, seeming nonplussed that a lady should travel so lightly. "Very well, then we shall proceed at once." He took the bag and offered her his arm. She stifled an urge to giggle—there was something terribly grand about parading before so many people on the arm of such a fine-looking young gentleman.

The journey from the depot to the Montague estate occupied a good hour, but Serenity found the time passed quickly as her escort pointed out places of interest and entertained her with a ready supply of amusing stories. By the time they reached the gates leading up to a large two-story house with graceful columns on either side of a wide entryway, she felt they were old friends.

Jerome escorted her up the front steps to a double door that was opened by a maid who quickly left them to summon Mrs. Montague. She and Jerome waited but a moment in the marble entry.

"Dear child," exclaimed a tiny woman with blond curls piled high on her head and the widest skirts Serenity had ever seen. The skirts crackled as she rushed across the foyer. "Rupert has told me so much about you, I feel that we can't possibly be strangers." She took Serenity's hands in her own small ones and gazed at her in admiration. "I've waited eighteen years to make your acquaintance, ever since your father announced your arrival."

Serenity didn't quite know how to respond. "Papa seldom spoke of the people he knew in New York," she stammered.

"Be that as it may, I knew your dear father, may God rest his soul, and have longed to express my condolences to you. His company was always a pleasure, and he shall be greatly missed in the years to come."

"Thank you," Serenity murmured.

"Oh, it shall be a delight to accompany a young lady, especially one of such pleasing aspects, as you acquire a new wardrobe and are introduced to society. We must begin first thing in the morning, as the Pendergast soiree is but two days away. We shall begin with a few ready-made frocks, then later we'll make the rounds of the tailoring establishments."

Serenity wasn't certain she relished the prospect of traipsing to the various shops and standing still for fittings. She was only in need of a couple of wool gowns and a thick coat and bonnet to keep her warm through the winter. She was more anxious to begin organizing the committee and selecting projects than she was to spend her time shopping. "There is much business I must attend to . . ." she began.

"Oh pshaw! There's always business. You mustn't let Rupert monopolize your visit. Come, let me show you to your room. After riding on one of those dreadful steam cars, you no doubt need to refresh yourself and rest before dinner." She linked her arm through Serenity's and led the way up a wide, curved staircase, chattering in a delightful way. When they reached the curve of the stairway, Serenity glanced back. Jerome smiled in a good-natured way and waved two fingers before disappearing through a door.

Serenity gasped when she saw the room to which Mrs. Montague had led her. A bed wide enough for four sat on a dais. Yards of sheer silk formed a canopy over the bed, hung at the windows, and looped in swags beneath the bed and over two paintings of idealized English gardens. A pale green carpet liberally sprinkled with pink roses the size of cabbages covered the floor, and two moss-green chairs and a divan formed a sitting area. A dainty rosewood secretary was positioned before the large window that overlooked an immense expanse of lawn and garden. An armoire and several tables completed the furnishings, and a bouquet of fresh roses graced the largest of the tables. Her bedroom at the cottage and the one she'd slept in while growing up would both fit in just one corner of this grand room.

"I shall send a maid to fetch you when dinner is served," Mrs. Montague promised before sweeping out of the room.

Serenity looked around in awe. She'd grown up surrounded by beautiful things and high-quality furnishings, but she had never seen anything like this house and the marvels it contained. She wasn't certain what anyone would do with so much space, and the abundance of paintings and decorations made her almost dizzy. Each piece taken separately was no doubt beautiful, but altogether, they seemed overwhelming. Perhaps she only thought so because her mother had been raised a Quaker and had retained a taste for simpler things. Upon reflection, she remembered her home had been furnished much more austerely before her mother's death and that it was Papa who had added most of the paintings and art objects that filled it later.

She dressed in the best gown she'd brought with her and was suddenly conscious of the dull color and plain white cuffs and collar. She fussed with her hair, feeling quite certain that her normal style would not do for such high society. Finally, she gathered it in a loose knot atop her head and allowed a profusion of tiny ringlets to cascade from either side to her shoulders. She had a few nice pieces of jewelry, which had been gifts from her father. She retrieved these from her carpet bag and decided to add a pair of ruby-and-pearl earrings to her ensemble. They weren't large jewels, nor nearly as impressive as her mother's ring, but they were dear to her because Papa had given them to her on her fifteenth birthday.

A maid tapped on her door to let her know that it was time for dinner and that Jerome was waiting to conduct her to the dining hall. He met her at the foot of the staircase and tucked her arm through his.

"You look lovely," he whispered as he whisked her through double doors leading off the hall. It was a good thing he had a firm grip on her arm, or she might have swooned. At least twenty people were seated at a long table, and several servers stood at attention beside a long sideboard. They all turned to watch her enter. More crystal and silver than she'd ever imagined existed glittered down the length of the table.

The gentlemen all rose to their feet as Jerome escorted her down the length of the table to where Rupert stood. Rupert stepped toward her and lightly kissed her cheek.

"I'm so pleased to see you have arrived safely," he said. And in a softer voice he added, "I requested a simple family dinner for tonight to give you a chance to get to know us, but Emmaline doesn't know the meaning of a simple meal."

Jerome pulled out a chair to seat her, then took the chair on her right for himself. Seated between Rupert and Jerome, Serenity found that the meal passed in a blur of food and more conversation than she could absorb. She discovered that the young man seated across from her was Rupert's other son, Delbert, who appeared to be much more studious and quiet than his younger brother. After the meal, he whispered something to his father and left the gathering. The others retired to a long drawing room, where several ladies took turns playing the pianoforte or singing.

As Serenity sat on a divan and tried to give her attention to the young woman who was singing, she found her head nodding and had to struggle to stay awake. After all the excitement of her first trip to New York, the four-hour train ride, and too much to eat, she only wished to lay her head down and sleep.

The young lady who was singing looked her way several times and didn't seem pleased with what she saw. Her disapproval reminded Serenity to keep her back straight and pretend interest in the endless songs. At length, Jerome took pity on her and invited her for a stroll on the verandah to clear her head.

The cooler evening air proved beneficial, and Serenity stood at the rail sniffing the few late roses that trailed up several columns and were putting forth their final burst of bloom before cold weather descended. She listened absently as Jerome listed several recent social events he had attended and then described an upcoming event he felt certain she would enjoy. She didn't respond but breathed deeply.

"Your garden is lovely," she remarked. "I shall look forward to exploring it tomorrow."

"I shall be happy to escort you now," Jerome offered.

"Thank you, but no. The evening is beginning to grow chill, and I shall enjoy the colors more fully by daylight."

"There you are," a voice called. Serenity looked up to see Rupert approaching them. Beside him was the young lady who had been singing when they left the parlor. She ignored Serenity but beamed at Jerome.

"I had hoped to find you before you retired for the evening," Rupert said. "I've some plans I hoped you'd have time to look over before we meet with the rest of the committee." He drew her deftly away from Jerome. Her last glimpse of Jerome showed him directing a look of sharp disapproval at the young woman who clutched at his coat sleeve.

Soon Serenity and Rupert were ensconced in the library with blueprints for a proposed college spread across the desk. Serenity examined them eagerly, though several times she found herself attempting to conceal a yawn.

"My apologies for keeping you up so late," Rupert said, sounding tired himself. He rolled the blueprint into a cylinder and tucked it inside a cabinet. He then pulled from the cabinet a large, stiff envelope. "I know you must be tired from your journey. Take this file of proposals upstairs with you to look over. Julia and Rosie will be arriving in two days, and we shall begin our meetings the following day. I shall be involved at the bank until then, so you should have plenty of time to rest and read the file."

He showed her another staircase, suggesting she avoid the drawing room where guests were still gathered. "I shall say your good nights for you," he promised.

* * *

Serenity slept better than she'd expected to in a strange bed. She also arose later than was her custom. She dressed quickly, then was uncertain whether she should go downstairs or wait to be summoned. Not feeling particularly hungry, she opened the file Rupert had given her, settled on a small sofa, and began to read. She was still reading when a soft tap sounded on her door, followed by the door opening silently to admit the maid who had summoned her to dinner the previous evening.

"Ah, you are awake. Would you care to go downstairs for breakfast or would you like a tray delivered here?"

"Goodness! There's no need to carry up a tray. I shall be happy to go downstairs for breakfast if you will show me the way." She smiled at the maid, who hesitantly returned the smile.

A few minutes later she was seated in a sunny room with a full plate before her. She nibbled at toast and took a few bites of a fluffy egg concoction before she was joined by Jerome.

"An early riser, I see." He heaped his plate from a sideboard laid out with various dishes, then carried it to the table and seated himself across from her. He bit into his jelly-laden toast and drank deeply from his cup before sending one of his lazy smiles her way, causing a slight flutter in her chest.

"You must think me a slug-a-bed for not rising as early as Father and Delbert," he said, though his smile indicated he wasn't unduly concerned. "Father always heads for his bank before the sun is fully up, and Delbert has been accompanying him of late. Now that old 'Bert is through with school, he has quite set his mind to learning Father's dull business."

"Will you work at the bank too when you've finished with school?" Serenity asked, making polite conversation.

Jerome laughed. "Not likely. I've no wish to be tied down to a stuffy old bank."

Serenity remembered Rupert commenting that his younger son was attending a university near their home in New York, while the older one had studied in Boston. "Have you no classes today?" she asked.

"It makes little difference whether I return to school today or tomorrow. Mother is taking you shopping today, and I prefer to escort the two of you and collect parcels for you."

"Shopping? But I had planned—"

"I won't listen to objections," Emmaline Montague called from the doorway as she sailed into the room. "I really must see that you are properly attired before Rupert drags you off to his dreadful meetings. I have instructed the maid to retrieve your cloak and reticule for you."

* * *

Serenity had done little shopping in her life other than for produce at local markets. When she needed a new gown, she'd visited the village seamstress or one of the Quaker women who was happy to trade her skill with a needle for a bushel of apples.

On this first excursion into the fashionable New York City shops, she was measured and measured again. An endless array of fabrics was held before her to see if the colors would do, and there were dozens of laces and ribbons that had to be matched. When she tried to protest, her objections were ignored.

When Emmaline was finally finished ordering cloaks, gowns, and the petticoats and underpinnings to go with them, Jerome drove them to an elegant tea room. There Serenity nibbled on tiny cucumber sandwiches and elaborately decorated cakes. She found the delicate strawberry ice Jerome ordered for her a delightful new experience, and she soon relaxed and found herself giggling as Jerome set about entertaining her with witty tales of life in the bustling city. New York was proving to be just as romantic and exciting as she'd once dreamed.

At the conclusion of tea, she was disappointed to discover that their shopping wasn't finished. She had hoped she could return to her room at the Montague house to study her papers, but there were still shoes and hats to order. She feared she might need to hire an entire train car to haul all the things Emmaline ordered for her back to Philadelphia.

She didn't see Rupert or Delbert that evening, and Emmaline ordered a tray delivered to her room, leaving Serenity and Jerome to dine alone in the spacious dining room. Seated across from each other at one end of the long table, the two young people discussed their foray into the city. Jerome was witty and in high spirits, causing Serenity to laugh several times. Still, the rich food and the exhausting day began to take their toll and she found herself struggling to keep her eyes open. At length the meal was finished.

"Should you care to join me for a game of cards in the drawing room?" Jerome asked.

"I must beg off," she protested. "I am quite weary and wish to retire."

"Very well," he agreed. "I shall escort you to your room." He tucked her hand in the crook of his arm and moved at a leisurely pace toward the stairs, sharing amusing anecdotes as he walked beside her. When they reached her room she pulled her hand free, but before she could twist the doorknob, he captured both of her hands in his, leaving her unsure how she should react.

"It has been a pleasure to share this day with you," he said.

"It has been both interesting and amusing," she replied. "I appreciate the time you and your mother have spent helping me."

"The pleasure has been ours." He smiled, then pressed a kiss to the back of her hand before allowing her to enter her room.

With her back to the closed door, she sighed deeply. She wished Jerome hadn't kissed her hand. She was sure there was nothing improper about the gesture, but she was unaccustomed to such familiarity and something about the pressure of his lips on the back of her hand disturbed her in some vague way. She was a married woman, she reminded herself, but a small voice in the back of her head suggested she wasn't really a wife.

She picked up the file of papers, then set it back down. She was too tired for the file. She knelt hastily beside the bed to pray, then crawled beneath the quilt. Tomorrow she would have more time.

The next day became a repeat in most ways of the first day, though this time she was poked and measured as she tried on gowns that were already sewn, but which would require altering before they would fit her to Emmaline's exacting standards.

Turning one way, then another to better see in a tall cheval glass, she hardly recognized herself in the dusty rose gown. Emmaline had insisted she try it on, even though a half dozen other dresses had already been selected. Ivory lace and deep rose braid trimmed the bodice and formed wide bands across the skirt. It was the most elegant dress Serenity had ever seen, and it fit as though it had been made especially for her. At last Emmaline said that it would do and proceeded to search out slippers to match. Taking the dress and slippers with them, they left the shop to find Jerome waiting for them. He took charge of the parcel and tucked it in the boot at the back of the buggy before assisting the two ladies into the seats.

Serenity was pleased when he urged the horses away from the shops. Shopping had been an exciting adventure, but she was glad to be done with it. It was still early, and she would have time to study the papers Rupert had given her.

When they reached the Montague home, which she'd learned was generally called Montague House, Jerome turned the horses over to a waiting servant at the foot of the porch stairs, then linked his arms with those of the two ladies and escorted them inside.

"Now dear," Emmaline said as she paused before a mirror in the grand foyer to inspect her reflection, "I shall instruct the kitchen to send up a light lunch, then you must sleep for a time. I shall send someone to wake you when it is time to begin dressing. The rose gown will do, and it is sure to start you off in splendid style."

Serenity tried to smile. "You have invited guests for dinner again?" She felt disappointed. A formal dinner followed by entertainment would cut sadly into the time she meant to study.

"No, no." Emmaline's laugh was like the tinkling of a tiny bell. "I thought I had explained. The Rothchilds are holding a ball this evening and are expecting us for dinner before the dancing begins."

Serenity's heart sank. She'd never danced a step in her life, unless one counted dancing with the fairies as a small child each spring, when the orchard was filled with blossoms and a lilting breeze beckoned. "But I can't—"

"I won't hear any objections," Emmaline insisted. "The Rothchilds are dear friends and they would be offended if they weren't allowed to be the first to entertain you."

Serenity nodded. She would just have to read quickly instead of taking a nap, she decided.

In her room, Serenity removed her shoes and curled up on the divan with the thick packet of project plans in her lap. She read until the words began to blur. Her head sank lower and lower.

"Miss. Miss!" An insistent whisper awakened her. "Madam Montague said I should wake you and tell you that you have just enough time to dress before the carriage is brought around."

20

The Rothchild mansion was even larger than Montague House, which in Serenity's estimation was practically a castle. The ceiling of the ballroom was covered with a vast painting of a bucolic country scene enlivened with cherubs and pixies. A riot of late-blooming flowers and colorful leaves filled massive urns on every table. Gentlemen attired in dark trousers and evening coats with their hair tied back in short queues twirled brightly gowned ladies across a gleaming dance floor.

Serenity felt confident that her gown was as lovely as any in the room. The maid who had come to awaken her had also pressed the gown and stayed to create an elegant hairstyle for her. Serenity had known the maid's efforts were successful the moment she descended the staircase and all three of the Montague men expressed their approval of her appearance. She felt pretty and stylish, a condition she'd never given much thought to until her arrival in New York.

The music kept her feet tapping, and she regretted that she'd never learned to dance. The Quakers disapproved of dancing, and her father had never shown any interest in teaching her dance steps. She imagined that swaying to the delightful music would be almost heaven.

Jerome's voice startled her from her thoughts. "May I have this dance?" he asked, bending low before her in a courtly bow.

Blushing and stammering, she explained that she'd never learned to dance. He seemed startled by her admission, then leaned forward to whisper, "There's a small balcony just off the sitting room on the north side of the ballroom. Meet me there in ten minutes and I shall teach you to dance."

After he turned away, she considered whether or not she should allow Jerome to instruct her. She didn't know whether it was proper for a married woman to dance with a man other than her husband. Thinking of her marriage brought a frown to her face. When the butler had announced the Montagues and her as they'd entered the ballroom, he'd called out "Miss Serenity Caswell." Not wishing to make a scene, she'd made no attempt to correct him, but she'd felt like a fraud for staying silent. She knew little about society rules, but come to think of it, she supposed it would make no difference if she danced with Jerome, since no one other than Rupert and his family even knew of her marriage.

Most of the time she tried not to think about being married. Sometimes she doubted the marriage was even valid, since she and Edward didn't live together and their relationship was more that of dear friends than of husband and wife. Thinking of Edward, she wished he were present. It would be perfectly acceptable to dance with him, and he wouldn't laugh if she made mistakes.

Her foot was tapping again. This might be her only opportunity to dance. Soon she'd be traveling to Utah, and she had no idea whether Mormons allowed dancing. She rose to her feet and casually crossed to the sitting room. A curtain at the far end of the room blew gently, indicating an open door beyond it.

Serenity stepped onto the balcony and was conscious first of gas lights glowing in the dark as far as she could see, then of a chill breeze that warned winter was not far off. Jerome stepped out of the darkness into the puddle of light coming from the window behind her. He reached for her hands.

"I knew you would come." There was a note of triumph in his voice that awakened a hint of concern as she wondered how he could have been so certain of her actions. She hadn't known herself that she would meet him on the balcony until she'd made her way to the open door. His hands tightened on hers as if he would draw her closer to prevent her from changing her mind.

She took a step backward. "All right, teach me to dance."

The pressure on her fingers tightened, then relented. "Watch my feet," he instructed before demonstrating three simple steps. Soon she was duplicating his movements, then she graduated to moving with him to the music that drifted from the ballroom. After a momentary awkwardness, she let him lead and found she didn't need to think about the steps.

"Excellent," Jerome whispered in her ear as he twirled her around the small space. She smiled, pleased with his praise. The music seemed to flow through her and out her feet. She forgot the chill breeze and saw only the stars in the sky and the lights of the city. Dancing seemed to be the most beautiful and natural movement in the world.

After a short time the music stopped, and then it commenced again with an entirely different rhythm. Once more Jerome demonstrated the steps. Then, holding each other's hands crossed in front of them, they tried it together, with much laughter and several missed steps.

"This one is meant to be danced in a set of four couples," Jerome explained, giving up on the dance. Leading her to the balustrade that ran around the balcony, he rested his elbows on the stone ledge without releasing her hand. Standing close together, they looked out over the vast park that surrounded the mansion. Neither of them spoke for several minutes. A bright harvest moon hung low over the bare trees, bathing their view with silvery rays.

"I'm glad you are here," Jerome said finally in a low voice. "The city has been brightened considerably by your presence."

Serenity didn't know how to respond. She hadn't been the recipient of enough compliments in her life, particularly from gentlemen, to feel comfortable with the lavish remarks Jerome so easily showered on her. His words made her conscious of how closely they stood, and she withdrew her hand from his.

"I think I should return to the ballroom," she told him.

"Yes," Jerome sighed as though greatly disappointed. "It would not do for our absence to be noted. I shall step back into the sitting room, then signal when it is clear for you to leave the balcony.

Make your way to the powder room at the end of the hall, then after a few minutes return to the ballroom by way of the hall."

Serenity shivered while waiting for Jerome's signal. The light wind had grown stronger and leaves drifted in the air. A faint whistle came from beyond the open window. When at last she stepped from behind the curtain into the sitting room, there was no sign of Jerome, but by following his instructions she made her way to the powder room. There, she studied herself in the glass and was embarrassed to find that a dried leaf was caught in her upswept hair and that several tendrils of the dark mass had slipped from their pins, assisted no doubt by both the breeze and her exertions. She removed the leaf immediately and repaired her hairstyle.

A sense of guilt, though she didn't feel she'd done anything wrong, caused her to glance around to see if any of the ladies preening before the mirror had noticed. One set of cornflower blue eyes met hers. They were filled with laughing amusement.

Before she could make an excuse and claim she'd stepped outside because the ballroom had grown stuffy, the young lady leaned close to whisper, "I won't tell. Everyone steps outside for a whiff of fresh air. No one, except a few cranky old ladies, cares." Linking her arm through Serenity's, she continued. "Come, we shall return together with none the wiser. My name is Pauline Sebastian," the young woman introduced herself. "Please call me Pauline."

"And I am Serenity B—Caswell," Serenity amended, thinking it might be best to keep her marital status secret from Pauline, who seemed to be a little too knowing and quick to make assumptions.

Arm in arm, the two young women made their way to the ballroom, easily discussing the decorations and the crush of people filling the mansion. Serenity noticed that Pauline's gown was a bit worn and her slippers showed signs of use. There were lines around her eyes, and she wasn't quite as young as Serenity had at first supposed.

Emmaline Montague met Serenity at the door to the ballroom and hurried her inside. "It just isn't proper for a young lady to disappear for more than a few minutes," Emmaline scolded, though in a perfectly kind voice.

"I'm sorry. It's my fault," Pauline said, appearing close to tears. "I don't know many people here, and I felt self-conscious about my lack of dance partners. Father is occupied with cards, and I was feeling alone, so I fled to the powder room. Miss Caswell saw me there. She consoled me and gave me encouragement to give the gentlemen another chance."

Emmaline gave the girl a sharp glance, then, taking Serenity's arm, began to lead her away from her new friend.

"Good-bye," Serenity whispered. "Perhaps we shall have a chance to get better acquainted another time."

Emmaline steered her to a distant sofa, leaving Pauline behind. Serenity couldn't imagine why the girl had created such a fantastic story. She considered telling Emmaline the truth, but she feared doing so would bring maternal wrath down on Jerome's head. By this time, she was certain that it had indeed been improper for her to spend so much time alone in his company. It annoyed her that Jerome had been so careless with her reputation, but she could easily forgive him since he'd only intended to teach her to dance and since it had been a delightful experience.

Delbert appeared at her side to request a dance, and she graciously accepted. His movements were stiff, but she managed to follow his lead. His conversation consisted of a few polite phrases, and he seemed relieved when the dance ended, leading her to conclude he'd only asked her to dance out of social courtesy. That stilted dance, however, seemed to open a floodgate, releasing a deluge of young gentlemen eager to waltz her onto the ballroom floor.

Jerome stood before her, crowding out all other contenders for the final dance. Slipping into his arms felt easy and natural. He was by far her most accomplished partner of the evening, and his conversation the most entertaining. It was with regret that she made her final curtsy when the song ended.

He offered his arm, and she walked from the ballroom between him and Delbert. Rupert and Emmaline preceded them. Just as Jerome handed her into the carriage, she caught sight of a figure standing behind a hedge watching. It was just a glimpse of long blond hair and a familiar gown, but she felt certain the woman standing in the shadows was Pauline Sebastian.

* * *

"Julia, Rosie." Serenity embraced the two women who had arrived at the bank prior to her own arrival. "I have missed you so. When did you arrive? Did you have a good journey?" She was glad Rosie had accompanied her mother and that the older woman hadn't had to travel alone.

Julia sniffed. "We come yesterday. Mistah Rupert send us train tickets. The train be much faster than horses or walkin', but cold an' drafty. An' the soot took three washings to get out of our clothes. We was right glad for the nice room that Professor Carter took us to with plenty of water."

"Goodness, did you sit in an open car?"

"That uppity conductor boy, he say covered cars is for white folks only."

Serenity hugged Julia and Rosie again and said, "I'm so sorry! I guess it'll take time for society to change."

Rupert escorted two scholarly looking gentlemen into his office at the rear of the bank. The older one was black, slightly heavyset, and wearing wire-rimmed eyeglasses. He was introduced as Professor Carver. The younger man, Professor Osgood, was white and seemed to bounce with each step he took. Both were equally excited about laying the groundwork for a Negro college in New York.

Serenity felt overwhelmed as the three men discussed several properties that could be leased for the college. The discussion then turned to teacher qualifications, whether women should be admitted as well as men, dormitories for students, and whether the college should employ only Negroes. She wished she could just sit back like Rosie and simply be an observer, but Rupert would not allow that. He made a point of drawing her and Julia into the discussion, and Julia was soon making her presence felt. It took a little longer for Serenity to feel comfortable expressing her views. It was only when she remembered that it was her grandfather's money that would fund the college that she became more free about asking questions and stating her opinions.

"A budget for the college needs to be drawn up before we vote on it," she said. "Though there is a need for such a college, there is a greater need for village schools." She didn't want her grandfather's entire fortune spent on a college when most freed slaves couldn't write their own names or work simple math problems. And there was the matter of land. Until the freed slaves became landholders, their progress would be limited. She suggested that Congress be lobbied to ensure that black heads of households were eligible for homestead rights.

Their discussion continued most of the morning, and it was well past lunchtime when Rupert called a halt. Serenity was surprised to find that so much time had passed.

"I have bank business to attend to this afternoon," Rupert explained. "But we shall meet again tomorrow morning to work out details. I shall have my secretary prepare papers outlining the specific costs of the proposals we have discussed."

Serenity was disappointed to learn that Julia and Rosie wouldn't be returning to the Montague House with her but would be staying at the boardinghouse Professor Carver had taken them to the previous evening after meeting their train.

She waved to Delbert as she left the bank and was surprised to see Jerome waiting for her with the buggy instead of the man the Montagues employed to run errands and care for the horses. He seated her and took care to tuck a robe across her lap. Seating himself beside her, he snapped the reins and the horses trotted forward.

Snuggled beneath the thick wool robe, Serenity's thoughts remained with the meeting she'd just left. It was exciting to be part of such an important venture. She felt confident Papa would be proud of the steps the committee was taking to right the wrongs perpetrated by her grandfather. She decided to study her notes more thoroughly when she reached her room.

She covered her mouth to hide a yawn. She had retired to bed late following the ball the previous evening, and she'd arisen early to accompany Rupert and Delbert to the bank. Traffic was heavy, and Jerome was occupied driving. Gradually, Serenity's eyes closed and her head tilted toward Jerome's shoulder.

The sharp turn into the long lane leading to Montague House jostled her awake. She looked around sleepily without raising her head. As her senses returned, she discovered to her acute embarrassment that she was curled against Jerome's side, her head resting on his shoulder, and that he had his arm wrapped possessively around her.

She sat up at once, feeling a flush of embarrassment creep up her face. "I'm so sorry," she said. "I'm not accustomed to late nights."

"I'm not complaining," Jerome responded with a smile. "I like the feel of you beside me."

Serenity blushed furiously. "You shouldn't say things like that," she admonished him. "You forget, I am a married woman."

He looked at her oddly. "It's my understanding that your marriage was just a temporary convenience to prevent a thief from stealing your inheritance, and that it would be a simple matter to apply for an annulment."

"Edward is studying to become a doctor. He hasn't had time to think about an annulment." She didn't like explaining anything so personal as her marriage. Neither was she pleased that Rupert had shared information about her personal life with his family. To be fair, though, she had to admit he'd likely had to explain to Emmaline why she was visiting them instead of coming to live in their household as his ward.

When they reached the house, a servant came rushing toward them to take over the care of the horses. Jerome handed Serenity down from the buggy, his hold on her waist lingering in a familiar manner. "I'm sure Father could arrange the necessary paperwork. Your friend would only need to sign . . ." Jerome attempted to speak to her as they walked up the steps, but she hurried ahead to her room. She didn't want to discuss Edward or their marriage. She needed some time alone.

In the quiet of her room, she hung up her cloak and washed her face. She watched her reflection in the mirror that hung above her washstand and admitted to herself that she didn't want to think about ending her marriage to Edward. Theirs wasn't a real marriage, it was true, and Edward would probably be relieved to be free of responsibility for her. She'd been selfish and unfair to ask him to marry her. But he'd been kind to her and had put her needs before his own ever since the day her father died. She wished she could be as noble in setting him free, but something held her back.

Carrying her portfolio of papers and notes to the little rosewood desk, she seated herself on the matching graceful wooden chair. She wasn't going to repeat the mistake she'd made the day before of getting so comfortable that she'd fall asleep instead of studying the papers. At first, she had difficulty thinking of anything but the dilemma she faced over her marriage. After a time, however, the words on the papers spread before her brought vivid pictures to her mind of the plight faced by the many slaves who had gained freedom but who still lacked education, land, and political clout. She became so deeply engrossed that a knock on her door startled her.

Rising to her feet, she moved reluctantly toward the door. She halfway expected to find Jerome at her door, but she should have known he wouldn't commit such a grievous breach of manners under his mother's nose. Instead of Jerome, she discovered a maid who had been sent to inform her that it was time to dress for dinner.

She changed to one of the dresses that had been delivered in her absence. The soft fabric and smooth lines of the gown bolstered her confidence, and she set out for the dining room, anxious to not keep the family waiting. She was surprised to see Jerome waiting at the top of the stairs as he had each night since her arrival. Smiling his slow, lazy smile, he complimented her on her gown, then held out his arm. Behaving as though their earlier rift hadn't occurred, he escorted her to the dining room, where again more than a dozen guests awaited them.

21

The days passed quickly, with her mornings filled with meetings and her afternoons given to study, fittings for her new wardrobe, and short naps. The evenings continued in a mad social swirl. Jerome never brought up the matter of her marriage again, but if anything, he was more attentive than before. Though Serenity had little choice but to allow him to drive her back to Montague House each afternoon, she took care not to indulge in any more private dancing lessons.

The Montagues hadn't attended church her first Sunday in New York, and, not being in the habit of attending church services anyway, Serenity hadn't found it unusual. But as the second Sunday approached, Emmaline announced that they must all be ready to attend the noon service the following day. The announcement brought Serenity feelings of both excitement and guilt. She'd enjoyed the service she'd attended with Edward and now looked forward to again experiencing the feelings she'd felt that day. On the other hand, she felt guilty. In the whirl of activities since her arrival in New York, she'd found little time to think about her growing conviction that the Book of Mormon was true. Most nights she fell into bed too exhausted to even remember to kneel and pray.

More of the gowns that had been ordered arrived at the house, and Serenity was glad Emmaline had insisted that she order more than the two she had originally intended. Her estimation of her needs had missed the mark by a great deal, since she'd had no idea of the social demands that would be incumbent upon her during her stay in the city. Neither had she a prior inkling of the immense satisfaction to be derived from being attired in beautiful, fashionable gowns and being the recipient of so many compliments.

Looking around at the ladies alighting from various carriages, she was glad for the dark green velvet cloak and elaborately embroidered bonnet trimmed with black braid that Emmaline had insisted she wear that morning. It set off her nearly black hair and pale complexion most satisfactorily. It also complimented exactly the lighter hue of her lavender gown with its gored skirt. The flat front panel extending from neckline to hem suited her thin shape and was flattering when she walked, but the wide hooped skirt took up a great deal of space when she was seated.

During the stroll up the steps and down a long aisle to the family's pew, she was awed by the multi-colored windows and the elaborately carved side panels of the pews and pulpit. The pulpit sat on a dais well above the pews. Behind it, light fell on a huge cross and the tortured face of the Man who hung there. It was both magnificent and horrible. It brought to mind something Edward had said when she'd asked him about the various stories she'd heard about Mormons not being Christians because they hadn't placed a cross on their temple. "We don't worship a dead god," he'd replied, "but One who triumphed over death. Instead of dwelling on His death, we believe He lives." She thought she'd rather dwell on a living God too.

Considerable angling was required to constrict the two women's skirts to the Montague family pew without forfeiting their modesty. Once Serenity was seated between Jerome and Delbert, she took in her surroundings and admired the high ceiling, the stained glass windows, and the soaring sound of an organ. This grand edifice differed greatly from the simple Quaker meetinghouse she had been in a few times while visiting the Nixons.

She soon discovered there was also little similarity between the services. At the Friends' meetings, a number of men and women had stood to deliver impromptu interpretations of various Bible verses. The sermon delivered by the Montagues' pastor, on the other hand, was long and tedious and made little sense to her. She thought longingly of the shipboard service she'd attended with Edward. The sermons there had interested her far more than the tiresome lecture delivered by the ornately robed man at the lectern.

Serenity was, however, enthralled by the music. She'd been raised with little exposure to music other than an occasional music box that passed through Papa's store and the soft sound of congregational singing that drifted from the town church on Sunday mornings. She promptly fell in love with the choir and the opportunity to stand between the Montague brothers and share their hymnal. By the second or third verse of each hymn, she was able to join her voice to those around her. She wondered briefly if God was offended by the music. But as she sang, a calm peace, the one Edward had taught her to recognize as the Holy Spirit, filled her heart and she knew God did not hold the soaring hymns in ill favor.

A warm shiver passed over her as she had a brief recollection of her mother holding her on her lap and singing to her when she was a small child. The memory further calmed her concerns. Mamma wouldn't have sung to her if it were wrong to expose her to music. She remembered too from Mamma's Book of Mormon that the Nephites broke into song in celebration of their victory over the Gadianton robbers. She'd marked the passage in Third Nephi because she could identify with their happiness and gratitude. It seemed to describe her own feelings when Sheriff Compton and Fenton Simmons rescued her and Edward from the robbers who had attempted to steal her mother's missing ring.

Once the singing ended, she lost interest in the church service and made no more attempt to listen to the sermon. A kind of melancholy filled her heart. She wished she knew what had become of Mamma's topaz ring. She also wished she had brought Mamma's book with her to New York.

* * *

By mid-week she could see the committee wouldn't be finished by the end of the week, when she had planned to return to Philadelphia. There was no pressing reason for her to return as originally planned, so she extended her stay another week. That week turned into two. Then two more.

She didn't think about the cottage or her father as much. Edward seemed almost like a distant memory. Everywhere she turned, Jerome was there to make her laugh and give her entry to the best of New York society. Now her afternoons often included callers or visits with Emmaline to the homes of some of her friends.

It no longer seemed strange to wear beautiful gowns or dance until dawn. It was flattering, too, that she never lacked for partners. Several young women her own age from prominent families extended frequent invitations to her, and they giggled and whispered with her between dances and at the entertainments where they met.

Pauline Sebastian often sought her out at the various entertainments, and they became close confidantes. It was a new and rewarding experience to have such a good friend. The discovery that Pauline had also lost her mother at a young age seemed to bind them closer, and Serenity sympathized with her friend because unlike her own dear Papa, Pauline's father had drowned his grief in liquor and cards. Serenity sensed that Emmaline didn't approve of their friendship and she began to suspect her hostess was a bit of a snob who found fault with Pauline because her gowns were not as elegant as those worn by most of the other young ladies. Whenever they chanced on each other while strolling in the park or at less formal functions, they managed to slip away from Emmaline for a few precious minutes. On one such occasion, Pauline requested that Serenity meet her alone in the park the following afternoon.

Knowing of Emmaline's habit of taking an afternoon nap, Serenity walked the few short blocks to the meeting place without fear of discovery. She found Pauline in tears. Wrapping her arms around the other young woman, she begged to know the cause of her unhappiness.

"Papa insists that I journey to the country for a time. He wishes me to visit an aging aunt from whom he hopes to inherit. Aunt Agatha is a most disagreeable woman, and I shall be so lonely there with no hope of seeing you." Pauline wiped at her eyes.

Serenity felt close to tears herself at the news. "How soon must you leave and when shall you return?"

"I shall be leaving almost at once and do not know when I shall return. Oh, Serenity, will you write to me?"

"Of course. You only need give me your address."

"I'm not certain of the address, but shall send it to you as soon as I arrive at my aunt's home. You never said how long your stay at Montague House would be. If you plan to leave soon, how should I direct a post to you?"

"I'm not certain how long I shall be in New York, but if I should return to Philadelphia before you arrive back here, Mr. Montague will forward your missive to me," Serenity assured her friend.

Pauline appeared about to say something more, then changed her mind as a carriage turned into the park and moved toward them. "There's Papa. I must go." She hugged Serenity, then offered to drop her off at Montague House.

"Thank you, but I shall enjoy the short walk."

Pauline appeared reluctant to part, putting out her hand as though she would stay Serenity from walking away.

"You mustn't keep your papa waiting." Serenity turned quickly to hurry down the walkway, fearing if she lingered she would burst into tears and make their departure from each other more difficult. "I shall look forward to your letters," she called over her shoulder.

* * *

Early one afternoon a few days later, Serenity returned from a meeting to find a letter resting on a silver tray in her room. Never having received a letter by post before, she examined it closely. There was her name scrawled across the front of the envelope. Seating herself at the small desk, she smoothed her skirt on either side of her chair before reaching for the ornate letter opener she'd never had cause to use until that moment.

Carefully inserting the blade beneath the seal, she lifted the daub of wax the sender had used to seal the missive and withdrew a single sheet of foolscap. It was dated a week earlier. "Dear Serenity," she read. "I stopped by the cottage today and discovered you still had not returned." The letter was from Edward, not Pauline as she had supposed. "The little house seemed dark and bare without your presence in spite of the pretty trimmings I credited with enlivening it before. I immediately wired Rupert at his office to enquire about your welfare. By return wire, he informed me that you were extending your stay, perhaps permanently, and that he would begin the paperwork immediately to have our marriage set aside. The formal nature of his wire left me somewhat confused concerning your failure to contact me directly to discuss this matter. Before your departure you were adamant in your desire to travel to Salt Lake to meet your uncle, and you seemed eager to learn more about your mother's beliefs. I would like to know what has caused you to change your mind. Before proceeding further, I respectfully request that you postpone any action until we are able to meet again. If you cannot come here, I shall be free to go to you at the end of February. With kindest regards, Edward."

It makes no sense. She reread the letter. *Why would Rupert tell Edward I mean to stay in New York? And I have never discussed the matter of an annulment with him. Why would he assume to begin the appeal for me?* Rupert was a busy man, but still she felt hurt that he hadn't mentioned Edward's wire and that he had sent an answer without discussing the matter with her. She would insist on sitting down with him in his study when he returned from the bank that evening.

After a few moments she folded the letter along its original creases and returned it to its envelope. She placed the letter in the little drawer of the secretary before wandering to the settee, where she sat deep in thought for a long time. She wished she could discuss the matter with Pauline, but her marriage to Edward and the events surrounding her departure from her childhood home were the only subject she'd avoided with Pauline. Besides, her friend was out of town.

She didn't wish for others to make decisions for her, but she'd done little to make choices of her own lately. Beyond the whirlwind of social activities, she had thought of little else besides the committee meetings concerning the disposal of her father's inherited fortune. In that forum, she'd learned to be decisive and had long since overcome her reluctance to disagree with the two professors. They wished to see the entire sum used for establishing a college, while she felt certain her father would want those former slaves who would never set foot in a college to have access to education that would equip them to go west. There they could prove up on homestead land and become reunited with their families. Through the participation of all five members of the committee, progress was being made toward both goals, and another day or two would see their plans completed and beginning to be set in action. It was only in her personal life that Serenity had allowed herself to drift. And it was in her personal life that others seemed to be stepping forward to make choices for her.

She tried to think about what she wanted. She loved New York, the balls, and the beautiful clothing. She enjoyed the company of young people who were bright and witty. She wasn't certain what she felt for Jerome Montague, but there was a good possibility she might come to care for him enough to wish for her marriage to Edward to be set aside. It was pleasant to have servants wait on her. She'd like to meet Uncle Reliance, but it would occupy at least two years of her life to travel to the Utah territory and back. She wasn't certain she wished to give up the life she'd grown attached to for something so vague as learning about her mother's people. Also, there was a big push to extend the railroad all the way to California. If she waited, she could visit Utah when travel would be easier and much faster.

She considered sending Edward a wire, asking that he send her things on to her, but he had requested that they meet before she made definite decisions concerning her future. Edward had rescued her from an unbearable life with Percy Tolson. He'd risked his life for her, and he'd been there for her when no one else was. Though he credited her with saving his life in the river, she felt she owed him more than she could ever repay. The least she could do would be to travel back to Philadelphia to meet with him before making a decision.

* * *

An air of excitement prevailed as Serenity joined the family to wait for the carriage to be brought around. Rupert didn't seem to share his wife and younger son's enthusiasm for the dinner and entertainment they would be attending, but rather appeared first annoyed and then resigned. Delbert was his usual self, exhibiting an air of polite boredom. Serenity found herself feeling somewhat out of sorts. There had been no opportunity to speak with Rupert about the telegrams he and Edward had exchanged, and given the arrangements Emmaline had made for the evening, their talk would have to wait until tomorrow.

She didn't remember ordering the elegant red velvet gown she found laid out in her room for this evening, nor the fur-trimmed cape and muff that matched its rich color. The deep red offset her dark hair and brought a flush of color to her cheeks. It was the most beautiful gown she'd ever seen, but it left her feeling half-dressed. She tugged at the neckline, which bared far too great an expanse of skin with its fashionable off-shoulder cut that dipped to a deep V in front. The maid and Emmaline assured her the dress was perfectly acceptable and very much in fashion. She eyed herself critically in the cheval glass and knew she really did look splendid.

The beautiful gown almost restored the sense of well-being she'd felt earlier, but not quite. A new steel crinoline frame gave the many yards of soft fabric an alluring shape, but it made Serenity wonder whether she'd be able to sit in the carriage when it was brought around. As she struggled to adjust her skirt and the awkward crinoline cage to the reality of a narrow carriage seat, she wondered why women's fashions couldn't be lovely and practical too. It was enough to make her wish Amelia Bloomer's innovative fashions for women were more acceptable.

Dinner didn't improve her frame of mind. She was seated between two congenial gentlemen who were at pains to entertain her, but she found their conversation childish and silly. She was hungry, but the maid had tightened her corset strings so severely she couldn't eat more than a few bites without risking becoming seriously ill. During the fish course her mind drifted back to the morning when Edward had caught fish in the river and grilled them over an open fire. She'd cheerfully trade every morsel of the elaborate dish before her to be able to go back to that morning when she'd dressed in a simple dress with cotton petticoats and no stays and had stuffed herself with a breakfast of simple river trout.

Jerome's proprietary air toward her further added to her annoyance as the party left the dining room and moved toward a salon decorated for the purpose of entertaining. A few gentlemen disappeared with their host into his library, where Serenity was aware they would be served glasses of port and some would indulge in smoking cigars, a filthy habit she'd come to abhor. She had made her feelings clear to Jerome some weeks earlier when he'd approached her for a dance, reeking of the foul odor. He'd avoided cigars ever since.

Seating herself on a small divan beside Emmaline, Serenity took care to spread her skirts properly and was amused to discover that their voluminous skirts left no room for any of the gentlemen to sit beside them. Rupert and Delbert wandered away and were soon absorbed in conversation with a portly gentleman who appeared to be an important figure. Jerome remained standing behind Serenity and his mother with one hand resting on the back of the divan, mere inches from Serenity's bare shoulder. She wasn't certain why the gesture annoyed her nor why she felt out of sorts that evening. She supposed it was because she hadn't found an opportunity to discuss Edward's letter with Rupert.

A young man lifted a violin to his shoulder, and a woman dressed in a severe black gown—minus the wire cage that made sitting uncomfortable for Serenity—seated herself before a large, black grand piano. The first sounds were enthralling, but as the duo continued to perform, the room grew stuffy and warm. The stench of cigar smoke drifted from the library, and Serenity fanned herself vigorously.

When the musicians at last paused for an intermission, Jerome leaned forward to whisper, "You look like you could both use a little air. May I escort you to the solarium? It's bound to be cooler there."

"Thank you, dear boy," Emmaline murmured. "I am feeling a mite faint." She rose gracefully to her feet, and Serenity did her best to copy Emmaline's smooth transition.

As the three wandered down a hall with which both Emmaline and Jerome seemed familiar, Emmaline paused several times to chat with friends. When one conversation seemed destined to go on for some time, she whispered to her son and Serenity, "Go on. I shall catch up with you in a moment."

Serenity hesitated, but Jerome secured her hand on his arm and continued walking down the long hall. When they reached a point where the hall branched, Jerome chose the direction that seemed darker to Serenity.

"That seems to be the direction others are going." She pointed down the well-lit hall Jerome had turned his back on.

He continued walking. "This way is shorter," he explained.

"We should go back," Serenity said after taking a few steps. "We seem to have strayed into the private portion of the house."

"The solarium is just ahead."

"The wall sconces haven't been lit in this part of the house," she protested.

"We're almost there."

"I'm going back." She stopped, pulled her hand free of where Jerome held it captive on his arm, and turned toward the lighted part of the hall.

Jerome moved quickly. Clasping her about her waist, he spun her into a darkened room.

"What are you doing?" She gasped for breath and struggled to free herself from his hold.

"I merely wish a moment alone with you." He chuckled, releasing his hold on her waist, but retaining her hand in his. "I have quite fallen in love with you," he announced. "Since you are without father or guardian from whom I might request permission to court you, I have determined to ask you outright. Will you do me the honor of becoming my wife?"

Something about the satisfaction she sensed in her suitor's voice served to increase her irritation with his tactics. "You tricked me into this dark room to propose marriage?"

Jerome defended his action. "I've tried for a week to find you alone in a more suitable setting where I might kneel and do the pretty, but you've been elusive and seldom alone of late."

"This is ridiculous. I have a husband, as you well know." She took a step back, pulling her hand free again as she did so. She wished the room weren't so dark. She could barely see Jerome's outline, but the object behind her felt suspiciously like a bed. *Surely, Jerome wouldn't be so careless as to arrange an ill-advised meeting in a bedchamber to propose marriage!*

"I've taken care of that obstacle," he stated in an airy voice. "The paperwork has been completed and only awaits signatures. Then Judge Moore, a man with political ambitions but little wealth, will set your coerced marriage aside. No one need know that the marriage ever took place."

"Edward won't sign your papers." She hoped that was true, but the letter she'd received from him that day didn't offer her a great deal of reassurance except that he wished to speak with her before proceeding with the annulment.

"He'll sign. His only interest is in becoming a doctor and returning to his Mormon friends. He doesn't need you for a wife, and he doesn't know about the money. He can have all the wives he wants when he goes back to Utah, and money is of no importance anyway to religious fanatics like him."

Jerome's sneering explanation incited her to defend Edward. "He's not a fanatic. He's a good man who cares about me and the people I'm trying to help with Papa's money."

His voice turned hard. "You can forget about any plans you've made to give away that money to poor black people," he hissed.

"My father's will—"

"You never read your grandfather's will. I did. Your father was a foolish man who tried to subvert the law to his own liking. Your grandfather's will left his money to his sons and his son's children, with the stipulation that should your father have female children, their husbands should inherit equally with his sons. Since you, a female, are the only descendent, your husband is the only heir."

"Edward is my husband."

"A mere technicality that will soon be resolved."

"You have no right to—" She had no words to express her anger.

"As your future husband, I have every right."

How could she have been so wrong about Jerome? She'd trusted him and thought him her friend. She'd even been flattered by his attention. The reality of his motive for courting her brought pain and embarrassment. He cared nothing for her, only for the money he thought he would gain by marrying her.

"You're not my future husband. I have not consented to marry you and I never will."

"Come, don't be such a naive child. You've been compromised and will have no choice but to marry me or forever be a social pariah. We were seen strolling off from the others in the direction of this room, and when we leave here, Mother and several of her friends will see us."

"Emmaline knew of your plan?" She felt a painful stab in her heart, knowing the answer before his harsh chuckle confirmed his mother's complicity.

"Is your father aware of your meddling in my life?"

"He's anxious to welcome you as his daughter-in-law. Once our engagement is announced, he can halt this nonsense about giving away your fortune to illiterate slaves who would be better off returning to their masters."

"No." She couldn't believe she'd been as wrong about Rupert as she'd been about Jerome.

"It's time to end this nonsense." Jerome's voice was cold, but then it softened slightly. "We get along well enough. You've no reason to feel put upon. I shall be a generous husband and see that

you have the finest wardrobe and attend the most exclusive entertainments. Give me your hand. When we meet Mother and her
friends, you can blush prettily and then we'll proceed to the salon,
where we shall announce our engagement."

She wouldn't do it. She couldn't. But how could she escape the
fate planned for her? Slowly, she sidled along the side of the bed.
Jerome kept talking, first coaxing, then becoming more demanding
when she didn't respond. She'd reached the end of the bed and
ducked behind it before he realized she was no longer standing
near him.

"Hiding will do you no good." There was anger in his voice now.
She could hear him moving about the room. Several times he
stumbled into furniture and swore bitterly. She considered making
a run for the door, but if she miscalculated, he'd catch her and
force her to leave the room with him.

The air around her stirred as though a door had opened. Could
Jerome have given up and left the room? No, it was more likely a
trick to lure her from her hiding place. She crouched lower.

A familiar sound reached her ears, one she heard every morning
when the Montague's maid flung open the heavy drapes in her
room to admit the morning sun. Her heart beat faster. Jerome
intended to let in enough moonlight to allow him to discover her
hiding place.

"There you are!" His voice was grim.

To her astonishment, she saw two shadowy figures silhouetted
in front of a tall window that now let in a little light. She felt a
moment's gratitude for the overcast sky and approaching storm.
Jerome lunged toward the other figure—obviously a woman, as
revealed by her wide skirt—but he was not quick enough to catch
her. The woman raised something high above her head and then,
without hesitation, crashed it against Jerome's head. There was a
splintering sound of breaking glass and Jerome slowly slumped to
the floor.

22

"Come, Serenity. We must hurry," a woman's voice hissed. "His mother is looking for him and will arrive any moment to discover her son and the Caswell heiress having a tête-à-tête in a darkened guest chamber."

There was something familiar about the voice, but there was no time to think on it. Taking a chance, Serenity scrambled toward the woman, who now stood in front of the pale outline of a window. By the time she had skirted Jerome's limp form and stepped over bits of glass that crunched beneath her slippers, the window was open. Without hesitation, she followed her benefactress through the window onto a balcony. She heard the click as the window closed behind her.

"I wish we could close the curtains too," she heard the woman mutter.

Pauline! A jolt of recognition ran through Serenity. Why was Pauline in New York instead of at her aunt's in the country? And how did she know Serenity needed her help? A gust of icy wind reminded Serenity she'd left the house without her cloak. But there was no time for questions or worrying about being cold now. Putting as much distance as possible between herself and Jerome was her greatest concern. She hurried to the balcony rail where Pauline stood.

"We're on the second floor," her friend said before Serenity could speak. "We'll have to go over the rail and drop to the ground. The gardener recently turned the soil and piled leaves in the flowerbeds to prepare them for winter. Together they will cushion our fall." Pauline's words were not particularly reassuring. Even with the prospect of a soft landing, jumping from a second-story balcony filled Serenity's heart with dread.

Serenity looked over the rail. She might break her neck, but that was preferable to being forced to wed Jerome. He dressed better, smelled better, and had better manners than Percy Tolson, but they were two of a kind—except Percy truly liked her, not just her money. She sniffed back a sob. There was no time to indulge in self-pity. When she was safely away from New York, she'd have time to feel sorry for herself and wonder why she was once again fleeing an objectionable forced marriage.

Pauline caught her arm before she could climb over the rail. "You'll have to take off your crinoline. You'll kill yourself if you jump wearing a steel cage."

Pauline was right. "Help me, please," Serenity conceded. It took both of them to maneuver her voluminous skirt out of the way so they could reach the ribbons holding in place the cage that created a fashionably full back to her gown.

With that impediment out of the way, Serenity was still hampered by stays and an excess of fabric that threatened to trip her and send her sprawling instead of allowing her to drop safely to the ground below. A tree much like the one that grew outside the storage room back home branched up close to the balcony. It gave her an idea.

"I think we can climb down that tree," she whispered.

"All right. Follow me." Pauline stepped onto the rail and leaped toward a sturdy limb a few feet away. Serenity prepared to follow but stumbled over the trailing yards of fabric no longer held clear of her feet by the crinoline.

There was nothing to do but to tie snatches of the hem into knots to raise her hemline. Before she finished tying the knots, she became aware of a change behind her. A glance over her shoulder revealed light streaming into the room she'd recently vacated. Whether she tripped on her skirt or not, she realized she had to jump now.

She scrambled over the rail and reached for a nearby tree limb. Except for the necessity of frequently pausing to work her snagged skirt free from the tree's clutches and to gasp for breath, she was able to move rapidly down the huge skeletal tree. Reaching the ground without mishap, she searched the shadows for her friend. A hand touched her shoulder and she jumped.

"Shhh." Pauline pulled her into deeper shadows near the house. The two women huddled together for what seemed like a long time, waiting to see if an alarm would be raised and a search begun.

Serenity wasn't certain whether the tremors causing her body to shake were from the cold night air or fear. Perhaps the answer was both. Her fervent wish at the moment was to somehow exchange some of the copious amounts of velvet in her skirt for a greater amount in the bodice.

When no one dashed from the house in search of them, the two young women began moving with great caution toward the street. They paused just short of the gatehouse.

"Stay here while I distract the gatekeeper," Pauline whispered. "Watch for an opportunity to slip out undetected." She darted away, and as she passed near the gatekeeper's lantern, Serenity noticed Pauline's gown resembled those worn by maids instead of the lace and satin of their previous encounters.

The gatekeeper seemed to know Pauline rather well, not as the young lady Serenity had met a few weeks previously, but as a practiced flirt. As Pauline absorbed the attention of the gatekeeper, Serenity slipped through the gate and into the shadow of the wall that circled the estate. Uncertain whether Pauline meant to continue on with her or remain with the guard, she began walking.

She wasn't certain where she should go. Boarding a train for Philadelphia was the most appealing option, but the tiny velvet bag that matched her gown had been lost somewhere between the music salon and her present predicament. It wouldn't have done her much good anyway, since there was no money in it—just a fan and a lace handkerchief. Unless she returned to her room at Montague House, she'd have no money with which to purchase a train ticket.

She considered walking to the tiny room Julia and Rosie shared, but the distance was too great. It would take all night and half of tomorrow to reach the part of town where they were staying. Tears welled in her eyes.

"Serenity." She heard someone call her name. She shrank farther into the shadows, but apparently she had been seen because a light horse-drawn cabriolet stopped beside her. "It is only I," Pauline whispered. "Climb aboard and we'll be off."

Gratefully, Serenity climbed over the wheel onto the single seat beside Pauline. Before she was quite settled, Pauline snapped the reins and the cart horse plunged ahead in a rapid trot.

"There's a carriage robe on the seat. Pull it over our shoulders." Pauline's teeth were chattering as badly as her own. Serenity felt around until she located the robe. Shaking from the cold, she could scarcely hold the robe in place as Pauline concentrated on exacting the greatest possible speed from the horse.

"How did you know . . . I thought you were . . . I never expected Jerome to . . . What shall I . . ." Serenity found she couldn't complete a thought, never mind a sentence.

Pauline urged the horse to a faster pace. "I haven't been completely honest with you. My only excuse is that I wanted you to like me and be my friend. Like you, I'm an orphan, but quite without funds. Occasionally, one of my mother's old friends invites me to an entertainment, but I've been forced to fend for myself since I turned sixteen. That's what I was doing tonight. Mrs. Stapleton hired extra staff, and I was glad to get the work. I saw Jerome Montague slip one of the waiters a gold piece to make certain all of the lights along the south hall were extinguished. Being of a curious nature, I went along to see why. Hearing raised voices coming from an unused guest chamber, I succumbed to my unladylike curiosity and put my ear to the keyhole."

"Well, I'm glad you did. I don't know how I would have escaped Jerome without your timely intervention."

"Are you going to return to your husband?"

"I never left him in the way Jerome implied. He's busy finishing his training to become a doctor. While he is occupied, it seemed a good time to travel to New York to put into place some plans that my father charged me to carry out upon his death."

"Is your husband studying at one of the medical schools in Boston?"

"No, he's in Philadelphia and I shall rejoin him as soon as I can find the funds to purchase passage on the steam train."

"Have you no funds or valuables in your room at Montague House? Or you might wire your husband to purchase your ticket." Pauline began to slow the horse that she'd urged to a mad pace earlier.

"Why didn't I think of that? I shall go to Julia, if you should be so kind as to drive me into the city. Then I shall send a wire to Edward."

"We are almost to Montague House, and your dress is quite ruined. Surely you don't wish to appear in public in a torn and soiled evening gown. Would it not be better to change your dress, pack a bag, and gather whatever valuables you might wish to exchange for cash? You needn't fear Jerome's return. It will be some time before he arrives, and I shall keep watch for you. Should he return, I shall give you ample warning."

"I won't need to exchange valuables for cash. The only jewelry I brought with me to New York are the ruby-and-pearl earrings I'm wearing, and I have sufficient cash in my room to purchase my ticket. I never considered returning to the house, as I thought it the first place Jerome would search for me."

"He's sure to search the house and grounds of the Stapleton mansion first. There should be sufficient time to retrieve money and those items you most wish to take with you. I shall remain with the horse if you promise to hurry." She slowed the horse further and drove around the side of the house to the servants' entrance.

After climbing down from the cabriolet, Serenity eased the back door of the house open. Seeing no one in the kitchen, she hurried across a short hall to the servants' stairs. Again luck was with her, for there were no servants in the upstairs hall either, and she made her way to her room without incident.

Without the assistance of a maid, it took several minutes to free herself of the tattered red velvet gown. She tugged on the buttons, sending them flying about the room. Once the dress lay in a heap on the floor, she quickly scrambled into one of her simpler gowns, vowing silently to never allow herself to be imprisoned by fashion again.

After she was dressed, she searched out the traveling case she'd brought to New York and stuffed it with a couple of the less cumbersome dresses, a change of underpinnings, and her papers. Then she grasped her fur-lined cloak and the bag that held the remainder of the cash she'd brought with her. She refused to think about the room filled with her papa's purchases that Rupert had promised to sell for her.

With the strap tightened on her bag, she crept toward her door. She listened, then twisted the glass knob. The door opened and she found herself facing Rupert.

"Oh-h!" A small scream escaped her lips and she took a hasty step back.

"It's all right. You don't need to be afraid of me." He extended a hand as though to touch her arm. She drew farther back.

"Serenity, Jerome was just found unconscious in an unused bed chamber at the Stapletons'. A red velvet bag was in the room with him and the window was unlocked. Your cloak was still in the cloakroom, but you were nowhere to be found. I have a pretty good idea what happened, but I want to hear it from you."

"I'm leaving." She gathered her courage and stepped toward the door, hoping she could push her way past him.

"You can't leave like this," Rupert protested. "If Jerome insulted you, I shall insist that he apologize."

"Apologize?" Serenity turned on him. Her anger outstripped her sense of caution. "You and Jerome are no better than the Tolsons. Jerome meant to compromise me and force me to marry him so he could gain control of the money Papa intended to use to help the former slaves. I thought you were Papa's friend, but you and your wife schemed with Jerome to steal that money from the people who need it and should have it."

"What!" Rupert looked taken aback. "I have done little else over the past couple of months other than work with our committee to devise a plan for benefitting the freed slaves with your grandfather's fortune."

"So I thought. I believed you really cared, but Jerome told me Papa's will doesn't matter. He said that the money will go to my husband and that you've already applied for an annulment for my marriage so Jerome can marry me and take charge of my grandfather's ill-gotten fortune."

The color drained from Rupert's face. "Jerome could not know about your grandfather's will unless . . . I can only assume Emmaline was involved in my son's scheme to force you to wed him. She was present when your father and I discussed the particulars of his will. I think you may be right to flee my household and return to Edward." He reached for her bag. "We can discuss the details of this matter on the way to the train station."

"My friend is waiting—"

"I found her on the stairs and sent her on her way. I almost threatened to have her arrested for trespassing, but she seemed eager to be on her way once I asked what her business was."

Serenity wasn't certain she could trust Rupert, but her only choices seemed to be to go with him or remain in his house for the night. She knew she couldn't bear to see Jerome and Emmaline again. Drawing her cloak close about her, she followed Rupert down the stairs and out the front door and allowed him to assist her into his carriage.

"To the train station," she heard him instruct his driver as she leaned back against the cushions and adjusted her skirt. When Rupert climbed inside the carriage, he sat across from her and leaned slightly forward. "Tell me everything that happened this evening."

She considered whether it was wise to tell Rupert all that had happened. She still wasn't certain whether she could trust him. But if she didn't tell him and he was innocent of involvement in the plot, then might all the work she'd done these many weeks be for naught?

Slowly she began. Rupert didn't interrupt, save to urge her to go on whenever she seemed to hesitate. When she finished, he was silent for some time. Then, when he did speak, she thought she could detect sadness in his voice.

"I have devoted too much time to my business," he lamented. "In my absence my wife has turned to society to fill her time. I have allowed her to spoil my second son, flattering and coddling him into believing his looks and his charming manners entitle him to an elite station in life. I think it's time to accompany Emmaline to Europe to reestablish our marriage and to enroll Jerome at Oxford, where he will learn something of discipline and the futility of assuming wealth and birth entitle him to privileges he has not earned. I shall turn over the management of the bank to Delbert and instruct him to send your quarterly allowance to you at whatever address you choose."

Serenity didn't comment. Silence filled the carriage until they reached the train station, and then Rupert spoke again. "There is more I wish to say. Jerome is correct when he says your husband could choose to set your father's will aside and claim your grandfather's fortune. I apologize for my failure to tell you of that possibility. I can only hope to redeem myself by explaining that I knew how strongly Charles felt about this matter, and I didn't know whether you might attempt to subvert his intention. But in my defense, you should know I did explain it all to Edward, who was in perfect agreement with your father on the matter. Also, I never saw the telegram Edward sent me nor have I corresponded with him since your arrival in New York. It seems that telegrams in which I have an interest have a habit of going astray. That matter was entirely Jerome's doing. I can only guess that he visited my office and found the telegram on my desk while he waited to drive you home after one of our meetings, and that he presumed to use it to his advantage."

Tears spilled from Serenity's eyes. She wasn't certain whether it was because Edward had known about the will and, being an honorable man, had made no move to claim the money, or because her faith in Rupert was restored and her heart ached because she knew he suffered as she did because of his family's betrayal.

Rupert assisted her from the carriage and escorted her into the station to purchase her ticket. Before he walked away, he stooped to kiss her cheek. "Rest assured that the black college will be built and that colored children will attend village schools. Your father's money cannot resolve all of the problems the blight of slavery brought to this country, but it can begin the healing. Now you must begin to heal too from all the wrongs you have suffered. Let Edward and your mother's people help you."

She watched him walk away before she seated herself to wait for the train. She glanced around, seeing few people, mostly men. A heavyset woman with a sleeping child on either side of her sat near the stove. Serenity seated herself on a bench opposite her. The woman nodded in greeting but didn't speak.

The stationmaster assured her it wouldn't be a long wait. It was almost morning, and the train to Philadelphia would leave at five. She grew warm in her heavy cloak and felt her head begin to nod. The sharp blast of a train whistle jerked her head up. Gathering up her bag, she moved toward the platform. The brisk air cleared her mind. When the conductor placed a small stool near a coach and began taking tickets, she hurried toward the car. Once settled aboard the train, she could sleep.

The train car wasn't crowded, and there were plenty of open seats. Serenity was pleased to see she would have a bench to herself. After settling her traveling case and smoothing her cloak, she looked out the smoky window toward the city, where night was beginning to fade but a few lanterns still spilled their light across the train platform. The area around the train station wasn't as brightly lit or glamorous as the opulent surroundings she'd grown accustomed to during her brief stay, but she still felt a kind of relief at bidding good-bye to them and the city they represented.

A woman darted from the station, running toward a car several yards down the track from the one Serenity had boarded. In the dim light Serenity couldn't see her clearly, but something about the woman reminded her of Pauline. She wished she could have thanked Pauline properly and offered her a reward for her kindness . . . that the running woman really was Pauline and they could continue their friendship in Philadelphia . . . that she'd been able to say good-bye to Julia and Rosie.

As the train left New York City, snow began to fall and Serenity snuggled deeper into her cloak. She leaned her head against the back of the bench seat and attempted to rest, but sleep wouldn't come. She couldn't shake the nagging feeling that she had brought misfortune on herself. Though her marriage wasn't a true marriage in the fullest sense of the word, she should have conducted herself as a married woman until she determined her future course. Instead, she'd allowed pleasure and vanity to lead her astray from the values she'd been taught as a child and those she'd adopted during her weeks of studying her mother's book. She was disappointed in Emmaline and Jerome, but most of all she was disappointed in herself. At the first opportunity, she must sit down with Edward and discuss their situation.

23

Serenity was surprised to find Edward waiting for her when the train pulled into the Philadelphia station. He came striding toward her with a hesitant smile on his face. A burning warmth filled her chest and only an awareness that they were standing on a train platform within view of dozens of people restrained her from flinging her arms around his neck. He greeted her quietly and took her traveling case from her hand.

"How did you know—?" she began.

"Rupert sent me a wire, telling me to meet your train. He also said to hear you out before believing anything his son may have said in his name."

"I fear Jerome Montague has created a great deal of pain with his manipulating and misrepresentations. I shall tell you all about it when we reach the cottage."

"Do you have a trunk?" He eyed her one small bag skeptically. "You said you planned to purchase a few winter clothes. I see you are wearing a new cloak, but I expected you might choose several gowns as well."

"I'm afraid I purchased more than a few new gowns and more than one cloak. Rupert promised to send the rest of my wardrobe on to me."

He took her hand to assist her in boarding the city train, then took the seat beside her. "I won't be able to stay at the cottage to hear the details of your adventure. I must hurry straight to the hospital. My friend Richard Deerfield is covering for me until I can get back."

"Very well then." She looked around to assure herself that no one was close enough to overhear. "The visit started out splendidly. It was grand to see the city, and Montague House is a marvel. Rupert's wife and his two sons welcomed me warmly. Emmaline and I spent the first week shopping and selecting a suitable city wardrobe for me. There was a different entertainment to attend almost every evening. But lest you think my visit was all frivolity, let me assure you that most days Rupert and I, with Julia and the two professors, met together to prepare a plan for the wise use of Grandfather's money. Once a plan was agreed upon, we began arrangements to set our plan in motion." She looked down, twisting her hands together before continuing.

"Being hopelessly naive and knowing little of the interaction between ladies and gentlemen, I allowed myself to be tricked into a compromising situation." She went on to tell Edward of Jerome's plot to annul her marriage to Edward and force her into marriage with him.

"That bounder!" Edward exclaimed. "Excuse my blunt language, but that young man deserves a horsewhipping. You were fortunate indeed to be rescued by your friend. I hope she doesn't suffer unemployment because of her courageous act."

"If only I'd had the presence of mind to obtain her address, I would help her." Serenity continued filling Edward in on the details of her escape for several minutes until Edward interrupted her.

"We've reached our stop. We must hurry or we shall be carried beyond the cottage." Edward stood and made his way to the steps with Serenity clinging to one arm and her bag in the other.

From the corner where they disembarked, it was a mere four blocks to the cottage. Snow was no longer falling, but a dusting of white covered the road. Seeing the dear cottage with a winter cap of white on its roof, looking bleak and alone through the bare trees, Serenity felt an ache. She'd missed the cottage. It wasn't so grand as Montague House, but she couldn't help thinking it was as happy to see her as she was to see it. When Edward pressed a hand against the small of her back to urge her inside, it seemed to welcome them. And when he departed a few minutes later to catch a train to the hospital, she imagined it shared her disappointment at his hasty departure.

* * *

Serenity took pleasure in setting her small house in order, and she was pleased when a large trunk arrived from Rupert bearing the many gowns she'd purchased and a few items Rupert believed her father had selected specifically for her. There were a pair of small bronze pieces she set on the mantle above the fireplace beside the candlestick she'd brought from her previous home. There were also some simple but elegant pieces of jewelry, which she put away with her ruby-and-pearl earrings in a carved wooden box that her father had given her a long time ago.

When the first business of arranging her home was completed, she sat in a chair before the fireplace and read. Her mother's Book of Mormon seemed like an old friend, long missed, and she wiled away many of the coming evenings poring over its pages. It became a daily gesture to kneel and ask her Heavenly Father to help her understand the passages she read.

When she finished reading the last page, she didn't immediately close the book and turn to other tasks. Instead, she sat for a long time with the open book on her lap. She thought long of the people who had allowed greed to destroy their faith, their government, and their entire civilization. Shame tore at her heart as she remembered her own absorption in fashionable finery and flattery and how easily she'd allowed herself to be distracted from her purpose in traveling to New York. The fire burned low, but warmth filled her being. The book was true. That knowledge burned like an ember within her breast.

For several days she spent every waking minute reviewing each passage that had touched her heart, lingering over the words that brought hope and joy to her. She tried to reconcile the things she'd heard and the things she knew about the Mormons with the book she now knew to be true. Accepting the story James had told of a boy prophet who spoke face-to-face with God was far more difficult than believing Christ had appeared to ancient people.

One afternoon when she'd been back in her cottage for a little more than a week, a tap sounded on her door. Peering out before opening the door, she noticed candles in several windows and Christmas wreaths on doors along the street. To her delight Edward was standing on the doorstep. She lost no time opening the door.

"Come inside!" She brushed at a dusting of snow on his collar. Recent flurries had accumulated several inches of snow.

She poured Edward a cup of hot chocolate and insisted he take the seat closest to the brisk fire burning in the fireplace. He took a deep swallow of the chocolate and sighed contentedly.

He picked up her Book of Mormon, which was lying near the chair where he sat. "Have you finished reading?" he asked.

She nodded.

"And do you believe it to be a true record?"

"Yes," she admitted. "You told me of the promise in Moroni chapter ten, verses four and five, but I still felt uncertain until a short time ago." They talked for a while about her slowly growing conviction and then the consuming certainty she'd felt as she sat quietly contemplating all she'd read.

"Have you considered baptism?"

"I'm not ready yet, though baptism has become the desire of my heart. I've only recently discovered my feelings for the Book of Mormon, but I know little of your church and must learn more before taking that step. I feel some of my willingness to accept what I read was because much of the book seemed familiar to me and I think my mother must have taught me many things from it."

"From what James told me of your mother, she had a deep and tender testimony of its truthfulness. She only left Nauvoo because she felt the Lord desired her to rescue the Hayes family and do all she could to free an enslaved people."

"Sometimes as I read I felt close to my mother, so close that several times I listened intently, thinking there was a message coming to me from her lips. Other times I became so caught up in the story of two quarrelsome groups of people that I grew angry with their greed and their quickness to fall away. I was studying that verse on recognizing truth when I heard your knock on the door."

"I'm sorry I interrupted your meditation."

"I'm not," Serenity assured him. "I'm glad to be able to talk to you about it. Mamma marked many verses in the book, including that one. I think Papa read that verse many times too and asked the same questions that trouble me. He penned, 'What is my real intent?' in the margin so lightly I could scarcely read it, and he underlined, 'if ye shall ask with a sincere heart, with real intent.'"

"Many people read the Book of Mormon more from curiosity than from a serious intent to know whether or not it's true. Do you feel that's why you and your father read it?"

"Not from curiosity exactly. I think Papa read it because he missed Mamma and felt closer to her when he read the book she loved. I think, too, that he began to hope for the truthfulness of the things she told him about the Mormon temple being a place where a man and wife could be married forever instead of only until death."

"And what of your reason for reading it?" Edward's attention seemed to center solely on her, making her want to squirm but also telling her that her answer concerned him.

"Papa's reasons matter to me too. I want with all my heart to be with my parents again. But I admit that some of my reason was curiosity. When you read to me while we were traveling on the river, the story interested me and I wanted to know how it ended. Also, I've felt a sense that Uncle Reliance would be disappointed if I arrived at his home without trying to read the book he and my grandparents surely must love as much as my mother did. And . . ." She hesitated, uncertain how to put her last reason into words.

"Come here." He beckoned her to come closer.

Slowly she approached the chair where he sat. He reached for her hand, pulling her down on the footstool before him. He continued to hold her hand. When she gained the courage to meet his gaze, she was surprised by the soft expression on his face. "Tell me your other reason," he urged.

"You," she said at last. "Every night you opened the book and read from it. I thought you might like me better if I read the Book of Mormon." Her eyes dropped to their joined hands, but she didn't attempt to break his grasp.

"I already liked you. I liked you the moment I saw you standing in the kitchen when I walked into your home from your father's store." He smiled, the old mischievous smile that she hadn't seen much of lately.

"That was before I trapped you into marrying me."

At first he didn't respond but seemed exceptionally still. Serenity's cautious glance revealed a troubled look on his face.

"Perhaps I wasn't as unwilling as you think."

"You're being kind. I thought only of myself that day. I was so angry that the Tolsons were trying to force me into turning over Papa's property and my person to them, and that the judge seemed to be in complicity with them. I proved to be no better than they were by forcing you to marry me. I don't know how I can ever gain your forgiveness."

"Understand one thing, Serenity." Edward emphasized each word. "Neither you nor Judge Detweiler forced me to marry you. I'm a man quite accustomed to making my own decisions. No one prevented me from walking out of that room. I'll concede that I didn't plan to marry you that day and that I didn't choose the place. But I did choose my bride."

"You what?" Surely she'd misunderstood him.

"From the day I first saw you, I planned to marry you."

She stared at him in bewilderment, unsure what to say or even think. An awareness of him she couldn't explain spread through her, both frightening and thrilling her. Slowly she withdrew her hand from his.

"You never . . . I didn't know . . ."

"There was little opportunity. You were just beginning to know me and were still blushing prettily at my teasing when your father was killed. Only an insensitive cad would have attempted to secure your affections at such a time. I could only hope you would learn to trust me and that caring would follow. If you're wondering why I haven't insisted on what polite society terms my husbandly rights, be assured it isn't because I do not desire you, but because I respect your right to choose."

"I don't understand." Edward was her dearest friend, and though they were married, she'd never thought of him as her husband. She'd been flattered those first few weeks by his flirting and had been grateful for his steady support and protection through her trials. Even in fleeing New York and Jerome, she'd been anxious to return to Edward and the cottage much the way she'd looked forward to Papa's return from New York at the conclusion of each of his trips.

"You're young, just eighteen, and have lived a sheltered life," Edward began. "Facing the laws and manipulations of men following your father's death was your first experience with the injustices that can be heaped on one of your youth and gender. I saw your frustration and indignation at being unable to grasp the reins of your own life. Lack of self-determination leads to resentment. I don't want a resentful wife. I want a wife who is my wife because she chooses to be. You had fewer choices the day we wed than did I. I understood that, even if you didn't, and I determined that day that I would wait as long as needed for you to decide to become my wife or to choose an annulment."

"How can I know what I want?" Knowing what she didn't want seemed much simpler than knowing what she did. She stepped away from Edward, feeling flushed and confused. She'd been nearly forced into marriage with two different men she did *not* want, but how could she know if she *did* want to be Edward's wife or someone else's? In spite of Edward's words, she couldn't help feeling she'd forced Edward into a position as untenable as those she'd faced. It was only his kind nature that brought about his denial.

"It's a lot like that verse in Moroni we were discussing." Edward spoke softly now. He closed the space between them and took both of her hands in his. "When we want to know if something is right or true, we must study it carefully, then get down on our knees and ask Heavenly Father about it. If we really want an answer to our question, He will give us that answer. But if we ask merely from curiosity to see if asking works or because we think it a duty, we have no promise."

"I know the Book of Mormon is true, but discovering truth doesn't seem to work the same way concerning my personal life. I'm not sure He even cares what happens to me. I thought it right that I should go to New York and work with Rupert Montague to provide relief and better opportunities for the freed slaves. You said the warmth and peace I felt that night we discussed that verse beside the Susquehanna were the Holy Spirit assuring me it was the right thing to do. I prayed about going to New York and believed it to be the right decision."

"Do you doubt the plans you made with Rupert were right?"

"No. When those plans are carried out, they will alleviate much suffering and provide essential opportunities to many former slaves and their children. But Jerome and Emmaline . . ."

". . . were thwarted in their plans. Don't you think God's will and the many prayers offered for your protection while you were away had a part in your escape?"

"You prayed for me?"

"I pray for you every day."

Serenity was touched by the thought of Edward praying for her. She'd been grateful for Pauline's help and Rupert's too, but she hadn't considered that God might have had a hand in her rescue or that Edward had asked for divine protection for her.

She couldn't look at him. Edward hadn't come right out and said he loved her, but his revelations left her feeling awkward and unsure of what to say to him. She needed time to think and to examine her feelings.

"Come now." He stood, bringing her to her feet. "It's Christmas Day and time is short before I must return to the hospital.

"Today is Christmas? I lost track of the days and didn't know, but if you can stay until evening I shall prepare us a Christmas supper." She'd purchased a plump hen the previous day and planned to roast it for her supper, and she could quickly prepare an apple cobbler. Preparing supper would keep her busy, she thought, and distract her from the awkwardness.

Edward smiled with boyish pleasure. "I needn't return to the hospital for a few hours."

She set about preparing the chicken and the cobbler at once. Instead of settling himself comfortably beside the fire to rest, Edward joined in her preparations, sometimes getting in her way and sometimes anticipating her needs. By the time they sat down to eat, the discomfort had dissolved into laughter and an exchange of each other's stories.

"Did you not celebrate Christmas as a child?" he asked.

"Since Mamma was raised a Quaker, she had little experience with holidays. But Papa used to slip a coin and a sweet on my pillow while I slept, then pretend to be as surprised as I when I discovered them there in the morning." She smiled, remembering that happy time. "Was Christmas a special day in your home when you were a small boy?" she asked in turn.

"When I was small, St. Nicholas arrived to fill my and my brothers' shoes with sweets and a small gift. My mother made new shirts for us when she had enough money to buy the cloth. She always prepared a special dinner too. After she remarried, her new husband and all of his family would come for dinner and the farm-house would ring with laughter and children running everywhere. Before he returned to the city, my step-father would press a five-dollar gold piece into my hand and tell me to study hard and come to him if I needed more."

When the dishes were cleared, Edward surprised her by insisting on washing the dishes while she dried them. When they finished, he picked up the jacket he'd discarded much earlier. "I must go now," he said. There was a reluctance in his voice that Serenity found she shared. "But before I leave, I have a small gift for you." He drew an object from his coat pocket. Holding it in his closed hand, he stepped closer to her.

"I worked extra hours for some of the doctors while you were away to purchase this for you. It's not so grand as the one your mother wore, but it's a reminder that you must think clearly and seek the Lord's protection." He lifted her hand and slipped a ring on her finger. It fit perfectly.

Through tear-filled eyes, Serenity stared at the small amber stone surrounded by tiny diamond chips, a small replica of the ring she'd hoped to someday wear. She remembered telling Edward of how she longed for the strength and clarity of thought her mother's ring was reputed to possess. His gesture touched her heart. Wordlessly, she stood on her toes to kiss his cheek. Then he was gone into a swirling flurry of snow.

24

Through January, Edward was usually at the cottage one day each week. Once he came early in the morning, heavily bundled against the severe cold, to announce that a few nights earlier had been the coldest night known in Philadelphia and that the Delaware River had frozen over. He cautioned Serenity against going out for any reason save an emergency.

His visits were filled with laughter and descriptions of the happenings around town. Serenity was appalled by his accounts of several fires that had caused great damage and sent victims to the hospital with terrible burns. And she commiserated with him in his frustration over not being able to do enough for burn victims, who often died—or, if they survived, were grossly disfigured. She felt a sense of pride that Edward was trying to make a difference for these people.

Each time he came, he brought her a small gift: a bag of walnuts, an orange from some exotic foreign port, a lace handkerchief with a tiny embroidered violet in one corner, and once a few chocolate creams. He never spoke of their marriage, but she understood that he was courting her, and she began to suspect her feelings for him were more involved than she'd previously thought.

With the extreme cold that blanketed the city, she didn't venture out often but devoted her time to studying the Book of Mormon. She found answers to many of the questions her reading brought to mind by searching out other passages that discussed the same concept, but when she couldn't find an answer, she wrote her question down to ask Edward when he came again.

Her anticipation of his visits went beyond an opportunity to gain answers to her questions and to escape from loneliness. Each day brought greater proof that Edward himself was the reason she listened for his knock on her door.

Not even her fur-lined cape was sufficient protection against the cold when she found she must visit the outhouse hidden in the woods a short distance behind the cottage, or dash to the main house kitchen pump for water. Once upon returning from the main house, she saw a figure hurrying up the lane that led from the street to the cottage. Her heart leaped and she walked more rapidly with the bucket she carried, but when she reached the lane, no one was there. Her first thought had been that Edward had come, then that Stephen Rappleton had found her, but once she was back in her cottage warming her fingers at her fire, she couldn't shake the impression that her almost-visitor had been a woman.

Edward's visits became less frequent in February due to the approaching end of his course. Knowing that his professors' lectures would soon end and that he desired to return to Utah with the first wagon train in the spring, Serenity grew anxious concerning her own future. She enjoyed Edward's company, and she trusted him to look after her without trying to control her or her inheritance. He was also a fine-looking man. That thought brought a flush of heat to her cheeks, and she was certain it differed from the warmth she felt when she pondered the teachings in the Book of Mormon.

She thought often about being baptized and prayed for guidance in the matter. She read the Book of Mormon again and became familiar with the gentle warmth and peace it brought her. Gradually she became convinced that her testimony of the Book of Mormon required her to be baptized, and she decided to ask Edward to baptize her as soon as his studies were completed.

To better prepare herself for the trek across the plains and mountains to Utah Territory, and to take her mind off Edward, she pulled her gowns from their trunk and began to study them critically. Handling the dresses brought a mixture of memories and sensations. She truly had enjoyed wearing the lovely dresses, and she would never forget the pleasure of dancing or just listening to music. Holding one of the gowns close to her cheek, she closed her eyes and hummed a remembered tune, imagining herself swaying gracefully across a ballroom floor in Edward's arms. Edward? She had never danced with Edward. She set the ball gown aside. The last time she'd worn such a gown had been anything but pleasant.

Her experience of fleeing Jerome in her red velvet dress served as a caution, however, against paying heed to fashion when choosing gowns for the journey ahead. She set aside the ball gowns with their wide skirts, bare shoulders, and low necklines. That left nearly a dozen walking dresses and morning gowns, far more than she'd owned at any one time before her trip to New York. Of those, she chose four with less full skirts and a minimum of lace and trim that might snag or fray. Her favorites since returning to the cottage were the matching skirts and jackets worn with white bodices, which she'd worn to her committee meetings. She'd take those, she decided.

Though she reasoned that darker colors would be more suitable, her eyes returned over and over to a gown the color of sunshine that she'd worn once to church with the Montagues. She loved it for the contrasting colors of the pale yellow satin and the bronze lace that edged the neckline and ruffles, reminding her of her mother's topaz ring and the smaller ring Edward had given her.

Her hands caressed the dress. She loved the way Edward's ring looked shining against the satin and the way it blended into the lace. After a few moments she folded the dress and returned it to the trunk. She wouldn't wear it on the journey, but surely when she reached her destination she would have need of one special dress. She couldn't help picturing her mother's ring on her hand when she wore the gown.

She shook off thoughts of her mother's ring. She'd never see it again, and it served no purpose to dwell on it. Besides, her hands were smaller than her mother's had been, so it wouldn't look as striking on her. The ring Edward had given her suited her well enough.

One day near the end of February, Edward arrived with the welcome news that he was free all day. His exams were finished and he had only two more assigned shifts to complete. Though the temperature was still uncomfortably cold and a chill breeze was blowing, they decided to spend the day exploring the city. Serenity was bundled in her warm fur-lined cloak and matching fur-lined gloves and walking boots. She fastened the hood tightly to protect her head. Edward wore a thick coat he'd purchased in Denmark. They set out for the center of town together.

Even with a cold wind blowing off the river, Serenity savored her first real outing since returning to Philadelphia before Christmas. Not even the thick coal smoke that hung in the air could dampen their spirits. Serenity marveled again that some of the buildings were over a hundred years old and had been standing since before the Revolutionary War. They stared in awe at Independence Hall and felt a hush-like reverence viewing the Liberty Bell.

"It's like a page out of one of Papa's books. It can't possibly be real!" Serenity whispered, thinking she would never grow tired of viewing such grand sights.

"I felt the same way in Denmark," Edward told her. "There I was, newly come from a city less than twenty years old, gaping at buildings that had stood for hundreds of years. It was a humbling experience."

They found a dining room in a stately hotel and enjoyed their luncheon immensely. A warm glow seemed to surround them, and Serenity suspected she knew the answer concerning her future with the man who smiled across the table at her.

They were just finishing their lunch when a wild-eyed boy dashed into the hotel shouting, "George H. Roberts's hardware store is on fire, and all of the businesses close to it are burning too."

Several gentlemen jumped to their feet and raced toward the exit. The clang of fire bells could be heard when they opened the door. Leaving money on the table, Edward scarcely gave Serenity time to fasten her hood and pull on her gloves before conducting her outside to the street. He peered anxiously toward a billowing cloud of smoke, and Serenity knew he was thinking of the horrible burn victims he'd told her of earlier. The sharp blast of a steam whistle kept them from stepping onto the street, and they watched in amazement as a steam fire engine rushed past.

"The fire isn't far from here," Edward said. "I'd best see you home, then return to see if I can be of assistance." They saw a streetcar halted at the end of the street and hurried toward it, swinging aboard just as it began to move. Looking around, Serenity could see the car was filled mostly with men and older boys, who spoke excitedly about the fire and their intentions of fighting it to save their city.

The city train traveled only a few blocks before it stopped and most of the passengers began to jump down. From the car window, Serenity could see flames leaping high in the air. Smoke streamed far in the distance beyond the blaze. More than an entire block of businesses and warehouses was on fire.

"Would you mind continuing on by yourself?" Edward asked. "This fire is going to spread to the whole city if it isn't brought under control soon, and the odds of survival for those people caught in the flames will increase if they receive immediate care."

"No, I don't mind. Go ahead. I'll be fine," she told him. "But be careful."

"I shall." He leaped to his feet and hurried to exit the train before it began to move again. She watched until he disappeared into a crowd of smoke-shrouded figures running to assist in the firefighting effort.

There was a jolt, then the car began to move forward. Less than a city block passed before the train stopped again. Serenity sat with her face pressed against the window, catching glimpses of flames only a short distance away. Thick acrid smoke swirled around the train and began to fill the passenger car.

A man wearing a railroad uniform entered the car and raised his voice. "This is as far as this train is going. The fire is dangerously close to the tracks a short distance ahead, so the engineer is going to back the car to the last crossing. Anyone wishing to continue on foot must exit now."

An older gentleman took a small boy by the hand and stepped toward the exit. Serenity hesitated, uncertain whether to make her way to the cottage—a distance of several miles—or return to the hotel to wait until the fire was extinguished. If Edward returned to the cottage and didn't find her, he would worry, and she had no way of knowing how long it would be before another train ventured in the direction she needed to go. Making up her mind, she hurried toward the exit.

Stepping from the train, she had to wait for a horse-drawn fire wagon to pass before continuing on. As the wagon disappeared into the smoke, she caught sight of a woman hurrying in the direction of the fire. Something about her seemed familiar. She watched as the woman reached an alley that cut through the block and then glanced behind her before running into the narrow space. For just a moment Serenity saw the woman's face.

"Pauline," she whispered. But how could that be? The woman was in New York, not Philadelphia. Serenity began to run, dodging men and wagons. She must catch up to the woman to make certain she wasn't mistaken. And if the woman really was Pauline, she would offer her whatever help she needed, especially if her home was somewhere in the burning inferno ahead of them.

Serenity reached the alleyway and didn't hesitate. Her boots slipped on the mud and patches of ice as she hurried along, carefully sidestepping the clutter and unsavory deposits that littered its length. When her boots clattered against stone once more, she knew she'd reached the next street. She paused, gasping for breath and choking on the thick smoke. She attempted to look about and realized she was directly across the street from the fire. Clouds of vapor from the fire engines formed a fog that mixed with the dank, black smoke, making it nearly impossible to see more than a short distance ahead. There was no sign of the woman.

A cacophony of sound reached her from farther down the street, where a crowd of men and horses were gathered. Thinking Pauline might have gone toward the crowd, she hurried in that direction.

The crowd surged back, and Serenity was nearly trampled by a couple of men who took off running.

"What is it? What happened?" she asked an urchin who was jumping wildly around the edge of the crowd.

"I seen it!" he shouted. "The whole wall of that warehouse fell over. Bricks and burning timbers were flying. I ducked, I did, thinking I was about to be beaned by them flyin' bits."

"Was anyone hurt?"

"I reckon there's lots of dead folks . . . firemen and such." The boy thrust out his chest, somehow taking pride in being the bearer of sad news.

"Edward!" she screamed, turning her back on the child to elbow her way through the crowd, all thoughts of Pauline forgotten. She must find Edward and make certain he was safe.

She reached the front of the crowd at last and could scarcely breathe. Heat hit her like a slap in the face. The air was thick with smoke and dust, and just across from where she stood was a massive pile of rubble. Men were swarming over it, digging frantically to free those who had been trapped when the wall gave way. Bricks flew through the air as would-be rescuers tossed them toward the street. Several policemen rushed about in a vain attempt to hold onlookers back.

She searched the rescuers, looking for Edward. If he were alive, he would be among those giving aid to the injured. When she couldn't see him, she attempted to get closer but was thwarted by a burly policeman. She paced the length of the fallen wall from across the street, ignoring warnings to flee the fire and speculation that it was about to jump the street.

The din rose in an ear-splitting crescendo, and she backed into a doorway as the police cleared a path for a closed wagon marked by a clanging bell and the name *Philadelphia Hospital* stenciled on its side. When the wagon stopped, she crept closer.

Two men leaped from the back of the wagon. Carrying a stretcher, they hurried into the chaos. Before they returned with a groaning victim on the stretcher, another wagon appeared and the same procedure was repeated. The men bearing stretchers made several trips from the wagons to the rubble pile, and each time they returned with an injured man. She strained to see any identifying feature or piece of clothing. Each time she became certain the new victim wasn't Edward, she felt a guilty sense of relief, then her mind plunged into fear once more that he was buried beneath the bricks and burning framework of the building.

With their wagons filled with patients, the men who had carried the stretchers began to secure the wagon doors.

"Here's one more," a voice called from farther down the street. Three men stumbled from behind the debris. The one in the middle hung weakly from the arms of the other two, who were holding him upright. They had almost reached the wagons when the man on the right collapsed, carrying the other two with him to the ground.

"Edward!" Serenity screamed. Even covered in soot and grime, she knew the rescuer who lay crumpled in a heap on the ground. Ignoring orders to stay back, she dashed toward him. When she reach him, she knelt at his side, attempting to gather him in her arms. He didn't move, and his breath seemed faint. Fear stronger than she'd ever known filled her heart. She couldn't lose Edward. She just couldn't.

"Stand back, miss," one of the hospital workers warned, tugging at her shoulder.

"He's my husband." She refused to move. With her eyes and hands she searched for an injury.

"Said he was a doctor," the other rescuer said as he scrambled to his feet. "Took off his coat and tore up his shirt. He was bandaging wounds and helping everyone until some clumsy dolt stumbled against him and shoved him into a burning pillar. He recovered his balance and offered to help me bring that fellow out." He pointed to the man who lay on the ground beside Edward. "I had no idea he was hurt too."

"Get him loaded," the other attendant barked. "Some of these men are in pretty serious condition, and we'd better get them to the hospital before they die on us." The men roughly pushed Serenity aside to load the two fallen men into one of the ambulances.

Serenity ran after them and scrambled inside just before the door slammed shut.

"Hey! There's no room—"

"Let her come. We can use an extra pair of hands."

* * *

The journey to the hospital was harrowing. The injured men groaned and cursed as the ambulance jolted over cobbled streets and tilted precariously around corners. Finally the vehicle came to a stop and the attendants flung open the doors. One at a time, the men were hurried inside a large imposing structure, where they were met by a pair of harried doctors. Serenity remained beside Edward until it was his turn to be given a cursory examination.

"Ho! I know this fellow," the younger doctor shouted to the other. "He attended your lectures."

The older doctor looked over at Edward. "It's Dr. Benson. How did he come to be at the Third Street fire?"

Serenity looked up at the gray-haired doctor. "He's my husband, and we were returning from an outing when he stopped to help. Please help him."

"By all means," the doctor responded. "He will likely be much improved when you stop by to see him tomorrow."

Serenity shook her head. "I'm staying with him until he awakens." There was an unmistakable fierceness in her reply.

The doctor looked at her thoughtfully, then gave her a gentle smile. "There's a small chapel just down that hall and to your left," he said, pointing. "I must examine your husband more thoroughly and assign him to a ward. Go there and I'll come for you when I've finished."

She resisted leaving Edward's side, but the doctor was adamant that she leave until his patients were examined and a course prescribed for each. Reluctantly, she went in search of the chapel. On her way, she noticed a pump just beyond the back door where she could wash the blood and soot from her hands. The icy water felt so good, she splashed her face too in spite of the chill in the early evening air.

Feeling more refreshed, she continued following the doctor's directions until she found a small room with a few wooden pews. There was a pulpit at the far end with a crucifix behind it, much smaller and simpler than the one in the Montagues' church. She looked about and, seeing that she was the only person in the chapel, sank onto one of the pews at the back.

She leaned her head back and closed her eyes. Fears and questions ran through her mind, and she found herself trembling. Lowering her head, she clasped her hands together and began to pray. "Please, Father," she whispered. "Spare Edward. He is good and kind and I need him."

Warmth stole through her chest, and she knew she loved him. It was so simple, she wondered why she hadn't discovered the true nature of her feelings for him before. Perhaps she hadn't understood that love was friendship that went far beyond pleasant acquaintance and pleasurable outings. It was knowing that without Edward, an important part of herself would be missing. It was wishing she could bear his pain for him.

"Please, help him to awaken and be safe and whole," she prayed. When she finished, she didn't move for several minutes as a quiet calm crept over her.

The calm remained for a long time, then was replaced by a sense that she was being watched. She lifted her head, expecting to see the doctor enter the chapel. When he didn't, she let her gaze wander as she studied each detail of the small room. She almost missed a tiny movement near the front of the chapel. A curtain fluttered, then was still. Prickles of alarm formed goose bumps along her arms, warning that danger lurked nearby.

She stood, intending to discover whether the chapel had a second door, but as she moved into the aisle, she heard steps behind her.

"Mrs. Benson." She turned to see the doctor who had sent her to the chapel. He motioned for her to be seated again and sat on the pew in front of her with his body turned so that he faced her. He gave her a tired smile and spoke in blunt, direct language.

"Your husband was hit by falling debris when the wall collapsed, and he suffered multiple burns, cuts, and bruises. His head struck a pillar, causing a deep gash that lost a great deal of blood. His worst injury comes from mortar dust and soot in his lungs. Unless an infection sets in, he will recover, though his lungs may always be weak. This type of exposure often results in pneumonia. He will require careful watching, but for now, he needs rest more than anything."

* * *

For three days, Serenity refused to leave the hospital. The doctor, taking pity on her, provided her with a mat she could spread beside Edward's bed when exhaustion overcame her. He told her that Edward was one of his best students, and he brought her a small basket of apples and rolls.

The overworked nursing staff left most of Edward's care to Serenity. Knowing of his belief that illnesses were spread by contact with unclean hands and equipment, she scrubbed every bit of grime from his face and hands. She demanded clean sheets for his bed and fussed over him like a hen with one lone chick.

He coughed and mumbled through the first night and opened his eyes sometime around dawn.

"Good morning," she said, struggling to hold back the tears that suddenly dampened her weary eyes. He tried to speak, but no words passed his lips. Seeing the puzzlement and worry in his eyes, she sat on the edge of his bed and placed a finger on his lips. Then she told him all she knew of the fire and his injury, and she assured him that he would get well.

By the second day Edward could speak well enough to ask why she had left the train and made her way to the fire. She explained about the train traveling only a short distance before turning back, and about following the woman who looked like Pauline.

After awakening the third morning, Edward demanded in a hoarse whisper to be allowed to go home. As the hospital was in need of beds and Serenity was taking care of his nursing anyway, the doctor agreed to his release. A young physician, a man she'd been introduced to as Dr. Deerfield, had frequently come to examine Edward, and Edward reminded her that he and Dr. Deerfield shared the same dormitory and were accustomed to attending lectures together. Now Dr. Deerfield told them that he was just finishing his shift, and he offered to drive them to the cottage in a carriage he had borrowed from a friend.

Serenity adjusted Edward's scorched and tattered coat. Finding a scarf in its pocket, she wrapped it around him three times before she was satisfied, and then she pulled the carriage rug up to his chin. There had been no new snow while they'd been in the hospital, and the earlier snowfall had turned gray, giving the streets a dismal appearance. The sky was overcast with clouds, and a pall of coal smoke hung in the air. By the time they arrived at the cottage, Edward was exhausted, but he refused his friend's offer of assistance in moving inside.

"No, be on your way," he croaked. "I'll manage the few steps to the cottage without trouble." Reluctantly, Dr. Deerfield slapped the reins across the horses' backs to set them in motion. Soon the carriage was out of sight.

Serenity walked beside Edward with her arm about his waist, watching carefully for patches of ice and supporting him when he almost stumbled. He reached the door and she pushed it open.

Both of them stopped cold. *It can't be.* It was like opening the door to her father's room all those months ago. The room was a shambles—tables overturned, her trunk emptied, her kitchen supplies spilled across the floor, and feathers from her slashed tick floating in the draft they'd caused by opening the door.

25

Edward sagged against the doorpost for just a moment, then drew himself up to step inside the cottage. Serenity hurried to right a chair and then, taking Edward's arm, helped him to be seated before turning back to close and lock the door. She couldn't allow herself to think about the destruction or the reason behind it. Her first concern was Edward.

Without saying a word about the broken and scattered contents of her home, she knelt beside the fireplace to start a fire. The kindling and chunks of firewood had been dumped from their box but were still close at hand. She arranged them in the fireplace, then searched for a match. The sulphur matchsticks were scattered too, but she gathered up those she could find and struck one. Carefully she held it to the kindling until a tiny curl of wood burst into flame. She nurtured the small blaze, gradually adding larger pieces of wood until a steady flame began to heat the house.

Once the fire was started, she turned back to Edward. "Are you all right?" she asked.

"I'm fine." His attempt to reassure her ended in a strangled cough. "But who . . . ?"

"You need to lie down. The sofa will be faster to right than the bed." She pushed and tugged the heavy piece of furniture back into its place, then began her search for quilts. The cushions were ruined, but the frame was intact, and he could use quilts for padding.

Once she had the quilts arranged, Edward tried to stand. Fearing he might collapse, Serenity rushed to his side. "Lean on me," she suggested. She placed her arm around his waist and her shoulder beneath his arm. Slowly they made their way to the makeshift bed, where she insisted he lie down. She helped him remove his boots and pulled one of the quilts over him. It wouldn't do for him to catch a chill, and since the cottage had been empty for three days, it would take some time to warm it sufficiently.

"To think you've been here alone all these months, and now that I'm here I'm useless to protect you," he lamented in a raspy voice. She could see it pained him greatly to be unable to look after her as he thought he should. She knelt beside the sofa and placed her hand lightly on his chest.

"Hush," she whispered, trying to soothe him. "I locked the door each night and was in no danger. It was leaving the cottage vacant so long that attracted vandals. Now that I'm back, I don't expect any further trouble."

"But . . ." His voice trailed off.

"I know what you're thinking, but there's no way Rappleton could have found us in Philadelphia. Try to sleep. You need to rest. We'll talk later."

He lifted a hand and settled it over hers, pressing gently. His eyes closed.

She brushed his hair, which had grown long, back from his brow and stayed beside him until she was certain he'd fallen asleep. As she freed her hand, he moaned but remained asleep. She rose to her feet and stood looking down at him. Peace filled her heart, and she marveled again that it had taken her so long to recognize her love for him.

She couldn't stand around watching him sleep; many hours of work awaited her. She squared her shoulders and set about the task of restoring order to the cottage. Both the flour and sugar had been dumped from their containers and would have to be sifted before they'd be usable. As she put away her supplies, it seemed there were fewer than she remembered. She was fairly certain she'd had more apples and potatoes in her bins. Once the kitchen corner of the room was organized and swept, she turned to the bedroom.

Using pillowcases as receptacles, she began gathering the mounds of feathers that lay around her bed, then went on to those that had drifted about the cabin. Then she began the arduous task of mending and refilling the mattress and pillows. When her fingers tired, she set down her needle and began gathering up the clothing that had been flung from the trunk. Two gowns were missing, as were their matching petticoats. She hurried to the small wardrobe that stood with its doors gaping open. All of the dresses she'd hung there were accounted for, though the hems had been ripped open and the trim damaged on several, including the plain gowns she'd owned before her trip to New York. Her mother's saddlebag lay open in the bottom of the wardrobe. The toys were scattered among the clothing and other objects on the floor. She bent to gather them up.

Noticing undergarments lying on the floor and hanging from the wardrobe drawer, she quickly snatched them up but felt reluctant to return them to their drawer. The thought of wearing what the intruder had touched offended her sensibilities. She'd have to wash and somehow dry them without offending Edward.

Returning to the trunk, she discovered to her dismay that several holes had been punched in the bottom of it.

"That's odd," she murmured, sitting back on her heels.

"What's odd?"

She turned to see that Edward had awakened and pulled himself to a sitting position, from which he could see her through the open door.

She hurried to his side. "Are you feeling better? I put on a kettle of water to heat. Would you like a cup of tea?"

"Yes, to both of your questions, but the tea can wait. What did you find to be odd?"

She told him about the missing food and clothing. "That isn't so surprising as finding hems opened and holes punched in the bottom of my trunk."

"A hungry thief might have taken the food to eat and your gowns to sell," Edward speculated. "But tearing open mattresses and hems, dumping flower and sugar, and looking for a false bottom in your trunk suggest the intruder was looking for the ring."

Serenity's face fell. "Mr. Brown is in prison, but do you suppose Mr. Rappleton has found me after all?"

Edward urged her down beside him and continued in his whispery voice. "It could be that he has discovered your whereabouts. He clearly didn't believe you when you told him the ring was lost."

"I wish it weren't lost, but I can accept that it is. I wish those who would steal it could accept that as well." She sat quietly thinking for several minutes, then jumped to her feet. "I don't remember seeing the small wooden box Papa gave me. It's where I keep my few pieces of jewelry and a small amount of cash."

Standing on her toes, she searched the top shelf of the wardrobe and found it bare. No hats and no small wooden box met her searching fingers. She knelt to sift through the items remaining on the floor. She found the hats, or what remained of them—most had been torn apart. The box was missing. Running to the fireplace, she searched the mantle. The candlestick and the small brass figurines were also gone.

She burst into tears. "My money and all of my gifts from Papa are gone," she wailed, lamenting the loss of her ruby-and-pearl earrings, the necklace Rupert found that her father had bought for her on his last trip, and even the brass candlestick.

"It's all right to cry." Edward struggled to his feet and made his way to her side. His arms went around her, and she clasped him about his waist. She buried her face in his shirtfront and sobbed for a long time with an intensity she couldn't control. Little sleep for the past three days, worry about Edward, and the huge task of putting the cottage in order made her loss nearly unbearable.

When at last her emotional storm passed, she felt embarrassed. She insisted that Edward sit back down while she begin supper preparations. She fussed with placing some of the cushions she had repaired on the sofa and adding more fuel to the fire.

"I need water," she told him as she picked up the water bucket.

"I'll accompany you." He moved to stand.

"No, you aren't ready to walk so far."

"If the intruder is still nearby, it could be dangerous for you to be out alone, as it's almost dark. Can't water wait until morning?"

"I'll be careful." The water was truly needed. She couldn't prepare dinner, wash, or keep Edward's wounds clean without it. She didn't wish him to know that she was fearful of the long walk. She'd spoken bravely of being alone in the cottage, and she hadn't been afraid at first, but now that had changed.

Though it was only five o'clock in the afternoon, evening was already upon them. As Serenity walked down the long lane, she was conscious of Edward watching her from the cottage window. Though he was weak, just knowing he could see her aided her confidence. Once out of sight of the cottage, she grew more fearful. A sharp breeze rattled bare branches on the trees and sent the firs dipping and swaying. Dried leaves escaping the grasp of the frozen, gray piles of snow caused her to jump.

Reaching the pump at last, she filled her bucket and started the trek back to the cottage.

"Good evening, miss," the elderly Mr. Frampton called. Serenity turned to acknowledge her landlord's greeting.

"Hello, Mr. Frampton."

"I haven't seen you about of late. Have you been ill?" He was bundled warmly against the cold and seemed about to enter a closed carriage.

She walked nearer. "My husband was injured while he was attempting to aid the firefighters on North Third Street a few days ago and has been in the hospital."

"And is he recovering?"

"Yes, but he's still weak." She set the heavy water pail down before going on. "Today we arrived back at the cottage to find that an intruder had broken in during our absence. He stole a few items and caused a great deal of damage to the furniture, which I will endeavor to repair. I will reimburse you for what cannot be saved."

"An intruder, you say?" He appeared indignant.

She nodded her head.

"The furniture is old and worn. I shall not expect you to replace it. I will, however, send Donald and Belle down to help you with repairs tomorrow morning," he informed her, naming two of the servants who worked in his house. "What can't be suitably fixed, I shall instruct them to discard. I shall also have Donald patrol the park each evening and keep an eye on the cottage until Mr. Benson has recovered."

"Thank you," Serenity said sincerely.

Serenity followed the slow-moving carriage until the lane split, then it was only a short walk to the cottage. Though the water bucket was heavy and she had to set it down twice, she was no longer nervous. If anyone approached her, she could scream and both the carriage driver and Edward would come, she assured herself.

Once back in the cottage with the door locked and a bar placed across it for good measure, she set about preparing supper. Edward insisted on sitting at the small table with her to dine, though she tried to convince him that she'd prepare him a tray. Before the meal was finished, she could see he was greatly fatigued. He didn't argue when she suggested he return to the sofa while she cleared the table and washed the dishes.

Once those tasks were finished, she resumed mending the mattress. As she worked, she found herself wishing the task was finished. She was exhausted. Several times her head nodded. If she had any place to lie down other than the bed, she'd go to sleep and finish the task in the morning. One thing was certain: as soon as the feathers were back in the mattress, she'd pull off her walking boots and fall onto the bed.

She looked over at Edward. He appeared to be sleeping. Rising to her feet once more, she tucked another quilt around him to keep him warm should the fire go out before morning. She stood for a few minutes watching him sleep, then moved to the fireplace to bank the fire. When she was assured all was ready for the night, she picked up the lantern, carried it to the side of the bed, and set it on the small table, which she'd righted earlier and returned to its proper place. Sinking to the floor, she picked up the heavy ticking and her needle to resume stitching the mattress.

When only a small gap remained in the ticking, she began transferring the feathers from the pillowcases to the mattress. Holding onto the heavy fabric while getting the feathers into the gap she'd left proved to be an aggravating task. Repeatedly she found it necessary to set down the slowly filling mattress and chase down escaped feathers.

"That job doesn't look too heavy for me to attempt."

Startled, she looked up to see Edward standing beside the bed with a quilt wrapped around his shoulders. He dropped the quilt and sank down beside her on the floor. "Do you want me to scoop feathers or hold the seam open?" he asked.

Working together, it didn't take them long to fill the mattress. Then Serenity picked up her needle and began a whipstitch to close the seam. When she finished, she stretched and yawned. That's when she noticed that Edward had fallen asleep again. He was lying across the mattress near the lantern with his face turned toward her.

Gathering up the quilt he'd dropped on the floor, she crawled across the mattress toward him. When she reached his side, she rose up on her knees to extinguish the lantern, then lay the quilt across his sleeping form. Meaning to let him continue sleeping on the mattress, she began to back up. She'd sleep on the sofa.

A hand circled her wrist. "Don't go," Edward whispered. She found herself powerless to resist the slight tug that brought her sprawling beside him, her head beside his—especially since there was nothing she wanted more than to give in to sleep with Edward's arms around her. She scarcely had time to savor the soft feathertick beneath her tired body and the delicious warmth of lying beside Edward, sharing the quilt, before her conscious mind surrendered to sleep.

She awoke to find Edward's face smiling down at her. He lay propped up on one elbow watching her. She flushed self-consciously.

"Good morning, sleepyhead," he said with a grin—the flirtatious smile she'd seen little of for many months. She marveled again at how handsome and kind she found him. His head came closer to hers, and she couldn't take her eyes from his lips. Her hand crept toward the corner of his smile, then she snatched it back quickly, remembering Mr. Frampton's promise. Donald and Belle might arrive at any moment.

Her eyes opened wider as she noticed the sun shining through the cottage window. She rolled away from Edward and scrambled to her feet while keeping her face averted. She'd only just barely straightened her gown and splashed water on her face when a knock sounded at the cottage door.

It didn't take Donald and Belle long to finish straightening the cottage and repairing the pieces of furniture that had been damaged.

"Mr. Frampton said I should undertake nightly patrols of the grounds," Donald informed Edward. "If you remember to lock the cottage whenever you leave it, you shall be perfectly safe."

"Thank you, Donald," Edward said. "I certainly hope that will be the case. At any rate, my wife will no longer be alone here, as I have finished my classes and mean to stay in the cottage with her until early summer, when we shall be returning to Utah."

By noon the two servants had finished their task and were on their way back to the main house, leaving Serenity and Edward alone again. Serenity felt an awkwardness for a time, but Edward never mentioned that she'd slept through the night beside him. He didn't refer again to his intention of remaining at the cottage with her either, though his declaration had greatly relieved her concern about the intruder returning.

The next two weeks brought a renewal of the camaraderie Serenity and Edward had experienced while floating down the river. He began sleeping less each day, and on the occasional day when the sun shone brightly, they took short walks together around the estate. It seemed natural to read together again each evening, too.

Dr. Deerfield arrived one day with Edward's bag and a message from the older doctor, offering Edward a job with a small salary as soon as he felt ready to take the position. The offer excited Edward, and he expressed an eagerness to put his skills to use while waiting to begin his journey west.

Serenity refused to listen to Edward's arguments concerning where each should sleep at night. Edward had been injured and needed to rest comfortably to regain his strength, therefore he would use the bed and she would make do with the shorter, more narrow sofa. Sometimes, just before she fell asleep, she thought of the night they had shared the mattress and wished herself back beside him, listening to the even thump of his heart beneath her ear.

Sometimes she caught him watching her and recognized the longing in his eyes. She shared that longing, but she didn't know how to tell him of her feelings. He'd made it clear that the direction of their relationship was in her hands, but she couldn't bring herself to say, "Oh, by the by, I've decided I want to remain married to you, share your bed, and bear your children." She couldn't possibly be so forward, so she tried in more subtle ways to let him know she cared for him. She prepared the dishes he expressed a liking for, accompanied him on his walks even after he was strong enough to walk alone, and let her fingers linger any time she found a reason to touch him.

* * *

"I believe I shall visit the hospital today," Edward announced one morning as they sat at breakfast. Pale green buds were showing on the trees surrounding the cottage, and the air smelled of spring. "Professor Wickham assured me that I completed my course satisfactorily, but I need to sign some papers and pick up the certificate that states I am now a licensed doctor of medicine. I also wish to discuss with him his offer to allow me to work at the hospital until we begin our journey to Salt Lake. President Young will not give orders for the Church trains and teamsters to leave Salt Lake until April, so June is the earliest we can expect to meet up with them. That gives me two more months to study Dr. Wickham's methods. It's a wonderful opportunity and will better prepare me for my life's work."

"Are you certain you are well enough?" Serenity wasn't convinced she liked the idea of him walking to the street where the train ran and then traveling all the way to the hospital. And she didn't even want to think about being alone for extended periods of time again while Edward worked. But Edward was chafing at being idle now that he was stronger, especially with spring making an early arrival.

"I'll be fine," he assured her. "I feel quite invigorated, and the cough is nearly gone." He reached a hand across the table, taking her hand in his. She could tell he guessed at her fear that the intruder might return, because he added, "Donald keeps watch for trespassers, and if you keep the door locked, you shall be perfectly safe." He handed her the key to the cottage door, which she dropped into her apron pocket. "I shall return before evening."

Serenity felt strange being alone in the cottage after Edward left. She mixed a batch of bread and washed her more personal laundry, setting the items to dry before the fire. Several times she went to the window to gaze down the lane toward the street, though she knew it was too early to expect Edward's return.

There was a hint of spring in the air, and she considered scrubbing the floor, but on going to the water bucket, she found it nearly empty. Lifting her eyes from the empty bucket, she saw Donald ambling along the lane. Snatching up the bucket, she opened the door and hurried after him, pausing only long enough to turn the key in the lock and drop it back into her pocket.

Knowing she was safe while the burly servant was about, she walked quickly to keep him in sight. Hearing her footsteps, he turned, then waited for her to catch up to him.

"Hello, Donald," she greeted him. "I believe spring will soon be here."

"'Tis a false spring, I fear," the servant responded. "Each year we have a brief period in March that suggests an early spring, then foul weather returns in all its fury for a few more weeks. From the end of the lane, I could see the clouds gathering to the north."

"I must hurry with the water then," she responded and added a silent prayer that Edward would return before the storm arrived.

She filled the bucket while chatting with Donald. He then hoisted it, offering to carry it back to the cottage for her.

"Donald!" The back door of the house opened and the large woman Serenity had learned was the cook came out on the stoop. "Mrs. Frampton has asked for the carriage to be brought around. She has been invited to tea and has been waiting for your return. You must hurry."

Donald looked at Serenity apologetically.

"Don't worry, I shall be fine," she said, taking back the heavy bucket.

Reluctantly, he allowed her to take it, then hurried off to do his mistress's bidding. Serenity walked quickly, though at frequent intervals she had to set the bucket down to rest her arm.

On reaching the cottage, she set down the bucket to unlock the door, then reached back for the bucket.

"Excuse me," a voice called from behind her. She whirled around, splashing water against her skirt, her heart thudding. When she saw a small boy of seven or eight extending a paper toward her, her fright began to dissipate.

"A lady said I should give this to you," the boy said. He was dirty and dressed shabbily, but he was perfectly polite. She glanced around to see if an adult were present. Seeing no one, she accepted the paper. She glanced down at it, reading with haste:

Serenity, come quickly. I am dreadfully ill and have no one but you to turn to.

It was signed "Pauline Sebastian," followed by an address in a distant part of the city.

26

Serenity looked up to question the child, but he was gone. After all Pauline had done for her, she hesitated for only a moment before deciding to go to her friend's aid. She ran for her purse. She would need money to ride the train. Thankfully, she'd had her purse with her the day Edward was injured, else she'd have nothing with which to buy a train ticket. There had been no opportunity for Edward to withdraw funds for her from the bank since then.

Not wishing Edward to return to an empty cottage and worry about her absence, she scribbled a note telling him Pauline was ill and had sent for her. She propped the note on the table and set her key beside it. With fumbling fingers she closed the cottage door and hurried toward the tree-lined street, arriving in time to see the Frampton carriage turn the corner some distance away and disappear from sight. She began a brisk walk in the opposite direction.

Just as she glanced up at the dark clouds that seemed to be rushing toward her, she heard quick steps behind her. Before she could turn, an arm encircled her throat and a rag reeking of an unpleasant odor covered her face, filling her mouth with a sweet, burning taste. She struggled to free herself, but it was no use. Deep blackness filled her head, and she seemed to be falling into a long, dark void.

* * *

She awoke to a world that swirled in frantic waves around her. Deep convulsions shook her slender frame, resulting in heaves that soiled her clothing and the place where she lay. She struggled to turn to her side, resting her head against the coarse mattress and trying to regain her senses. After a few moments, she remembered hurrying down the street to catch a train that would take her to Pauline, and then the attack that came from behind.

Pauline! Pauline would think her a faithless friend when she didn't arrive to care for her.

Eventually, the dizziness began to subside and she was able to look around. She was in a narrow room with only one small, high window that let in little light. She lay on a metal cot with a thin mattress that smelled of moldy straw, smoke, and other undesirable odors. She lifted her right hand to touch her left, seeking comfort from the ring Edward had given her. It was gone!

In her struggle to sit up, she discovered that her hands were free, but some kind of shackle circled one ankle and attached her to the cot with a short chain. There was a cluttered washstand beside the cot, and several articles of clothing hung from a row of nails hammered into the wall. Two of the hanging items bore a remarkable resemblance to her own missing gowns. A trunk rested beneath the clothing. Its lid was up, and various items hung over its sides and lay scattered about the floor. Amid the clutter on the stand beside the cot sat the wooden box her father had given her. Clearly she had fallen into the hands of the intruder who had ransacked the cottage a few weeks earlier.

She appeared to be alone at the moment. Feeling ill and confused, she tried to make sense of the situation. She had no idea where she was nor who had brought her to the small, dingy room. She vaguely remembered being forced up a long flight of stairs wearing a blindfold. She considered screaming for help but feared her screams might bring her captor. Her head ached and her stomach threatened to rebel again.

The metal cuff on her ankle cut into her tender skin as she tried to change position so she could see it better. Once she achieved a better view of it, she attempted to free herself, but it soon became apparent she could not open the clasp nor break the heavy band. The chain was equally secure. She squirmed until she could see where the chain attached to the iron bed frame. She had hoped it was merely looped beneath one of the legs of the bed and that by lifting the bed leg she could pull the chain free, but it was secured by a second cuff to one of the bed frame's crosspieces. She was a prisoner with no way of freeing herself. A wave of nausea rose in her throat, and she struggled to contain it.

She sat still with her head down until her stomach settled once more. The floor was in need of a good sweeping and scrubbing, she noted in an abstract way. Her gown was soiled and her hair matted with vomit. She wondered if she was going to die or if her captor had something more sinister in mind. A verse she'd read just the evening before in Third Nephi came to mind. "No unclean thing can enter into his kingdom . . ." She couldn't recall the rest of the verse. She knew that the filth that surrounded her was not the filth of which the Lord spoke. Nor would He hold her responsible for the unclean acts of others, should her capture result in violation. A brief moment of peace filled her mind.

As time dragged by, her mind filled with those things she'd failed to do. She regretted that she hadn't been baptized, but with Edward being the only man of her acquaintance holding the priesthood, she'd delayed asking him to perform the ordinance, fearing the cold water would further weaken him. She regretted, too, that she'd never shared with Edward her feelings for him. She loved him and wished to be his wife. Now it might be too late.

Her thoughts turned to the cause that had brought her parents together. She had done her best to carry out her father's instructions to provide opportunities for the former slaves, but she'd committed none of her own personal fortune to the cause.

Footsteps beyond the door to the room brought a hasty end to her prayer. Lifting her eyes, she noticed the room had grown darker, but she had no way of knowing whether night had fallen or if the storm was darkening the sky. She watched with fearful eyes as the door swung open. In the gloom she could barely make out two forms in the doorway. One appeared to be female. The woman stepped closer.

Pauline! A surge of hope lifted Serenity's spirits for a brief moment, but then she saw Pauline's eyes. They were hard and sparked with venom. Pauline raised her hand as though to strike her, and Serenity shrank back as far as her shackles permitted.

"Why?" Serenity whispered through a knot of pain that constricted her throat. She'd liked and admired Pauline. She'd believed they were friends. The dawning realization that Pauline's friendship was a lie hurt more than a physical blow.

"You have something I want," Pauline sneered, stepping closer. "Josh promised that ring to me. It's mine."

The fingers of Serenity's right hand hesitantly touched her bare ring finger, and her mind grappled with the mention of Josh. There was no doubt that Pauline meant Joshua Brown.

"Not that ring," Pauline spat. "The candlestick fetched more than it did."

"It was the only ring I possessed." Serenity spoke with real sorrow. Edward had told her the ring was of little monetary worth, but she'd valued it because he had given it to her.

"Don't think us fools." The man who had remained in the shadows stepped forward, and her eyes widened in fear as she recognized Stephen Rappleton. He grabbed her arm and gave it a vicious twist. "You know the ring we want. It wasn't lost, it was hidden. And you know where it is. Tell me at once where it is."

"I don't know. My father and I have both searched, but it's not to be found."

"I don't believe you!" Pauline nearly screamed. "Josh didn't search properly. He knows nothing of women. A woman wouldn't hide a valuable piece of jewelry in a saddlebag; she'd slip it in a loose seam or conceal it in her hat, or even in her hair."

"Papa never found it—"

Pauline slapped her face, making her ears ring. "It will do no good to lie. I need that ring and I mean to have it."

"But, I don't—"

Pauline snatched a fistful of Serenity's hair and yanked. Serenity fought back, screaming as she tried to free her hair from the other woman's painful grasp.

"Screaming will do you no good," Rappleton snarled. "The fire took half of this building last month, and the rest is about to collapse. There's no one other than us living here now."

Weak from her bout of nausea and hampered by the short chain, Serenity was no match for the older, stronger woman, who knew a great deal more than Serenity did about kicking and punching. Serenity slumped to the floor, her leg twisted painfully above her.

Rappleton pounced on her, roughly binding her hands behind her back.

"If I didn't need that ring, I'd kill you," Pauline whispered, her voice full of hate. "You're spoiled and rich and care nothing of the poverty you thrust on me and my brother. Because of you, my husband is in prison and Stephen has been forced to abandon his business."

Serenity was beginning to have a sense of this woman's connection to the earlier events surrounding her mother's ring. She turned her eyes toward Rappleton. "It's because of you my parents are dead," she accused.

"I didn't know your mother, and it was only chance that led Josh to her. If she hadn't been engaged in an illegal activity, she'd still be alive."

"You're saying Joshua Brown killed my mother?" Serenity choked on the words.

"He'd been trailing those blacks for weeks and was watching from the trees when that woman took off her gloves. He recognized the ring at once from the description I'd given him years earlier. He figured he could get it, then go back for the runaways. After he fired, it only took a few minutes to reach the woman, but the ring was gone and he could hear riders approaching. He grabbed her saddlebag, figuring she'd hid the ring in it, and got out of there. He swore that as soon as the war ended he'd find that ring."

Serenity's mind swirled through a sea of blackness. She couldn't breathe. Her mother had been murdered and Rappleton spoke of her death like it was of little consequence. As though from a great distance, she heard Pauline laugh on a high, almost hysterical note.

"Stephen was supposed to find out the ring's location when Charles returned to New York, but the arrogant fool invited your father for a weekend visit and didn't watch him closely enough. Instead of Stephen getting him to talk, Charles discovered the valuables Joshua and I took to Stephen to hide until they were safe to sell. With them was the saddlebag he'd promised to get rid of five years ago. Josh had to stop Charles from telling what he knew."

Pain tore through Serenity's heart. Pauline obviously derived some twisted satisfaction from sharing the details of her father's death with her.

Pauline paced the floor, kicking debris aside or walking over it. Eventually she seated herself on a chair beside a small table Serenity hadn't been able to see from the cot. The dark expression on her face frightened Serenity, and she feared Pauline would kill her when she didn't produce the ring.

"But didn't Joshua tell you the ring was lost?"

"He doesn't believe that any more than I do. He couldn't find out where you'd gone, so he told me to watch Rupert Montague and that eventually you would show up in New York. I was unable to find employment in his household and had to settle for temporary positions in the Montague's social circle. We hadn't counted on young Jerome making a fool of himself over you and never leaving your side."

Serenity's feelings toward Jerome softened somewhat. He'd schemed to steal from her too, but he'd never threatened her with bodily harm.

"Why did you pretend to be my friend?" Serenity was scarcely aware she asked the question.

"I had to get close to you to find out where you hid the ring. I've followed you for months, ever since your arrival in New York, though Stephen lost you for a time after you returned here."

"That was your fault," Rappleton said, glaring at his sister.

"No matter, I knew that dolt you married was at Philadelphia Hospital and would eventually lead us to you. That husband of yours would have died in the fire, but for Stephen's incompetence."

"You didn't do any better after you followed that ambulance to the hospital." The pair glared at each other. Serenity remembered the rescuer's assertion that Edward had been pushed toward the flames and had struck a support, and her own uneasiness in the hospital chapel before the doctor had found her.

Pauline rose to her feet and advanced toward her. In her hand was a small silver pistol. "It's time."

She's going to kill me. Serenity closed her eyes. *Comfort Edward and let him know I really do love him,* she prayed.

The chain dropped from around her ankle. The toe of Pauline's boot nudged Serenity's side.

"Get to your feet," she ordered.

Opening her eyes, Serenity blinked in confusion. The room had been almost completely dark, but now she could see the stubborn set of Pauline's jaw. Stephen had lit a lantern and set it on the table while she'd prayed.

"You fool!" Pauline turned on Stephen. "I told you no light until we reach the stairs." The small weapon in Pauline's hand flashed with an astonishing burst of sound. Stephen looked startled, then pitched forward, sprawling at Pauline's feet. Serenity was horrified.

Pauline reached for the lantern, turning its wick low before once again ordering Serenity to stand. Serenity struggled to her feet. Pauline motioned with the gun for her to walk toward the door. Serenity opened it and took a single step onto a narrow landing.

The lantern provided just enough light to reveal a gaping stairwell. Narrow stairs ran downward for at least two floors before they disappeared into blackness. Serenity could also see a hall stretching to the left and right with several closed doors. No light showed beneath any of the doors.

Pauline shoved her toward the stairs. "Get going."

Serenity stumbled, barely regaining her balance in time to avoid tumbling down the seemingly endless flights of stairs that stretched before her. Her heart hammered. She knew with a certainty that Pauline meant to kill her sooner or later, and she wondered if it was her erstwhile friend's intention to send her crashing to her death in the blackness below.

"You can take me to that ring or we can end it right here," Pauline hissed. "But if you choose to die, I'll burn your cottage

down while your Mormon husband is inside. I'll have that ring or
no one will."

Serenity's heart filled with anguish. She couldn't produce the
ring and she couldn't bear to be responsible for Edward's death.

Pauline nudged her with the gun, and Serenity took a hesitant step
forward. With her hands bound, the stairs were more formidable.
Hesitantly, she felt for the first stair, then the next. The wooden steps
were old and warped, and the air was thick with stale smoke. Trash
littered nearly every stair, increasing her trepidation. Each step creaked
or groaned, and occasionally one cracked as though splintering, filling
her with a new fear of crashing through a rotten step to her death.

"Hurry!" Pauline urged her, poking her in the ribs with the pistol.
Serenity tried to increase her speed, but her fear of falling and her
bound hands made it difficult. The garbage-strewn stairs stretched
downward beyond the lantern's light like a never-ending nightmare.

A sound came from the darkness below them. "Wait! What's
that?" Pauline hissed, catching at Serenity's sleeve and bringing her
to a teetering halt.

"A storm was heading this way. The wind probably blew a door
open." Serenity answered as calmly as she could manage, though
her heart was pounding and she hoped someone, not just the
wind, had opened a door—someone who would see her predicament and come to her rescue. A draft of air floated up the stairs,
making her explanation more credible.

"Keep moving." Pauline's voice was pitched lower. She turned
the wick on the lantern so low Serenity had difficulty seeing the
next step. With each gingerly placed foot, her fear escalated.

They came to a narrow landing similar to the one outside the
room where Serenity had been held prisoner. She paused, gathering
her courage to begin descending the next flight of stairs. In the
silence of that brief pause, she heard footsteps coming up the stairs.
Pauline heard the sound too. She lifted the lantern higher as though
trying to see farther. A cat-sized rodent scuttled across their shoes.

Pauline shuddered, then nudged Serenity toward the stairs again.
"Just a stupid rat!"

Serenity squeezed back tears of disappointment. Her imagination had conjured up a rescuer when it was only rats sharing the stairway. Her foot collided with an empty can and she listened to it clatter against the stairs and walls for a long time before it reached the bottom.

"Who goes there?" a man's voice drifted upward, causing both women to draw in sharp breaths. A faint glow appeared far below and seemed to be growing stronger.

Pauline extinguished her lantern and pressed the gun into Serenity's neck before Serenity could shout a warning. With one hand Pauline gripped Serenity's shoulder, and she hissed in her ear, "I'll kill you both if you make a sound."

Serenity didn't dare respond to the voice at the bottom of the stairs. She stood rooted to the step, watching as the light grew brighter until she could distinguish its source. The stairs continued downward for one flight more beyond the one on which they stood, then turned sharply to the right. Someone with a lantern was coming up the stairs toward the corner where the stairway turned.

It seemed like an eternity, but it was only a few moments until a man rounded the corner two floors below with a brightly lit lantern. Something about him looked familiar. Serenity had only a brief glimpse before a second man turned the corner, and she gasped. Revealed in the lantern light was Edward. Joy filled her heart, then was replaced by icy fear.

Hearing a slight click behind her, she knew Pauline had drawn back the hammer on the tiny gun she held to the back of Serenity's neck. Though a cold draft rushed up the stairs, perspiration formed wet patches across Serenity's bodice and her lips felt dry and cracked. Pauline was going to shoot her, then turn the gun on Edward.

The pressure against her neck suddenly ceased. Pauline released her hold on Serenity's shoulder, and she knew what was about to happen. Edward was spotlighted in the circle of light coming from the lantern below. Her captor intended to kill him first.

She couldn't let Pauline kill Edward. Throwing herself backward, she sought to hinder the woman's aim. Her head struck something soft, and she heard the whoosh of air leaving Pauline's lungs, accompanied by the sound of her lantern shattering. In the darkness, the gun exploded, the sound reverberating inside the enclosed stairwell. Excited shouts drifted upward, and the distant lantern went out too, plunging the stairwell into complete darkness.

Hands clutched at her, grasping for her throat, and she felt herself sway. Frenzied, fear-filled obscenities filled the air. Pauline too was off-balance and clutching for something to hold onto. Serenity's hands, bound at the wrists, opened and closed helplessly. Finally they caught at a handful of fabric, but in the darkness she didn't know whether she clutched her own skirt or Pauline's.

There was no way to halt the inevitable. One minute they teetered precariously on a narrow step, then the next they were falling. She heard Pauline scream, or perhaps it was her own screams that echoed through the blackness. First one shoulder struck a step, then the other. She bounced against a wall and cried out. Pauline's screams and curses echoed in her ears.

Pauline clasped her in a fearful embrace. Their legs tangled as together they tumbled and rolled down the long flight of stairs, helplessly wrapped in the fabric of two full skirts and all their petticoats. Yards of cloth wrapped about Serenity's head, nearly suffocating her.

Pauline's moans ended abruptly just before Serenity slammed into something solid. Hands tore at the fabric gathered around her head. A sliver of light squeezed past her eyelids. She recognized Edward's voice, and now she recognized the other man: Dr. Deerfield was saying the blond woman was dead of a broken neck. Then she knew no more.

27

"Darling, you're safe now, but don't try to move." There was desperation in Edward's voice. Serenity tried to talk, to assure him she was all right, but she didn't have the strength and she hurt so terribly much.

"I think the blond woman inadvertently saved your wife's life," Dr. Deerfield said. "She buffered Serenity from the support she slammed into that broke her neck."

"All those blasted yards of petticoat did some good too," Edward added. "They protected her from the glass ground into the other woman's face."

Edward continued his examination of Serenity as he talked, assuring himself and her that neither her arms nor legs were broken. And though she'd suffered several deep lacerations and possibly a few sprains, he couldn't detect any internal damage.

Serenity was vaguely aware of a constable arriving and of Pauline's body being taken away.

"Rappleton. Upstairs," she gasped. Pain in her chest made the light from the lantern near her seem to flicker eerily and then go black. When she became conscious again, several more lanterns surrounded her and she no longer lay in the stairwell but was propped in Edward's arms in a curricle.

"Be still," he whispered, smoothing her tangled curls from her face. "It's best that you move as little as possible. The constable wishes you to answer a few questions before I take you home. Are you able to do so?" Serenity attempted to nod, but the motion brought a stabbing pain to her head.

Edward and his friend answered most of the constable's questions, but neither the questions nor the answers made much sense to Serenity. She was only able to stammer out simple answers to a few questions herself before Dr. Deerfield insisted his patient must rest. She fell asleep, feeling secure in her husband's arms as they journeyed back to the cottage.

It was morning when she awoke. Tears filled her eyes as she looked around the familiar little cottage she had thought she would never see again. She attempted to arise and gasped with pain. She hurt everywhere. Bandages covered her arms and there was something strange on her head.

"Don't try to move without assistance, my dear," Edward said, coming into her line of vision. "You've suffered a terrible battering and are quite covered in bruises and welts. You may have a broken rib. I bandaged your ribs, just in case, and Richard—that is, Dr. Deerfield—did a superb job of bandaging the gashes on your temple and arms." Seeing her tears, he seated himself beside her on the bed and gently took her hands in his. "The bruises will heal and you'll be strong and well again in a few weeks."

"How did you know where to find me?"

"Your note said you'd gone to help Pauline, who was ill, but you left no address. I was afraid she might need medical help, so I prevailed on Richard to help me find you. I remembered you thought you saw her on a street near the fire. As we drove down Third Street, I spotted a light in a window near the top of a partially burned building that has been condemned by the city, and I felt we should investigate."

After a slight pause, he whispered, "I love you."

Her attempt to respond ended in a sob as she remembered Pauline had shot her brother because he lit that lantern.

"Is that so terrible?" he asked with just a hint of a wry smile, mistaking her tears for a response to his declaration.

"It is. Because I love you and have dreamed for weeks of your strong arms around me. Now I hurt so much that even the smallest embrace would surely mean the end of me."

"Well, we mustn't take any chances." Edward smiled the old smile that had enchanted her from the start. "I shall feed you and fuss over you until every bruise and ache is gone, and then I shall go down on bended knee to invite you to become my wife."

She felt an urge to giggle. "I'm already your wife."

"Ah, but this time our marriage shall be quite different."

"Could we start over with another wedding?" she asked wistfully. "I should like to wear my best gown and repeat our vows before a minister."

"I'm sure that we can find an elder arriving on one of the first immigrant ships in a few weeks who can be persuaded to perform our marriage."

"When you told me about the temple that is being built in Salt Lake you said eternal marriages were being performed in an endowment house near the temple site. Will you marry me again there?" she asked.

A roar of laughter erupted from deep in his chest. "You've proposed to me twice now. Whatever happened to a man's prerogative in matters of marriage? And there's a little matter of becoming a member of the Church before you can get President Young's permission to enter the Endowment House."

A flush of heat crept up her cheeks. "I'm sorry. I didn't mean to be so bold. I shall wait patiently for your proposal—if you don't take too long. As for becoming a member of the Church, you know that for some time I've known the Book of Mormon is a true record. I feared asking you to baptize me until you were completely healed from the smoke damage to your lungs. I didn't want to risk you contracting pneumonia."

He leaned forward to place a gentle kiss on her lips.

Serenity closed her eyes and smiled, savoring the sweetness of his kiss. Then she thought of the ring Edward had given her and her thoughts abruptly returned to the ordeal she'd just endured.

"Pauline took the ring you gave me, the earrings that were Papa's gift, and the money I kept in the little box. She wasn't satisfied with the things she stole from me. I think she truly convinced herself that she had a greater claim to my mother's topaz ring than I did. She was incapable of accepting that her husband's and brother's actions, and her own, were responsible for her plight." Serenity was silent for a moment, reviewing in her mind the lengths Pauline, Joshua Brown, and Stephen Rappleton had gone to in their attempt to steal the topaz.

"I wonder where that topaz is," she said. "Do you think it's buried so far beneath twigs and rotting leaves in the forest that it shall never be found?"

"Sometimes birds scavenge bright bits of metal and carry them off. It may adorn a bird's nest miles from where it was dropped."

"Sometimes I fancy that it has been found by a child and is worn by her doll, but wherever it is, I just hope no more thieves come searching for it."

"Stephen and Pauline are dead, and Joshua will be tried for murder. Even if he doesn't hang, he'll never be free to torment you again."

* * *

Before the first immigrant ship docked at the Philadelphia port, a party of missionaries arrived in the city from Salt Lake on their way to New York. James had entreated them to look up Edward before journeying on. When Edward learned of the missionaries' arrival, he took the opportunity to ask them to assist him in baptizing Serenity and to perform a marriage ceremony for them.

It was a beautiful spring morning, a full year since she and Edward had first met, when they joined the missionaries in a rented carriage for a brief ride to a forested spot outside the city. Serenity wore a simple white dress beneath her cloak, and her hands trembled with nervous excitement. They followed a meandering stream to a spot where a fallen tree had collected deadwood behind it, forming a small pond. There she and Edward waded into the water until it was almost to Serenity's waist. The water was cold, but bearable.

Edward held her gently with one hand and raised his right arm. He spoke slowly and distinctly the words she'd longed to hear, then swiftly swept her under the water. She recognized the stillness and peace that encompassed her as she rose out of the water. A picture of Papa flashed through her mind, and she wished he were present to rejoice with her. A voice whispered in her heart, *I am here.* Warmth filled her near to bursting, and she smiled happily as Edward helped her out of the water.

Wrapped in a towel, Serenity hurried toward the thick brush she'd chosen as her dressing room. She stripped off the sodden dress, then donned the dry apparel she'd brought. In moments, she was pulling the sunshine yellow gown over her head and fastening it with nimble fingers. She vigorously toweled her hair before sweeping her damp, unruly locks into a fashionable twist at the back of her head.

She was ready. She looked down at herself and felt a moment's gladness that she'd kept the yellow satin gown and that her bruises had almost faded away. She thought of the long mirror in her room at the Montague House, then dismissed the thought. Her mother's voice seemed to whisper in her ear, *You are lovely inside and out—as a bride should be.* The thought warmed her, and she hurried to join Edward.

Seated on a stool, she felt hands on her head. Then Edward bestowed upon her the gift of the Holy Ghost. Joy filled her heart, magnifying the peace and warmth of her baptism. When the blessing was complete, Edward took her hand and raised her to stand beside him. Each of the missionaries shook her hand, and then Edward led her a short distance away to stand amid a sprinkling of early wild flowers.

She looked around the small clearing. Sunshine shone through the trees, which were showing the pale green of new leaves. The splendor was as great as that of the multi-colored windows of the church in New York. The buzz of bees was as sweet as organ music. Edward was handsome in his dark suit with a tiny yellow buttercup in his lapel. One elder came to stand before them, and the rest of the missionaries formed a small semi-circle behind them.

The ceremony was brief and simple. Serenity knew it meant nothing as far as the law was concerned, but to her it meant far more than had the brief, rushed ceremony before Judge Detweiler the previous spring. This time Edward kissed her briefly on her lips. He slipped a ring on her finger and she gasped in surprise, seeing the small bronze stone surrounded by a ring of diamond chips.

"I searched every pawnbroker for ten blocks around where Pauline held you captive until I found the one who had purchased the ring from her," he whispered. "If it were possible, I would place your mother's topaz on your finger."

Suddenly Edward went down on one knee. "Serenity," he said. "I love you with a love that will not allow me to be parted from you by death. Before fall turns to winter, we shall be in Salt Lake City. Would you do me the honor of becoming my eternal bride in the Endowment House as soon as we can get permission from President Young?"

Laughing and crying, she urged him to his feet. "Oh yes, Edward. I shall marry you a third time." Still smiling, she added, "Have you noticed that each of our weddings is better than the last?"

* * *

Serenity handed dolls to two little girls, then set a carved toy wagon before a little boy who sat in the dust crying. "Here is something you can play with while I fix dinner," she told them.

The poor, fatherless children were tired and afraid. Their father had died before reaching America, and their mother had been in her wagon for hours. Several times they had heard her cry out.

Ever since leaving Omaha with the Saints traveling to Salt Lake, Serenity had looked forward to reaching Fort Laramie and discovering whether Timothy was still there. Though they now were camped only a short distance from the fort, Clarissa Nelson was about to give birth and Serenity had committed to watch her friend's older children while their mother delivered her baby. Since there was a midwife in their wagon company, Serenity had insisted that Edward accompany those who were visiting the fort.

She peeled potatoes and added them to the piece of meat simmering in a heavy kettle over the fire. Supper was almost ready. She glanced toward the Nelson wagon. A woman who had been assisting the midwife stepped down and hurried to Serenity's side. "Is your husband available? There is need for a doctor."

"He went to the fort with . . ." Over the other woman's shoulder she saw a cloud of dust and several riders approaching camp. Some were men from the camp, but the lead rider was wearing a blue uniform and rode a familiar mount. Seated behind the rider was Edward, grinning broadly and waving his hat.

"Look who I found," he shouted.

"Sister Nelson has need of a doctor," she called back. Edward's smile disappeared and, as the horse came to a stop, he leaped from its back. He ran to their wagon for his bag, then disappeared inside the wagon parked a short distance away from the others. The woman turned to run after Edward.

Serenity felt small hands grip her skirt. Glancing up to see what the children had seen, Serenity's eyes met those of a large, black soldier she barely recognized.

"Timothy!" He was no longer the skinny youth she'd bid farewell to a year ago. She reached for him but found herself hampered by the frightened children. He stepped forward and gripped her hands.

"Miss Serenity." He smiled and doffed his hat. "I couldn't believe my eyes when Mr. Edward came walking into the fort. When he told me you were here too, I had to come see for myself."

"Do you know that soldier?" the little boy whispered hesitantly as he eyed Timothy's menacing rifle.

"Yes, Davy." She brushed the child's hair from his eyes. "Corporal Timothy is a dear friend. And don't worry, he's a very kind man."

The children continued to eye Timothy warily, but they returned to their play and Serenity and Timothy seated themselves on stools to talk. Serenity told him about Joshua Brown and the Rappletons, and Timothy confided that his enlistment would be up in another year and that he planned to seek a wife who would accompany him west to homestead.

Several times Serenity rose to her feet to stir the contents of the kettle hanging over the fire. When it finished cooking, she invited Timothy to stay for supper.

"There's no telling how long Edward will be," she said. "Will you be so kind as to lift the wagon seat down for us to use as a table?"

Timothy reached for the wooden box that served as a wagon seat while the wagon was in motion and as a table when camp was set up.

While Serenity set the table, Timothy crouched down to the children's level. He watched them play for several minutes before picking up the wooden wagon.

"I had a wagon like this when I was a little boy," he told Davy.

Serenity came to stand behind him. "That *is* your wagon. I hope you don't mind that I let little Davy play with it. I brought it with me because I hoped we'd find you here at Fort Laramie. I thought you might like to have it to remind you of the man who carved it for you." She arched an eyebrow and added, "You might one day have a son you'll want to give it to."

Timothy turned the wagon over several times in his hands. "Grandpa Soren was a craftsman. See all the detail? It looks just like the wagons parked here in your camp. See the buckets hanging on the sides? Even the wagon box lifts off just like . . ." He gave the box a sharp twist, then lifted it forward. A ring with a large golden stone surrounded by small glittering diamonds fell to the packed earth at his feet.

Time seemed to freeze. Neither Serenity nor Timothy could take their eyes from the ring. Not even the children moved. Then from somewhere behind them came the cry of a newborn baby.

One of the little girls picked up the ring. She held it out to Serenity. "Is this yours?" she asked with awe in her voice.

Serenity slipped the ring on her finger. She stared at the huge stone but didn't really see it. Removing it from her hand, she said, "No, I believe it belongs to Timothy." Serenity placed the ring in his hand.

"That ring belonged to your Mamma. I can't—" he began to object.

"I made my mother a promise," Serenity interrupted. "Her ring was precious to her, and she asked me to wear it until the Lord told me to pass it on to someone who had a greater need for it. As she was dying, I think Mamma knew the topaz was never really hers to keep and that was why she put it in your wagon. She was returning it to you and your family. Now I'm passing it on to you with the instruction she gave me: 'Trust in the Lord to let you know what to do with it.'"

Long after Timothy returned to the fort, taking the topaz with him, Serenity took the Nelson children to see their new brother, then tucked them in bed. Edward turned the care of his patient back to the midwife and followed Serenity to their campfire to eat his supper. Later still, he lay beside her in their wagon and she told him about the ring.

"Are you sure you won't regret giving away your mother's ring?" he asked, pulling her close against his side.

"I don't need a memento to remind me of my parents' love for me. The day of my baptism and our real marriage, I received the assurance that I shall be with Mamma and Papa again one day. That topaz brought Mamma to Papa, and I credit it with the events that brought us together, but in my heart I know it's time to pass it on. Timothy and his people have greater need of sunshine, protection, and clear vision now than do I."

About the Author

Photo courtesy of Olan Mills

Jennie Hansen graduated from Ricks College in Idaho, then Westminster College in Utah. She has been a newspaper reporter, editor, and librarian. In addition to writing novels, she reviews LDS fiction in a monthly column for Meridian Magazine.

She was born in Idaho Falls, Idaho, and has lived in Idaho, Montana, and Utah. She has received numerous writing awards.

Jennie and her husband, Boyd, live in Salt Lake County. They have five married children and ten grandchildren.

Jennie enjoys hearing from her readers, who can visit her website, www.jennielhansen.com, or who can write to her in care of Covenant Communications, P.O. Box 416, American Fork, UT 84003-0416, or via e-mail at info@covenant-lds.com.